PRAISE FOR
THE OTHER SIDE O...

"Raw, confronting, and deeply insightful, *The Other Side of Nothing* is for anyone who has held on tight to a loved one's life and felt it slipping through their fingers. Anastasia Zadeik has infused her exquisitely written narrative with the powerful voice of experience. Heart-wrenching, riveting, and hopeful, this is a no-holds barred glimpse into the agony of emerging through a mental health crisis, told from the inside out and from the outside in. An important read."
—**Emma Grey**, author of *The Last Love Note*

"Riveting, devastating, redemptive. *The Other Side of Nothing* is both intimate and cosmic—intellectually, physically, and emotionally. I was holding my breath until the final pages."
—**Shelley Blanton-Stroud**, author of
the Jane Benjamin novels

"Mental illness is still something we don't talk about enough. Anastasia Zadeik tackles it head-on in this moving portrayal of two suicidal young adults searching for meaning in their lives. With sensitivity and compassion, the author explores the effects of the demon of mental illness not just on the patients but also on their loved ones. Heartbreaking yet also hopeful, *The Other Side of Nothing* takes the reader on an unforgettable journey."
—**Jody Hadlock**, author of *The Lives of Diamond Bessie*

"*The Other Side of Nothing* is a page-turning novel about young love, art, philosophy, motherhood, grief, and healing. Zadeik writes with tremendous empathy and compassion for her characters, exploring the complexities and nuances of mental illness. The characters in these pages are beautifully alive."
—**Tammy Greenwood**, author of *The Still Point,*
Keeping Lucy, and *Two Rivers*

"This is an immediately engaging, emotionally raw novel that weaves together grief, art, secrets, family dynamics, class, and mental disorder. In the end, it is a moving and important account of love—its costs and its rewards."
—Sue William Silverman, author of *Acetylene Torch Songs: Writing True Stories to Ignite the Soul*

"This book has everything: vivid characters with distinctive and specific arcs, an accelerating narrative pace, evocative prose, and heart—so much heart. Rich with moral and ethical questions about consent, personal freedom, and how hard it is know the right thing to do when someone you love is at risk, it will help to educate and build empathetic understanding of the vagaries of the mind."
—Deborah Serra, author of *Lost in Thought*

"*The Other Side of Nothing* takes readers on a journey into the complex world of mental illness and its effects of both luminosity and shadow on the fully realized characters who inhabit this novel. Zadeik's deep knowledge of the intricacies of mental illness and her compassionate portrayal of its ramifications make this an important and timely book."
—Judy Reeves, author of *When Your Heart Says Go*

"Anastasia Zadeik's characters grab the reader from the first page as a young couple embarks on a suspenseful journey in search of beauty, connection, and meaning—heading toward a perilous precipice. The story reveals the complex and misunderstood layers of mental illness, offering insights and nurturing empathy for those who suffer and the people who love them. Recommended reading to enhance understanding of mental illness through a heart-wrenching story."
—Linda Moore, author of *Attribution*

PRAISE FOR ANASTASIA ZADEIK'S
BLURRED FATES

"The author's tale is as chilling as it is affecting. . . . A hypnotic page-turner . . ."
—*Kirkus Reviews*

"Mental and emotional health and healing from trauma are the book's main foci, and it handles them with utmost care . . . a tense, emotional thriller about betrayal and strength."
—*Foreword Reviews*

"Zadeik writes viscerally, Kate's anger, pain, and uncertainty suffusing every scene. The multifaceted plot deftly juxtaposes Kate's present and previous traumas, sensitively exploring several fraught topics while generating suspense and maintaining drive. Complex characters and nuanced relationships further distinguish this stunner from the pack."
—**Katrina Niidas Holm**, *Mystery Scene* review

"*Blurred Fates* is an unerring portrayal of the realities of trauma survival in an enthralling tale of tragedy, love, and betrayal. Zadeik's elegance on the page is captivating from start to finish."
—**Amelia Zachry**, author of *Enough: A Memoir of Mistakes, Mania, and Motherhood*

THE
OTHER SIDE
OF NOTHING

Also by Anastasia Zadeik

Blurred Fates

THE
OTHER SIDE
OF NOTHING

A Novel

ANASTASIA ZADEIK

SHE WRITES PRESS

Published 2024
Printed in the United States of America
Print ISBN: 978-1-64742-668-2
E-ISBN: 978-1-64742-669-9
Library of Congress Control Number: 2023921757

For information, address:
She Writes Press
1569 Solano Ave #546
Berkeley, CA 94707

Interior Design by Tabitha Lahr

Excerpts from Albert Camus's *The Myth of Sisyphus* are courtesy of Random House.

She Writes Press is a division of SparkPoint Studio, LLC.

For Olivia and Jack,
my answer

MORNING

November 10, 2016

"I'LL BE WAITING FOR YOU on the other side," he'd said.

She'd nodded. Tried to smile.

"Don't be afraid," he'd added, gripping her shoulders, the intensity in his voice exhilarating but also frightening somehow. "Five minutes. Don't talk to anyone. Don't look back. And whatever you do, don't run."

With that, he'd dropped his hands and left her there, feeling the loss of his presence like a phantom limb. She looked at the clock on the wall. Watched as the minute hand crept forward. Then, though everything in her screamed *run!*, she walked down the antiseptic hallway, avoiding the gaze of the psych tech on duty. She exited quietly through the French doors at the back of the building and proceeded at a measured pace to the barn where she'd learned to love him. She kept her eyes fixed on the weathered red door until she was almost upon it, then turned and skirted the side of the building, heading for a break in the trees, remembering what he'd said earlier. "It may not seem like a trail, but trust me, it will take you where you need to be."

But fifteen feet into the small woods, the trail ended. Julia looked left, right, left, trying to catch her breath as dizziness poured over her. She blinked slowly, deliberately, hoping the world would stop swirling. Instead, the swirling spiraled upward, pulling Julia with it until she was gazing at the tops of trees, at sunlight slanting down through a profusion of scarlet, mustard, and orange. She saw herself, small, nearly hidden in the shadows.

For an indeterminable amount of time—seconds, perhaps minutes—she watched herself, swaying, ever so slightly, until the crack of a branch brought her back. Fear beat in her chest. Her vision grew spotty, turning the ground beneath her into thick daubs of paint. Burnt Umber. Pale Gold. Terre Verte.

Breathe, she told herself. *It's just underbrush.* Leaves, earth, moss, stones.

Only moments ago, in the courtyard, it had been gravel, shifting under his boots—*outside shoes*—as he performed a 360-degree sweep of the walls and windows surrounding them. "Come with me," he'd said, and he'd had a plan. He'd flipped her hand over to draw an escape route on her palm with the tip of his finger, sending currents along pathways she hadn't known existed until he revealed them.

"Here's the barn," he'd said, tracing a square under her pinkie. "And here, eight feet from the back corner, that's where the trail begins." From the bottom of her ring finger, across her palm toward the fleshy part of her thumb and the scar on her wrist, the path was clear, measuring in centimeters. In reality, it was hundreds of meters, and it wasn't clear at all.

Julia scanned the trees. She heard him whisper, "Look for light on the other side. That's where I'll be." And then her father's voice flooded in, reciting, "The woods are lovely, dark and deep," followed by the plea that had become a refrain in her head, *Please help me.*

The voices collided. Julia stumbled. Something pulled on her sleeve.

She turned.

And then, she ran.

JULIA

Ten days earlier

"WHY ARE YOU HERE?" the doctor asked.

Julia sat across from the guy, the latest psychologist her mother had found, staring at the edge of a bandage under the wrist cuff of her black hoodie, realizing she needed to change. She'd been wearing the same clothes for two days. Or maybe it was three. Time and space had gone wonky lately; weaving in and out of weeks, an hour could feel like a year, while a day went by in a blur. The world couldn't be counted upon to keep its form and shape. One moment she was—

"Julia? Can you tell me why you're here?"

Julia looked up, pointedly down to her wrists, then back at the doctor.

Seriously? she wanted to say but didn't.

She lifted her eyes higher and took in three framed diplomas on the wall. The largest one announced David P. Stein had been awarded a Doctor of Philosophy in Counseling Psychology. She couldn't make out the date, but Dr. Stein was old—grandfather old, with gray hair, corduroy pants, and reading glasses. Clearly experienced. Backed by floor-to-ceiling cases of books discussing every psychiatric malady in existence. The leather-bound notepad he held in his lap had not been blank when she walked into his dull beige office to sit upon his dull beige couch; background information had been provided, judgments made, boxes checked.

Why am *I here?*

Julia sighed and turned toward the window, where dust motes floated in slivers of light filtering through the wooden blinds.

Dust, she thought. *Of course there would be dust.*

She closed her eyes as a scorching emptiness filled her chest, the feeling of memories she wanted to forget. Mourners in black, like rows of crows. A crescent of flowers around a small wooden box that impossibly held what remained of her father. Her mother, dry-eyed, leaning toward the arrangement as a minister Julia didn't know read the same words her father had asked her to read only weeks ago under a canopy of stars—"Dust thou art to dust returneth, was not spoken of the soul"—ruining the Longfellow po—

"Let's try a different way," Dr. Stein said, interrupting her thoughts. "How about you tell me what's been going on that brought you here?"

Eyes still closed, Julia shook her head. She couldn't put it into words. She never could. And even if she were able to do so, Dr. Stein wouldn't understand.

No one did.

It was endless days engulfed in a fog. Nights that became black holes; lying awake while the whole world slept. Ordinary, unavoidable things transformed into land mines: her reflection in the mirror; former friends at school who looked away; books stacked on her father's desk, never to be read.

It was despair that struck like an avalanche—the ground sliding out underfoot, snowflakes compressed into cement, asphyxiating her with her own exhalations. She'd read about that, about how you literally kill yourself under the snow.

"Julia?"

She couldn't breathe. She couldn't move. Her head was so ridiculously heavy, she was pretty sure her neck might snap any day.

On cue, in what was becoming an alarmingly common occurrence, Julia saw the neck snap from above: a young woman, too thin, dressed in black, ankles crossed at her Doc Martens, shaking her head until it toppled off and tumbled forward. Matted dreadlocks spilling. Hands reaching up, too late—

"Julia, are you with me?"

Am I?

Julia opened her eyes. She *was* back on Dr. Stein's dull beige couch, her curtain of hair restored, a single lock of dread in her fingertips. *Don't,* she thought, even as she gave the lock a fierce tug, whispering "trichotillomania." A familiar sensation traveled along her scalp as the syllables tripped across her tongue. Though she hated the behavior, she loved the name for it: the rolling *r*, the staccato *ch* and *t*. She missed the clicking of her tongue ring. She recalled awakening in the hospital to its absence—and the presence of her mother, stoic, silent, undoubtedly pleased the ER docs had removed all her piercings. Her mother hated the piercings, the pulling, maybe even Julia herse—

"I'm sorry, what was that?" Dr. Stein asked.

Julia dropped the lock of hair. She did not want to talk about trichotillomania or dreadlocks, or how the latter was supposed to be a solution for the former, or how this solution had failed, like all the others.

Dr. Stein was waiting, though. She had to say something. *Here goes nothing.*

"There are times," she said. "When I leave my body and see myself, from above, like a scene in a movie."

Dr. Stein remained perfectly still.

Julia went on. "Most of the time, it's real, what I'm doing, but sometimes, it isn't. Sometimes it's all in my head. I see things that aren't actually happening."

"Like?"

"Like, just now." Julia hesitated. "I saw my head fall from my neck."

"I see." Dr. Stein spoke with practiced evenness. "And how did that make you feel?"

"How did it make me feel?" *Honestly?*

"Yes. As in, did your head falling off provoke an emotion?"

Provoke an emotion? My God, is he serious? Yes, he is. Pen poised.

"No," Julia replied, then paused. "Actually, yes. Well, maybe. Relief."

"You felt relief."

Julia nodded tentatively, still thinking about the fragility of her neck.

"Relief from . . . ?" Dr. Stein peered at her over the edge of his glasses.

From you. From this. From all of it, Julia wanted to say. *Is this supposed to be helping?* Exhaustion swept over her. She closed her eyes again and dropped her face into her hands, bringing her wrists into contact with her collarbones, reminding her of wounds just starting to heal, the matching cuts on her thighs. Attempts to end the agonizing numbness and emptiness failing again and again, even the last one; she'd even failed at ending it all.

And yet.

And yet, she recalled the warmth of the water holding her, the slow deceleration of whirling thoughts, soaring out of her body to float overhead for the first time. Watching the scene below with unexpected, unburdening detachment as the edges faded into a calm stillness. A stillness broken by her mother's muffled voice, louder and clearer as she approached. "Julia! Julia, answer me!" Fists on a door. Flashing stars. White lights.

Then, something hard in her throat. Realizing she was still alive. Trading pain for more—

"Julia?" Dr. Stein's even voice returned. "Relief from . . . ?"

Fine.

" . . . pain. I want relief from the pain."

"You want relief from the pain."

Julia nodded into her hands.

Dr. Stein was silent. Silent enough for Julia to hear her own breathing. She assumed this was some sort of therapeutic technique, but the silence simply served as a vacuum, sucking in more fog. She wanted to leave. Perhaps it was unfair, but

Julia did not like Dr. Stein. She did not want to be there in his dreary beige office.

Then again, she didn't want to be anywhere. Not at school. Not at home. *Definitely not at home.* Though she'd been out of the hospital only a week, she was suffocating. Dust and memories everywhere. Her father gone. Guilt and complications rising. Texts she couldn't answer. Her mother abruptly switching from avoiding her to hovering. Watching her. Filling the house with an iterative loop of questions she didn't really want the answers to: "How are you feeling? What are you feeling? Is there something—"

"Is that what you are feeling now?" Dr. Stein asked. "Pain?"

Julia sighed. *What's the point?*

She'd tried to explain what she was feeling to the last doctor she'd encountered, a young guy in a stereotypical white coat on the psych ward. Young enough to relate, she'd thought. She'd told him about the pen and ink self-portrait she'd been working on in AP Studio Art, and how, one day, she'd felt the urge to destroy it; how she'd opened the ink and spilled it, first a drop on the middle of the smooth forehead, then another on the chin, then a slow dribble across the left cheekbone. How her index finger had pressed into the ink, pushing it deeper into the weave of the paper, smearing and pouring and smearing. How she'd watched her face disappear. She'd hoped the young doctor would understand. That he'd get it, but he hadn't. He'd been brusque. Taken notes. Checked boxes. Decided she was stable enough to go home with her mother if they switched her from Lexapro to Prozac, *the wonder drug,* combined with counseling, which landed her here, in Dr. Stein's dreary beige office.

So, really, *why* am *I here? Why is* anyone *here? What's the point of any of it? We're all here, and then we die. Dr. Stein, so old he wears corduroy? He might die soon. Can I say that? Jesus, Julia, no.*

Dr. Stein broke through. "Julia? Can you tell me what you're thinking about right now?"

The word slipped out into her hands before Julia could censor it. "Death."

"You're thinking about death." Not a question. Not a statement. Something in between.

Yes, she was thinking about death. But as soon as the word was out of her mouth, Julia knew she shouldn't have said it aloud, because no one wanted to talk about death. If there was anything she'd learned in the last year, it was this—no one wanted to talk about death. Or sadness. Or her father, who should have had more time. Who'd once believed in a world of beauty and poetry, grace and second chances. As had she. But then—

Please help me. Shit. Shit. Shit.

The scorching emptiness returned. Over the sound of her own breath, she could hear the ticking of a clock. Slowing.

"I want to disappear," she whispered into her hands.

"I'm sorry," Dr. Stein said. "I didn't catch that. Did you say you want to disappear?"

Yes, she wanted to go away. Somewhere else. She couldn't go—

"Julia?"

Not for the first time, *Girl, Interrupted* popped into Julia's head. She'd read the book three years earlier, when she was fifteen and life was still good. Back then, it hadn't seemed right that the narrator was in a mental hospital when it wasn't clear she was crazy, at least not to Julia. But now? Now, the idea of being somewhere else—away from the memories and mistakes, the pain she felt, the pain she'd caused—

"Julia? Do you want to die?"

Julia lifted her head, opened her eyes. Dr. Stein sat, pen still poised.

"Are you planning to hurt yourself again?"

No. Yes. She didn't know.

Dr. Stein did not understand. She just wanted it all to stop: the guilt, the cutting, the trich, the whispering, the drugs, the turning away from everyone and everything she'd once loved. She wanted to believe again—in something. She also knew the requirements for an involuntary hold, "a danger to self or others." A simple affirmative response might get her back into the hospital. Into a residential program. Away. Dr. Stein could do for her what she could not do for herself. He could give her another chance.

Julia knew, suddenly, ironically, she had to want to die to get a chance to live.

And Dr. Stein might be her last best shot.

"Yes," she said. "Yes."

LAURA

DUSK WAS FALLING: the sky gray, with menacing steel-wool clouds; the air, cool and damp, with that just-about-to-rain feeling. Laura Reeves maneuvered out of her car, computer bag and keys in one hand, the strap of her daughter's backpack in the other. As she pushed the car door closed with her hip and turned toward the house, a cluster of costumed children approached on the sidewalk—a small princess in a pale blue gown, a fairy with wings, three superheroes. Two women trailed them by several feet, holding wine glasses and closed umbrellas.

Laura's thoughts tripped forward. Trick-or-treaters. Halloween.

Paul.

She dropped her head. Inhaled sharply.

Her husband, Paul, had loved all holidays, but Halloween was his favorite. Every year on October first, he'd purchase bags and bags of candy, chortling as he opened the first tiny pack of peanut M&Ms or a mini Snickers bar. He'd place Styrofoam headstones, fake bones, and mechanized spiders in the lawn, hang frothy spider webs from the eaves and the back half of a witch mid-splatter on the front window. The afternoon of the thirty-first, he'd load dry ice in the mood machine, put on a black onesie embossed with a glow-in-the-dark skeleton, and stand at the front door ready for the deluge of children.

He'd gasp in faux fear, enthuse over creative costumes, and quote Edgar Alan Poe using his best Vincent Price impression.

Until last year.

Last year, he hadn't felt well enough to man the door, so he'd corralled Julia into decorating and handing out treats. This year, Laura had purchased a bag of candy only because it was displayed near the register at the grocery store. She had not retrieved the boxes from the basement that bore Paul's handwriting in thick black Sharpie: "Open at your own risk, BWA-HA-HA."

She couldn't have faced the onesie or the gravestones.

Laura waited by the car, eyes downcast, praying the happy troupe didn't stop at her door. Only when the voices faded did she look up and down the street. Nearly every other house on the block was decorated. Porch lights on. Jack-o-lanterns glowing.

How did I miss this driving home? she wondered, before acknowledging she didn't recall the drive home itself. Not really. Epic-level distraction had become her new normal. It was as if a sledgehammer kept striking, breaking her thoughts apart and sending them scattering.

As she walked to the side door of the house, the day came back in fragments: the look of resignation on Julia's face when Laura presented her with water and one of the new little white pills; the stack of worn magazines in the waiting room of yet another psychologist, one Dr. Stein, who'd recommended placing Julia on a 72-hour hold "for her own safety"; the back of Julia's hoodie as a nurse led her away before Laura could say goodbye; a white desk placard bearing the words "Christine Renner, M.D., Medical Director, Brookfield Health" that Laura couldn't help staring at as the woman explained Dr. Stein's 72-hour hold was unnecessary, because "Julia has requested a voluntary admission."

Nothing made sense anymore. Laura had stood there, dumbfounded, wondering how it was that her just-turned-eighteen-year-old daughter, who was clearly unable to think clearly, was being allowed to make any decisions at all. The doctor had asked Laura to sit, gesturing toward the chairs across from her desk, and Laura had noticed Julia's backpack on one of the chairs, top open, Doc Martens visible.

"Her shoes—" Laura said without thinking.

"Laces," Dr. Renner had replied, "are disallowed."

It had taken a moment for Laura to catch up. And then the questions had come at her, like flying knives. Upon completion of the interview and signing away a large portion of Paul's life insurance, she had not known what to do or where to go, so she'd driven straight to her office only to stare blankly at the screens on her desk until her half sister, Lilly, called.

"You checked Julia into a psych hospital and went to work?" Lilly had said. And then, softer, "Go home, Laura. I'll meet you there as soon as I can."

But home was no longer home.

Laura turned the key in the door and the deadbolt clicked open.

The emptiness inside was palpable. Gone were the smells of good things to eat, the glow of the hanging lamp over the kitchen table where Paul and Julia used to sit, computers open before them. The warmth of Paul's baritone voice. "There she is. How was your day?"

Tonight, sounds reverberated in the void: the thud of Julia's backpack on the floor; the clatter of keys hitting the countertop; the sigh that escaped when Laura saw the stack of homemade mood trackers recommended in the *Surviving a Suicide* booklet she'd been given by a hospital social worker just ten days earlier. Laura had read the booklet over and over, trying to understand something—anything—as she sat next to a hospital bed where Julia lay in the medically induced coma doctors hoped would protect vulnerable organs—her liver and kidneys, her heart.

Her heart.

Laura recalled being asked to leave the room while they brought Julia out of the coma, the nurse saying, "She needs to feel safe when she regains consciousness, and until we can talk to her, we won't know what caused her to take this step. You understand, right?"

She did. They thought Laura might be the reason Julia wanted to die.

Now, as then, anguish struck like an ice pick to her sternum. Laura's right hand flew to her chest, palm flat, fingers splayed. For a second, she couldn't breathe, but then hardwired childhood reproaches filled her head. Her mother's favorites: "Stop now or go to your room. Bear up, no one wants to see you cry." The one her stepfather, Carl, preferred: "Buck the fuck up, or I'll give you something to cry about."

Stop, she told herself. *Stop now. Buck—*

THE DOORBELL RANG, A LONG angry buzz. Laura startled, then remembered. Trick-or-treaters. Superheroes. Princesses. *But why?* The inside of the house was dark. Unwelcoming. Laura walked across the room, peered down the hall, and saw the front porch light was on. She must not have turned it off before they left the house that morning. Julia had been moving slowly, and Laura had been distracted, worried they'd be late for the 8:00 a.m. appointment with Dr. Stein she'd made, thinking Julia might go to school afterward.

In retrospect, as with nearly everything it seemed, Laura had been shockingly naïve in this assumption. Julia had not gone to school; around the time Laura had imagined watching her daughter walk through the front doors of her high school, she'd been watching a nurse lead her away instead, listening to Dr. Renner explain that Julia wanted to be there.

In a psychiatric facility. Brookfield Health.

Rather than with Laura.

The ice pick to the sternum had struck then too, but Laura hadn't let on. She'd straightened her spine and clutched Julia's backpack of disallowed items as if it could save her. Even when Dr. Renner had misinterpreted her reaction, saying, "It can be difficult for family members to understand how overwhelming and unrelenting the pain is—actual physical pain," Laura had not argued or objected, though she knew that kind of pain.

She'd felt it and borne it.

She'd bucked the fuck up. Done what needed to be done. The evening after Paul's memorial service, Laura had gone to her room, set her alarm, and allowed herself to cry. The next morning, she'd showered, dressed in business attire, woken Julia for school, and gone to work. She'd weathered the initial shows of sympathy and been thankful when they ceased. Day after day, she'd gone through the motions, making sure there was cereal in the pantry, milk in the refrigerator, gas in the cars. Sheets and towels and clothes had been laundered. Bills were paid.

Lilly had urged her to attend a support group, claiming Laura wasn't "allowing herself to grieve." One meeting had been enough to confirm drinking coffee in a church basement with sad total strangers was not for her. The truth was that it had done more harm than good. The rift that had been forming between her and Julia after Paul's death had begun opening into a chasm, so when the young group leader said, "Everyone grieves differently. Give your loved ones time and space to grieve in their own way," Laura had taken his words to heart.

At the time, this approach sounded rationale, reasonable even. Only later, when things had gone terribly wrong, could Laura see she'd zealously followed the advice because giving Julia time and space had been easier.

Time and space had allowed her to ignore Julia's loss of appetite, the monosyllabic responses to every query, the hurt embedded in each interaction.

Time and space had given Laura permission to accept she'd never fill the hole Paul left behind. To pretend silence was not surrender.

Giving Julia time and space had given Laura time and space.

She just hadn't anticipated the unintended consequences.

It had been weeks before Laura noticed Julia's grades had slipped and her friends had dropped away; her taste in music tilted louder and angrier as she grew quieter and quieter; she'd disappeared for hours. One evening she'd come home late, defiant, with newly formed dreadlocks—dark snakes that overwhelmed her features, and though Laura had been shocked, she'd thought, *time and space*. The next week, they'd been enduring another silent meal when Laura had seen the flash of something dark in Julia's mouth and heard a strange muted clicking noise, the sound of metal against something hard.

"What was that?" Laura had asked.

Julia had looked up, briefly, then away. "Nothing."

"It was definitely something, Julia."

"Fine," Julia said, frustrated. "It's a tongue ring."

"A tongue ring? You have a tongue ring?"

In response, Julia made the clicking noise again, like a taunt, following it with the twirl of a dreadlock and a whispered "trichotillomania," the habitual coupling of the obsessive hair twirling she'd exhibited on and off since she was a child with the psychological label for it that Laura had come to despise.

"When did you—Did you even think about asking me?"

Click. Twirl. Whisper.

Laura could feel her heart beating faster. Her lungs tightened. She knew it was an explosive situation, yet she'd gone on, aware her tone sounded more angry than concerned. "I'd have liked to know. You shouldn't have gone alone. Something might have gone wrong."

"Right, like you would have gone with me. Besides, I didn't go alone. Cheyenne took me."

Cheyenne. Dreadlock stylist. Wardrobe consultant. A 21-year-old musician Julia claimed to have met online who was now her one and only friend. Though Laura had heard the woman's voice on Julia's phone several times, she'd seen her only once, sitting in the passenger seat of a car at the curb, dressed all in black with kohl-lined eyes and reddish-purple ombre hair that resembled a bad wig; her appearance so stereotypical it felt manipulative.

Click. Twirl. Whisp—

THE DOORBELL RANG AGAIN, ONCE. *Stop.* Then twice, in rapid succession. *Stop now.*

Laura needed to turn off the porch light. She grabbed a bag of candy from the pantry and walked to the front of the house, tugging at the end seam. She turned the bolt, pulled open the door, yanked the seam harder, and just as she heard "Trick or treat!" the seam gave way.

Candy exploded onto the floor.

There was laughter, teenage laughter, jarring and unexpected. These trick-or-treaters were not superheroes and princesses. Laura took in a severed arm, a brutally scarred face, weapons, blood dripping from wounds and lips. Though her eyes remained open, the sledgehammer hit again, splintering her thoughts. An image flashed across the back of her brain: Julia sitting against the bathroom wall, dreadlocks against white tile, a small knife in her hand, bloody curved lines on her thighs.

Laura heard a strangled cry.

"Is she all right?" one of the teenagers asked.

"They're just costumes," another said.

Laura shifted her gaze from blood and gore to the candy littering the floor. She bent down, hastily scooped up handfuls, and dropped them into the bags held before her. She knew the words "Happy Halloween" were expected, but she could not say them. *Leave*, she thought. *Please leave.*

Before their backs had fully turned against her, Laura retreated into the house, shut the door, and flicked off the porch light. "Guess you don't need a costume to be a witch," she heard one of them say.

And then, as Laura walked back toward the kitchen, another memory fragment rose, hazy with the passage of time. A dusty blackboard. Posters of the alphabet. Costumed children marching in a Halloween parade. The six-year-old version of herself is not taking part in the parade because the six-year-old version of herself is not wearing a costume because Carl doesn't believe in six-year-olds dressing up and Carl's rules rule and little girls who cannot buck up are given something to cry about. Laura remembers her first-grade teacher kneeling beside her, noticing her stricken expression, saying, "You can tell me." Laura remembers knowing, even as a six-year-old, the woman is wrong. "No one needs to know our business,"

Carl says to Laura and her mother, and Laura understands she cannot tell the truth about what is happening at home, because the truth will sound bad.

This was the very thought she'd had that morning while talking to Dr. Renner. Under questioning, Laura heard just how bad her fragmented answers had sounded: the mistaken giving of time and space; finding Julia on the bathroom floor with the self-inflicted wounds on her thighs; frantically driving her to the ER for nothing but butterfly bandages; the incomprehensibly interminable ten-day wait for a psych consult. Laura could hear her own frustration as she explained to Dr. Renner how the first psychiatrist had spent only twenty minutes with Julia before prescribing Lexapro, using phrases like "Selective Serotonin Reuptake Inhibitors," "non-suicidal self-harming," and "impulse control disorder," as if these were ordinary, adding, "SSRIs, like Lexapro, can increase suicidal ideation," as if it was somehow acceptable, and then replying to Laura's "Excuse me, did you say *increase* suicidal ideation?" with the equally unacceptable response, "It works for some. These aren't perfect drugs, Mrs. Reeves. It's not a perfect science."

Laura had tried, she told Dr. Renner. She'd Googled "Selective Serotonin Reuptake Inhibitors" and "non-suicidal self-harming." She'd read the small print under "Suicidality and Antidepressants" on the prescription insert advising her to "monitor appropriately and observe closely for clinical worsening," and though she'd had no idea what "clinical worsening" would look like, she'd rearranged her schedule to handle client meetings during school hours and kept a closer eye on Julia at home. She'd touched base. Created mood trackers with Sharpies and index cards.

And, initially, it had seemed the medicine was working; Julia was engaged, relieved even.

So, feeling relieved herself, Laura had gone to a dinner meeting.

One dinner meeting.

Twelve days into the Lexapro.

LAURA HAD SEEN DR. RENNER'S neutral look falter then, when she admitted she'd forgotten about Paul's pre-cancer prescriptions stored on the top shelf of the medicine cabinet in their master bathroom—pain medication, sleeping pills, muscle relaxants. How she hadn't noticed the careful repositioning that concealed the absence of orange plastic bottles.

She'd missed the clinical worsening, the formulation of a plan.

She'd come home from the business dinner to a silent house. The upstairs hall bathroom door locked.

LAURA HAD KEPT TO HERSELF the fragments that looped every night as she tried to fall asleep. Calling *JuliaJuliaJulia*. Sirens blaring. Flashing lights. Heavy boots on the stairs. A limp body lifted by uniformed men, water dripping from black fabric, a lifeless hand, a slit wrist—

A CAR PULLED INTO THE DRIVEWAY. The noise of the engine quieted. A car door closed.

"That would be Lilly," Laura said to no one. She picked up the stack of index cards and the *Surviving a Suicide* booklet and opened the junk drawer.

The door to the mudroom opened. Light flooded the kitchen. Laura blinked hard.

"Lor?" came Lilly's voice. "What are you doing in the dark?"

Laura did not reply. She stood, frozen. Lilly would never understand that Laura welcomed the darkness because she couldn't have what she really wanted—to go back two years to a fall Sunday in the park, a day marked by normalcy: the smell of freshly mown grass mingling with fallen leaves; Paul and Julia throwing a football; Julia playing peekaboo with a toddler nearby. Laura could not adequately explain what she knew now but couldn't have known then—that she'd been living her last best day.

Laura dropped the cards and booklet into the drawer.

The doorbell rang again. A long, sustained buzz.

"Do you want me to get that?" Lilly asked.

Laura did not answer.

"Wait here," Lilly said, touching Laura's back gently. "I'll be right back." Then, as she entered the hall, she said, "Jesus, Lor, what happened? There's candy all over the floor."

Laura closed the drawer and stood, listening, as her sister scooped up the candy and opened the front door. She waited to hear "trick or treat," candy being dropped into bags, Lilly saying "Happy Halloween." But instead, she heard a vaguely familiar voice demanding, "Where is she? Where's Julia?"

JULIA

JULIA'S ROOMMATE, CLAUDIA, was in a constant state of motion: pacing or bouncing on her toes, flexing her hands, tapping her fingers. A tech was glued to her side for an hour after every meal. "The food police," Claudia told her after lunch on her second day. "You'd think I'm a fucking criminal, the way they follow me."

"It's to keep her from sticking her finger down her throat," Rita stage-whispered, laying her hand gently on Julia's arm. "Claudia has issues with food, and authority."

Julia knew this without being told. Despite the fog, some things were clear. By the end of that second day, she knew the names and diagnoses of the three women with whom she shared a suite, or "pod" as the staff referred to it: one double and two singles grouped around a small living room. Rita, the matriarch of the unit, a silver-haired, puffy-eyed woman who wore flowing patterned caftans, suffered from depression with chronic insomnia. Claudia was twenty-two but looked fourteen. Years of anorexia had left her gaunt, nearly ghostlike, camouflaged in the achromatic setting except for a thin shock of short copper hair that brought to mind a candlestick burning bright. And Emily Rose, age unknown, nondescript brown hair, average height and weight, the sort of woman who'd escape notice were it not for her entirely non-average schizophrenic behavior— furtive glances, handwringing, soft murmuring.

Julia felt a sense of belonging, both confirmation and affirmation: she was insanely depressed, or at least she had been, and she wasn't alone—other "others" were here, right in front of her, not out in the ethersphere. This knowledge was strangely comforting. So, too, were the crisp, slightly scratchy white sheets and sage fleece blanket, the wood floors and cream walls, the tiny clear plastic cup of pills with its big sister plastic cup of water, the daily routine with its circumscribed activities and time constraints.

Day three had been nearly identical to the day before:

7:15 am: morning check by the pod-tech, medication/vital signs

7:30 am: breakfast in the common dining room

8:30 am: group therapy. Intros, sharing, goal setting. Breakdown of new patient, Rachel: obese, brassy hair with dark roots, crying incessantly, story nearly unintelligible and totally uncomfortable—depressed, addicted to pain meds, mother-hatred issues.

9:30 am: activity therapy in the form of yoga with Ashni—compensation for Rachel decompensation

10:30 am: individual therapy with "please call me Tanya." Young, pretty, with honey-colored, shoulder-length hair and a voice like a marshmallow.

Yesterday, the intake assessment with Tanya had been all about forms and questionnaires Julia was starting to recognize. The Beck Depression Inventory. The PHQ.

Checking boxes. Establishing a baseline.

Today, Tanya's hands were empty. No clipboard. No pen. No leather-bound notebook. And no white coats at Brookfield. Tanya was wearing a bright turquoise sweater.

Really bright, practically neon. Maybe this wardrobe choice was intentional. Some kind of casual cheeriness.

"So, Julia," Tanya said. "Tell me, why are you here?"

Julia had known this question was coming — or something like it. That morning, lying in bed, the sheet over her head like a blank canvas, she'd deliberated over how to answer. Who could she trust? Now, the whisper of her subconscious swirled to the surface: *Who will understand?* If this didn't work, nothing would. She could feel pressure building under her rib cage, like a bubble bursting to be released.

"I — " she began. "I can't explain it. I never can. I want to, it's just so fucking hard."

"I know," Tanya said with a barely perceptible nod. "It's hard to put into words."

"It's like . . . like the world has gone dark and I can't control . . . anything. I can't sleep. I can't eat. Sometimes, it's hard to breathe."

Tanya was still nodding.

"At first, I tried to find ways to help myself, like these." Julia grabbed a handful of dreadlocks. "This trich site said it might help stop the pulling. It's not like I want to be falling apart, despite what my mom — " The pressure inside Julia's chest moved up, increasing as it ascended. "I can't talk to her. To anyone. It's like people expect me to be the way I was before. But after what I've done — " *Stop, stop there,* she told herself. The pressure kept building. "I don't care about any of it — grades, SAT scores, getting into college. This girl at school, Sara, she actually said losing a parent is good material for an essay. 'Good material,' that's what she said. Literally, 'good material.' And my best friend, she — "

Julia heard her voice shaking as the memory surfaced. They'd been sitting in the cafeteria. Her best friend, Jess, had nodded as Sara spoke, and Julia had known she couldn't sit there another second. She'd banged her leg on the table as she rose to leave and heard Jess murmuring comforting words — *to Sara, to SARA* — as Julia walked away. "Don't worry, she'll be okay. Just still kind of sensitive about her dad." *If only she knew.* The bruise on Julia's leg had faded about the time she stopped receiving text messages from Jess, the last one reading "I'm here but it's hard 2 know what 2 say around u."

"But that's not it," Julia said now, to Tanya. "I don't care about them or that they don't care about me. I just think everyone should tell the truth and stop hiding. But—" Julia sighed heavily. "That's not it either."

She wasn't telling the truth herself. This wasn't what she'd meant to say. The pressure inside wasn't abating. It started to choke her thoughts and words. She lifted a hand to her throat.

"I can't—"

"I know," Tanya said softly. "It's okay, Julia." She paused, tilted her head. "Maybe you could tell me about when this all started."

That, Julia could do.

Her dad. The seizures. Everything taken from him: his energy, his laugh, his dignity—at the end, his will. His vision. Death robbing him blind. Lines of poetry muddled and reinterpreted.

Please help me.

An involuntary shiver shuddered through her, and then her words spilled like a river overflowing its boundaries: losing the only person who truly saw her and loved her without limits or expectations; the guilt and loneliness and emptiness; not being able to sleep despite feeling ridiculously tired, all the time; the irresistible urge to cut herself and the temporary relief it provided; the drugs that provided only slightly more relief before making things worse, and then, trying to stop it all, the cloying, counterfeit response from her mother and the people who were supposed to care; losing herself in a world spiraling out of control; the utter hopelessness of the whole, fucking mess.

Tanya listened, her face open, nodding, an occasional "hmm, mm," until Julia said, "the whole fucking mess," at which point Tanya shook her head softly.

"God, I'm sorry, Julia," she said. "You're dealing with a lot that pretty much sucks."

For a fraction of a second, Julia thought Tanya might actually understand: "pretty much sucks" was the only valid response.

"And yet," Tanya said, "you're here, in my office, struggling to hold on. You don't want to give up. Simply being here tells me that. You're sad and tired and lonely, but you're here." Tanya's voice slowed. "Losing your dad was devastating." She paused. "And what I'm hearing you say is you feel disconnected. People don't understand, so you avoid them, but then you feel isolated, even numb. You want to feel something—anything—instead of nothing. You want to tell the truth. And you want to believe in something. Am I getting close?"

Closer than anyone else, Julia thought, *except for the part about telling the truth.* She realized she couldn't tell the whole truth. Not now. Maybe not ever. To anyone. She pushed her hands hard across the cutting marks on her thighs, feeling relief as sensation radiated down her legs, up into her arms. She watched Tanya watching her. Nodded.

Tanya raised her own hands into a half steeple, fingertips pressing together, palms apart, almost as if in prayer. "And I want you to know," she said, "you have something important going for you—you're incredibly smart and self-aware. And this"—Julia watched the praying hands move apart gently as if now holding something delicate in between—"this is a huge strength."

The hands dropped to Tanya's lap, loosely folded.

Julia reached up to twirl her hair, expecting to encounter the bandana she'd taken to wearing, another technique prescribed on a trich site. Then she remembered bandanas were prohibited, along with her shoelaces, the drawstrings in her hoodie and joggers. All withdrawn. "It hasn't helped much," she said.

Tanya nodded. "I get why you'd feel that way. But here's the thing, Julia, you came here of your own free will, which tells me you want to deal with this—how did you phrase it?—this 'whole fucking mess.' And I believe we can do it." Tanya gave her a rueful half smile. "Have you heard of cognitive behavioral therapy?"

"Mm-hmm."

Julia did not admit that, in addition to repeatedly googling pain medication contraindications and warnings, hoping for different answers, she'd developed an obsession with psychology and psychiatry on the Internet. In an effort to get past her inability to concentrate, she'd taken to rereading certain web pages—one of which was about CBT. She'd been drawn to a graphic of emotions, thoughts, and behaviors in a triad with arrows—feelings of darkness leading to not wanting to be around people, leading to loneliness and more darkness, and so on and so on. It made sense, the idea that changing the direction of the arrows might start with changing behaviors rather than focusing on "how do you feel?" and it was one of the few techniques with actual self-help parameters. Julia had even downloaded a PDF manual and left it out on her dresser with a bunch of other stuff she'd found online, hoping her mom would notice it.

But her mom had stopped coming into her room to say goodnight. Every interaction now was about medicine or index cards—forced, prescribed, contentious.

Regardless of what Laura professed, Julia was convinced her very existence caused her mother pain—because of what she'd done and what her mother hadn't. Couldn't.

Her mother would eventually be relieved if she were gone.

"Well, while you're here at Brookfield," Tanya said, "we're going to use CBT and a few other things to work through all this. Help you find a way to think about things differently. Give you tools to regain control, so you can reengage and see that there's good in the world. I want to be honest with you, Julia. Some of the things you're feeling—like missing your dad—they won't ever go away completely. But, together, we can get you out of the hole you're in. At first, it'll be like finding a shovel to toss some of the shit out over the top, but then, hopefully, we'll find you a ladder, so you can climb out and start looking forward to where you want to be."

Hopefully.

A welling up inside, a cresting wave, and then, tears.

"Can you tell me what you're feeling?" Tanya asked.

For once, Julia had an answer to this question. "Hope scares me."

ALL AFTERNOON, JULIA COULDN'T shake the image of herself standing in a chasm of steaming shit with a tiny plastic beach shovel like the one featured in her favorite childhood photograph—age two, plump and pot-bellied in a lavender polka-dot bathing suit, standing with one small pudgy hand in her father's, the other clutching a pink sand shovel, a castle with twin lookout towers and a moat in front of them, clearly his design and construction. Written unevenly in the sand, "Princess Julia."

From the recesses came another memory, more recent—lying on the family room sectional watching *The Graduate* with her parents. "One word: plastics," her dad had said along with one of the male characters, like it meant something, something outside of Julia's worldview.

"I don't get it," she'd said to her father. "Benjamin's sort of a jerk, isn't he?" Which had prompted a long conversation about the 1960s, generation gaps, the meaning of life and the malaise of youthful uncertainty, about symbolism, art, materialism, and idealism. Her father's eyes bright, his hands gesticulating, words spilling.

Her mother had left ten minutes in, saying, "It's just a movie, Paul." And yet, Julia knew that for her dad, it wasn't just a movie. She didn't understand what it was just yet, only that it must be important, so post-*Graduate,* Julia decided she ought to give the movie another chance.

Her father had always encouraged her to give things another chance: pickle relish, snowboarding, *The Catcher in the Rye*. While he was sick, Julia had created a "Second Chance Bucket List," a combination bargain-with-fate and a challenge to her father: if he stayed alive, she'd continue to give things another chance. But then everything had gone sideways and upside down, and then he'd died, leaving her and the list behind. She'd folded it and placed it inside her favorite childhood book. Promises notwithstanding, Julia couldn't bear to look at the list, let alone give any of the items their second chance.

And yet, she couldn't throw it away either.

IT HADN'T TAKEN LONG FOR HER to understand that lists were big at Brookfield. So were metrics, cards, goals, strategies, and big reveals.

> **3:15 pm:** Process group. Stated purpose: discussion of separating self from thoughts. Psychiatric detour: Rachel redux.

Julia's skepticism about group therapy ramped up. Certain that hearing painful story after painful story had little chance of helping her feel better about the world, she'd focused on the floor until Rachel had started to cry again, really hard.

Looking up had been a bad idea.

The immediate judgment she felt toward Rachel was as uncomfortable as Rachel herself, shifting on the molded plastic chair, head bowed, greasy dark roots reminding Julia of black oil, as if Rachel's depression was seeping out of her head. Julia thought it possible that Rachel's chair could break, which brought back thoughts about her own neck snapping, and she wondered how she was supposed to be responding. *How is any of it helpful?*

"Goddamn," muttered a twenty-something guy Julia didn't know as he retrieved a pack of cigarettes from his back pocket.

The social worker, Beverly, a middle-aged Black woman with a bronze-tipped halo of hair, interrupted him. "You know the rules, Brett. You can't smoke in here. Outside only."

A collective cleansing sigh filled the room as everyone turned away from Rachel to Brett.

Julia stared at Brett as he tapped the Marlboro box on his leg, black, white, and red against the blue fabric of his jeans. She studied the images that appeared like carved statues on his sinewy arm: a Botticelli cherub in the embrace of a Bernini archangel with a strong patrician nose and folded wings that disappeared beneath Brett's gray t-shirt. The fingertips of Julia's right hand dropped to her thigh, caressing an arc over the wounds on her leg, sculpting the curve of a wing.

"Just kinda tense in here," Brett said. He glanced at Julia and took in the movement of her hand, then raised an eyebrow, smirking, as if he'd caught her doing something forbidden.

God, maybe he had.

Julia looked away, scanning the circle of faces for a safe place to land, finding Beverly.

"Julia? We didn't hear from you this morning. Do you feel ready to share?"

Wrong landing place. Julia did not feel safe. She did not want to share. At all. For an instant, she floated up, saw the circle from above, tops of heads, Beverly's bronze curls, Rachel's roots—

"Start with your name and why you're here," Beverly said. "Maybe your goal for today and how it's going?"

Back in her chair, Julia felt her lungs constrict. "I'm Julia." A slow, abridged reveal. "Depression. Trich. Cutting." She crossed her arms wrist to wrist in her lap, each hand gripping the opposite arm. "Drug overdose."

"That last one your goal?" Brett asked. He leaned forward, an unlit cigarette perched between his lips. "My kind of girl."

Julia found herself turning inward, hating Brett, hating Rachel, hating process group until she heard someone say "capture the light." She looked up to see a dark-haired guy with a scruffy beard leaning in the doorway. "That's the goal for today. Still working."

"Sam? Can you join us?" Beverly asked. She swept her hand in the direction of an empty seat in the circle.

Sam surveyed the group. His gaze passed over Julia to Rita, reversed, and then, dead stop, his eyes locked on to Julia's. Impossibly blue. One second. Maybe two. Before Julia could register what had happened, the door was closing, with Sam on the other side. "Not happening today, Beverly. Maybe tomorrow."

As quickly as he had appeared, he was gone.

LAURA

"MENTAL MASTURBATION." That's what Laura's stepfather, Carl, had labeled self-analysis one evening after hearing from Laura's mother about a neighborhood kid landing in therapy. Laura had been thirteen at the time and feeling depressed and lost herself, though she never could have admitted it. Her mother and Carl rarely discussed such things, but they'd made their opinions clear—if the unexamined life might not be worth living, the over-examined one was an exercise in self-absorption. Allowing one's emotions to run amok was pathetic, and as for dissecting dreams, rehashing childhood events, and drawing parallels between the past and the present, all of it was foolhardy at best, downright dangerous at worst.

Yet this was what Laura now had to do—all this and more—for Julia. Family therapy started in four hours, with yet another psychologist or social worker. The she-said, she-said. Julia and Laura telling the story again, with all the warts and missteps.

From the beginning, the end, somewhere in the middle.

Looking for answers.

Laura took the morning off and began the search on her own. Holding her breath, she walked past the hall bathroom and opened the door into Julia's too-quiet bedroom.

She straightened the comforter and, lifting the pillow to fluff it, spied Julia's cuddly, Max, a stuffed dog with floppy ears named for the main character in her favorite childhood book, *Where the Wild Things Are.* Laura brought the toy close, inhaled deeply and then, out of habit, placed him on top of the fluffed pillow.

She turned and studied the posters tacked on the wall that had replaced framed prints from the Met, the bulletin board laden with drawings and cartoons. She took in skulls with empty eye sockets and swirls of purple and black, spiraling inward like collapsing galaxies; the desktop cluttered with papers; the dresser top with more papers, jewelry, and an ancient Howard University sweatshirt of Paul's that Julia had taken to wearing, crumpled and inside out. Laura walked to the open closet and stood for a moment, gazing at the clothing her daughter had purchased at thrift stores under Cheyenne's tutelage, trying not to dwell on the obvious disconnect with items pushed to the back of the closet, the things purchased with Laura and Paul. "You don't know her at all," Cheyenne had said Halloween night. "And you weren't there for her."

In the back, on a high shelf, Laura found the flat boxes in which she'd stored Julia's baby book, photo albums, and memorabilia. It took two trips to retrieve them. She sat on the floor, brushed dust from the tops, and opened them in succession, looking for the baby book.

Starting at the beginning.

Laura had been a diligent chronicler; dates filled each line for turning over, sitting up, first tooth, first day of school. The albums were similarly complete. She'd taken pleasure in organizing and documenting, carefully selecting each image, placing the photos into the white adhesive corners, creating the labels underneath: "Julia in utero, 32 weeks"; "First day of pre-school, age 3"; "League MVP, age 13." Julia blowing out candles. Julia playing with the neighbor's golden retriever, Buddy. Julia holding Max, curled up next to Paul as he read aloud to her. Julia dressed up for Halloween with her best friend Jess as twin cats.

Two of the boxes were devoted to artwork, and Laura lingered over each piece in a way she hadn't had time for when they were created: the obligatory finger-paint handprints, the reproduction of Van Gogh's sunflowers that had taken the teacher's breath away, the first comic book about Buddy the puppy, and a more elaborate one, about a girl living at the foot of a mountain, with precisely drawn characters and bubbles of remarkably realistic dialogue.

Julia had been an easy baby and a sweet, empathetic child. "All the makings of an ideal big sister," Paul had said. However, four years after Julia's complicated caesarian birth, following three miscarriages, two D&Cs, and an intra-uterine photo shoot that revealed excessive scarring, Laura was informed she could not have any more children—news she'd borne up and away.

Paul's death was not the only one Laura had mourned silently.

As she sat on the floor with boxes of Julia strewn around her, Laura realized contributions to the memory-lane repository ceased about the time Paul's headaches began to darken their lives. Literally darken them—Paul couldn't stand bright light or loud noises. Curtains were drawn. Voices muted. Pain stifled.

There were no pictures of Julia with dreadlocks or heavy eyeliner. Laura hadn't smoothed and scrapbooked the academic probation notice she'd found in Julia's garbage pail. She hadn't saved the plastic hospital wristband with the label "First suicide attempt."

Stop. Now. There would be no answers here.

Laura tidied up the boxes and placed them back on the shelf. She walked past the dresser, lifted Paul's inside-out sweatshirt, and saw a yellow Post-it note with "For Mom" written on it, stuck to a sheaf of paper. On top was an article on the genetic component of mental illness. Underneath were dozens of articles and website printouts. A piece on childhood trauma. Another on cutting and self-harm. Assisted suicide legalization and "Being there" for teenagers dealing with grief, both of which caught Laura's breath. A blog about dreadlocks as treatment for trichotillomania, featuring a young woman with bright orange snakes of hair. And at the very bottom, a section stapled together called "A Parent's Guide to Cognitive Behavioral Therapy." Laura looked up at herself in the mirror on the wall, and like a bolt out of the blue, it came to her—she'd been looking in the wrong place.

"It's not your fault," everyone had told her: Lilly; the paramedics who'd pulled Julia from the bathtub; an ICU nurse who'd monitored Julia during the coma; the social worker who'd given her the Suicide Survivor booklet; the young psychiatrist whose name she could not recall, who'd switched Julia's medicine and referred her to Dr. Stein; Dr. Stein himself; Dr. Renner.

They were all wrong, but Julia knew. Fucking Cheyenne knew. "For Mom."

The fault *was* hers, somewhere along the way. Perhaps as early as when Paul's sperm hit the egg loaded with her genes, the head of a pin carrying hidden maladaptive codes. Or maybe it was that she hadn't picked Julia up fast enough when she was crying as an infant, leading to a deep-seated fear of abandonment. Then again, it could have been the unconscious squelching of weakness when Julia was young, when Laura's own programming came out in phrases like "that's not worth crying over" or "please stop, you're going to ruin your hair." Refusing to discuss the changes Paul's illness had wrought or giving Julia time and space when it was clear she was falling and needed her mother to catch her.

As if the universe decided to confirm her thoughts, Laura spied a photograph that had slipped onto the floor. She reached down and picked it up. Julia from the back, at LaGuardia, age eleven, about to embark on a trip with Paul to Chicago. The picture was blurry, taken by Laura through a rain-covered windshield, a wiper mid-arc, ineffective against a late summer downpour. The image reminded Laura of the day the last-minute father-daughter consolation getaway had been planned, when Julia had discovered she hadn't been invited to the class queen bee's birthday party—an improbably inappropriate day of beauty for a select group of prepubescent girls. Laura could picture Julia's fingers wiping at tears ineffectively; as soon as Julia wiped, more tears fell. And Laura could remember her own response: Stifling anger at the queen bee and the queen-bee's mother, she'd been dismissive of the event—Julia didn't need that girl or her silly party.

"She's clearly not your friend," Laura had said. "Besides, you don't really want to spend an entire day primping with those girls, do you?"

Julia had shaken her head bravely, yet her face crumpled as she admitted, "I do."

The memory burned. Paul had swept Julia into his arms and, cradling the top of her head with his hand, shaken his head at Laura, eyebrows raised, before saying aloud, "Even if it wasn't something you'd have chosen, it hurts to feel left out, doesn't it?"

Julia had nodded into Paul's chest while Laura stood there, awkwardly, realizing she'd said the wrong thing, again, and she'd wondered for the umpteenth time how she and her husband had found their way together—Paul, the sensitive, empathic poet who'd found his calling through Teach for America, and Laura, the stoic but highly efficient financial consultant, whose demanding job was simply a means to an end, not a calling. Unaware at the time of what was to come, Laura had thanked the stars that Paul had seen something in her, because it was clear that without him, she would be lost.

And then, remarkably, Julia's left hand had dropped and reached for hers.

Before Laura could recall her daughter's touch, her phone vibrated—Family Therapy @ Brookfield started in one hour. Her eyes shifted from phone to photo to dresser top, taking in Julia under a deluge, Paul's inside-out sweatshirt, and the sheaf with the "For Mom" Post-it note.

Bucking the fuck up took on new meaning.

Laura lifted the sheaf of paper, flipped to the first page, and began to read.

5

JULIA

THE SKETCH LAY NEXT TO HER cafeteria tray when Julia returned from refilling a water glass with ice chips. A few lines of charcoal on ivory paper, it wasn't like any portrait she'd ever drawn. It reminded her of something she'd seen in AP History, but she quickly realized it was her face, in profile, from the left. She recognized the jaw, the curve of her cheek, the small arc of an asymmetrical dimple, the shape of her eyebrow.

"Sam left it for you," Rita said. "Said it's a token, whatever that means."

Julia didn't know whether to be flattered or freaked out. She stood behind her chair, the glass cool in her hand, and looked around the dining room, her eyes flitting from table to table before landing on Sam's back.

He sat alone, facing windows that looked onto a sterile gravel-lined courtyard.

"Got a bit of a reputation, that one," Rita said. As she leaned over, reaching for the drawing, the sleeve of her purple and green peacock caftan slid over the rim of Julia's plate. "Be careful."

"You, too," Julia said. She gestured to the paper.

"I'm not going to hurt it," Rita said, frowning.

"No, I meant your sleeve. The dressing—"

Rita lifted her arm, saw the silken fabric resting in a pool of balsamic vinegar and oil, and dropped the picture onto the plate. Julia retrieved it hastily, but not before two spots of oil appeared to the right of paper-Julia's nose.

"Oh, shit," Rita said. "Oh, shit. I'm so sorry." The older woman's mouth trembled.

"It's okay. Really. It doesn't matter," Julia said. She patted Rita awkwardly on the shoulder. "I'm going to go over and . . . thank him . . . I guess."

Julia wasn't certain she wanted to go over and thank Sam, but she also couldn't handle another breakdown, and Rita was fragile. Morning group day four had been a shit show. Drifting up and away, Julia had been imagining how she might draw the scene when, quite abruptly, Rachel had gone after Rita when she tried to say something comforting, and then Brett went after Rachel, which set Emily Rose on edge, who'd started rocking in her chair, moaning, louder and louder, until Beverly had to bring in reinforcements—the whole mess convincing Julia that processing in a group was the very definition of letting the inmates run the asylum.

Family therapy that afternoon hadn't been much better. Her mother's discomfort with delving, oddly combined with her statement to "do whatever I have to do to help Julia," made for a truly painful hour with "call me Donna," the family therapist. Julia wondered how any of it was going to fit together: she pictured pieces of herself, like jagged-edged bits of a photo-mosaic puzzle, spread out on a conference table with Donna, Tanya, Beverly, Dr. Renner, and her mother all poring over them, flipping them, looking for edge pieces that might give her definition, searching for patterns, and then, realizing there was no box top to guide them and pieces were clearly missing, sliding the sharp little shapes around to look busy, waiting for someone else to be the first to give up.

As Julia approached Sam's back, she noticed his elbow moving, his arm, his hand arcing over the sketchpad, effortlessly, as though directed by a higher power. She stopped and watched the charcoal block rise and dip, creating a series of concentric circles with connecting swirls.

Passages. A six-petal flower at the heart.

An image that was both otherworldly and intimately familiar. Sam turned to look at her.

"It's beautiful," she said.

Sam stared into her face. "It is." He looked toward the sketch she held. "Though I don't think I did the model justice. I had to pull it from memory because I hadn't obtained proper permissions. I assure you, under ideal conditions, I can do better."

Julia felt her pulse quicken, a flush spread across her chest, up her neck, and into her cheeks. Her hand moved up to twirl her hair. Julia wondered how she looked and instantly wanted to deflect Sam's attention elsewhere.

"Oh, no, I meant—" Julia tilted her head toward the unfinished drawing on the table. "The maze. It looks Gaelic."

Sam didn't take his eyes off her. "It's a labyrinth, for meditation. I want to build one, here." Sam gestured with his head to the courtyard. "I've been offering to design it, build it, for years, but, well, management isn't convinced."

"Years?" The word slipped out. Questions and answers pinged and bounced off each other: *Does he live here?* Not possible; she'd been told it was a short-stay facility. *Maybe he works here, except then why would Beverly invite him to join group?*

Sam gave her a wry smile that conveyed both pity and amusement at her confusion.

"Sorry," Julia said. "I, I didn't—"

"Nah, it's okay," Sam said. "But yeah, years. On and off." He slid his own chair back six inches and pulled out the chair next to it. "Have a seat."

The room was clearing. Julia looked back at Rita. Eyes wide open, hands pressed to her lips and cheeks, the older woman shook her head, mouthing the words, "no, don't." Julia recalled the warning she'd been given during her entrance interview: "Fraternization of any kind is strictly prohibited."

Sam leaned his head down and whispered conspiratorially. "It's okay. We're allowed to talk to each other."

"Oh, I know, I just . . ." Julia's voice fell off for the third, or was it the fourth, time. She pictured herself—a skinny girl with a piece of paper fluttering from her fingers, standing in front of a drop-dead gorgeous guy with a bemused look on his face, a dialogue bubble over her head filled with *I just* and a slew of ellipses.

Oh my god, get a grip, she told herself. *He's another patient. And he's at least five years older than you.*

Julia placed the sketch of her face down on the table and sat in the offered chair. Sam's tray of food was nearly untouched.

"Where should we start?" Sam said. He flipped the labyrinth drawing over on the binding, revealing a blank page and a tangled scar on his wrist, then looked up at her from under a messy fringe of dark brown hair. "May I?"

It took Julia a moment to realize what he was asking. "You want to draw me?"

"While we talk." Sam paused, his hand suspended over the paper. "If it's okay with you."

Julia nodded. Though she was accustomed to being on the other side of the equation, she'd had a teacher who required her students to sit for others to understand how it felt—the vulnerability, the gift of giving oneself. Julia's thoughts turned back to her art classes, the outside world, Cheyenne, the mess she'd left behind. Her chest tightened.

"Are you sure?" Sam said. "Body language conflicted."

"Yeah, it's okay."

"Excellent. See, I've been thinking about your face since yesterday afternoon. I tried to pull the lines from my faulty gray matter, hence the Matisse-like sketch, not that I'm comparing myself to Matisse or saying that Matisse was faulty." Sam looked up, then back at the paper. "But *I* am. Quite faulty. Most of the time I can hold images in memory, but as you've probably guessed, my brain isn't totally cooperative. If it were, I wouldn't be here, engaged in the Sisyphean task of finding the balance of thoughts and behavior that most men take for granted, men without awareness of true depth, uninterested in the passionate pursuit of an epic sunrise or the perfect margarita. The ice, the salt, the sting. But I digress."

Sam looked up again, this time smiling broadly. "Digression can be a beautiful thing, though, can't it? God knows I've provided psychologists across this magnificent state with enough contradictory material to send a previously stable mind into a maelstrom of doubt and, perhaps, surrender. There was this postdoc, a couple of years ago, I almost felt sorry for him. I was going on about the Hell's Angel on Rorschach's Card IV and how it wasn't a father thing for me."

Sam's hand did not stop moving while he spoke. His eyes darted up, then back.

"Talking about how my dad is an international banker whose ass has never hit the leather seat of a bike, given his strong preference for the heated seat of a classic BMW, the 'true driver's car.' Not that we discuss things like that. I can't remember the last time my father and I had a conversation about anything other than my general fucked-up-ed-ness, which he has labeled 'beyond worse.'"

Sam lifted his head, gave another smile, one-sided and crooked, halfway to a frown.

"I heard him use those exact words in one of his heated arguments with my mom right before he left — 'this is beyond worse' — which I learned, later, was a reference to their marriage vows." His eyes continued darting. "Apparently, my grandmother expected the standard vows at my parents' society wedding, the whole 'for better or for worse,' which became a point of contention between her and my dad. Not that my dad wanted to write his own vows. That would require creativity, which he abhors, as it's a reminder of our family history of insane genius, which, I explained to the postdoc, explains his difficulty in dealing with me. 'Guilt of self runs deep in my blood,' I said, and the postdoc just stared at me, kind of like you are now —"

Sam stopped, hand poised. "Of course, I wasn't trying to draw the postdoc, so the quizzical expression was not an issue." He tilted his head. Raised an eyebrow.

Julia had been staring, drawn in by the angles of Sam's face, the shape of his mouth as he spoke. Her face was likely a mirror reflecting alternating fascination and bewilderment at the tangential world of words he'd created. Her thoughts flitted to the graphic novel she'd started and abandoned; how difficult it would be to capture Sam's moods visually as a cartoon figure; and how impossible it would be to fit his words into dialogue bubbles. *So many words.*

"Sorry," she said. She pressed her fingertips across her cheeks and up over her eyebrows, smoothing out her features.

"Just kidding." Sam placed the charcoal block on the table and pulled a kneaded eraser from his pocket. "Nothing to be sorry for; sometimes I can't even follow my own logic. Hence, my presence here for what I call 'a maintenance visit,' though my mother prefers the term 'recalibration.' I don't have the heart to tell her the correct definition of the word. Truth is I suppose we're both right . . . and we're both wrong. It's the same thing over and over: new meds, old meds, a few sessions with Tanya, recasting the absurd struggle over how I live my life, if it's worth living, whether I have choices about any of it."

If it's worth living? Sam's "years on and off" comment started making sense. *How many times has he been here? How many years?* The spilling speech, untouched food, and arcing charcoal now presented as symptoms she'd read about online, which made Julia think of her own—the obvious ones and those hidden from view. Her fingers migrated up to her dreadlocks, down to her thighs, pressing where she knew nerves would respond, grounding her. A powerful urge to run away broke over her like a wave, competing with an equally compelling urge to stay. A psychic alarm bell clanged in her head, cautioning her to silence her questions.

Sam looked from her to the drawing, back to her, dabbed the eraser. "So, enough about me. What's your story?"

"My story?" The alarm bells continued to clang. Julia imagined a spiky cartoon bubble over her head displaying *CLANG!* in a bright red comic font.

"Yeah. What's a girl like you doing in a place like this?"

Julia's chest tightened and the bubble popped. She quickly rewound the ways she'd presented her narrative in the last few weeks: the dark Prozac-hasn't-fully-kicked-in version given to Dr. Stein, the dangerous hope-inducing version with call-me-Tanya, the abridged version for group. Images and their accompanying feelings flashed: her head falling, the little plastic shovel, Brett's Bernini wings and angels. And then her dad's face, the pronounced cheekbones, the rattling in his chest, her mother's stoic silence, and her own gulping tears.

What have I done?

"My dad. He was—"

Despair flooded in. Her words halted as the urge to run overwhelmed the urge to stay.

Julia stood up abruptly, banging her leg on the table and more memories flooded in. The day in the cafeteria, losing Jess, the old version of herself, the one her father had loved and trusted, perhaps more than anyone. *Would he even recognize me now?*

She sensed rather than saw Sam moving. His hand grasped her elbow to steady her, but it had the reverse effect. She could feel his touch radiating in and out, up and down, nerve endings awakening—a cut without a blade.

"Come with me," he said. "I know what you need."

6

LAURA

LAURA ENTERED HER SISTER Lilly's house through the side door, adjacent to the kitchen, warm with golden light and laughter, the latter of which ceased immediately when she crossed the threshold. For the briefest of moments, the four other women in the room froze as if a remote control pause button had been pressed, creating a post-modern tableau of discomfort. Julia had once called these moments "Generational Installation Art." Lilly by the stove, one hand holding a glass of red wine, the other a wooden spoon mid-stir in the contents of a cast iron pot on the stove; Lilly and Laura's mother, Frances, sitting regally in a high-back slatted wooden chair at the head of the kitchen table, silvery blond hair perfectly coiffed, cheekbones sharp; Lilly's younger daughter, fifteen-year old Grace, cross-legged on the window seat, dark blond hair in a ponytail, a yellow highlighter poised over the textbook in front of her; and Lilly's older daughter, Isabella—Izzy to those who loved her—mere inches from Laura, skin smooth, green eyes wide, arms extended toward a stack of Italian ceramic dishes in the cupboard next to the door.

"How's Julia?" Izzy blurted. "I mean . . . is she feeling any better?"

Before Laura could speak, Frances broke in. "Isabella, I thought we'd decided not to discuss this. Your mother has spent a great deal of time preparing a dinner that we've all been waiting to enjoy." The statement punctuated by raised eyebrows, tight lips. The unspoken message: "Enough of that. Leave the elephant alone."

There was another pause, a new tableau, just as frozen, yet more awkward than the first. Izzy's green eyes flitted from Laura to her grandmother, back to Laura, then to her mother.

Lilly's voice melted the silence. "It's okay, Izzy. We didn't *decide* anything of the sort. We all want to know how Julia's feeling, don't we, girls?" Lilly placed the spoon onto a ceramic spoon rest that matched the dishes in Izzy's hands, the window valances, and a wall clock. She turned from the stove and took a few steps in Laura's direction. "Did you see her? How is she?"

"I went," Laura said. "But, well, she wasn't ready, yet, for visitors. I did see her yesterday, though, for family therapy, which was—"

Loud scraping of wood against wood interrupted Laura's words. She turned to see her mother push away from the table dramatically, her mouth set in a firm line.

"Family therapy." Frances spat out the words, "My God, these places prey on your generation—everyone's a victim, always blaming others for your problems. Julia's not the first moody, rebellious teenager, and she won't be the last." Frances sent a knowing glance directly at Laura, somehow sundering the half sisters who stood shoulder to shoulder: Lilly, calm, cool, with a sleek, smooth blond bob; Laura, tense and awkward, with unmanageable curly brown hair Frances had declared over and over to be "so like your father's," a comment clearly not meant to be complimentary.

"This isn't about me," Laura said, then stopped. *For Mom.* She'd been reading the documents Julia left her. And though she didn't understand much of it, if any of it was right, this wasn't just about Julia and her, it was about all of them—Frances and Carl and Lilly and Paul.

Patterns and relics and layers.

"I am fully aware what this is about." Frances stood in the doorway, shoulders back, head high, glass of Chardonnay held aloft.

Laura stood, frozen in place.

"*I'll* be in the living room," Frances said. "*Waiting. Again.* Grace, come keep me company."

"No." Lilly's voice stopped her daughter as she rose from her chair. "I'd like Grace to stay and hear about her cousin. Of course, you're welcome to wait in the living room. The *Times* is on the coffee table for you." Lilly pointedly turned away. She spun Laura gently, pulled on the sleeve of her dark wool coat. "Come, take off your coat. Sit down."

Laura saw her mother's withering look over her sister's shoulder. "I see," Frances said, a biting emphasis on the "see."

Laura closed her eyes to avoid watching her mother's back recede down the hall, the tightness in her chest increasing with each heel click on the hardwood floor.

Lilly shook her head. "I'll be right back," she said.

Laura heard Lilly calling "Mother?" as she followed their mother into the living room and then only bits of the conversation, mostly Frances' voice, as if she wanted to be heard.

"The girl needs to pick herself up, stop choosing misery like it's a badge of honor. My God, the hair and piercings. All the darkness and brooding. Laura needs to—"

"Stop," Laura heard Lilly say, and then again, more quietly, "Stop." Then just a few words emerging. "...struggling ...loss..."

"I do not need a lecture on loss," Frances said abruptly. "I've buried two husbands and dwelling on it does no good."

Lilly's voice again, even softer but firm. Short bursts of words. Then footsteps returning.

"Wine?" she said, reentering the room.

"Lil—" Laura began.

Lilly shook her head. "Don't let her do it."

A few minutes of surface-deep questions and answers later—how far away was Brookfield, what was it like, how long would Julia be there—Lilly sent her daughters upstairs to "write a note to your cousin and let her know you're thinking of her," before asking Laura how it really went. With dark red liquid courage under her belt, Laura admitted she was lost; family therapy had been awful, and she couldn't help but wonder if Frances might be right. Yet she didn't believe Julia was simply seeking attention; the emotions were too raw, too real. She pulled an envelope from her purse and showed its contents to her sister—a charcoal drawing of a whorled shell that Julia had asked the nurse to give her when they'd turned her away at the reception desk for visiting hours.

"She's drawing again?" Lilly asked. "That's great, no?"

Laura shook her head. "It isn't hers. Another patient gave it to her. But Julia wrote me a note. She said it reminded her of me, but also of Georgia O'Keeffe, which reminded her of Paul. You might not remember, but last summer, we'd planned a trip to Arizona to see his mother, but then he fell, and his mother got sick . . . well, anyway, he'd wanted to take us to O'Keeffe's museum in New Mexico. He said he'd wanted to see the desert one more time. The mountains and colors—"

Laura didn't say that, before reading the note, the shell had reminded her of Julia—hard yet fragile, with so much hidden, folded in on herself.

"Anyway, Julia asked the guy who drew it if she could give it to me."

"Oh?" Lilly raised her eyebrows ever so slightly. "It was a guy?"

"What? No, it's not like that. Not at all," Laura said, instantly defensive, though the truth was that she didn't know what it was like.

Lilly gave her a half smile as she slowly rose from the table. "Well, whatever it is, she's connecting with people again, and that has to be good, no?" She rested her hand lightly on Laura's shoulder. "I better get Mom before she combusts."

Laura pressed her lips tightly between her teeth, resisting the urge to shrug off her sister's hand. She watched Lilly walk away, wondering—too late—if she should call her back. Should she tell Lilly how, earlier that day, she'd been waiting in line at CVS when one of the super moms from Julia's school had come around the corner, looked right at her, and darted away? Should she share how this woman had organized casseroles and unsolicited prayer chains when Paul was ill and now she avoided Laura like the plague, or how there hadn't been any get-well cards or "sending thoughts and prayers" texts when Julia was in the hospital? Should she admit she understood—that she would have behaved the same way?

Laura remembered seeing an article a few years earlier, about a town in which three or four teenagers had taken their own lives in a short period of time, raising concerns of suicide pacts and the contagion of behavior. At the time, she had given only minimal consideration to the topic, convinced such things did not touch her. She'd been so quick to dismiss—or maybe it was barricade against—the tragedy of other people's lives.

Even when tragedy struck the ones she loved, she hadn't broken down the barricades in time.

And even now, she had no idea how to do it.

JULIA

THROUGH A SET OF WINDOWS on the far wall, Julia took
in the crisp autumn day—a Phthalo Blue and white sky, with
wisps of cotton-candy clouds—the kind of day she associated
with falling leaves, her father reciting poetry over the sound
of metal rake teeth scraping across the grass, "We Alone," "O
Captain, my Captain," or the first lines of the only poem Julia
knew completely by heart, "Whose woods these are I think I
know." She remembered how her dad changed the last repet-
itive lines to "leaves to rake before I sleep," as he'd done with
other tasks, "dishes to wash, clothes to fold"; how he'd never
ceased to try engaging her in discussions about metaphor and
interpretation, the duality of beauty and ferocity, the power of
words; and how she hadn't appreciated most of it until it was
being taken from her. From him.

  And then she recalled the night, toward the end, when
he'd asked her to read to him in the glow of a flashlight, the
classic Walker, Frost, and Blake offerings supplanted by Longfellow's "A Psalm of Life" and Henley's "Invictus," her father
joining in on the last stanza, his voice both defeated and determined: "I am the master of my fate: I am the captain of my
soul." Her mother's face turning to stone. The argument Julia
had heard between her parents suddenly making sense, the
words, "I can't do it, Paul. Please don't ask me to."

She inhaled sharply. Her breath caught as if she'd been hit by a stiff gust of wind.

"You okay?" Sam said. He handed her a wedge of moist gray modeling clay, his fingers lingering against hers. "Art therapy . . . ?"

Julia swallowed hard before replying. ". . . is good for the soul."

"Indeed. Indeed." Sam turned back to the granite counter that ran the length of the wall, open shelves above, locked cabinets below. He chose two more lumps of clay, weighing them in his hands before announcing, "Together, these are perfect. Come, Julia." He drew out her name, extending the long *u* vowel, his voice loud and deep, artificially melodious. "Let us create."

"Samuel, please," the art therapist, a petite dark-haired, dark-eyed woman with an accent Julia couldn't quite place, called out. "Respect the space. There are others working here."

Julia saw only one other person in the room. A woman in her young twenties with dark circles under her eyes sat at a table near the windows, stretching clay into a linear figure with elongated limbs, arms pinned to its torso. She'd arrived the day before. Anne? Anna? No, Hannah, that was it. Hannah looked up briefly at Sam and Julia. She did not seem negatively affected by their presence, a fact Sam clearly felt duty-bound to acknowledge.

"My apologies, Dr. Tarvas. I do not believe that our esteemed colleague"—Sam looked over at Hannah and her long strands of clay—"Ms. Giacometti, has been disrespected, nor has the space. Nevertheless . . ." Sam stopped, gave a mini-bow with a flourish of his right hand, still holding a lump of clay. "I will accede to your request for proper behavior during art therapy."

"Thank you," Dr. Tarvas said to Sam, treating his clearly sardonic words with typical Brookfieldian therapeutic seriousness as she turned to address Julia. "I understand you two have been here quite a bit on your own."

There was no reproach or accusation in the doctor's tone, and yet Julia felt a tightening in her chest. The barn had become a haven, and she was loath to tarnish it.

Sam had brought her here four days earlier after giving her the Matisse-like portrait. He'd led her on a circuitous route to the barn's red-paneled door, quickly unlocked it, ushered her in, and pocketed the key. Once inside, he'd presented the space as if it were a gift, with what she now recognized as his signature bow and flourish. Though it had the same ash wood floors, cream walls, and fixed overhead lights as every other room in the clinic, the barn's interior had a warm familiarity, with waist-high tables, metal stools, pottery wheels, and wooden French sketch box easels. Shelves holding stacks of paper and wooden storage bins bearing labels in a rainbow of colors.

"Art therapy is good for the soul," Sam said slowly, watching Julia taking it all in. "Or as Tanya says"—Sam imitated Tanya's marshmallow voice—"'Art is healing, and healing is an art.' She'll tell you, if she hasn't already, how it works on different pathways in the brain. Helps to reveal our true selves."

In response, Julia recited words she'd heard a dozen times from her studio art teacher, Mr. Wardel, a six-foot-two, two-hundred-pound ex-football-player turned teacher/coach with a penchant for quoting famous novelists, artists, and poets, chalking them in surprisingly elegant script on a blackboard before reading them aloud. Quotes Julia used to share with her father, anticipating his smile. "'It is art, and art only, that reveals us to ourselves.'" She looked over at Sam. "Oscar Wilde."

Sam stared at her, eyes narrowed, head tilted, like he couldn't believe what he was hearing, but had expected it all along. "Oscar Wilde," he said, nodding slowly.

Julia smiled and shrugged. "My studio art teacher, Mr. Wardel. Big fan of quotations."

"Goddamn," Sam said, still nodding. "Okay, okay. I've got one for you." Placing his hand over his heart, he said slowly, with gravity, "'Creativity takes courage.'"

Julia racked her brain, polling memories of Mr. Wardel, his deep bass resonating in the vast studio space. "Matisse?"

"Indeed." Sam's smile broadened as his voice deepened. "Your turn."

Julia re-racked her brain for a moment.

"'Art is not what you see, but what you make others see.'"

"Yes. Excellent." Sam confirmed his approval with a now-exaggerated nod. "And that was . . . Monet. No, wait . . . Degas?"

"Yes," Julia said, surprised. "Degas."

"One more," Sam said. "'Art washes away from the soul the dust of everyday life.'"

This one was not a Mr. Wardel quote, nor a line from any poem Julia could recall.

"Art washes away from the soul the dust of everyday life," Sam repeated.

Julia felt the words as she heard them. *Dust.* Sadness billowed up, the familiar scorching ache. She dropped her chin as she shook her head, hoping Sam would not notice instant tears forming. "Sorry."

"Hey, hey, it's just a game." Sam's voice was gentle. Julia looked up into his face; his eyes were bright and clear. "Picasso. Beautiful, right?"

"Yes," Julia said.

Sam took a step forward. "And true." His head bent toward hers. Julia held her breath, wondering if he would kiss her. But Sam backed away, breaking the spell. "My mother is a believer. She funded all of this—years ago—made a 'qualified gift' for the express purpose of building the barn, buying supplies, providing art therapists, on and on, in perpetuity. I'm not sure what she gave in terms of an actual dollar figure, but whatever it was, it established the Lorenzo Fund." Sam directed a flourishing wave toward a small wood-framed silver plaque on the wall near the light switch.

"Hence, my unfettered access." He held up the key on a leather strap. "Well, not entirely unfettered, as I am not permitted keys for the cabinets, wherein sharps may lie. I am, however, permitted to use the room during time periods designated as therapeutic, so long as I also participate in a predetermined number of other sessions—mindfulness, yoga—which my mother also believes in."

Julia took a few tentative steps into the room.

"I've never used the key for anyone else, but I saw you drawing your first day."

Julia tried to recall that first day.

"You were sitting in the window seat by the door."

The memory came to her. It had been shitty work, and she'd been so frustrated. The cartoon drawing of a woman drawing, Julia *but not Julia*, with an empty dialogue bubble, had ended up a crumpled ball in the trash bin, a teabag dropped on top, saturating it. She'd envisioned the paper recolored splotchy sepia, wondering if she would ever create anything worthwhile again. *And he's been watching me?* Her expression must have given her thoughts away because Sam put up his hands defensively.

"Anyway." He returned the key to his back pocket. "Access is precious. Something I protect, so as not to lose."

"Could they take it away?"

"Honestly? I don't know, but I'm not planning to tell anyone we're here."

"And they won't come looking for us?"

Sam shook his head, crossed the space between them in two steps, and reached for her hand. "Doubt it. I rarely do as I'm told, and they'll just assume you're skipping group—you wouldn't be the first—which just means a chat about committing to the process. Another warning about fraternization."

"I don't want you risking anything for me," Julia said, even as she realized she was lying. Sam holding her hand, the idea of him fighting for her in any way, made her feel something she'd thought she couldn't feel.

"Well . . ." A look passed over Sam's face—as if he were contemplating saying something and deciding not to say it—before he continued, "If there's one thing I've learned over the last few years, it's that nothing worth having comes easy. Every day is a risk." He gave her hand a tight squeeze and pulled her toward the row of shelves and cabinets. "Now, let's be courageous."

And she'd allowed herself to be led, wanting her hand to stay in his.

That first day, he'd pulled out a bin that contained wooden boxes of used oil pastels in various stages of stubby with paper wrappers torn or missing. Large sheets of creamy ingres paper were pulled from a top shelf. "My hidden stash," Sam had said as he laid the sheets on two side-by-side tables.

Julia felt the absence of Sam's touch. She jealously watched his fingers passing over the pastels in a movement that was part Ouija board, part caress.

"Not a time to overthink, Julia," he said. "Don't judge. Let the spirit move you. Just be."

She stood quietly for a long while, staring at the blank paper, waiting for inspiration. Her thoughts swirled. She leaned forward, closed her eyes, and tried to visualize the color welling up inside, swelling up and over her. She saw herself from above, the skinny girl with tangled hair, floating. She opened her eyes and moved her hand to hover over the array of pastels until her fingertips settled on deep purple. Holding it gently, Julia took in its texture.

Just be. Be here.

With the tips of her fingers, strokes of aubergine, black, and blue became sweeping petals, patches of peach and white, and smudges of ivory, black, and gray smoothed into pale blush interiors around a dark center. Flowers that weren't flowers, blooming, large and glorious. The emotions she couldn't name spilled onto the paper, bleeding into one another, becoming something she hadn't seen coming. Something almost beautiful.

And freeing. She looked toward Sam. She wondered if he felt it too.

"Art therapy," he said, reaching for her fingertips, now the color of pale bruises.

As her gaze drifted back to her drawing, she'd identified the emotion. "Is good for the soul," she replied.

In the four days since, other activities—group, call me Tanya, meals, even sleeping and showering—became a frame around the time she spent with Sam. Watching him as he spoke, shrugging, grinning, grimacing, laughing, holding back tears. Feeling his touch: his thigh against hers under the table at lunch, his fingertips fluttering across the small of her back as they walked to yoga, his breath on her neck as he stood behind her at an easel.

Thinking about him in the dark.

It felt as though a bubble of Samness surrounded her, a buffer against Claudia's brittle resentment, Rita's disapproval, Brett's cynical glances, even her own self-loathing. Only an hour before Sam handed her the lump of clay, while reviewing her CBT homework with Tanya, Julia had noticed that, though the boxes on the positive thought checklist were still mostly empty, the Xs on the negative list numbered fewer as well. She'd surprised Tanya, and herself, laughing when she read a statement halfway down the negative list: "I'll probably have to be placed in a mental institution someday."

"Guess this form isn't ideal for those of us already inside," she'd said to Tanya.

"You have a lovely laugh," Tanya had responded.

And Julia hadn't immediately dismissed the compliment.

As she and Tanya had discussed another worksheet that conceptualized how Julia's beliefs impacted her actions, how she might consciously dispute negative "all or nothing" thoughts and shift them by changing her behaviors, she realized the fog was lifting. The print on the page was crisp with clean lines delineating spaces. She noticed a lavender scent and spied a diffuser on the bookcase that Tanya told her had been there all along. She felt the heaviness of the dreadlocks on her head and wanted them gone.

She wanted to look in the mirror and see the girl her father had loved. She wanted to believe that girl was still there, inside her, worth redeeming. She wanted Tanya to help that girl.

She wanted Sam to know her.

When she and Tanya talked about possible reasons for the change in her perceptions—the Prozac kicking in, having her feelings acknowledged without judgment, feeling safe, doing the work—Tanya told her reconnecting with creativity might contribute further to the fog clearing. Julia worried she'd given something away, that Tanya could sense her feelings for Sam or his risking his leather-chained key for her.

But as Sam predicted, Tanya had simply said, "Art is healing, and healing is an art."

Poetic words. Pulling her out of the darkness.

Picasso washing her soul. Matisse encouraging her to be courageous.

And today, now, Sam handing her clay. "Let us sit and create."

Though Julia knew by now Sam was prone to hyperbole, she also knew he meant every word. The power of creation was real and validating. It was more than capturing a moment or an expression or a feeling—it was immortalizing that moment or expression or feeling, of saying "this happened." She wondered if it were possible to create a piece of pottery that represented her darkest hours, something she could point to and say, "Here, hold this. Feel its colors and contours. Don't look away."

The clay was supple. Pliable. It gave way. She sat at the wheel. The movement of her hands traveled up into her forearms and shoulders.

Into her chest. Into her head.

She thought about her deep purple flowers that weren't flowers, how Sam had placed them between two sheets of wax paper "to preserve it 'til we can frame it someday."

She turned from the wheel, watched Sam dip his thumb into a small dish of water before sliding it down over a curve of what appeared to be the start of a female figure.

And for a moment, she silenced her inner judge and the psychic alarms she was growing to despise. She allowed herself to go further than just being; she imagined the existence of a future. A future in which she was drawing again. A future filled with beauty instead of guilt. A future with Sam.

Someday.

LAURA

THE CLASSICAL MUSIC STOPPED abruptly as Laura turned the key in the ignition. Sweeping violins and elegiac cellos ceased, leaving behind a hum of silence. Laura sat, absorbing the quiet. She leaned forward and turned her face to the night sky.

The moon was still low on the horizon—waxing gibbous.

Paul had been a double English/Astronomy major, a dubious choice in terms of career potential, according to Carl, who famously said to his future son-in-law, "I suppose two useless majors is better than one."

It was no secret Carl considered Paul a lightweight, only marginally better than the string of "losers" Laura had been drawn to for years: a musician, a masseuse, an apiarist—men Carl had no interest in relating to in the least. Her mother's judgment was different, though no less harsh: Frances was certain Laura's decision to marry an idealistic teacher, and a person of color to boot, was just another form of rebellion, a way to complicate things, to bring judgment down upon Frances in some way.

Thankfully, Paul was able to put it all aside. He even took the "useless major" comment with typical aplomb, chuckling as he said, "I'll have to share that one with my mom."

Which he did because, though, like Laura, he'd lost his dad when he was young, unlike Laura, Paul had a good relationship with his mother. He loved to share jokes and inspirational messages he'd heard, obscure facts he'd learned, the last spoon of his hot fudge sundae. In particular, he was passionate about sharing the subjects about which he was passionate: reading aloud after dinner from C. S. Lewis, Angelou, and Whitman—of lions and the power of literature and nature to inspire and heal; rolling out down-filled sleeping bags in the backyard upon which they lay as he explained the stages of the moon and its influence on the tides, the mythology of constellations, and the history of celestial navigation. Laura could picture him, cropped curly hair, khaki corduroy jeans and Patagonia fleece, arm aloft, voice filled with wonder. He'd been wearing a fleece over his pajamas the night she and Julia had enlisted an aide to bring him outside onto a makeshift bed of couch cushions and down sleeping bags.

"This is heaven," Paul had said, his voice a shadow before asking Julia to read aloud by flashlight the poetry he'd specifically selected—poetry worth fighting over, poetry that made her husband and daughter weep and made Laura question her own decisions, whether she'd let him down in the end, when pain had redefined the noblest of goals.

Laura could see Paul now, lying there, eyes wide and wet with tears. The moon and stars bright in the sky.

Tonight, a layer of gray clouds filtered the starlight.

Visiting hours were three to four on weekend days and rotating evenings. When the admissions nurse had given Laura the weekly schedule, she'd passed along Dr. Renner's suggestion that Laura give Julia at least a few days to adjust before visiting.

Prescribed time and space.

So Laura had waited until the Saturday after Friday's family therapy, only to hear Julia wasn't feeling up to a visit, news delivered by another nurse, Roberta, a sturdy middle-aged woman with a kind face. "Try again in a few days," Roberta said. "Sometimes, it takes a little time to feel ready for stressors from home."

Laura was learning this new vocabulary. According to Frances, Julia was an "issue." According to Roberta, Laura was a "stressor from home."

Getting out of the car, she forced herself to *Stop. Breathe. Count to ten.*

To look up at the waxing gibbous moon and channel Paul: *Be patient. Listen.*

Roberta greeted her without saying anything about the previous visit, handing her printed guidelines and helpful tips. "When you're finished reading, she's waiting for you in the common room."

Guidelines, helpful tips, rules, order, supervision—Julia was safe here, safer than at home.

The common room had three matching seating areas that looked like pages from a Pottery Barn catalogue. Entering from the lobby area, Laura glanced at the clusters of people already present, looking for and failing to locate Julia's signature dreadlocks. Her eyes came to rest upon the back of a head of a woman with warm tawny skin and dark hair in a pixie cut.

Laura froze.

She recognized the nape of the neck.

She hadn't seen it in months, and then it had lain under a high ponytail or loose bun. She remembered washing wispy curls, kneeling over a bathtub, holding her baby daughter's head and neck in the palm of her hand.

"Julia?"

As the young woman turned, Laura recognized the jaw, the cheekbones, the nose, and lips. The eyes—beautiful brown doe eyes.

"Hey, Mom."

And that soft half smile—a smile Laura hadn't seen in months, maybe a year.

Julia looked both younger, and older, than ever.

"Hey," Laura said. Her thoughts tripped over themselves, self-doubt silencing her next words. If she said, "You look beautiful," would Julia take it to mean she looked awful with the dreadlocks? If she said, "You cut your hair," would Julia scoff at the obviousness of her observation? If she said, "How are you?" would Julia close off with a "How do you think I am, I'm in a psychiatric treatment facility?"

No good options came to mind.

"I've missed you," Laura finally said, because it was true. She had. Seeing her daughter without the heavy dreadlocks filled Laura with an emotion that encompassed both nostalgia and melancholy, a longing for something she loved and thought she'd lost.

The soft smile faded, only a little, but enough. Enough to hurt.

Laura continued her slow approach toward her daughter. "How are you?"

"Good. I'm good," Julia said, then tentatively added, "better, I guess."

"That's good. That's great," Laura said, hating how bright her voice sounded. Sharp. Tinny. "I mean—" Laura stopped. She didn't know what she meant. She did not know what to say to her own daughter, and this cut her to the quick. Cutting "is a cry for help," the psychiatrist had said. And in an instant, the memory fragment was there: Julia on the bathroom floor, the blood on her thighs. The cuts. Julia's pain becoming her own. Laura's failings pooling on the floor, deep dark red. A "For Mom" article explaining physical pain can be preferable to feeling nothing at all.

She heard a noise between an inhalation and a gasp and realized she had made it.

"Mom?" Julia's voice, here and now. "Do you want to sit down?"

Laura rounded the side of the couch and sat beside Julia. "Sorry."

"For what?"

The two women looked at each other, down, out, back at each other.

Laura knew it was on her. She had to say something, but not the wrong thing. "I like your hair," she said.

Julia lifted her right hand a few inches, then dropped it and gripped it tightly with her left.

Aware her statement could be interpreted in myriad ways, Laura also believed it to be true, and she'd decided to stick with true. "I'm undoubtedly going to keep saying the wrong thing, so I want to apologize in advance. Can I do that? Or is that bad too—it probably is."

Julia's eyes dropped to her hands. "I don't know. It's not like I'm some expert at this."

Buck up. You can do this, Laura told herself. She reached out to rub the back of Julia's hand. "I know. I've been reading the packet you left for me—"

Julia stiffened. "You have?"

Laura nodded. "I'm sorry. I want to do the right thing. I just don't know what that is."

Julia removed her hand from under her mother's and raked it through her short hair, hard.

Laura reminded herself not to take Julia's actions personally. *Channel Paul*, she told herself again. "Do you want to tell me about the last few days?"

"What about them?"

"Anything. Whatever you want to talk about. How are things going with your therapist?"

"Which one?"

"Tanya?"

"I like her." Julia raked her hands again. Raked and pulled. "She helped with this. Her sister-in-law is a hairdresser."

"She did a good job. It looks really nice. Do you like it?"

Julia shrugged her shoulders. Laura noticed how impossibly long Julia's neck seemed, how pronounced her collarbones were, how thin she'd become.

"Is the food good?"

"It's not bad."

Laura was aware she sounded like an inquisitor, even as she asked, "Are you sleeping okay?" Recalling how she'd found Julia's cuddly under her pillow, Laura lowered her voice. "Do you want me to bring Max?"

"No, I'm good." Though her voice bore the irritation Laura had grown used to, a hint of Julia's soft smile returned as well. "I don't know if I could have him here anyway. There're all sorts of restrictions. Maybe the book, but no—" Julia cut off her own words, the hint of a smile gone. "No, thank you though. I'll be out of here soon anyway."

An awkward silence fell. Laura looked around at the other families, wondering if, like her, they wished for privacy. If, like her, they wished they weren't there at all. Voices were muted. There was no laughter.

Laura noticed Julia's eyes following hers.

"Let the wild rumpus start."

Laura wondered how to interpret this statement. Was it simply a line from the story or was it a comment about the scene in front of them: the group "shit-show" Julia had described during family therapy? This visit? All of it?

So many wild things.

Again, true seemed safest. "You used to love that book."

"I did," Julia said. Her hands began to migrate toward her hair. She pulled the left one down with the right, gripped them tightly again in her lap.

Laura found herself longing to go back in time again, to nights when she'd stood in the hall outside Julia's bedroom, listening to Paul's voice rising and falling, the pauses he'd insert before certain lines, encouraging Julia to chime in. Waiting for the last line, "and it was still hot."

"I miss him," Julia said. "All the time."

"So do I," Laura replied.

"I wish I could go back and—" Julia stopped short.

"What?"

"It doesn't matter."

Laura saw Julia's eyes were filling with tears. A surprising surge of protective desire overwhelmed Laura. She felt an urge to fold Julia into her arms and keep her safe from all the monsters, figurative and literal. But sitting there Laura realized, as always, she didn't know who or what the monsters were—let alone how to combat them.

"You can tell me," Laura said.

Julia shook her head, quickly wiping her eyes. "No, I can't."

A woman's voice called across the room, crisp, British. "Roberta, have you seen Maximilian?" Julia and Laura both turned. A willowy blond had entered the room. She was dressed entirely in black, from a soft-looking cape down to high-heeled boots. As she strode toward an unoccupied couch, she called out, "Could you please let him know I've arrived?" Laura watched her place a clearly expensive handbag on the side table, remove the cape in a dramatic swoop, and settle onto the couch, ankles decorously crossed. Mid-thirties maybe, the woman was striking, with deep blue eyes that drew immediate attention and bone structure Laura guessed was perfectly asymmetrical.

"Mom," Julia whispered. "Don't stare."

Laura turned away and whispered back. "I wasn't—"

Julia raised an eyebrow in a gesture that reminded Laura of herself, issuing that same admonition over the years. "Okay, maybe I was," Laura confessed, voice low. "My bad."

"My bad?" Julia said, now with an expression more like Paul's when he'd heard something surprisingly humorous. "I've never heard you say that before." Julia leaned toward her, a small gesture that meant worlds to Laura. "I get it, though—the staring—kind of makes you wonder what Maximilian is like."

"You don't know him?"

"Nope. Must be new today."

Some unseen ice broken, for a few minutes she and Julia spoke with less discomfort. Feeling an odd indebtedness to the elegant blond, Laura listened as Julia told her about the vase she'd thrown on the pottery wheel, watching her daughter's hands move through air as she tried to convey the shape, seeing the wrinkle form in her brow as she described the transparent midnight blue and mica glaze she'd mixed and the mystery the blended color would be until after firing. When Julia added that she'd bring it tomorrow to visiting hours, Laura must have sounded overly enthusiastic because the discomfort returned. Laura remembered the notes from Izzy and Grace and pulled them from a pocket in her purse.

"I almost forgot about these," Laura said, holding them out. But Julia ignored her outstretched hand, her eyes focused on something behind Laura.

A tall young man was bounding into the room. Mid-twenties, clean-shaven with dark hair. Ruggedly handsome.

"What a delightful surprise," he said, heading for the blond woman, who rose to greet him.

"Happy early birthday, darling. I know I'll see you tomorrow, but I simply couldn't wait." The woman opened her arms to embrace him.

Despite her statuesque height, the young man enveloped her and lifted her easily off her feet, boots dangling.

Laura felt Julia stiffen next to her on the couch, heard a sharp intake of breath. The blond woman's eyes darted over to see Julia standing abruptly, Laura reaching for her. As if sensing the blond's attention shifting, the young man turned.

Looking startled, he lowered the woman's feet to the ground. His hands unloosed hers from around his shoulders, and he took two steps in Julia and Laura's direction. Stopped. Turned back. Cleared his throat. Took hold of the blond woman's hand and led her a few steps closer.

Laura watched her daughter try to contain what looked like desperation.

"Arabella," the young man said, "I'd like you to meet a friend of mine." He stretched his free hand toward Julia.

"Julia, this is — "

Before he could say another word, Julia bolted from the room, leaving Laura, Arabella, and Maximilian staring after her.

9

JULIA

JULIA TOOK A GULP OF HOT TEA. It scorched her throat yet did nothing to dilute the sludge in her veins, pounding into the small spaces in her brain. Her head hurt. Lowering the mug to the table took effort.

Everything was heavy. Laden.

"Hey, are you okay?" Rita slid into a chair across from her.

"I don't feel well." Not feeling well did not begin to describe it. "I can't go to group. Can you tell Beverly?"

"What's wrong?"

Julia sighed. She was exhausted. She'd avoided everyone at breakfast and, during yoga, had stayed in child's pose as long as possible, face down, longing to disappear into her mat. She could not face group: Beverly's "Are you ready to share?"; the stares of the others; Brett asking, "What'd you do to your hair?" She clutched her mug with both hands, staring at the reflected flicker of overhead lights in her tea.

"Are you ill?"

The irony of this question seemed to slip Rita's grasp. Julia thought, *We're all ill, Rita, that's why we're here.* Without looking up, she said, "Sorry . . . can you just tell them I don't feel well?"

In her peripheral vision, she saw Rita's shape move away. Heard her footsteps receding. A murmur of voices, her name

Julia, Julia, Julia in dialogue bubbles floating everywhere. People were talking about her. She'd known they would be. Rita saying she'd warned Julia to stay away from Sam, how she'd tried explaining the rumors circulating about him, but Julia wouldn't listen. Claudia, glad not to be the focus of staff attention, narcing on how Julia had left their room during quiet time and hadn't returned for nearly an hour. Arabella—Sam's leggy blond—whose crisp accent would make every comment sound sordid and sad. "Really, Sam"—or Maximilian or whatever the hell his name really was—"She's not your sort at all. Dreadfully thin and that hair." *Too bad*, Julia thought, that her dreads had been cut off. That would have really given Sam's leggy blond ammo. Ammo. Ami, the name she'd called Frances as a child. Her grandmother and Aunt Lilly huddled around the kitchen table, speaking in hushed tones so Izzy and Grace wouldn't hear about Julia's mini-breakdown at visiting hours "over a man at least five or six years older than her." And Sam. Explaining to Dr. Renner that he hadn't meant to encourage her; he was only trying to help. How he didn't understand her reaction yesterday evening. How he was leaving anyway, clean-shaven and ready for the lovely, leggy Arabella.

Perhaps he'd already gone.

Awake most of the night, Julia had revisited her interactions with Sam under the microscope—no, the floodlight—of the truth, and realized she'd read too much into each touch, each glance, each sliver of attention—granting significance where none existed.

He'd never been interested in her. *Of course he hadn't.*

She'd talked about high school. Fucking high school. She'd been an idiot: opening up about losing her friends, getting entangled with Cheyenne and drugs, grasping for meaning in her existence only to realize all she'd gotten was in over her head. She'd written him a note, putting into words how she felt, failing to express it adequately, and then telling him that too.

Worst of all, she'd shared her dad with him, his favorite poems, his belief in second chances. She'd told Sam about the flashlight night, about "Invictus," and the list in *Where the*

Wild Things Are. She'd only just stopped herself from telling him everything, but she'd allowed herself to imagine some-day she might be able to—and that he might understand. That they'd save each other.

She'd given in to hope.

Humiliation washed over her as she recalled watching dreadlocks fall to the ground in the pod bathroom, imagining what Sam might say when he saw her, the real her. Thinking once they both got out, soon, they could be together. Now, instead, she heard Arabella in her head saying, "He introduced her as 'a friend'—and how could it be otherwise? I mean, look at her."

Julia heard movement in the hallway. She opened her eyes. Looked over to the clock on the wall, aware she didn't know how much time had passed. She drained the last of the tea, now resembling watercolor rinse water. Pale brown. Cold.

In the end, everything was cold. Empty.

Julia pushed the mug across the table, crossed her arms where the mug had been, laid her forehead upon them, and closed her eyes. She heard footsteps walking across the wood floor, stopping in front of her. She waited for the ubiquitous pod tech asking, "Is there somewhere you're supposed to be?"

There was nowhere to go.

She lifted her head to say those exact words, except it wasn't a member of the staff. With both hands, she pushed from the table and began to rise. Her eyes sought an escape route.

"Thank God I found you." Sam reached for her. "Julia, wait."

Julia shrank from his touch and began moving toward the nearest exit, French doors that led to the courtyard, before remembering this space was walled in. She spun around and collided with Sam, who stepped back, holding up both hands as if settling a wild animal. Not wanting to meet his gaze, Julia looked down. Sam wasn't wearing his standard canvas Toms but sturdy black leather boots with buckles—outside shoes. She scanned up: black jeans, white t-shirt, charcoal-gray fleece jacket.

He was leaving.

"Julia, stop. I need to talk to you."

Julia buried her face in her hands. "I know. You're leaving."

"Yeah. The driver's here, so I don't have much time, and there's a lot I need to tell you."

Julia lifted her head.

"You could start with your real name."

"My real name?" Recognition dawned. "Oh, right, Max." He sighed, paused. "My full name is Maximilian Samuel Lorenzo, Junior, for my father." Sam's jaw clenched.

"Your name is Maximillian?"

"Yes, which, you can imagine, has not been great for me. I was 'Little Max' until my grandpa died, and I decided to go by Sam, my middle name, in his honor. It took a while, but most people call me Sam now, except my mom, who reverts to Max when she's angry or excited. As for my dad, he can't decide which he hates more—me having his father's name, or his."

Julia recalled one of Sam's stories from group about an argument he'd overheard between his parents when he was twenty, a year or so into his cycling: his father yelling he'd been fucked over by one Sam Lorenzo and wouldn't let it happen again, telling his mom she could have it all—the house in the city, the beach house, the art—as long as she took Sam too. And his mom crying, but angry, saying Sam wasn't some cat his dad could put out on the street, hoping it would run away or get hit by a car.

Sam had gone on to reveal that the first time he'd come home from the hospital, his cat, Geronimo, was missing. How his dad told him the cat had disappeared, and his mom had hugged him, shaking her head at his dad. And how the day of the argument, several months later, he realized what his father had done with Geronimo. His father didn't love him, Sam had said. His father wished to be rid of him.

"I'm so sorry," Julia heard herself say now. "Where will you go? Home?"

"Yeah, to pick some stuff up, but I'm not staying. I have places to see, things to create, beauty to immortalize."

Sam's eyes bore into hers. Bright blue intensified.

Julia dropped her gaze back to his boots. She should have anticipated he would leave; he'd explained he wouldn't stay any longer than necessary, only enough to reset his medicine regimen. She realized that while he talked nonstop most of the time, she didn't know basic things about him: how many times he'd been at Brookfield; if he had siblings; if he'd finished school or had a job; where home was.

As if he could read her mind, Sam said, "My apartment's in Brooklyn. Ground floor of my mom's brownstone. One of the reasons she came was to tell me it's cleaned up from . . . well, it's cleaned up. 'Habitable again,' she said." Sam's voice took on an English accent for the last two words.

Julia lifted her head yet again.

"That was your mother?" Impossible. The woman visiting him last night was not old enough to be his mother. "But she's—" Julia paused, censoring herself. "English," she finished lamely.

"Indeed." Sam kept the English accent going. "She is."

"But you don't have an accent."

"Because I'm not from England. Born and bred New Yorker. We used to go back to visit my grandparents, before all this started." Sam moved his hand in a vague circle. "But my mom's lived here since she met my dad at some party in Ibiza when she was eighteen. He used to love to tell the story about how she was a runway model and someone else's date. Typical assholey perspective—how it made her a conquest and gave him a victory of sorts." Sam paused. "Ironically, now she's the victorious one."

"She is?"

Sam looked furtively around the clearly empty room, then whispered, "We should go outside." He pulled her through the French doors. The air was cold. Sharp. Sam closed the doors firmly, then turned and stepped toward her, stopping inches away. He reached up and wound his fingers into her cropped hair.

"You're the most beautiful thing I've ever seen," he began. "And I've known from the first time I saw you, we were meant to be together."

Sam lowered his face to within inches of hers, and Julia

instinctively closed her eyes. Sam whispered, "I'm coming into serious money," and then his lips brushed hers. *Or did they?* Julia wasn't sure. She also wasn't sure she'd heard him correctly. His hands dropped away.

She opened her eyes and saw he'd stepped back.

"What?"

Sam now spoke just above a whisper. "I said, I'm coming into serious money. From my grandfather, not the English one. My dad's dad. See, when I was little, he decided to leave everything to me, much of which I'd be granted access to today, my twenty-third birthday." Sam's voice ratcheted up. He began pacing in a tight circle. "My father, the conquistador asshole, doesn't think I'm worthy of these spoils nor 'capable of this responsibility.'" Sam threw up air quotes. "Which is why he's been trying to have me declared mentally unfit for years. Meanwhile, my mother—" Sam stopped.

"Arabella," Julia filled in.

"Yes." Sam nodded dramatically and resumed pacing. "Yes, Arabella. She came up with this strategy to thwart my father: coming here of my own accord and moving me into my own apartment to prove my independence. She's always said"—Sam's voice continued to increase in volume—"that coming here was to make me whole. You know, bring the two sides of me into balance. But now? Now, I find out it was to establish not only that I'm fully aware of my condition, but also that I acknowledge the need for this safety net and can, therefore, be trusted."

Sam stopped in his tracks and scrunched his face as though he were in pain. Just as Julia was about to ask if he was okay, he opened his eyes, scanned rapidly left and right, and resumed circling. "So, while my father has been arguing with the staff in some bizarre antithetical effort to get them to take his side, my mother has been subtly wielding her upper-crusty manners and checkbook to convince them to take hers."

Sam stopped again, this time in front of Julia. "And she's won."

Though his body was coiled with barely contained energy, other than the changes in volume Sam was speaking with a deliberate, almost mechanical rhythm. Even so, the circling made Julia dizzy, and she struggled to follow what he was saying.

"Accordingly, I will soon be in possession of a large sum of cash." Sam held his hands as if clutching a handful of gold. "I can go anywhere, do whatever I want. And I want many things." His hands flew up and apart, as if releasing the invisible gold into the air. "But the thing I want most—" Sam wove his fingers into her hair again. "Is you."

This time, the kiss was not fleeting. It was long and soft and deep. And there was no mistaking the meaning of his next words.

"Come with me."

LAURA

LILLY'S DISEMBODIED VOICE ROSE from the dashboard. "What do you suppose set her off?"

Modern parking lots were not designed for Hummers or Escalades, Laura decided, as she pulled her Honda into a tight space, begrudging the owner of a massive black SUV the space they'd stolen by parking well over the line. She squinted against a shaft of sunlight refracting through her streaky windshield and sighed with frustration.

"Let me guess, you don't want to talk about it," Lilly said.

"Oh, no, that wasn't directed at you. I parked next to this massive SUV, and my car is filthy. Honestly, I don't know what set her off. She seemed better at first. I didn't tell you, she cut her hair. No more dreadlocks."

No more tongue ring. No bandanas. No clicking or twirling. *Jury still out on the whispering.*

"Wow. How does she look?"

"Much better. Like she used to, but older somehow, and so thin."

"She's been getting thinner for a while, though, no? I mean, you didn't say anything about that, did you? That'd send my two into a tailspin."

Laura recalled the nape of Julia's neck, the fragile openness she had revealed while describing the vase she'd made, and the desperation that had replaced it.

"No, I think it was related to this young man, Maximilian. He was in the middle of introducing Julia to the woman visiting him, who was drop-dead gorgeous, and then she took off. I mean Julia, not the woman. It all happened so fast. One second, she was fine, and the next—"

The pattern repeating: Julia pulling away; Laura uncertain what to do, so doing nothing.

"I didn't know if I was allowed to go after her or—Shit . . . hold on."

Hearing the sound effect of a battery dying, it occurred to Laura her phone had been lying next to her pillow all night, rather than resting on the bedside table attached to its assigned outlet. She glanced down to see a low power warning.

"Sorry," she said. "My phone."

"What'd you do?" Lilly said.

"I forgot to plug it in, and I don't have my extra charger."

"No," Lilly said. "I meant last night, when Julia took off. Did you go after her?"

"Oh. No. I apologized and talked to the nurse."

"Apologized to whom?"

"To the young man, Maximilian, and the gorgeous woman."

Laura heard her sister laugh softly. "Sorry. That sounds like a children's book: *Maximilian and the Gorgeous Woman.*"

Laura thought about Max and the wild things. All the Maxes. The wild things. The irony.

"So, what did the nurse say?" Lilly asked.

"That this happens all the time, behavior coming out of nowhere. She said sometimes clients get homesick and want to leave *with* you—other times, they just want *you* to leave. With Julia, it must be the latter because when I called this morning, this other nurse said she was fine. She got up, went to breakfast, was on her way to yoga."

"Maybe it *was* something with this Maximillian. Was he the one who gave her the shell drawing?"

"I don't think so. Julia said he was new and she'd never met him. But then he introduced her as a friend, which made no sense. Anyway, the nurse suggested I call later. Give her some time and space, though that certainly hasn't helped before."

"Please don't take this the wrong way, Lor, but she's safe there," Lilly said. "In good hands. With people who can help her." Lilly paused. "It's you I'm worried about."

For Mom.

"Laura?"

"I'm fine. Listen, I need to go—"

"Of course you do. Will you at least call me later?"

"I will."

"No, you won't. One day, though, I hope you'll realize it's okay not to be fine."

The new-age music Laura had been listening to prior to her sister's call returned, filling the car. Despite promising meditative relief, the sitar and flute weren't working. Laura recalled the nurse's deliberately soothing voice—her advice to review the web page of advice for families, the importance of keeping oneself healthy, well rested, and calm.

Laura was none of those things. She'd stayed up until the wee hours, reading about how fucked up she was, about the patterns and relics and layers. Generational. Familial. Personal. How she'd inflicted on Julia the painful adaptations and unhealthy behaviors instilled in her by Frances and Carl. About how much she'd clearly failed her daughter.

Worse, efforts to change her ways also seemed to be failing. She looked down at the phone in her hand and thought about her obsessive checking throughout the night. Memories of Paul's last day intruded: the rapid decline; him wanting his pain to end, her wanting him to stay; the argument they'd had only days earlier clouding her last moments with him; Julia, the horrified look on her face when she saw him—*Stop.*

Stop now.

Laura rubbed her forehead and temples and whispered her sister's words. "She's safe. In good hands." Then she turned her phone off to save what little battery was left, placed it face down on the passenger seat, and squeezed out of her car, directing a curse to the absent Escalade owner and, for the first time since she was six, a prayer to whatever god or gods might be out there—and listening.

ARABELLA

THOUGH TROUBLING IN NATURE, at least the call came at an opportune time. Arabella Marks Lorenzo had spent nearly an hour with a couple that bore obvious hatred for one another and viewed an art gallery as an appropriate battlefield. Arabella wondered if the large contemporary landscapes on the walls had contributed; executed in shades of orange and red, they resembled explosions. The woman's surgically pinched expression had grown tighter each time her husband asked Arabella a question, and he had many—about the artist's background, themes of his work, previous sales, logistics related to shipping and handling.

The three of them—Arabella, husband, and wife—engaged in an elaborate dance. With each query, the husband invaded Arabella's personal space like a honeybee drawn to a flower as the wife moved farther away, shooting Arabella with psychic poisoned arrows. Arabella, meanwhile, struggled to find a comfortable, non-insulting distance between them.

Just before her phone vibrated in her back pocket, the husband had murmured, "Perhaps I should come back tomorrow—on my own," as he returned psychic arrows aimed at his wife's retreating ass. "I am terribly interested."

Arabella excused herself. "And I'm terribly sorry, but I really must take this call."

She took four strides toward her floor-to-ceiling glass office in the back. Pressed accept.

"Arabella? It's Kristine Renner. Do you have a moment?"

Dr. Renner. Max. Sam.

"Yes, is everything all right?" Arabella had learned to dread telephone calls about her son. She knew it was difficult for the caller to begin with "everything's all right" when this was a blatant untruth. Nonetheless, having one's heart in one's throat on a regular basis was distinctly awful. "I haven't spoken to Sam yet—"

"Yes, no, the discharge went smoothly, no paperwork issues. And I personally reviewed his medication during rounds. I'm actually calling regarding another patient, Julia Reeves? Roberta mentioned you met her yesterday, during visiting hours."

Through the window into the gallery, Arabella watched the tightly pinched wife light into her husband. He shot one last pained hopeful glance in Arabella's direction. She met his gaze, then turned away.

There would be no sale.

Arabella thought back to her visit to Brookfield. The friend Sam had introduced. "If you mean the young woman with the cropped hair, Sam introduced her, but I did not speak with her. Why? Has something happened to her?"

After a brief silence on the other end, Dr. Renner said, "She left. This morning. Without clearance and without telling anyone."

"Oh, I see," Arabella said, cutting her reply short, thinking *Oh, shit.*

"She was last seen just before Sam left. I was hoping you might be willing to check with him, see if he might know her whereabouts, or plans."

Dr. Renner's tone was conciliatory yet firm. Quid pro quo.

"Is there reason to believe my son would know these things?"

As soon as the question left her mouth, Arabella feared the answer.

Dr. Renner's voice remained calm and even. "Julia's an artist. They struck up a friendship, of sorts."

"I assume you are not suggesting something untoward. My son is well aware of Brookfield's policies." Arabella knew, perhaps better than the doctor, that her son was both aware of the policies—and how to skirt them. She also knew, notwithstanding having never set foot on an athletic pitch of any sort, that a good offense is the best defense.

"I don't mean to suggest he's done anything wrong. It is possible her departure aligning with his is simply coincidental."

"Yes, quite possible. I assume you've spoken with her family?"

"We haven't been able to reach anyone yet. In the meantime, perhaps you'd be willing to check with Sam—see if he knows anything? Of course, that would be voluntary, on his part, but we'd appreciate it. I'm sure her family will as well."

Striking the family chord: Shared experience. Shared pain. Fear. Loss.

An appeal to empathy.

"I'll see him this afternoon. It's his birthday. I'll call and let you know what he says."

"Thank you, Arabella. Really, thanks."

By the time she'd signed off, Arabella had tidied the top of her desk and sent an automated away-from-office email. It took only a minute to gather her coat and bag, adjust the lighting, and lock up. A brisk wind blew her hair into her face. She shook her head in a fruitless attempt to clear her hair or her thoughts and, arm held high to hail a cab, she approached the curb.

What had her son done now?

JULIA

ARABELLA'S BROWNSTONE WAS located on a quiet street near a park.

"Prospect Park," Sam narrated, as the black sedan drove by. "I grew up coming here. Played Little League when I was a kid, which did not go well. Putting a kid with an attention deficit in the outfield is a truly horrific idea. Let's just say" — he gave her a rueful smile— "I was not a star right fielder. Lacrosse, on the other hand, was awesome: running, scoring, hitting people with a stick. . . . Here we are."

Sam had been talking the entire drive—about the conversation with his mother the night before and his father's decision to get out of the country rather than face him; his mother's reassurance that she believed in him, and that she knew he'd do the right thing; how he knew exactly what the right thing was since, after watching *The Big Short*, he'd become fascinated with the world of finance, reading for days about investing strategies, real estate, income generation, and bond yields; and how now he could embark on living the life he knew he was meant to live.

Julia tried to focus on his words, a task made difficult by the spinning of her own thoughts and unanswered questions: Had they discovered she'd left? Had anyone seen her walk toward the art barn before she darted into the woods? Should she call her mom, or would that get Sam in trouble? Could they make her go back?

Sam's physical proximity only made concentrating harder. It had been bad enough when, twenty minutes into the journey, he'd moved forward to speak with the driver and settled back with his leg touching hers, but then a few minutes ago, he'd dropped his hand down onto her thigh. Julia felt nerve endings awakening in a completely new way, rippling out and in and down. For the briefest of moments, she marveled at the intricacy of her own body—of neurons and neurotransmitters and invisible signals, cognition and emotion and behavior tied together in ways she was only starting to understand.

"Hold on a sec, Joe," Sam said to the driver as he exited the sedan. He raised his hand in the universal "Stop" sign to Julia, who'd been sliding toward the back door on the passenger side. "Wait here. I'll be right back."

So Julia remained, perched awkwardly on the leather seat, watching Sam cross the sidewalk, open the wrought-iron gate, and traverse a small courtyard. He dropped his duffle at the base of the stairs, took the stone steps leading to the main front door two at a time, unlocked the heavy coffered front door, and disappeared inside. The front window suddenly shone with light, revealing a room with high ceilings, a geometric chandelier, and a large modern painting of flowers or maybe fireworks—bursting in pink, Cadmium Orange, and yellow. Julia looked up and down the block of brownstones. There was a noticeable lack of pedestrians in comparison to the bustling streets they'd traversed crossing into this section of Brooklyn.

A new set of questions floated up: What were they waiting for? Were they leaving again? Going inside? What was Sam doing on the main floor—*didn't he say he lived downstairs?*

The driver, Joe, cleared his throat. Other than the brief consultation with Sam regarding the preferred route home, the man had been silent. Julia wondered if she should try to make conversation while they waited for Sam to reemerge. She wanted to hear a voice other than Sam's, a counter to his tempest of words, and yet, she didn't know what to say.

As the silence became acutely uncomfortable, Joe turned. "So you're a friend of Mr. Lorenzo's?" he asked.

Julia looked away from the front of the house to respond. "Yes." She considered how to proceed. "We met—"

"Hey, hey." Sam was back. He leaned in, reaching over Julia to hand the driver several folded bills, outer-wrapped with a hundred. "It'd be great if you didn't mention I had anyone with me. Kept it between us. You know, not that anyone would ask, but—"

"Yes, sir, I understand," Joe said, in a way that led Julia to wonder if this wasn't the first time Sam had made such a request.

"Any chance you could wait for thirty, forty minutes," Sam went on, "maybe get a coffee or something and come back? We've got a couple more stops to make today, and it would be great if you could take us."

"No problem, sir. Take your time."

Taking one's time was not in Sam's playbook. He, Julia, and the duffle were through a wrought-iron security door, an inner door with two bolts, and across the threshold of the apartment under the stone staircase in thirty seconds.

Julia surveyed Sam's living room—reclaimed ash wood furniture with clean lines, off-white upholstered sectional sofa with assorted throw pillows artfully placed, black-and-white photographs hanging on the walls and books—everywhere— filling bookcases, stacked against the wall and piled on flat surfaces, along with canvases and more photographs, loose and matted.

She turned to see Sam staring at her, his blue eyes bright. Brilliant.

And then his hands were on either side of her face, and his mouth was on hers. She felt herself moving with him down the hall, her sweatshirt over her head. His hands on her body. Stumbling over each other's feet. Into a bedroom. Later, she would not recall how or when clothing was removed or covers pulled back. Skin met skin; sensations overwhelmed thought. The longing of days compressed and fulfilled in minutes. Sam's lips gentle on the palms of her hands, sliding down over the inside of her wrists, and then his own scars pressed against hers as their fingertips entwined over her head. Julia yielded to desire that had become an aching need, flooding over her and through her. Her mind emptied of reason and worry and uncertainty.

Just being.

Afterward, eyes closed, lying on her side, her limbs entangled with his and a soft sheet, Julia relished not thinking.

But it was fleeting.

In the space of a breath, Sam disentangled. Leaning on his elbow next to her, he slid the sheet away, exposing her body. Fingertips feather soft, he traced a path down over her hip onto her thigh, lingering over the cutting scars. Julia's thoughts flooded back in.

Inexplicably, she felt tears forming. Melancholy washed over her.

"Did it hurt?" Sam asked.

She wasn't sure if he was referring to what had just transpired or the cutting.

She shook her head. *Hurt* was the wrong word in both instances.

Sam was up, away.

"Don't move," he said, grabbing his jeans off the floor. "I'll be right back." He took a few steps into the hall and then returned, leaning his head and shoulders back into the doorframe. "Sorry, *please* don't move."

Like the living room, the bedroom was done in shades of ash, black, white, and gray. Decorative pillows Julia didn't recall seeing when they came into the room now lay scattered on the floor. It occurred to her that everything surrounding Sam had little color, as though he lived in a vintage black-and-white photograph.

From where she lay, Julia could see the titles of the books in the case. There were books about photography, lighting and exposure, real-estate investing, war, wrestling, and mountaineering. Books by George R. R. Martin, Hemingway, and Joyce, Socrates, Plato, and Nietzsche.

If he'd read them all, he was five years and a world apart from her.

A stack of thick coffee-table books sat on the floor next to the platform bedframe. On top was a very worn copy of *The Myth of Sisyphus* by Camus, its cover, fittingly for Sam, a black-and-white pattern. Underneath it, a book titled *Night Photography and Light Painting: Finding Your Way in the Dark*. She identified the edges of photographic prints emerging from between the pages.

She could also see piles of prints, curled, clearly pre-book-flattening, on top of and under the bookcase. She wanted to get up and look at them, to see what Sam considered worthy of capturing.

But then, he was back. He held something in his hand, tucked behind his leg.

"Thank you," he said.

For what? Julia thought but didn't say.

"You didn't move," he said.

"You asked me not to."

"I wanted to catch you, as you were, with your eyes closed, lying next to me," he said. He held up a camera, some sort of antique folding one, with bellows. He took two steps, stopped. "Is that okay?"

Julia rolled onto her side, closed her eyes. She heard Sam moving around her, over her, the opening and shutting of a camera lens.

Click. Click.

"You have a lot of books," she said.

"Indeed, I do. For me, bookstores are both solace and nemesis. My grandfather once told me that one can never have too many books, which is, quite obviously, a belief I share."

Julia thought her father would have liked Sam and his love of books.

Click.

All at once, a loud buzzing noise came from the hall.

Startled, Julia sat straight up and self-consciously scrambled for the sheet.

"Shit," Sam said, dropping the camera to his side. "That's probably my mother." He put the camera on the foot of the bed and bent to retrieve his t-shirt. "Stay here. I'll be right back." After taking a few steps into the hall, he returned, head and shoulders back in the doorframe. "Sorry, *please* stay here." And again, after only two steps, his head was back. "By the way, that was amazing. All of it. You. Are. Amazing."

Julia stood up and began to frantically search for her clothing; profession of amazingness and request for stillness notwithstanding, she had no intention of meeting the elegant Arabella naked in her son's bed. Julia quickly realized her sweatshirt was lying somewhere in the hall and her underwear were nowhere to be found. Panic set in. One second, she was standing next to the bed, holding her breath, feeling her heartbeat, and the next she was looking down at herself, clad only in leggings and a sports bra, head bowed, arms crossed, one hand pressed against her mouth.

She could hear murmured voices, blurry dialogue: Arabella questioning. Sam answering. Arabella sounding concerned. Sam reassuring. A door closed. Footsteps on the hardwood floor.

She was back in her body when Sam bounded in.

"You got up," he said, disappointed. He held out her sweatshirt. "Probably for the best, though, since we're facing a slight complication. I wouldn't give up the last half hour for anything, but we probably should've left before she got home. She's heading over to the bakery to pick up a cake, so we've got a little window, maybe fifteen minutes."

Sam opened a large flat drawer in the bedframe and removed another duffle and laid it on the bed. "I couldn't tell her I wouldn't be here to blow out the candles," he said. He threw a pair of black canvas high-top sneakers into the bag, then began pulling clothing from hangers and drawers in the closet: button-downs, t-shirts, sweaters, pants, underwear, socks—all of it black, white, and gray.

"If there's one thing I wish I'd never do again," he added, "it would be breaking my mother's heart. But if we don't get out of here now . . ."

Julia felt unmoored as questions rose again. Where were they going? What was she going to wear? She looked again for her underwear on the floor. She had nothing other than the clothes on her body. "Where are we going? I don't have anything. Not even a toothbrush. I left everything behind."

"Ah," Sam said, "but you're wrong." He pulled her close, enveloped her, tucking her head under his chin. "You have me. And I have you. And if we had more time, I'd make that clear. Which reminds me—" Sam loosened his arms, let her go. He grabbed the worn copy of *The Myth of Sisyphus* and dropped it on top of the duffle, then reached under the night-photography book to retrieve a boxed set of books.

"Stieglitz," he said softly. Then louder, "This must go with us. It contains prints of every mounted photograph he had at the time of his death."

He tipped the box toward her. On the cover was a photograph of hands holding grapes, fingers curved like a shadow animal. "Georgia O'Keeffe. His muse, his inspiration. They brought out the best in each other—passion, angst, beauty." He shifted the box to rest on his left arm, reached for Julia's chin, and tilted her face up. "I've been searching for that." He kissed her. "I've been searching for you." He dropped the boxed set on top of *The Myth* and grabbed her hand. "Come on, I've got something else to show you."

The bathroom was at the end of the hall, sleek, with a slate-gray floor and walls, large white soaking tub, and silver fixtures. "Room with the best view," Sam said. He gestured not to the frosted window over the bathtub but toward a single photograph of a craggy face of rock, a majestic black slab against a dark sky and white snow, all angles and texture and contrasts.

"It's beautiful," Julia said.

"'Monolith: the Face of Half Dome.' Ansel Adams's first masterpiece and a pivotal moment in his artistic life. It was, and I quote"—Sam smiled—"his 'first conscious visualization.'"

Julia took a step closer. Sam stepped behind her and wrapped his arms around her. His voice resonated into her body. "He said standing there on the edge, praying the wind wouldn't shake the camera, he could see the final image in his mind's eye. The mood. The substance. Back then, photography meant something. Adams, Weston, Stieglitz. They were creating something real, tying the visible to the invisible. Today, guys with digital cameras take hundreds of shots hoping to get one that works. Zooming, photoshopping, filtering with apps. Back then? It took fucking effort. It took courage."

Sam dropped his arms from around her waist and turned to the cabinet under the sink. He removed a small leather bag and began tossing items into it.

Julia studied the piece. She'd once had an Adams print hanging in her bedroom, and one of her doctor's offices had a series of them, all bearing the title of the work, his name, and the location at which the image was captured, in telltale clean print on a white background. The framed picture in the bathroom had none of those.

"Is this an actual photograph?" she asked.

Sam looked over his shoulder. Nodded. "Twenty-first birthday present from my mother. She's a masterful giver of gifts." He turned to stand behind her again but didn't touch her. "I spent so many days here, staring at it, dreaming. I see myself hiking up, Half Dome towering over the landscape. Magnificent not just for what's there, but also for what's missing. I imagine feeling the emptiness—the nothingness that is the other half—the part that makes it what it is, because without it, it's just another dome." His voice slowed, quieted. "And I imagine the moment when I see all of it in *my* mind's eye, the 'Monolith,' the missing half. I'll experience it—really experience it—and then, I'll make it my own." The not-touching was magnetic.

Julia reached back for Sam's hand. "You can do it," she said.

"No," he said. He dropped her hand and closed the space between them, his chest pressed against her back, his arms around her again in a tight embrace. "*We* can do it. You asked where we're going? That's where. Together. Ansel Adams had his wife. Stieglitz had O'Keeffe. And now . . ." Sam lifted his right hand and traced the hollow above her collarbone with a single fingertip as he kissed the side of her neck. "I have you."

Cool air hit the back of Julia's body as Sam stepped away. She turned to see him holding up two toothbrushes still in plastic wrapping. "And you'll have one of these. My mother must've restocked the drawers. So you have me and a toothbrush."

"Unfortunately, I can't wear you, or a toothbrush."

"No, you cannot, though it might be fun to see you try."

Sam plucked the framed photograph from the wall and moved back into the hallway. "We'll shop after we pick up money. Get the basics. Something to celebrate in."

"Celebrate?" Julia asked, following him.

"Yeah," Sam said, glancing back. "It's my birthday, remember?"

He dropped the small cosmetic bag in the duffle and continued down the hall, disappearing into the next doorway.

"Of course I remember," she said to his retreating back, but she hadn't.

Time and events were spinning by. Only a few hours earlier she'd been sitting with a tepid cup of tea, wondering how she was going to get through a day without Sam. Now she was standing in a hallway, looking at the bed on which she'd given all of herself to him, wondering where it would lead her. She thought back to that morning, to the moment after Sam had said, "Come with me." One of her last discussions with Tanya had entered her head — how the CBT was working; acknowledging the do-loop nature of her thoughts, behaviors, and emotions spinning positively or negatively; learning when to let go and when to reframe and take control; the art, the yoga, the SSRI. Believing she might be able to forgive herself someday.

The reality of what she had done slammed into her. Sam could say whatever he wanted, but she'd left everything behind — everything that was working. She'd left without finishing, without telling the whole truth. And even though it was only a few days until her discharge, running away was not part of the plan she and Tanya had developed. She had no Dr. Renner, no group, no therapist, no medication. Tanya's warning reverberated: "If you want to stop taking the antidepressant, you need to wean off. Going cold turkey can be awful, emotionally, physically. Headaches, insomnia, irritability, seizures, and depression, often worse than before."

Julia did not want to experience cold turkey.

But she also did not want to lose Sam.

"Sam?" Julia called, walking toward where he had disappeared. The door was open.

It was a darkroom. Small, cluttered, but surprisingly well-equipped, with two sink basins, a worktable, shelving on one wall containing dark brown bottles of toner and stop bath, thermometers, trays. Julia knew the steps involved, the equipment, the chemicals. She saw the signs for poison and Sam's form moving in a red glow of light, the framed photo in one hand, a small knife in the other.

"Another gift from my mother," Sam said. "She had it installed when I was away three years ago. Just packing a few things. Won't be long. Can you grab that?" He dipped his head toward a pale brown leather suitcase.

Julia bent to take the handle of the case. The leather was dry and cracked, the case heavy. She let go. Stood up. Watched Sam. She wanted to raise her concerns but could not find the right frame for her words. She realized she wasn't breathing.

"Hey," Sam called out. "You all right?"

Julia shook her head. "I don't have my meds, and Tanya said going cold turkey can be dangerous—"

Sam stopped and turned abruptly, cutting off her words with his expression—a combination of anger and fear and disgust. "I've got that more than covered," he said grimly. He crouched next to the bank of sinks and removed a metal box from a cabinet underneath. It bore a "Chemical Hazard Alert" tag.

"They've got you on Prozac, right?" Sam said. He handed her the box and stepped away. "Should be some in there."

Julia opened the box and took a quick, shallow breath. In the dim red glow, she could see it was filled with orange and white plastic bottles with childproof tops, a plethora of prescription medicine—medicine that Sam clearly had not taken. *Please help me.* Julia's vision blurred as she pictured other plastic bottles, stored in a medicine cabinet, hidden in the waistband of her yoga pants, tucked under a pillow, and then gone.

LAURA

AS SOON AS LAURA TURNED ON the ignition, the sound of sitar and flute filled the car. Loud, irritating. She closed her eyes, inhaled deeply, and sighed heavily, rolling her shoulders up, back, and down before reaching to retrieve the cell phone lying on the passenger seat.

Waiting for the phone to power up, she reversed her car out of the parking space. Messages popped up on the screen and her eyes were drawn immediately to two missed calls and voicemails from Brookfield's area code.

Habit guided her actions. She stopped at the lot's exit and sequentially clicked on icons, buttons, and arrows, and then Dr. Renner's voice filled the car, replacing the offending peaceful music. "Please call me as soon as you get this message."

Dr. Renner. Not a nurse or counselor. Dr. Renner.

The fear Laura had been fighting to keep at bay since she'd left her nearly dead phone in the car came howling. She quickly executed a U-turn, reentered the parking lot, located a new spot, pressed Call Back, threw the car into park, and pulled the emergency brake.

Dr. Renner was succinct. Julia was gone. She'd last been seen several hours earlier, walking in the direction of the art barn.

She hadn't been safe after all.

"I don't understand," Laura said. "What do you mean she's gone?"

Laura heard a rush of words. Dr. Renner explaining how they'd been trying to reach her. They'd left messages on her voicemail, sent an email. Laura felt the ice pick strike her chest. Instant nausea. Her words came in spurts. "My phone. The battery. I forgot my charger. You're sure she's gone? She didn't tell anyone? Leave a note?"

Laura felt disoriented. The air was suddenly thick, simple spoken words unintelligible, rational thought fraught with uncertainty. She tried to *Stop,* but the rules were being rewritten faster than she could keep up and the sledgehammer was back. As Dr. Renner answered her first questions—*Julia had not left a note nor told anyone she was leaving*—others rose and swirled. How could Julia walk away without anyone seeing her go? Did she take her things? Why had the nurse told her that Julia was fine, on her way to yoga?

Dr. Renner did not have answers to these questions. However, she assured Laura appropriate steps had been taken: a search of the grounds had been completed; interviews had been conducted with staff, patients, a UPS delivery man who'd dropped off some boxes around the time Julia left the premises. No one had seen anything out of the ordinary. Julia hadn't taken the things from her room, but there wasn't much to take. This kind of thing had happened before with other patients; Julia was there by choice and could leave by choice. Protocol had been followed, including best practices based on previous unexpected departures—which gave Laura no comfort.

"I should go home," Laura said. "Maybe she went home." She released the brake, put the car in reverse.

"It would be helpful to know if she returned home. However—" Dr. Renner's strained voice affirmed the thought that had crossed Laura's shattered brain: *Racing home won't make a difference. Julia is not at home. If she wanted to be at home, she would have called, not run away.*

Dr. Renner went on, her voice now both strained and hesitant. "There is something else I need to share with you, Mrs. Reeves—Laura."

In the moment that followed the clarification of her name, Laura knew what Dr. Renner's next words would be. Her daughter's departure had something to do with the events of the evening before, something to do with Maximilian, the young man Julia did not know, but knew—or was it knew, but did not know. Laura put the car back in park.

"This information is confidential," Dr. Renner said. "But given the circumstances, I feel you ought to know. Another client, a young man, Sam, was discharged shortly before Julia was last seen. Though he left alone, and we haven't been able to confirm he knows anything about her whereabouts, given the timing—"

Sam? Laura wondered.

"We're looking into the possibility the departures were related. We've contacted his mother in the hope—"

"Wait, who's Sam?"

"Sam Lorenzo. Roberta said you met him last night."

"No." Laura seemed to have found her voice. "I did *not* meet any Sam. I only met one young man, Maximilian, and the woman who was visiting him."

"Ah, yes," Dr. Renner said. "Well, Sam *is* Max, or should I say, Max is Sam."

"Excuse me?" Laura said, thinking *Oh my god, does this Sam have a multiple personality disorder?*

Dr. Renner went on. "His first name is Maximilian, Max, but he goes by his middle name, Sam. The woman you met, Arabella, is his mother."

"His *mother?*"

"Yes, and as I said, we called her and—"

"She doesn't know where he is."

"We don't—" Dr. Renner's voice reclaimed its hesitancy. "We don't know that yet. She's agreed to ask him about Julia and, of course, I'll call you if she has any information. Other than that, we've done everything we can at this point."

"What about the police? Shouldn't we call the police?"

Dr. Renner sighed. "It's been our experience the authorities won't get involved. Julia and Sam are both adults, here voluntarily, and Sam was discharged. Though we're concerned Julia left early, without her medication, she's been doing well the past few days. Unless there's an imminent risk to self or others, or evidence of foul play, there's little the police will do."

"Then what can *I* do?" Laura said softly, more to herself than to the doctor. The last time Julia had seemed better, Laura had been too complacent, too fucking stoic. She would not make that mistake again. She needed to do something. "I should go home."

There was a long pause.

"Laura," Dr. Renner began. Laura remembered Julia complaining about how everyone repeated her name—Julia this, Julia that—as if she were a loose helium balloon that needed to be tethered down with her name. Laura had not processed this complaint until now. So many things Julia had said that Laura had not processed properly. She'd heard without listening.

"I know this is upsetting," Dr. Renner was saying. "Please remember the oxygen mask analogy: secure your own before you help others. You need to take care of yourself to be there for Julia. Is there someone you can call, a friend, a family member?"

Laura's voice failed her again. *Paul*, she wanted to say. *I need my husband.*

Paul was gone. Julia was gone. She swallowed hard. "My sister. Lilly."

"Good. Call her. See if Julia's been home, and if you haven't heard from me by then, call and ask for Julia's therapist, Tanya. She'll let you know if we've heard anything, okay?"

Laura reached up. Her face was wet. As she forcefully pressed the backs of her hands to her cheeks, Laura remembered something else Julia had told her, right before she entered Brookfield. How she sometimes felt an invisible vise was tightening around her rib cage while a solid leaden mass invaded her lungs, crowding out air. How sometimes it was too overwhelming. How sometimes she wanted it all to end. At the time, Julia's words had been too painful to hear, reminiscent of Paul's toward the end.

Now, Laura felt an urge to say these words out loud. To validate them. She opened her mouth to speak, but she'd waited too long.

Dr. Renner was speaking again. "Julia was taking—"

Laura looked at the phone. The screen had gone black.

JULIA

LATE AFTERNOON DAYLIGHT PASSED through tinted windows as the driver, Joe, navigated the crowded streets of Manhattan. Julia sat cocooned in the backseat, watching an animated Sam recount the scene inside the private banking office: the quiet hush; paneled wood walls; an obsequious older man in a dark suit who'd spent countless billable hours working to keep him from his inheritance, now forced to help him claim it.

Julia tried to reconcile this Sam with the one who'd read *The Myth of Sisyphus* so often the spine was nearly split, highlighting so many passages that entire sections glared neon orange. The Sam who insisted they bring the book with them, as it was "essential reading for anyone who'd ever contemplated the meaning of life," which, he'd added, "is, sadly, not everyone."

Before they'd left his apartment, he'd tucked the book into his duffle and, while waiting for him during the banking, Julia had opened it—hoping for elucidation—only to find Camus held more questions than answers, right from the start: "There is but one truly philosophical problem, and that is suicide."

Her first thought was *what the fuck*, followed closely by *no, oh no.*

She'd looked up, startled, expecting to see someone watching her. Joe stood at attention outside, his back to the driver's side window. The street was quiet, the buildings primarily residential, though some bore small brass plates that appeared business-y. Subdued signage. Doormen. A woman dressed all in black walked past, talking on her cell phone.

No one was watching her.

Julia had turned back to *The Myth,* reading, then rereading the first few pages, wishing for a dictionary, a philosophy primer, and some Spark Notes.

Yet there'd been an eerie familiarity to Camus's torrent of words. Certain phrases resonated. Others reminded her of discussions she'd had with her dad about the universe and humanity, fate and free will, which reminded her of Sam's first monologue, delivered the day he gave her the abstract drawing of her face. She recalled how he'd used the phrase "Sisyphean task," wondering aloud whether his own life was his to determine, which brought her back to her dad again. *Invictus* under the stars.

She lifted a hand to her sternum and kept reading.

Camus read like a well-constructed distillation of Sam's ramblings. Perhaps, she thought, *The Myth* could be the key to understanding him, understanding herself, the decisions she'd made. Taking orange plastic bottles that didn't belong to her, not once, not twice, but three times now. Then again, perhaps it might lead her back to the black hole in her mind, an empty, silent place in her heart.

She recalled the pre-Brookfield session with Dr. Stein, when she'd longed to disappear, and how she'd put her trust in Tanya and the strategies she'd presented to exert control over her thoughts, behaviors, and emotions. She'd left too soon; she'd only begun to put those strategies into practice. She saw a cartoon version of herself at the edge of a black hole, her little pink shovel in hand, not at all certain she could keep from falling backward.

Maybe this was all a mistake.

And then, Julia had looked up to see Sam approaching the car, his backpack clutched to his chest, and she'd stuffed the book back into the duffle.

Within a minute, the hole, shovel, and Camus were all forgotten. She'd asked Sam a simple question, "How did it go with the bankers?" and after a brief look of confusion and puzzling initial response, "Bankers?" Sam had launched into the current monologue. His anti-centrifuge quality had kicked in, drawing her into his orbit and holding her there, spinning.

"Oh, right, the bankers. It was just this one guy really, going gray and trying to hide it, clinging to his youth, totally full of shit, acting like moving money around for a living is noble. I told him I needed seventy K, in hundreds—"

"Seventy thousand dollars?"

"Yeah, and get this, he's dead silent, doesn't even blink, like he deals with that kind of money every day, like it's no big deal." Sam sounded angry now. "Which, for him . . ." Sam paused, shook his head. "The money's in stacks. Crisp new bills with that smell, you know? He doesn't want me to have the money, but he's got no choice. So I signed a note, found this bag, and picked up the stacks one by one, put 'em in the bag, put the bag in my backpack, and left. The entire time, all I could think—" Sam turned to Julia. "All I could think was I wanted to get out of there. Back to you."

The centrifuge stalled. His lips met hers, abruptly stopping her spinning thoughts, dropping her into space.

Almost as abruptly, he pulled her back to the surface, breathless.

Sam's face was inches from hers. Eyes blazing.

The world paused.

The car wasn't moving. Joe opened his door.

Julia looked outside, saw people walking by a pale stone building with large display windows.

"Where are we?"

"Saks. Time to shop—for you. Clothes. Shoes. Celebratory attire. Remember, you can't wear me, or a toothbrush. Not to dinner, at least." Sam laughed to himself. He lifted her arm and brushed his lips over the back of her hand. It was totally distracting. "Which brings up an important point. Where to go for dinner? I thought we'd stay at the Pierre. I've always wanted to stay there, see the vast darkness of the park in the middle of the night from a high floor. What do you think?"

Focusing was proving impossible.

"Julia?"

"I don't know."

"You don't know what?"

So much, Julia thought. "I don't know any nice restaurants in the city."

Joe was standing outside the rear passenger door.

"But I do," Sam said. He grabbed his backpack and gestured to Joe in an effortless, familiar way. The door opened and Sam exited. "All you have to decide is what you want." Sam reached for her hand and said to Joe, "Give us an hour, maybe two? I'll text you." He pulled her toward the gold-framed entrance. "Pasta, sushi, steak. God, I haven't had a steak in weeks. We need to find a directory—"

A cacophony of sounds mixed with Sam's voice at the threshold: braying car horns and squealing bus brakes, piped music, and the low buzz of people conversing. Gorgeous glossy women stared down from posters and displays.

Julia couldn't keep up. She shook free of Sam's hand.

"Sam." Julia halted her forward motion, lifted her hands palms forward as if she were being held at gunpoint. "Hold on. Wait. Please. Stop."

"Stop?" Sam stopped several paces into the cosmetics department.

A man in a black sweater mechanically sprayed cologne onto a slip of cardboard, waving it toward them. "Tom Ford, Noir Extreme."

Sam ignored the proffered gift; nevertheless, the smell of wood and smoke and oranges filled the air. Sam stared at Julia. "Wait—do you not want to celebrate?" He seemed offended or maybe disappointed, Julia couldn't quite tell.

"No. It's not that I don't want to celebrate, per se. It's just . . . this is all happening so fast—"

And then Sam laughed, loud, startling her. With two steps,

he eliminated the space between them. "And *you* don't know any nice restaurants."

Julia had no idea what he found humorous about her statement. "I don't."

"Except you just happened to mention one of the best ones in the country." Sam retook her hand, began to lead her past counters bright with color and light—shimmering gold, reds, royal purple, cobalt blue—talking all the while. "Which also happens to be my father's go-to spot for entertaining clients and impressing beautiful women far too young for him. It's a genius choice, the ultimate 'Fuck you, you can't control me forever.'"

Julia felt herself resisting Sam's forward motion, her arm extended, tense. "I didn't mention a restaurant."

"Ah, but you did. Per Se." Sam called out to a saleswoman. "Dresses?"

The saleswoman looked Julia up and down. "Four."

Julia rewound her words. She had said *per se*. It was a phrase her father had used. Maybe she'd mispronounced it or used it the wrong way.

Sam went on as if uninterrupted. "Which happens to be on Columbus Circle, on the park, which is perfect. After dinner, we can walk through the vastness before taking it in from above."

Two women with a stroller were waiting at the bank of elevators, clearly a mother-daughter-grandchild situation: a carefully coiffed, nipped-and-tucked elderly woman, a younger Botoxed blond version of the same, and a little girl, maybe three, with curls and rosy cheeks. The women gave Julia the same up and down scan as the saleswoman.

She felt their judgment in an instant.

Sam tilted his head in their direction. "Ladies." He turned back to Julia with his left eyebrow raised, mouth in a half grimace, and whispered, "Yikes." He dropped her hand to slip his phone out of his pocket. He muttered "per se" as his fingers darted over the screen.

Though Julia's parents weren't big on expensive restaurants, on her sixteenth birthday her dad had been set on taking her to the nicest restaurant in their town, but he'd called too late and couldn't get a table. Surely one of the best restaurants in the world was full.

Sam put the phone up to his ear as an elevator door slid open to their left. Sam grabbed for her arm. "On hold," he said. He nodded to the women entering the elevator. "We'll catch the next one."

The elderly woman glanced back with a look that said she couldn't care less.

Sam gave her a huge smile in return. "Have a lovely day," he said as the door closed. His voice lowered and his tone changed—both dramatically. "Yes, good afternoon, this is Max Lorenzo." He paused to listen. "Yes, excellent." He raised his eyebrows to Julia. "Hello, Sandra, Yes, it's Max. I'm well, thank you. Listen, I'll need a table tonight, for two, 7:30. It's my son's birthday. Yes, Sam. You have a good memory. Indeed, he has quite the collection." Another pause. "Very good. See you then."

Sam slipped the phone back into his pocket and stepped forward to press the elevator button.

"What was that about?" Julia asked.

"That? Ah, the voice?"

She nodded, seeing a dialogue bubble forming, filled with "Very good" in something elegant. Cursive. Bold.

"I do a mean Max Lorenzo impression." Sam employed the voice again. "Basso profundo, with a touch of asshole."

The elevator door in front of them slid open.

Sam gestured toward the open space with his trademark flourishing mini-bow and added, "One small benefit of sharing his name—his voice literally opens doors. Point of fact, my father is known to many a maître d' as an NR."

"NR?"

Alone in the elevator, Sam wrapped his arms around her. He dropped an absentminded kiss onto her lips before answering. "Yeah, it's a thing. A code. Means 'never refuse.' Restaurants hold tables for people like him—as he'd be keen to tell you. He's got accounts at a bunch of 'em; they don't even bring a bill to the table. For him, it's a symbol of his cachet or the size of his dick. For me," Sam grinned, "it means dinner on Dad."

Julia watched the smile fade as Sam went on. "I've been to Per Se before. Twice. Both birthday dinners. Two menus signed by the chef. Of course, the second time, my father forgot I'd ever been there." Sam shook his head, his expression shifting to shaded sorrow. "Which goes to show how memorable my birthdays are for him."

"I'm sorry," Julia said.

Sam kissed her forehead.

"Nah, it's all right. Besides," he said, dropping his gaze to lock his eyes on hers, "tonight will make up for those. Tonight will be memorable." And then, his lips met hers purposefully, reminding her of the kisses in the courtyard and the hallway of his apartment—moments that changed her world. "Tonight, we will never forget."

The elevator door opened. Time suspended, hanging, waiting.

"And now," Sam said, smiling broadly, "now we shop."

ARABELLA

FALL HAD ARRIVED. It was getting dark earlier and earlier.

Arabella walked home with a carry bag containing butcher-wrapped beef in one hand and a cake box in the other. She looked up as the sun dropped behind the clouds, creating a soft halo at the edges of buildings on her street. The ephemeral glow led her thoughts to the candles she'd purchased for Sam's birthday and how, for as long as she could remember—long before the cycling began—she'd felt the need to cover for him. Every year since he'd been little, Arabella had made a wish, holding her breath as he let his out.

The candles on the cake were as much for her as they were for him: a fleeting bright, hopeful promise.

Promises. Promises.

The ones Max had showered upon her when she was young and impressionable. The ones they'd shared in front of a justice of the peace and two random witnesses, all three of whom she imagined judging her for the way her elegant white sheath pulled across her belly and breasts. The ones she'd made twenty-three years ago today when she first set eyes on her baby boy—that she would protect him and give him the unconditional love she'd always longed for and hitherto had not received.

As she ascended the stone steps of her home, Arabella remembered another promise, the one she'd made earlier that afternoon—to Dr. Renner.

She put the groceries away, poured herself a glass of crisp Chablis and curled up on the window seat with her legs folded under her, looking out at the garden in the back of the house. She stared at the top of the lone Yoshino cherry tree in the backyard, its remaining leaves yellow and bronze. Watched a lone leaf fall. Checked her watch.

And placed the call.

Not that she'd expected it to go swimmingly, but Arabella was surprised at how truly awful the conversation was. Even though she'd stated Sam had no knowledge of any plans Julia Reeves might have made, nor any information about where she might be, that he was behaving normally and had made plans with her for dinner, Dr. Renner had ended with this admonition: "I know you understand how painful not knowing can be when it comes to a child you fear may be unstable. Julia's only just turned eighteen. I trust that if you learn anything about her whereabouts or hear Sam had contact with her, you'll let me know."

Arabella had hung up feeling guilty and unsettled. Some sort of collective maternal consciousness took hold. Apprehension formed air bubbles inside her, displacing organs and crowding air from her lungs, because she *did* understand the pain Julia's mother was experiencing. Arabella replayed the scene from the night before: watching Julia fly away; her mother's hesitating, faltering steps; her arm reaching, finding nothing but air. Arabella could see, and feel, the despair on the woman's face. She heard and internalized the halting, uncomfortable words of apology.

She also recalled how Sam seemed to share some portion of Julia's mother's despair.

This reaction had worried Arabella. *What did it mean? Who is this girl to Sam?*

It still worried her now.

She replayed another scene: Sam at the door to his apartment earlier that afternoon, so relaxed, so confident.

"Julia?" he'd said, "Nah, no idea. Last time I saw her, she was drinking tea. Seemed a bit low but, well, that's why she was there, so . . . why do you ask?"

"It's nothing." Arabella had studied her son's face, looking for signs of evasion and culpability, all the while realizing she felt a bit of both. She'd taken a step toward Sam and, peeking over his shoulder into the hallway, had seen a faded black sweatshirt on the floor a few feet away. She remembered feeling an urge to pick it up. To fold it. "Do you need help with anything?"

"Nah, I've got this," Sam had replied with confidence. He'd placed his hands gently on her shoulders, exerting just enough pressure to keep her at the threshold. "I'm good. Really. Better than I've ever been in my life."

"So, dinner later?" she'd said then. "Maybe eightish? I've ordered the roast beef, and the cake—chocolate, with icing. And candles."

At that, Sam had given her an adult version of his six-year-old smile. "Guess I'll have to come up with a good wish." He'd leaned forward, dropped a kiss on her cheek. "You're the best."

And feeling buoyant and reassured her fears were for naught, Arabella had set off for the butcher shop and bakery. A line from a children's rhyme had floated up, a line about "the butcher, the baker, the candlestick maker." It wasn't until she stood at the register in the bakery, gazing upon the icing message on the cake that read "Happy 23rd Sam!" that she'd remembered the rhyme in question started with "Rub-a-dub-dub."

It was about men in a tub.

Arabella had gasped involuntarily. It would have been better not to dwell on that particular nursery rhyme. Sam reaching this birthday had often seemed a long shot in the past four years—an impossibility only six weeks ago.

"Is there a problem?" the bakery clerk had asked, looking concerned.

"Oh, no," she'd answered, tucking the cardboard flaps into the box, wishing it were as easy to close off memories, tuck away fears.

Now, looking into her darkened backyard at nearly barren tree limbs, Arabella drained the last of the Chablis, reminding herself that her son did not know where this Julia had gone. This was *not* a case of history repeating itself. Julia meant nothing to him. She must have mistaken the look on his face last night. He was home. It was his birthday. He would open his presents. There would be roast beef and Yorkshire pudding and cake and candles.

But only if she prepared it.

She rose, returned to the kitchen, and set about making dinner. She salted the beef, inserted garlic cloves into the fat, and put it in the oven, a cream-colored Aga Cooker. She closed the cast-iron door firmly and diverted her thoughts, turning them to the argument she had with Max in the kitchen design showroom about the merits of the solid stove that reminded her of childhood, of cold winter afternoons when she'd come home from school and linger in the kitchen with the cook, Marie Louise, who'd been more of a mother to her than her own. She allowed herself to dwell in memories, of crusty shepherd's pie, milky tea, and Marie Louise's quiet acceptance; of Max's devotion and desire to please her when she still enchanted him, before life became a twisting, topsy-turvy ride without end; and of her son and birthdays past.

Of love and loss.

Delight and pain.

One hour out from dinner, she wrapped Sam's presents: a soft gray V-necked cashmere sweater, a vintage pocket watch from the 1950s found in an antique shop in London, and a bundle of black moleskin journals, the sort Sam had used for nearly a decade. She signed the card that featured a road disappearing into a mountain range. "Happy Birthday, darling boy. A few things for the next stage of your journey."

She placed the gifts on the dining room table. Then, standing in the hall, she listened for sounds from Sam's apartment below—water running for one of his notoriously long showers or the low rhythmic bass of the music he loved that, despite trying, she could not appreciate.

Her ears met with silence.

Arabella tried to squelch the instant panic, the return of the air bubbles, the queasiness. She remained still, her hands unconsciously stacked over her heart. *It's nothing*, she told herself. Perhaps he'd fallen asleep, or was working in the darkroom, or reading. That was it, she decided, he was reading. How many times had she gone down to his apartment only to find him lying on the couch, earbuds firmly in place, completely absorbed by his latest fascination? And how many times had he pretended to believe she was there to drop off a frozen pizza, a half dozen bagels, toilet paper?

Unfortunately, it took only one suicide attempt to make periods of silence downstairs suspect. And Sam had had more than one.

Arabella glanced at her watch. It was only five minutes until their appointed meeting time. Should she wait 'til he didn't show up? Or should she grab the extra copy of his key from the drawer by the door and go downstairs with the cashmere sweater and an all-too-transparent story about how he might want to wear it to dinner?

Arabella turned back into the dining room and plucked the sweater box from the small stack of presents.

And then, as she turned to leave the room, she caught sight of herself in the beveled mirror on the wall, circles dark under her eyes, hollows in her cheeks. Instinct compelled her to reach for the dimmer switch for the chandelier overhead, to fill the room with sparkling light, to banish the shadows. But it wasn't the lighting. Worry and fear had the power to age and the truth was, at forty-one, she was no longer young.

Her baby was twenty-three.

And her ex-husband's latest conquest was a twenty-year-old Swedish model, Malin, who bore a frightening resemblance to Arabella herself at twenty: a blue-eyed blond with smooth skin and long legs. Arabella had seen a photo of them taken at a fund-raising gala. Max was with Malin now, in Paris, at the Hotel George V. He'd told her this during their call yesterday, with unnecessary relish, undoubtedly hoping to wound her.

It hadn't worked, not in the way he intended.

Before she'd hung up, Arabella had reminded herself she did not envy her ex-husband. She resented him, thought him weak, maybe even pitied him, but she did not envy him. While her own childhood and adolescence may have been defined by the institutional neglect of upper-crust British society, Max's young life had been a minefield loaded with his father's erratic behavior and eventual suicide, and, after years of therapy that he refused to join her in, Arabella understood that in some sad way, he was trying to relive his lost youth. Max felt trapped by the Sams in his life and, despite the exclusive restaurants and fine wines, the fancy cars and five-star hotels, the younger and younger women, he could not escape or rewrite his past.

Arabella lowered the dimmer switch gradually, watching her reflection fade.

The key to Sam's apartment was in a drawer in the side table next to the mahogany front door. Arabella's breath caught as she made her way down the stone stairs, whether from the early November evening chill or fear at what she might find in Sam's apartment, she couldn't be sure.

Probably both.

Diffuse light came through the front window shades, its source somewhere deep in the apartment. Arabella rang the bell. Waited. Shivered. Rang again. She hugged the wrapped box against her chest. Knocked. And then she used the key, calling "Sam? Darling, it's me," as she walked past the darkroom. "I brought you a gift, something to wear to dinner."

The bed was unmade, the sheets twisted.

Decorative pillows on the floor.

Stepping into the bathroom, she flicked on the light and her eyes darted to the deep soaking tub.

It was empty.

A sturdy triangular hook hung on the wall, revealing the absence of her gift of the "Monolith" photograph.

Air bubbles expanded yet her limbs felt weighted. Arabella reentered the bedroom as if moving through clear gelatin. Without thinking, she placed the gift on top of a stack of books on the bookcase, walked around the side of the bed and, with both hands, lifted the edge of the sheet to straighten it, longing to bring back order but mostly to have something to do. As the sheet billowed up, she spied the bare hangers in the closet and a pair of black lace underwear crumpled at the foot of the bed.

The sheet fell with her heart.

And she knew, with absolute certainty, Sam would not be there to blow out candles. Her wish would not be fulfilled.

Her son had smiled and kissed her cheek and lied.

He'd packed a bag and left for places unknown.

And he'd taken just-turned-eighteen Julia Reeves with him.

16

JULIA

JULIA HAD BEEN DROPPED INTO a world she didn't know existed — an intoxicating yet intimidating world with doting staff in dark suits, candlelit tables draped in white linens, and creamy roses in elegant arrangements. When presented with the menu, a leather folder holding two long lists labeled "Tasting of Vegetables" and "Chef's Tasting Menu," she found herself — for the second time in the span of a few hours — wishing for a dictionary. She instinctively reached up with her left hand, grasped a lock of short hair behind her ear and pulled down, feeling the tug. She sighed slowly, blowing air through her lips, consciously *not* whispering "trichotillomania."

Sam was sitting on her left side. He lifted his gaze from the iPad containing the wine list, reached for the hair-pulling hand, kissed the space between her thumb and wrist, grinned and said, "Honestly, you can't go wrong. It's all amazing. The biggest decision you've got to make is whether you want the foie gras and Wagyu beef, or the standard fare."

"Standard fare?" Julia whispered, noticing the maître d' hovering mere feet from their table. "I don't know what half these things are."

Sam leaned toward her. "Don't let it intimidate you. It's all a show. In fact" — he smiled conspiratorially — "I strongly suspect the chef made up some of the ingredients."

Within seconds, the maître d' was standing at attention at Julia's elbow. "May I be of assistance?" she asked.

"Oh," Julia said, "no, I'm fine."

Julia saw cartoon Julia in a fancy dress, clipped dialogue in a bubble over her head. She worried she sounded brusque and banished the image. At the same time, she realized she must be returning to normal, whatever that meant in the scheme of things. Normal, pre-depression Julia worried about things like sounding brusque and being an inconvenience to waiters—or maître d's, had she ever encountered one.

"Are we ready to order?" The maître d' managed to sound polite and assertive at the same time.

"We are," Sam said, nodding at Julia.

"Madame?"

Sam was right about the menu. There weren't many choices. And yet, according to the maître d', each selection Julia made was "splendid" or "lovely."

Sam's choices were also met with subdued superlatives.

The sommelier was summoned with a glance or signal imperceptible to Julia. He and the maître d' switched places by Sam's side seamlessly. Wines were discussed with gravity as fingers swiped left and right.

Julia glanced around the restaurant. Sixteen or so tables were spread across two levels connected by a short staircase in the center, across from a fireplace. She and Sam had been given a table located on the upper tier, along a railing separating them from the level below. Panoramic windows provided a sweeping view of a traffic circle teeming with cars, pedestrians, buses, and taxis—all light and movement and buzzing life. Beyond, the relative darkness of Central Park—streetlights illuminating paths leading into the trees. She could see it, fully drawn in her head.

"What a picture," she said softly.

"Right?" Sam said. "Got to hand it to my dad, he knows how to pick a restaurant." Sam raised his flute. "As do you."

"Well, I didn't really."

"Ah, but you did," Sam retorted. "I'd like to offer a toast, so, your glass?"

Julia complied.

"Eyes here," Sam said, tilting her face, engaging her eyes with his own. "It's a European tradition, looking into each other's eyes during a toast." The corners of his eyes crinkled as he smiled. "I know we're not in Europe, but it's nice, don't you think?"

Julia nodded, recalling his eyes locked on hers an hour earlier, lying on the huge king bed in their room at the Pierre, his fingers tracing her jawline, saying he could hardly wait to get his hands on some sculpting clay, to create a piece with her lines and curves.

Sam lifted his glass another inch. "To you, for coming into my life at precisely the right moment and making me feel completely present and astoundingly lucky to be alive."

Sam took a large sip from his glass.

Julia took a tiny sip from hers.

Even with no basis for comparison, Julia knew the champagne was exceptionally delicious. "Exquisite," as the maître d' had promised.

She also knew that she shouldn't be drinking it.

Besides being under twenty-one, which the waitstaff surprisingly did not seem to care about—"I think they're accustomed to my father's underage dates," Sam had said cavalierly—Julia recalled the list of "do nots" issued by Dr. Renner when reviewing her medication: "Do not skip a dose or stop taking the medication. Do not take other prescription or over-the-counter medications without approval. Do not use any recreational drugs. And do not drink alcohol."

Julia placed the slender flute of sparkling liquid gold back on the table.

"Wait," Sam said, motioning to her glass while raising his again.

As soon as Julia lifted hers, Sam went on. "To not only making me feel lucky to be alive, but *also* for making me want to stay that way."

Sam drained his glass.

Clearly, he wasn't concerned with Dr. Renner's do-nots. The first line of Camus's *Myth* rushed into Julia's head, joining the question she'd been suppressing ever since Sam handed her the box in the darkroom.

"Sam, do you ever take the medicine they give you?"

Sam's lips tightened into a thin line and his eyes narrowed. He turned his head toward the maître d', twirled the empty flute by the stem, and nodded his head. It was a move Julia guessed he'd learned from his father, a request made without a word.

"We're not going to talk about that tonight," he said, clearly forcing a smile. "There'll be plenty of time tomorrow, or the next day, or the one after that. Tomorrow we can debate free will and second chances and the meaning of life. But tonight, we are going to stay in the moment. Tonight is going to be light, and beautiful, and—"

The sommelier appeared tableside with another flute of champagne.

"Exquisite," Sam added.

The maître d' and another server appeared, each holding a plate. Simultaneously and ceremoniously, they placed the plates in front of Sam and Julia.

"An amuse-bouche," the maître d' said, launching into a description lost to Julia because Sam had reached under the table to place his hand on her thigh. The dress they'd selected with the ever-so-helpful Saks stylist was black, off-the-shoulder, fitted across the bodice to the waist, then flared to just above her knee. She'd felt like someone else modeling it for Sam and the stylist, twirling in front of the largest three-way mirror she'd ever seen. After sending the stylist off in search of shoes—Keds, heels, Uggs—Sam had followed Julia back into the dressing room to "help her unzip."

Now, as then, Sam's hand slipped under the fabric, his touch like a pebble in water, sending ripples in and out, up and down.

The maître d' finished the description with "Enjoy."

"Thank you, we will." Sam's fingers continued their path up her thigh. "An amuse-bouche: a small pleasure for the mouth."

Before Julia could react, he lifted his fingers from her flesh and returned his hand to the table.

Julia looked up to see the sommelier holding a bottle of wine toward Sam.

She reached for her champagne flute. Blushed. Took the last sip.

The sommelier glanced in her direction. "Another glass, miss?"

Do not drink alcohol. Julia shook her head, watched Sam nod toward the presented bottle. "Yes, perfect."

The sommelier made a gesture with his head to someone off-stage, presumably the "more champagne" signal, before engaging in an elaborate ritual for "opening the Insignia," a nearly black bottle with a gold and maroon label.

Gold Ochre with a touch of white and Alizarin Crimson.

Julia looked down. Her plate was a white canvas, the food a work of art, geometric shapes, and curls of color. Another flute of champagne arrived, inky purple red wine was poured, and the art kept coming, course after course: a tiny cone filled with salmon mousse; pale oysters and black caviar served in a pool of tapioca; six types of salt in a flower-shaped dish with a tiny silver spoon, pink and rust and black and white; butters shaped into petals and beehives; grilled fish with bright baby carrots and decorative green leaves veined deep red.

Her senses were engaged in a symphony of vibrant hues, textures, smells, and flavors. The maître d' and Sam had used the proper adjectives after all—it was splendid and lovely.

It was exquisite.

As she ate and the wine bottle emptied, Sam's eyes shone brighter, his hand motions grew more effusive, his voice more mesmerizing. He regaled her with stories prompted by a simple request, "Tell me about your favorite birthday." He'd started with birthdays and moved on to memories of experiences and places Julia had either only dreamed of or never heard of: feeding pigeons in Trafalgar Square and monkeys in Langkawi; skiing glaciers in Austria; diving with whale sharks in Belize.

Then Sam asked about her favorite birthday and watched her with an open look of wonder as she told the story of her fifteenth, before her dad had begun feeling unwell, when he'd pulled her out of school to take her to the Metropolitan Museum of Art and a late lunch in the café overlooking Central Park, not too far from where she and Sam were sitting. How patient her father had been when she stood forever in front of a Renoir still life of velvety peaches she would have sworn she could reach out and touch. How she'd been in awe of such beauty.

"As am I," Sam said, reaching for her. The caress of his fingers on her arm and delicate kisses dropped on her palm filled her with longing that was deeper even than that which she'd felt in the courtyard that morning. Then, she hadn't known exactly what she wanted.

Now, she knew.

She wanted Sam.

She wanted to be wanted by Sam. To be looked at with wonder, and held, and understood. She wanted to tell Sam everything, to explain what she had done—and why. She wanted him to save her, and she wanted to save him back.

And then, everything exploded.

LAURA

LAURA DIDN'T WANT TO BE ALONE in the house, but she couldn't leave either.

Lilly arrived shortly after a call from Dr. Renner asking Laura if she'd be willing to speak with Sam's mother. Arabella Lorenzo did not know where Sam was at present, Dr. Renner told Laura. Nevertheless, Arabella had reason to believe Julia was with him, that they'd been to Sam's apartment to pack bags.

Laura held out hope Julia, too, would come home to get her things.

"What if she comes and the door is locked against her. I have to be here."

So Lilly called her husband, Gary, told him she'd be home in the morning, and then, together, the two sisters took the late-night call from Arabella. Sitting side by side at the kitchen table, they listened to Sam's mother's crisp voice floating in the air as she explained how she'd found Julia's underwear and, when she couldn't reach Sam, had tracked his phone to a restaurant near Central Park and called to verify he was there. Meeting resistance from the staff, she'd raced into the city to find the phone purposefully stuck behind a couch cushion in the bar.

There had been no sign of Sam or Julia.

"The maître d' must have children," Arabella said. "When I explained the situation, she confirmed a young woman with short dark hair had been at dinner with Sam. Apparently, they left quite suddenly, no doubt a reaction to my call."

"You spoke with him?" Laura asked.

"No, regrettably, he didn't answer. I texted him, though."

Arabella had been careful, she said. She'd read and reread the message several times before hitting send. "My son can be impulsive," she said. "Impetuous, you might say. He doesn't always handle it well when he feels he's being controlled or censured."

Upon hearing the word "impetuous," Laura crossed her arms and pressed her lips tight between her teeth. On the word "censured," she shook her head, exhaling sharply through her nose. As she opened her mouth to speak, Lilly reached over to hit the mute button.

"She cannot be serious," Laura said. "He convinces Julia to leave against medical advice, has sex with her, and nothing can be done? And what in the world did she say to make him run?"

Lilly placed a restraining hand on Laura's arm. "I know. I get it, but . . ." Lilly paused. "How about I talk to her, okay?" Laura nodded, and Lilly unmuted the phone. "Hello, Arabella. This is Laura's sister, Lilly. Julia's aunt? Just curious, what did the text say?"

"Oh, hello, I didn't realize. One moment, I'll read it to you." Arabella's voice floated even higher, now double-speakered. "'Missing you at dinner. Assume you've made other plans. Are you with Julia, from Brookfield? Dr. Renner called. Call me, please.'"

"So you did ask about Julia," Lilly said, surprisingly evenly.

"Well, yes, I was obviously concerned. It's just texts can be misinterpreted, and I was worried he might cut off communication." Arabella paused. "Again, regrettably, I think he has."

Laura brought a hand up to her mouth, holding words inside.

"You may find this hard to believe," Arabella went on, "but I do understand how you feel. I've been sitting where you are, and I'm terribly sorry. I want to find them as much as you do. I was thinking perhaps we could meet. Share information. Join forces, as it were."

Laura shook her head again.

Lilly leaned in. "Sorry, Arabella, Lilly again. Can you give us a minute?" She reached over to remute the phone.

"She's been sitting where I am?" Laura blinked her eyes closed, seeing the nape of Julia's neck, a locked door, a gurney being loaded into an ambulance. Her daughter had been in Sam's apartment and then, again, in the restaurant, capable of being found and returned to safety. "Why didn't she just go to the restaurant? Why did she give him time to escape, again?"

Laura was drowning in a riptide of negative thoughts and struggling to stay afloat was only bringing her further from shore. *Buck up,* she told herself. *Buck the fuck up.*

Lilly gripped Laura's hand tightly with one of hers. "I know you want to blame someone, but it isn't her fault. This woman can't control her son any more than you can control Julia. And we need her. We can't turn away anyone with information that could help us. Listen, I'm on your side, but you need to think this through. Breathe, Lor. Take whatever time you need. But then we're going to meet this woman and do what we have to do to find Julia and bring her home."

Watching her sister make a waving motion of air flowing in and out of her lungs reminded Laura of Dr. Renner's advice about oxygen masks. *Stop. Stop now.* Three waves later, when Lilly unmuted the phone, Laura found she could speak without her voice shaking.

"Okay, yes, we should meet, but you'll have to come here."

JULIA

ACCORDING TO HER MOTHER, even as a child—long before she understood the concept of a giant tube under an unswimmable body of water or heavy mass of earth and rock—Julia had grown panicky when encountering a tunnel.

That's all this was. Just her old phobia.

Circumstances surrounding their midnight escape from the city had simply amplified her innate fear, she told herself, not the least of which was an eerie lack of car traffic. Lights placed periodically along the tunnel's length thinly illuminated the interior, bouncing off the tiled walls but not the dark painted ceiling, giving the illusion the space was open to a pitch-black night sky without stars.

Julia was not fooled. She wanted to see real stars, the moon. She wanted to stop thinking about drowning in a deathly quiet car.

She wanted Sam to reach over and hold her hand.

She wanted to hear his voice.

He'd been relatively silent for over two hours, ever since they hurriedly left the restaurant, the stunned waiters, sommelier, and maître d' scurrying about, distressed by courses that would not be served. "No Wagyu beef? No dessert?" It would have been comical had Sam not been equally distressed.

Sam's response—"I'm sorry. We must go straight away. Something's come up"—hadn't quelled their concern. Julia could relate. She'd been confused, anxious, even a little shaky, as she'd navigated the short staircase. The three-inch heels the stylist had chosen for her had become precarious with the consumption of two glasses of champagne and a glass of red wine.

The idyllic post-dinner walk through the park she'd envisioned had morphed into more of a mad dash—Julia four paces behind Sam, calling "Sam, please slow down. Who called you? What's wrong?"—until he'd stopped and suggested carrying her on his back the remainder of the way. Only with his arms wrapped around her legs had he finally answered. "It was my mother. She knows we're together. I don't know how, but she does, and if she knows, everyone knows, and now they'll be coming for us."

"I'm sorry," Julia said softly. "This is all my fault. If it weren't for me—"

"Stop." Over Sam's shoulder, Julia had seen they were thirty or so feet from the front entrance of the Pierre. Effortlessly and gently, he placed her on her feet, turned, and kissed her. Julia felt lightheaded and unsteady again.

"You're wrong," Sam said. "Without you, I wouldn't be feeling something I haven't felt in forever. You are everything. My mom knowing you're with me is just a complication, a complication we can manage, because even though they'll say we shouldn't be together, together is how we're going to do everything from now on."

Then he'd taken her hand and walked toward the door. "Having said that, we're going to have to move fast. My mother is wily and well connected and, as the saying goes, money talks. I'm sure by now she's headed to Per Se, and before long, she'll track us here."

The elevator doors closed. "I've got an angle on a car, but it'll be easier if I go alone," he said. "You should change those." He'd glanced at her shoes. "Go for the Keds or the Uggs. And wear something comfortable since we'll be driving for a while. We need to get as far as possible before they know we're gone."

As they walked into their hotel room, Julia remembered arriving after shopping, her astonishment at the elegance of the furnishings overshadowed by fevered removal of clothing, longing, belonging, exhilaration ebbing into feeling safe and treasured. Post–Per Se, she'd imagined falling back into the rumpled bed with Sam.

But instead, he'd been out of reach, shoving things into his duffle. Before zipping it, he'd pulled out the boxed set of Stieglitz and held it in his hands like it was precious and delicate, though having held it herself earlier, Julia knew it was sturdy as fuck.

"This," he'd said, as though the word conveyed a world of meaning. "That first pastel." He shook his head as if still in disbelief. "You're my O'Keeffe, but they won't understand."

Before Julia could ask who "they" were, Sam had gone on. "It'll be easier if we consolidate, and there's room in here for your stuff if you ditch the boxes."

Julia had nodded. With a few strides, he was next to her and she was in his arms, her head tucked under his chin. "Don't worry. I'll be back in thirty, forty minutes. Can you be ready?"

This time her nod was barely a nod. Sam dropped his arms from around her, grabbed his backpack, pulled his laptop out, and pushed it under the bed. "They may try to track this. Don't use it, okay?" Then he'd stood up, shouldered the pack, and stepped toward the door. "Don't worry," he said again. "Everything's going to work out. This could be good, you know, get us started right away."

Gripping the open door, he'd hesitated, repeated "Don't worry," and then he was gone.

When people repeatedly tell you not to worry, worrying is exactly what you should do. She'd heard this from a reputable source, a young women's self-defense program she'd attended with her best friend, Jess, before her dad had gotten sick and everything went sideways.

As Julia changed into a new pair of leggings, a soft pale blue sweater with a black drawstring hood, and new black Uggs, she'd recalled how a group of moms had arranged for the program after a nineteen-year-old nanny had been assaulted during an early-evening jog near their high school. The classes had included some basic Israeli Krav Maga self-defense moves interspersed with lectures and stories about staying alert and aware, recognizing signals, and listening to your instincts; warnings against ponytails and earbuds; advice about when to fight and when to run; that if someone is holding a weapon on you, it's better to drive your car into a fixed obstacle than drive to a remote location.

As Julia had carefully folded her dress, she recalled Sam helping her carry the Saks bags containing her hastily assembled wardrobe, and her thoughts turned to one of the Krav Maga classes. A young woman related a terrifying account of a man who'd gained access to her apartment by offering to help carry her groceries up the stairs, saying, "You don't need to be afraid. I won't hurt you or anything," and then, having placed the bags on the counter, had thrown her to the floor. "Trust your fear instinct," the woman had said. "When someone says, 'you don't need to be afraid,' there's a good chance you should be afraid. Listen to your gut."

Saks bags emptied, Julia had turned to pick up the shoes she'd worn to dinner. Sam was right, they were thoroughly impractical, the sort of shoes you wouldn't want to be wearing if someone was chasing you, although she supposed the heels themselves could be used as weapons. The Keds Sam had insisted she buy would be better for running.

God, why are you thinking about this? she asked herself. *Get a grip.*

Then she'd realized she had a grip, a firm one, on each heel. She'd have to be careful how she placed them in the duffle. They could puncture a hole in a shampoo bottle or tear a book cover. She'd pictured this, a book with a shoe heel stuck through it. Then she'd placed the shoes on the bed and moved to reshuffle the contents of the duffle. She'd lifted the Stieglitz box, saw the Camus lying underneath it. She couldn't handle any more Camus.

Not tonight.

"Nothing negative," Sam had said in the restaurant. But then his mother texted him and called. And the text or call had contained a threat to separate them. A threat from his mother—and others—them—whoever they were.

His mother. Hers. Dr. Renner. Dr. Stein. Tanya.

Maybe Julia could fix it. Although she'd promised Sam she wouldn't use the laptop—she could call her mother on the landline. She could tell her everything was okay, that she was choosing to be with Sam.

Julia had walked around the bed to the bedside table and picked up the phone handset.

Maybe Sam was right. She'll tell me this won't work. She'll want me to go back to Brookfield or come home. She won't understand. I can't go home.

Julia had placed the handset back down.

And she hadn't called anyone. Instead, she'd sat on the edge of the bed, picturing herself sitting on the edge of the bed, a girl with a pixie haircut dressed in clothes far too nice for her, staring out at Central Park's vastness, thinking she didn't really want to get any closer to the window—how when they'd first arrived that afternoon the view made her dizzy and nauseous.

The view was for Sam, and he wasn't there.

Sam is missing the vastness.

She wasn't supposed to be here alone.

The pixie girl's bubble popped.

Sam will be back soon.

Julia had reached down and pulled one of the Stieglitz books from the set. She'd scooted back against the padded leather headboard and flipped through the pages. As with the Camus, she'd felt a strange kinship with the contents, particularly the photos of Georgia O'Keeffe, but then she'd told herself this was only because Sam had compared her to O'Keeffe. Julia remembered her father's appreciation for the temperamental, brilliant artist, how he'd wanted to take her to see the landscape that inspired her work. And then she remembered the conversation at Brookfield when she'd told Sam about her list, about going to see O'Keeffe's museum, how he'd said, "it's a sign, don't you see."

Maybe it was *a sign.*

Sam had said he felt something he hadn't for forever.

Maybe it's hope. I can fix Sam. We can fix each other.

Then she'd heard the hotel door opening, signaling his return. She'd closed the book and attempted to place it back into the box, unsuccessfully, meeting resistance.

"Car's in front. You ready?"

Looking inside the box, Julia had identified the source of the jam—a few loose photographic prints. She assumed they'd been placed there to flatten them. She tipped the box, and as Sam had moved toward her, she'd glimpsed the photos before he said, "Come on, we've got to go."

In that moment, Julia had seen the subject of the photographs—another young woman—a beautiful young woman with long, wavy dark hair, lying in Sam's bed, on her side, with her eyes closed. A beautiful young woman lying in the same pose in which Sam had captured Julia earlier that day.

And Julia had known—before she'd forced the book back into the box; before they'd left the room and loaded a luxury SUV with duffle bags and camera cases, Sam's backpack, and the cardboard poster tube; before they'd driven out of the city into the tunnel in which she now sat, trying not to panic—that she wasn't Sam's first, or only, muse.

ARABELLA

SHE COULD IMAGINE MAX HALF-reclined, leaning on his elbow over a down pillow still crumpled in the shape of his head, pepper-and-salt hair tousled, eyes crinkled against the light of dawn peeking through heavy curtains. And she could imagine twenty-year-old Malin next to him, turning away from the sound of his voice, her long blond hair spilling over another down pillow, soft as a cloud.

"What the fuck, Arabella. It's the crack of dawn."

"I'm fully aware of the time, Max. I didn't choose the timing. I wouldn't be calling if it weren't important. The thing is, Sam's gone missing, and he took my key to your apartment. I don't know—"

"What? Hold on. Why do *you* still have a key to my apartment?"

"What do you mean, why do I still have a key? You gave it to me. You said I should have it, in case of an emergency."

"That had to have been years ago," Max snorted. "And you kept it?"

"Jesus, Max, that's what you're choosing to focus on? I'm calling to tell you Sam's gone missing, and you want to go on about a key you gave me?"

"I just don't understand why you kept it."

Arabella held the phone away from her ear, hand over the microphone, and sighed. *Because you told me to.* "Honestly, I didn't really think about it, and obviously, I never used it. Which is why I noticed it was missing, because it's always there, in the drawer, next to the front door, like you told me it should be. And now it's not there."

"So what are you saying? You think Sam's in my apartment?"

Arabella heard a female voice murmuring in the background, then Max's muted voice, kinder, as he replied. She could picture this too, Max putting the phone up against his chest, his free hand reaching out to touch her. Though it had been years, Arabella remembered that touch—tender, protective. She couldn't remember exactly when he stopped touching her that way, only that she hadn't realized what it meant at the time. She'd naively believed the abatement of tenderness was temporary, perhaps a manifestation of the clichéd ebbing and flowing of love, or a byproduct of stress created by clichéd late nights in the office and weekends away entertaining clients with golf outings and fishing trips he assured her she wouldn't enjoy. It wasn't long before she learned *she* was the cliché, the impressionable young girl who fell hard and believed too easily.

"Bloody hell." Max's kind voice was short-lived. "You call me at oh-dark-thirty and what, now you're not going to answer me?"

Arabella wondered if the impressionable young girl lying next to him understood that the quarrel she was overhearing was a harbinger of things to come.

"He might be in your apartment." Arabella didn't truly think Sam would stay in Max's apartment; he'd never liked it there. "But more likely, he only went to get something."

"Get something? You mean take something."

"I don't know, Max, but yes, maybe take something. I tracked him to the Pierre Hotel—"

"He's staying at the Pierre?"

"No, he's *not* staying there. He'd already left in an SUV, a BMW X5, which I'm thinking is probably yours."

"He couldn't have my SUV, Arabella. It's parked in a secure lot, and they wouldn't give it to him. They'd make him show ID."

Arabella waited for recognition to dawn.

It didn't.

"He has ID bearing your name, Max," she said. "Because he has your name." When Maximilian Samuel Lorenzo the First found out, via ultrasound, that she was carrying a boy, he'd puffed up like a peacock, as though he'd personally sorted out and destroyed the X-chromosome-carrying sperm, victoriously navigating the Ys until one pierced the egg. He'd scoffed at every other name Arabella proposed and begun calling their son "Little Max" in utero. "And he probably has a spare set of your keys, which I'm guessing would be in your apartment, in a drawer, by the front door." Max insisted on certain organizational habits—or rules—a spare key in a drawer by the front door was only one of them. "He knows your habits. He's your son."

"Don't try to put this on me," Max went on, his voice lower, a growl really. "This is what *you* fought for—this freedom for him. I told you this would happen, and I want no part of it."

"And I've told you, it doesn't work that way," Arabella said. "He's your son."

"Don't go there, Arabella. Don't you dare go there."

"I'm not going anywhere. You're the one that's always going somewhere—somewhere else. I'm simply stating a fact. He is your son."

"Pinning this on me is not going to work." Arabella could hear it in his voice—he'd risen from the bed, begun pacing, anger flowing into his muscles, his bones, his skin. "You allowed him to get to this point, not me. You enabled him every step of the way—making excuses, covering for him. My God, you fucking rewarded him, with cameras and darkrooms and art. You want to live your life for him, that's your choice."

On this, Max could not have been more wrong—she could no easier walk away from her son than she could give up her own life. Living her life for Sam was not a choice.

Neither was being alone, but finding someone to share her life with who understood her situation was proving to be nigh impossible.

She was alone.

The only one alone.

"We're pretty sure he's convinced a young girl to go with him," Arabella said softly. "A girl he met at Brookfield. She only just turned eighteen."

"Really?" Max said. At first, Arabella thought he might be embarrassed, but then she realized he was probably impressed. She was tempted to say something snarky about Sam taking after him in more ways than one when he said, "Last time I checked, eighteen was considered an adult. I don't suppose it's changed since you were that age."

Arabella bit her tongue. Tasted blood. "Can you at least call the garage, find out if he took the car?"

"I'm in Paris," Max said, the growl now biting. "And I'm not spending another minute on this. If Sam took the SUV, I'll deal with it when I get home. As I've said many times—I'm not going to allow Sam's behavior to dictate *my* life. This is a problem you've created. You want to call the garage and find out if he took one of my cars, go right ahead. It's the 24-hour IPark on 67th."

"One of those cars *is* an X5, isn't it?" Max was a dedicated BMW owner. He always had at least two of them.

"Yes."

"Well, that's what Sam was driving. Couldn't you call the dealer? You said they tracked Hank's car." One of Max's partner's cars had been stolen and returned within hours.

"Yes, they did, with a police report number. Do you want me to charge our son with felony grand theft auto?"

"Of course not. I thought—"

"You thought I'd step in, make a few calls, get the police to find Sam and this girl, bring him home to you, and send her packing," Max said. "But it's not going down that way. You've been arguing for years Sam is an adult, that he can be responsible for himself, and now, he's going to have to prove it."

"He *is* an adult. He's twenty-three, Max, yesterday, in case you forg—"

"Don't," Max interrupted. "You're in so deep, Arabella, you can't see the truth. But that doesn't matter. You're going to do what you're going to do. What I'm telling you is leave me the hell out of it. All of it. In fact, don't call me unless, well, unless—"

Max paused. Perhaps he didn't finish the thought, perhaps he did. Arabella would never know because she couldn't listen to another word. She pulled the phone away from her ear and, as quickly as possible, disconnected the call.

The physiological responses to the anger she was now feeling were old friends: heartbeat racing, ice-cold hands, sweat under her arms, tears in her eyes. Pressing her fingertips into her forehead, she told herself it had been worth it. At least she'd gotten the name and location of the parking garage.

She would not call them; she would go there. She might not be an eighteen-year-old model anymore, but Arabella Marks Lorenzo could still charm a parking attendant in the middle of the night.

Charm and a few Ben Franklins.

Arabella walked into the kitchen and opened a drawer in the island. She'd held onto another of Max's organizational habits while they were married—keeping a stash of cash underneath a custom-built flat knife block, in case of a run on the banks or some other crazy emergency.

Max always had at least $50,000 hidden.

Arabella had allowed her stash to dwindle to about twenty grand.

Lifting the wood, Arabella discovered Sam had reduced it to a single crisp hundred, on which he'd hastily scribbled "Sorry Mum."

She hadn't known Sam was even aware of the hidden stash.

It wasn't until she dropped the knife block back into place that she realized one of the knives was missing. A deboning knife she'd already replaced once.

And then, clinging to the sides of the drawer, Arabella bowed her head and wept.

JULIA

ACCORDING TO THE SUV'S CLOCK, it had officially been tomorrow for an hour and eight minutes, yet talking about negative things still seemed out of bounds. Sam remained silent, his coiled energy directed at the road in front of him— his jawline set, the muscles in his hands and forearms taut, his hands on the steering wheel in a vice grip.

Traffic had thinned—mostly 18-wheelers coming toward them with blindingly bright headlamps or, on their side of the road, appearing in the right lane up ahead, looming alongside and then disappearing behind them as Sam barreled past.

The speedometer wavered between 85 and 90.

Julia's mind operated in fits and starts. Questions rising, answers contemplated and discarded, questions reasserting themselves, spawning new ones: Where were they headed? Who was the dark-headed girl in the photograph? Where had she gone?

Despite exhaustion and an incredibly comfortable seat, Julia tried to stay alert, conscious that it would be wise to do so; the clanging of psychic bells warned of a wall-hitting event in the near future. She was reminded of the time Cheyenne convinced her to take a tiny bright pink pill imprinted with a rabbit—four hours of intensely empathic love followed by overwhelming fatigue tinged with anxiety. She'd read later,

during an Internet session dedicated to medications and contraindications, how ecstasy, the drug, impacted the brain.

Would ecstasy, the emotion, have the same effect?

And if it were hitting her, wouldn't it also hit Sam?

She rested her head against the window and reflexively
looked for the moon, unconsciously assessing its phase: way
more than a half circle, waxing gibbous. *There is something
about this moon.* She touched the cool glass with her fingertips.
Something I should remember.

She was so tired she felt sick.

Julia glanced toward Sam. "Do you think we could stop
somewhere," she said, "and get some sleep?"

His hands unclenched and retightened on the wheel. He
exhaled slowly with a barely perceptible shake of his head. It
wasn't clear if this was a no or a "I can't believe you're even
asking." He didn't say a word aloud.

"I know you wanted to get out of the city," Julia went
on. "And now we are, out of the city, I mean. Maybe we could
stop for the night. It's been a really long day."

Sam's eyes briefly closed, more than a blink. A reset.

"I'm not tired," he said. As if to emphasize the point, the
car accelerated, the speedometer above 90. "I can go another
couple hours, but you can sleep. There's a sleeping bag in the
duffle. You could make a pillow."

Julia couldn't ignore the psychic bell-clanging any longer.
The creep of fear climbed from her shoulders into her head,
settling behind her eyes. Rising nausea worsened. "I'm sorry,
Sam, it's not about sleeping. I'm not feeling well, and I don't
want to get sick in the car." Her voice broke. "If I could just
lie down for a few hours. Please?"

Sam turned to look at her and his face softened. "Yeah,
sure, of course we can stop." He reached for a small control
wheel located in the middle console under the screen and
turned it, bringing up a menu. "I don't know how to search
on this thing, but I bet we could figure it out, find a hotel."
He looked up to the windshield and down to the console, up,
down, up, down.

Ahead, a green sign indicated two exits for someplace called Bloomsburg. Also ahead was another eighteen-wheeler, amber lights framing its massive back door. Sam abandoned the screen controls. Simultaneously, he flipped on the right blinker, looked over his shoulder, and began to speed up. "Maybe there's a place here," he said, attempting to navigate in front of the truck, which promptly began to accelerate, keeping pace with their SUV.

"What the fuck?" Sam said, slowing down.

The truck slowed with them.

Julia could see an underpass bridge up ahead, after the first exit on the right.

"It's okay, Sam, let's go to the next town."

"They're far apart out here, and you're not feeling well. I can get around this guy."

Sam floored it.

Julia could hear the eighteen-wheeler's engine kicking in.

The SUV surged forward. The truck also gained ground, loudly.

Julia glanced over at the speedometer as it neared 100. She instinctively tensed and gripped the door handle with her right hand while bracing herself against the seat with the other. The nose of the SUV pulled even with the truck cab, and Julia looked up at the driver, who was looking back at her. For the briefest instant, she was in the cab next to him, seeing herself as he might see her—eyes wide open, pleading.

She didn't have time to register the driver's expression before the truck slowed and the cab dropped back. They passed the first exit and rapidly came upon the underpass and a sign for the second exit. Sam threw the wheel to the right. The SUV veered through the right lane, mere feet from the truck's grill and the cement wall, directly into the exit lane. Julia turned to watch the truck pass as the SUV careened around the cloverleaf.

She could feel her pulse quicken. Her palms were sweaty.

"What the fuck's wrong with that guy?" Sam said, pumping the brakes.

Julia had no reply. She took tiny sips of air, fighting the tight feeling in her chest. She turned toward the side window as the tears she'd been holding back for hours flowed freely, and silently, down her face.

"You okay?" Sam asked. Before she could answer, he went on. "Sorry about that, but it was worth it. Look, a Hampton Inn."

Julia hastily tried to dry her face with the back of her hand.

"Look okay to you?" Sam said.

Julia nodded, pressing her lips tightly together, so tight it hurt, trying to force down panicky tears that threatened to return full force. She was only partially successful. She wiped her eyes and nose and took two rapid gulping breaths. The sound reminded her of when she was a little girl, sitting in the backseat behind her mother, swallowing sadness. She could hear her mother's voice saying "A little cry is okay, but it's important to keep things in perspective." She could feel the emotion she had yet to call shame at her own weakness, her inability to keep things in perspective.

But then she thought of her mother the last time she'd seen her, reaching out to touch Julia's hand on the couch, watching her face as she spoke, and Julia felt a different kind of shame. Her mother had been trying, truly trying, and though it made Julia nearly as uncomfortable as it made her mother, the effort had meant something. She didn't know what it meant yet, but it meant something.

Julia wished she had called her mother from the Pierre, before she'd found the photos in the box, before the hurried departure and the silent drive. She wished she'd had the chance to let her mother know she was okay. To tell her that she needn't worry. That she was safe.

Now, sitting in a darkened Hampton Inn parking lot in Bloomsburg, in an SUV that clearly wasn't Sam's own, Julia realized it was too late—even if she had access to a phone, it might be difficult to convincingly make that call.

21

LAURA

ARABELLA LORENZO ARRIVED IN A black sedan at precisely 8:00 a.m.

Lilly had suggested they meet somewhere neutral, like a Starbucks, but still hoping Julia might come home, Laura had again refused to leave the house. She'd left the front porch and Julia's bedroom light on all night, stirring from sleepless rest whenever she thought she heard something outside.

Now she watched through the window in the living room as Arabella's driver, dressed in a dark suit and cap, walked around the rear of the car to open the back door. The man took Arabella's hand, assisted her exit from the car, and stood at attention as she made her way along the walkway to the front door.

Arabella was dressed all in black: ballet flats, slim pants, a form-fitting turtleneck, and large sunglasses. Her hair was pulled away from her face in a sleek ponytail that swung gently as she walked, her movement a daunting combination of striding and floating, reminding Laura of an elegant and subdued runway model.

"Wow," Lilly said at Laura's side. "She's something."

"I know," Laura said. She looked down at her faded yoga leggings and loose-fitting long-sleeved running shirt. She couldn't remember what she'd done to her hair that morning.

She'd undoubtedly brushed it, hair-brushing being one of the activities she'd done by rote, rather than with intention, most of her life. Even about this, her mother had always accused her of being rebellious. Laura could hear her now: "My God, Laura, you could have at least made an effort." The truth was, it wasn't that Laura was unaware of her appearance or didn't care, it simply didn't matter what she did. Her hair was a mass of curls that defied products of any kind, and makeup never felt natural to her.

As she approached the front door, Laura recalled a department-store makeover she agreed to do with Julia before Paul got sick. She could see her own face in the handheld mirror: gaudy, fake, her eyes like black holes. And she could see Julia, transformed into a glamorous young woman, her eyes bright and excited. Laura could hear her daughter's uncertain longing for approval: "What do you think, Mom?" And her own reply, characteristically missing the mark: "It looks . . . nice, but you don't need any of this. You're beautiful naturally."

Thought she'd meant well, Laura had known as soon as the words left her mouth that she'd said the wrong thing, because the expression on Julia's face, her newly grown-up face, could only be described as crestfallen. Julia had turned away, wiping her cheeks with the back of her hand. Laura could see now that she should've seen what the makeover meant to Julia, not what it looked like or what it cost. It wasn't about the makeup. Laura didn't need to buy every product the saleswoman was hawking, but she could have bought her daughter a tube of mascara or some blush. She could have acknowledged that Julia simply wanted her mother to be part of her growing up, to celebrate it with her.

And Laura hadn't.

Another opportunity lost.

There'd been so many.

Laura wondered which ones had been significant, which ones had landed them where they were now.

Where's Julia now?

The doorbell rang, loudly.

Laura shook her head, reaching up to push an unruly curl back behind her ear. She smoothed the nubby black fabric over her thighs.

"You're fine," Lilly said softly behind her.

Laura opened the door.

Arabella stood on the porch, just out of the sun. She'd placed her sunglasses on top of her head, revealing soft, pale purple circles under her eyes.

"Hello, Laura," she said, extending her right hand. "Thank you for meeting me."

Arabella's gaze was direct, her handshake firm, her manicure recent. When Laura simply nodded, Arabella let go of her hand and turned to Lilly. "You must be Lilly. I'm Arabella Marks Lorenzo, Sam's mother."

Laura found her voice; it sounded strained and awkward, even to her ears. "Oh, yes, sorry. This is my sister."

"My pleasure," Arabella said. "Though I am terribly sorry about the circumstances."

Lilly clasped Arabella's hand in both of hers. "Hopefully we can begin to understand those circumstances better. See what we might do to find Julia, and Sam."

Laura stared at her sister's hands around Arabella's. She felt a swell of anger rising, threatening to encompass everyone: Sam, for taking Julia from Brookfield; Arabella, for being Sam's mother; her own mother, Frances, for her remarkable lack of concern, for saying last night on the phone, "So now she's run away," like this was somehow inevitable; even Lilly, for her ease and graciousness.

"Can we offer you coffee, tea?" Lilly said, gesturing toward the seating area in the living room.

"Thank you. Coffee, please."

"Laura?" Lilly took a step toward the kitchen.

Laura stood off to one side, watching Arabella take in the room, the overstuffed sofa, upholstered armchairs, and coffee table all purchased years ago when they first moved into the house, the landscape she and Paul had splurged on at an art fair when Julia was three, and the framed family photos: Laura pushing five-year-old Julia on a swing; Laura in Paul's arms on their wedding day; Julia with Paul in front of one of her last oils, Julia looking at the camera, Paul looking at her, his smile one of unadulterated pride and joy.

It was a room rarely used. The last time was probably the brunch after Paul's memorial service, when it had been filled with extended family and Paul's colleagues, people standing about or sitting on folding chairs Lilly had somehow arranged to borrow, holding plates of food the casserole crowd had prepared.

Laura hesitated on the threshold.

"Do you want another cup?" Lilly asked. "I'll get it."

Laura realized Lilly had directed the question toward her. She was talking about coffee.

"No, you two sit. I'll get it." Laura sent Lilly a pleading glance. She wasn't ready to deal with Arabella, not alone.

Before her sister could object, Laura walked into the kitchen. She pushed the swinging door closed behind her and stood motionless, listening to Lilly asking Arabella about the drive, where she lived in the city; Arabella answering in her cool, crisp voice. "We, Sam and I, live in Brooklyn, Park Slope. His father, Max, lives on the Upper East side, which is where the garage is, where Max keeps his cars, including the one—"

"Maybe we should wait for Laura," Lilly said.

Laura startled at the mention of her name, a deer in headlights suddenly unfrozen. She turned to the tray that she'd organized earlier with mugs, a small pitcher of milk, and a sugar bowl. Laura filled the mugs with fresh coffee. She heard Arabella's voice again. "Is this Julia's father? Is he still in the picture?"

Lilly's voice dipped even lower. Though she heard Paul's name, Laura couldn't make out the response. She gripped the countertop, reminded herself to breathe. It was better Lilly was handling this question; she did not want to discuss Paul's loss with Arabella.

She waited a moment, heard Lilly ask, "So, you're from England originally?"

This was as innocuous of a question as Laura could expect. She picked up the tray and bumped the door open with her hip.

". . . I've been here since we married and Sam was born. Twenty-three years now. His birthday was yesterday. Max took him to Per Se two of the last four years, which I'm guessing is why Sam took Julia there. I'm sorry I didn't think of it earlier. Don't know why I didn't. I suppose because he'd made plans with me." Arabella's voice faltered. She picked up the mug Laura had placed in front of her. Held it to her lips without taking a sip.

Lilly looked over at Laura. Laura looked down at the tray, poured milk into a mug, and handed it to Lilly, keeping busy so she didn't have to speak.

"We've all been blindsided," Lilly said. "You couldn't have known." She raised her eyebrows at Laura as if to say *Now might be a good time to concur, open up the conversation.* She'd given Laura a mini-lecture on displaying empathy, even if she didn't really feel it. "You can make yourself feel it, Laura," she'd said. "Remember what you told me about what you were reading, about Julia's therapy? Behavior can impact emotions."

Laura hadn't wanted to hear this.

But she also knew Lilly was right.

Arabella took a real sip of the coffee, then held the mug between her hands, shoulders hunched, head down.

"No one could have known," Laura said.

Arabella looked up. Her face had a vulnerable quality that reminded Laura of Julia.

"Thank you for—" she paused, swallowed. "Well, thank you. I've learned a bit since we last spoke. I tracked Sam's laptop to the Pierre, on Central Park? I know the manager—we've met planning for charity events and the like. Anyway, he said Sam left with a young woman, shortly before midnight, in a BMW X5, which happens to be a car his father owns. I went to the garage. A young man resembling Sam picked it up late last night."

"So they have a car," Laura said, "which means they could be anywhere, going anywhere."

"Yes, I suppose, but I do have an idea about where they might be headed," Arabella said, her voice slow and hesitating,

as if she were contemplating each word. "I'm not certain—"
The hesitation became a full stop.

"Well . . ." Laura forced herself to stay calm. "We have
nothing, so . . .?"

"Yes, of course. You're right." Arabella sighed. "So a few
years ago, I gave Sam an Ansel Adams photograph of Half
Dome for his birthday. 'Monolith,' one of the most famous
photographs taken at Yosemite. I'm sure you've seen it."

Laura shook her head. Lilly said, "I don't believe so."

"Oh." Arabella was clearly surprised. "Well, it's beautiful,
magnificent really. Anyway, Sam's was in this custom frame,
and when I was looking to see what they'd taken, I found the
frame empty, in the darkroom. The paper back had been sliced
open and the photograph removed. Of course, it could be Sam
took it simply because it's meaningful. But I believe it might be
a clue as to where they're headed, because he also took camera
equipment, camping gear, and—"

Laura placed her mug down on the table, a dull thud of
heavy ceramic against wood.

"So you think they're headed there, to Yosemite?"

"Yes, because, well, there's more. Sam's told me the
photograph represents a pivotal moment in Ansel Adams's
career and he, Sam, has always wanted to experience a similar
moment, in the same place. He's tried to do this a couple of
times before, and . . ." Arabella paused. "Well, it didn't go well,
but he's convinced it's a calling of sorts and that he will succeed
eventually. Under the right circumstances."

Laura shifted in her chair. She was about to ask, *what do
you mean, didn't go well* when Lilly asked another question.
"As in?"

"As in now. He said the other night that he feels he's on
the cusp of something important. He's always believed if he
could find his muse—someone who understands and inspires
him—that he'd find the answers he's been looking for. His
truth, he says. A way to stay at the top of the mountain."

"And you think Julia could be this muse?" Lilly said.

"Yes, I think so. And therefore, it's highly possible Sam believes the time has come to create his own 'Monolith.' Give it another go. You know, another chance."

Laura startled. The words "another chance" flashed, along with a memory of sitting on the edge of Julia's bed shortly after Paul died, watching her cry into her pillow after saying she no longer believed in second chances. Laura had attempted a comforting touch on Julia's back, only to have Julia flinch and pull away. Laura had risen to her feet and seen *Where the Wild Things Are* partway under the bed, a folded piece of paper half inside. Laura had been exhausted, defeated, already well into the giving of time and space. She had only glanced briefly at the paper before tucking it away, placing the book back in the bookcase.

"Lor?" Lilly said. "You okay?"

Laura stood abruptly. "Excuse me, I'll be right back."

It only took a minute to find it, still there, hidden between pages of wild things howling at the moon.

22

JULIA

JULIA WOKE ALONE.

A sliver of bright light shone like a beam through a maroon-striped curtain. It took her a few seconds to remember where she was.

Bloomsburg.

Pennsylvania.

A Hampton Inn.

She sat up and pulled the sheet over her naked torso. "Sam?" she called, tentatively. She couldn't see if the bathroom door was open or closed. "Sam?"

No answer.

Where is he? Did he leave me behind?

Stop it, she told herself. *Control your thoughts.*

Her eyes darted to the foot of the bed. The duffle was still there, her clothes from the night before draped over the top: the leggings, the pale blue cashmere sweater.

Julia stood up. Within a few steps, she could see the bathroom door was open. The room was dark.

She spun to look at the digital clock between the two double beds. 9:02. The bed closest to the window remained exactly as it had been when they arrived, three crisp white pillows stacked diagonally in front of the dark wood headboard. Looking at the other bed, she remembered how tender

Sam had been with her. He'd curled up behind her, his coiled energy slowly ebbing as he gently stroked her head and neck until she fell asleep.

A small camera she hadn't seen before was on the round table by the window, along with Sam's sketchpad and the leather zip pencil case holding his supplies. The sketchpad was open to a charcoal drawing of a reclining figure under sheets and a blanket, and Julia marveled at the texture of the fabric Sam had created. She flipped the pages to other drawings he'd clearly worked on while she was sleeping: her face resting on a pillow, her hand curled under her chin, the hollow under her collarbone, the curve of her neck. Based on the number of sketches, Julia wondered whether Sam had slept at all. She placed the sketchpad back where she'd found it and picked up the camera. A classic Olympus, the kind that used 35mm film. The case held two black plastic film cartridges. *Are there older images on those cartridges, photographs of muse number one? Was the girl in the photos even his first muse? Have there been others?*

Where is he?

Stop. He was probably downstairs getting breakfast.

She needed to eat so she could take one of the Prozac tablets she'd found in Sam's box. *Take with food.*

When they'd checked in around two in the morning, the desk clerk had said breakfast was included. Julia had noticed a half-moon of dirt under his fingernails when he slid the paperwork across the counter. His long, tapered fingers didn't fit the rest of him—stocky shoulders, a hint of a tattoo under his shirt collar. She'd begun creating a cartoon version of him before she could stop herself, and he'd given them a furtive look, like he was in on something sordid she and Sam were doing, or he could tell she was drawing him in her head. Or maybe it was a response to Sam saying he didn't have a credit card, that they'd be paying with cash.

"You'll have to leave a cash deposit of $150.00," the clerk had said. "For incidentals."

"Incidentals?" Sam asked, reaching into his backpack for two more hundred-dollar bills.

"You know, like phone calls, damage to the room, missing stuff." The clerk had glanced sideways at Julia, like he knew she was the sort of girl that damaged things. Stole from others.

Which she supposed she did.

"So we get this back when we check out?" Sam held the money out.

"Yeah, aside from any incidentals," the clerk said. Then he'd given them the times for breakfast, but she'd been distracted by the dirt half-moons and the sideways glance—and now she couldn't remember the breakfast hours. Were they 'til 9:30 or 10:00?

Julia got dressed quickly, tugging the leggings up over her thighs, covering the scars. She remembered hesitating the night before when removing them, realizing she hadn't asked the Saks stylist to find her pajamas. She'd mentioned the lack to Sam as she'd watched him casually strip off his jeans. "You won't need them," he'd said. "I'll keep you warm."

"It's just—" Julia looked down.

"Julia," Sam said softly, "I've seen you. You don't have anything to hide."

Though he'd been wrong about the hiding, he'd reached for her then, and she'd been grateful. She'd put the dark-haired girl in the photos and the near collision with an eighteen-wheeler or concrete underpass out of her mind.

Her boots were under the bench holding the duffle, but only one boot held a sock. She knelt, running her fingers across the carpeting to find the other. The carpeting was sticky and stiff, like a drink had been spilled and not cleaned up. She glanced at her nails, expecting to see half-moons of sticky residue lodged underneath.

Julia wanted a shower, but she wanted to find Sam more; she'd have to settle for splashing cold water over her face. She entered the bathroom and was shocked to see her short dark hair in the mirror, curling off in different directions. She started the water, splashed her face, and ran her wet fingers through her hair, pulling lightly, trying not to dwell on the sensation, the tension along her scalp, thinking *trichotillomania,* but not whispering it. *Is this progress?* she wondered, wiping her face on a hand towel lying on the counter.

The towel was damp. Sam must have been there recently.

She hadn't heard water running, Sam getting dressed, or the door closing behind him. This surprised her, because one of the clearest symptoms on the first depression checklist Julia had completed online had been "Trouble falling or staying asleep." Yet last night, curled up in the bubble of Samness, she'd slept well enough to dream. She hadn't woken a single time.

Until she woke alone.

An empty cardboard key sleeve lay on top of the dresser.

"One or two keys?" the clerk had asked, and Sam had replied without hesitation. "Only one. We'll be together the whole time."

But they weren't together the whole time, and now she didn't have a key. As the door to the hall closed behind her, it occurred to her she had no way to prove she belonged to room 214. She had no identification, no phone, no money. She'd left everything behind.

She was completely dependent on Sam.

Julia heard loud voices arguing as soon as the elevator door opened on the first floor. The voices belonged to talking heads debating politics on a big-screen TV mounted on the wall of the breakfast room and an older couple sitting at one of the square tables, talking about the talking heads. The man was eating cereal out of a Styrofoam bowl with a plastic spoon. Two plates of half-eaten wilted waffles and sausages sat in the center of the table alongside Styrofoam coffee cups with plastic lids.

Sam was not in the room.

Julia inhaled sharply, smelled scorched coffee and something cloyingly sweet. Her fingertips migrated up to grip the ends of the short hair behind her ears. She tugged, exhaling through her mouth slowly, audibly, her eyes drifting closed, her body swaying involuntarily.

"Are you all right?" the woman asked.

Julia pressed her lips tightly between her teeth, willing herself not to cry. She nodded even as she felt her will failing.

Kindness often had this effect on her. Staying strong was easier when no one seemed to care.

The woman dropped her *USA Today* on the table. "Bob," she said, "I think she's gonna faint."

Swaying on her feet, Julia felt her perspective shift and then she was watching the scene from above: Bob turning in his chair; his wife demanding, "Bob, do something"; Bob pushing heavily against the table to stand up, upsetting his bowl of cereal, spilling milk and soggy brown flecks; saying "Aw, damn" as he took two lumbering steps.

And then, she was back, stepping away, saying, "No, I'm fine. Really." Her hands flexed in front of her in an attempt to stop Bob in his tracks. "Please, I'm okay."

It worked. Bob stopped. Looked back at his wife as if for instructions.

"If you say so," the woman said. "Looks like you need to eat. You young women in yoga pants never eat enough."

Bob shook his head slowly like a shaggy dog.

"I was going to eat," Julia said defensively, feeling she owed this woman an explanation without quite knowing why. "I'm just looking for someone."

"Tall, dark-haired young man?" the woman asked. "Blue eyes?"

"Yes, you've seen him?"

"He's in the business center. Nice young man. Said y'all are driving cross-country. Stopping in Chicago, he said, to ride a Ferris wheel. I told him there's a closer one, in Sandusky, at Cedar Point—you know, on Lake Erie. Much closer than Chicago. But he said no, it's got to be Chicago. Navy Pier, he said."

The Ferris wheel at Navy Pier.

Her bucket list.

Though Julia remembered telling Sam about the existence of the list at Brookfield, she wasn't certain which of the second-chance items she'd mentioned: the Ferris wheel at Navy Pier, Holden Caulfield, *The Graduate*? It hadn't been a long conversation. She hadn't told him any of the stories behind them, like how, when she was eleven, her dad had taken her to

Chicago to visit a friend from college who lived on the south side of the city with his wife and adorable twins that, at age two, "were a real handful," and Julia and her dad had escaped for a day. They'd gone to the Aquarium and the Planetarium, and then on a boat tour on the Chicago River that ended up on Lake Michigan, with a view of Navy Pier. She'd seen the big wheel, begged her dad to take her on it, and then gotten dizzy as it looped up. It hadn't gone well from there.

"And then heading to California," the woman went on, "which sounds just wonderful. I've never been that far west. I told your young man I've always wanted to go, but what with the kids and grandkids all living in the Midwest, or here in Pennsylvania, it's never worked out. We've been in Virginia our whole lives and now we're retired and can go places, all we do is visit the kids or go birding. Not that I'm complaining. There was that one summer—remember Bob?—when we looked into renting one of those campers, Cruise America—"

"Sheila, darlin'," Bob interrupted, shaking his head again, this time with a tender look toward his wife. "This young lady doesn't want to hear about the time we almost rented a camper." Bob sat back down. "She wants to go find her young man, get started on their journey."

Sheila nodded as Julia took a tentative step in the direction of the lobby.

"I'm just making conversation. And her young man isn't going anywhere without her. He said he's been waiting his whole life to find her."

"I know that feeling." Bob patted the back of Sheila's hand. "Finding you was the best thing ever happened to me."

"Oh, now," Sheila said, pushing his hand away playfully. "You go on," she said to Julia. "He's probably still in there."

Sam was standing next to the printer, holding loose pages, studying the top one. He looked up and his face broke into a grin. Walking toward her, he folded the papers lengthwise, stuck them into his back pocket, and opened his arms wide.

"Hey," he said. "I was just about to come get you."

"I didn't know where you were."

Sam pulled her in close, tight. "Well, I was here. Doing research on the interwebs. Printing stuff. You ready to go?"

"Sheila and Bob think I should eat."

Sam pulled away. "Sheila and Bob?"

"Sheila, the woman you met in here. She said she talked to you, about Chicago, and the Ferris wheel. Bob's her husband. I met them in the breakfast room. They were eating, and she said I should eat."

"Oh, right, Sheila. And eat you shall." Sam dropped a kiss on her forehead before dropping his arms and moving to the closest computer. Google Maps was open. A website with a map and dates and blocks of text, like a blog of some sort. "She was nice, Sheila. I didn't meet the husband, though. Bob, you say?"

"Yes, Sheila and Bob."

"Yeah, well, apparently Sheila and Bob's daughter lived outside Chicago awhile back, and said it's a great city. When I mentioned we were going to ride the Ferris wheel, she told me about this time she took her granddaughters to Cedar Point, this amusement park with a big Ferris wheel right on the lake, only to find out one of the girls was afraid of heights and the other was afraid of large bodies of water, so Cedar Point wasn't an ideal spot for a family vacay. Sheila said the one afraid of water had no problem with pools, but lakes or rivers freaked her the fuck out. Well, she didn't use that phrase, obviously—I mean, she's a grandma." Sam smiled. "She loves traveling with her kids and grandkids; she'd rather do that than go birding with Bob. He likes the quiet of birding, she said. Which I can imagine is tough for her. She's a real talker, that Sheila."

"Yeah." Julia lips bowed into a smile to match Sam's. *Sheila's a talker?* "She and Bob almost rented a camper one summer to go out West but didn't in the end because of the kids and grandkids." Sheila was the kind of grandmother whose grandchildren looked forward to seeing her. Warm. Overinvolved maybe, but in a good way. Julia thought of her own single remaining grandparent, Ami, and how disappointed Ami was in her. She wondered if Sheila would still be nice if she knew about Julia's issues. Dr. Stein popped into her head before Tanya and the little pink shovel displaced him. Throwing shit out. Climbing a ladder. *You control your behaviors.* She wanted to stay out of the shit. She needed to eat, take—

"Not a bad idea," Sam said. "Maybe we should do that."

"Do what?" Julia asked.

"Get a camper."

"A camper?"

"Yeah, like Sheila and Bob. Where'd you go? You're the one that brought it up, Jules."

Jules was what Cheyenne used to call her.

"Please don't call me that." Julia heard the pique in her voice.

"What? Jules?"

"Yes, please don't call me that."

"Okay, okay, no problem. Bad memory?"

"I'd rather not talk about it."

"No worries. I get it, but, just so you know, I'm an excellent listener, when listening is required. You can ask Sheila. I've had years of practice in group; in fact, I would venture to say, my listening skills rival Beverly's." While talking, Sam had logged out of the computer, closed every open window, and erased the search history for the last hour. "So I obviously couldn't print out *Catcher in the Rye,* but I did print this." Sam pulled the papers from his back pocket, rifled through them quickly, and then, finding the one he sought, began to read:

Out of the night that covers me,
Black as the pit from pole to pole,
I thank whatever gods may be
For my unconquerable soul.

"Sam—"

In the fell clutch of circumstance
I have not winced nor cried aloud.
Under the bludgeonings of chance
My head is bloody, but unbowed.

The poem "Invictus." Julia watched him reading, remembering her father asking for it, feeling a balloon grow in her chest.

Beyond this place of wrath and tears
Looms but the Horror of the shade,
And yet the menace of the years
Finds and shall find me unafraid.

It matters not how strait the gate,
How charged with punishments the scroll,
I am the master of my fate,
I am the captain of my soul.

As he'd gotten to the last two lines, Julia had felt herself whispering along as her father had done. She could hear her parents arguing. Her mother saying *you do not mean this.* The balloon inside her expanded, making it hard to breathe.

Sam paused. "Some poem. And the ending, phew." He shook his head slowly. "You'll have to explain why that's on your list 'cause I don't know why anyone would need a second chance to appreciate it. I realized I've heard it before—in some movie about South Africa, the one with the rugby team and Nelson Mandela."

Julia forced herself to exhale, prayed an inhale would follow.

Sam did not notice. "Also realized I haven't heard the whole list, but we'll have plenty of time to discuss it, more than enough. So, onward?" Holding his backpack in his left hand, he moved his right arm in the flourishing arc she'd grown accustomed to seeing at Brookfield.

Julia needed time. Space. Something. "I need to eat."

"Ah, yes, of course. Breakfast per Sheila and Bob."

"And I should go up. Get my meds," Julia said.

Sam changed in an instant. The flourishing arm dropped, accompanied by a harsh exhale. "Right," Sam said, his tone even harsher. He fished the key out of his back pocket and handed it to her. "Go ahead, get your meds." He turned away, back toward the business center, away from the breakfast room.

"Sam?" Julia called. "What about you?"

"What about me? I'm not hungry. I've got better things to do with my time." Sam's lack of hunger worried her, but his anger worried her more. "You go, though. Take your medicine and eat your breakfast. Don't worry. I won't leave without you."

ARABELLA

<u>Second Chance Bucket List</u>

The Graduate

Navy Pier Ferris wheel

Brussels sprouts

pickle relish

snowboarding—get a lesson? better snow out West. try not to break wrists!

The Catcher in the Rye though I don't know why . . . can't believe 95% of people love this book. Why?????

blue cheese (only thing more disgusting than sprouts)

getting a pedicure. wrong on so many levels—gross (people touching my feet), guilt-inducing (demeaning nature of task usually done by immigrants who deserve better), futility (I mean, who really needs their toenails painted), utter waste of money

flan—okay, haven't actually tried just plain creepy but Dad claims it's delicious so . . .

escargots aka snails—(see flan)

Georgia O'Keeffe's Museum (deal-breaker, promises matter)

~~A Psalm of Life~~

college

Jess?

self-portraiture

Mom

Hope

ARABELLA SAT ON THE COUCH, holding the list delicately between her fingertips—a tear-smudged paper window into the latest young girl with whom her son was falling in love. It was clear Laura hadn't wanted her to touch it. Maybe she hadn't wanted Arabella to see it at all, particularly given the item second from the bottom—Laura's inclusion on the list could be seen as incredibly sad—or hopeful—but since hope was also on the list, what good would hopeful be?

Just a few moments earlier, when Laura had reentered the living room, she'd held her arms crossed against her chest, partially obscuring what looked like a children's book. Arabella thought she recognized the image on the book's back cover: stylized palm trees with a full moon in shades of green, blue, and gray.

Lilly had gone to Laura, escorted her to an armchair, and crouched down in front of her.

"Lor, what is it?"

Wordlessly, Laura had glanced toward Arabella before opening the book and handing Lilly a sheet of paper.

Lilly read it, murmured "Oh, sweetie," and then, ignoring her sister's body language, she'd stood up and handed the paper to Arabella.

Arabella took in the list, conscious of two sets of eyes watching her, waiting for a reaction. A variety of ink and pencil and slightly different handwriting implied it had been composed at multiple points in time. Arabella wondered when Julia had written it. Had her father already been ill? Had he died? Had Julia talked to Laura about it?

Arabella quickly deemed these questions too invasive, but felt she needed to say something. "Where is Navy Pier?"

"It's in Chicago," Laura said. "On the lake."

Arabella nodded.

"Paul took her. Years ago." Laura gazed out the window as if she could see into the past. "She fainted on the Ferris wheel, right at the top. Paul didn't know why, perhaps because of the heat or because she hadn't had enough to eat, but later we wondered if it was a panic attack, claustrophobia maybe, or a fear of heights. She was fine in the end, but it stuck with her."

"And the O'Keeffe Museum in Santa Fe?" Arabella asked. At least she knew where *that* was.

"Paul grew up near there," Laura answered. "He said O'Keeffe captured New Mexico better than anyone, as if it were part of her soul . . . and she a part of it." Laura sighed. "We went to the museum once with Julia, the summer she was six. Paul promised to take her back, but . . ."

"Sam also admires Georgia O'Keeffe," Arabella said in a low voice.

Laura did not respond.

Arabella tried another approach. "Do you know what she means by it being a dealbreaker?"

"No." The shake of Laura's head was barely perceptible. "I guess I didn't realize it meant that much to her." It sounded as if she might snap.

Arabella was silent. She had no desire to be the one that caused the snap.

After a moment, Lilly gently asked, "Had she ever talked to you about this list?"

"No," Laura said. Her right hand floated up over her heart. "Not really. She talked about some of these things with Paul, the movie . . . the museum. And I guess I know why the poem is there. But the rest—" Her voice faded. "Julia and I weren't talking much, not about things like this. Not about Paul." She looked down at the book resting in her lap. "But I have a feeling this list matters. The other night, she asked me to bring the book—" Laura tipped it toward the other two women to show the cover: *Where the Wild Things Are*. "I thought it was about missing Paul. He used to read it to her all the time when she was little."

"Of course," Lilly said with gravity. "Max."

"My Max?" Arabella asked, realizing as soon as the words left her mouth it wasn't Sam to whom they were referring.

"No." Laura shook her head gently. "A stuffed dog named after the boy in the story. She's slept with it forever. I offered to bring him to her, with the book, but Julia said no, and then she changed her mind—about the book anyway. Maybe it wasn't about the book at all. Maybe it was about the list. Maybe she wanted to start working on it."

"Perhaps she and Sam are hoping to do it together," Arabella added. Sam was all about idealistic odysseys. "Maybe the list can help us find them."

"May I see it again?" Lilly held out her hand toward Arabella. She looked the list over. "You think this could have something to do with where they're headed? Chicago? New Mexico? Snowboarding somewhere out West? In November?"

Arabella did not respond.

Lilly looked back and forth between Arabella and the list, her brow furrowed. "Oh, wow, you *do*. You think it could be a clue. Listen, I don't want to a naysayer, but it's kind of a stretch to assume this is some kind of road map."

Laura still gripped the book in her arms. "It could be, though. We don't have anything else to go on."

Lilly shook her head, slowly, deliberately. "Okaaayyy. Let's assume they're on some cross-country trip. How in the world would they pay for it?" Lilly turned to Arabella. "Which raises the question: How could they afford dinner at—what was it called? Per Se?—and the Pierre? Aren't those incredibly expensive? Does Sam have some kind of great job or just access to your credit card?"

Arabella tried not to take offense. She gave a terse nod, consciously making another of a series of split-second decisions about how much to reveal about her son. She'd already made a few and each was a gamble of sorts: too much information and everyone would freak out; too little and she ran the risk of withholding things critical to keeping Sam and Julia safe. "There's a gallery showing his work and he's sold a few pieces, but not enough to live on. So yes, he has a credit card. In this particular instance, it would be good if he were using it, so we could track them. Unfortunately, I checked online, and he isn't. They must be using cash."

"Cash?" Laura asked. "Where would they get that kind of cash?"

Arabella rapidly reassessed her revelation decision-making. "Well, I keep some at home. As does Sam's father. He believes in having cash on hand to protect against a crisis or catastrophe. You know, like a run on the banks or—"

"A run on the banks?" Lilly sounded incredulous, as if this sort of thing never happened.

"Yes, you know, like after the Lehman debacle. We have friends who—" Arabella stopped herself, thinking *This isn't going in the right direction at all.* "The point is, Max has always insisted on keeping a significant sum in the house, and I've simply maintained the habit. To be honest, I hadn't given it much thought until I noticed the money was gone." It occurred to Arabella it was more than a habit; she'd been young and impressionable when she married Max, and it had been difficult to undo his influence in many ways. Not that these two women would understand or care about her middle-aged, suddenly-on-one's-own growing pains. "I can't be sure Sam has taken his father's money," she went on. "However, it does appear he's taken mine."

Arabella tried not to see the expressions on Laura and Lilly's faces turning from quizzical to judgmental. She knew this sounded awful, her son stealing from his parents. Sam's thievery would not endear him to Laura or Lilly the way Julia's list had endeared her to Arabella.

"A significant sum." Lilly began. "As in?"

"Tens of thousands of dollars."

"You keep tens of thousands of dollars in your house," Laura said, her tone matter-of-fact, shaded with disapproval.

"Yes." Arabella watched the two sisters exchange another look. She did not understand their apparent disbelief. Keeping a large amount of money in the house was not unusual amongst the circle in which she and Max had travelled for the last two decades.

"Wow," Lilly said, lifting her eyebrows. "So you have a safe or what?"

"No." Though most of their friends did keep their stash in a safe, Max did not. He maintained a safe wasn't safe, obvious and crackable by a thief worth his salt. A custom knife drawer with a hidden compartment, not so easy to discover. "The money was hidden."

"And Sam knew where."

"I was not aware he knew . . . until last night." Arabella's thoughts turned to the missing deboning knife. She felt an immediate, familiar need to defend her son. Again, she reconsidered her earlier revelation decisions. "I'm certain he intends to repay us. He—"

"So what you're telling us," Laura interrupted, "is your son has stolen from you, taken his father's car without permission, and convinced my daughter to leave against medical advice on some ill conceived journey to recreate an image that's going to change his life. Do I have it straight?"

Arabella pressed her lips together tightly and shook her head before saying in a clipped voice, "It certainly does not sound good when put that way."

"How else can it be put?" Laura's voice matched hers.

Arabella found herself questioning whether her underlying emotions bore any similarity to Laura's. She was reminded of something she'd heard from one of Sam's many therapists. She locked her eyes upon Laura's. "Surely, you've surmised—given where they met—Sam's thinking can be faulty at times, but being mentally unhealthy is not the same as being immoral."

Laura opened her mouth to reply, glanced toward Lilly, and slowly shut it, sighing. "Clearly, I do not know your son well, nor can I possibly understand his behavior." Laura looked down at the book in her hand. "The thing is, Dr. Renner said Julia was doing well before she left, but without the anti-depressant and the support, Julia could—well, she could—"

As her words fell away, Laura looked up at Arabella, her expression bleak. The space between them filled with unspoken words. Though it was clear Laura held Sam responsible for Julia's precarious psychological state, she did not say so. Though Arabella wanted to reassure Laura that Sam would take care of Julia, she could not say so, because she knew Sam's history—other odysseys with other girls. And Arabella had seen Sam manic, or worse, in a mixed state—mania colored black with depression, dark thoughts fueled by unbridled energy, capable of following through.

Laura's fears were not unfounded.

"I have to do something," Laura went on. "I can't just sit here waiting for the phone to ring. Waiting to find out—" She shook her head. "I can't do nothing."

All three women were silent for a moment. The sound of a garbage truck lifting a can could be heard, the punctuated cracks of waste falling onto more waste, the lowering of the can, and crunching of gears crushing and compressing the contents.

"We could go after them," Arabella said. "Try to find them."

"Go after them?" Lilly asked.

"Yes, go after them."

Lilly sighed and shook her head even more deliberately, but Laura's eyes opened wide.

"Yes, we could." she said. "We could go after them. The police won't do anything, and I'll be no good at work anyway."

"But Laura—" Lilly hesitated. "Oh, sweetie, you can't just get in your car and take off following some list and a missing photograph."

"Why not? If they're driving across the country to California, it's possible they might stop along the way to go on a Ferris wheel or visit a museum."

"Of course, it's *possible*," Lilly said. "Anything's possible. They could be driving across the country and stopping in Chicago or New Mexico. But they also could still be in the city or heading for Disney World—or Maine. We don't know where they are or what they're thinking. And even if they *are* heading for Yosemite, it's a huge country. There are lots of ways to get across it, and they've got a head start."

"I know," Laura said. "But if I don't try and I lose her? I couldn't live with that, knowing I just let it happen."

Arabella leaned forward and placed her hand gently on top of Laura's, still folded over the edge of the children's book. "I understand," she said. "I'll go with you."

"Please stop." Lilly looked intently at Arabella. "Both of you. We need to think this through. Seriously, you don't have enough to go on."

Arabella tried to decipher Lilly's expression, a warning of sorts.

"And behaving impulsively, or impetuously, won't help," Lilly added, with an emphasis on the words "impulsive" and "impetuous."

Yes, definitely a warning. Arabella lifted her hand from Laura's. Leaned back.

The concurrent sound and vibration of a text message came from behind Laura. She bent forward, retrieved her phone from the waistband of her leggings, and glanced down at the screen. Then she looked up, her mouth agape. "Oh my god."

"What?" Lilly asked.

"I think it's from Julia. It says 'ok w/S in PA.'" As she stood up, the book fell to the ground. "I don't recognize the number, but it must be her. Who else could it be?"

Laura held out the phone with the message in a green bubble.

"What's w/S?" Lilly murmured.

"With Sam?" Laura suggested.

"In PA?" Arabella said.

Laura and Lilly shared a glance. Lilly stood up.

"Pennsylvania?" Laura said as she placed the phone up to her ear.

Lilly and Arabella both spoke at once. "Are you calling?" "We should call."

Laura raised her hand, ducked her head, and closed her eyes.

Arabella watched Laura listening, saw her body shiver involuntarily. "Julia? Is this you? Please—" Laura swallowed. "Please call me back."

Laura stood, elbows bent, arms tense, holding the phone out in front of her. She stared at the screen as if willing it to ring back.

"What did the voicemail say?" Lilly asked. "Who was it?"

"It went straight to one of those automated responses, so I left a message," she said, as though the other two women hadn't just heard her. "Should I call again?"

Arabella's eyes met Lilly's. Before either of them could respond, Laura did indeed call again, this time turning and pacing toward the window in the front of the house.

"Lor, wait," Lilly said. "Let's think of what to say."

Arabella leaned forward to retrieve *Where the Wild Things Are*.

Laura shook her head. "Maybe she'll answer. Julia? If this isn't you, if it's someone else, my name is Laura Reeves and I'm trying to reach the person who just sent me a text message. Sorry. I'm . . . it's . . ." She spun around again to face Lilly and Arabella, placing her hand over the microphone. "What do I say?" She lifted her hand. "Julia, if this is you, please call. Or text, if you want to text, but I would really like to hear your voice, okay?" Laura's head dropped so her chin was nearly resting upon her chest, looking like a bird with a broken neck.

"I should have had a plan. I should have known what I was going to say. What if she doesn't call? What if—"

Lilly took the two steps necessary to wrap Laura in her arms. "She'll call. She texted. She'll call. The important thing is, she's okay."

Laura pulled away. "And she's with Sam. Somewhere in Pennsylvania."

24

JULIA

JULIA GRIPPED THE EDGE of her seat.

The SUV was on an entrance ramp, traveling at a speed she preferred were slower.

Sam glanced in her direction.

She preferred his eyes remained on the road.

"You know," he said, "you could do some sketching of the scenery, or . . ." He reached over to flip down Julia's sun visor and imitated the motion of sliding open the mirror cover.

She would prefer his hands remained on the wheel.

"Or you could work on a self-portrait," he went on. "For ease of access, I put a sketchpad and charcoals in the front pocket of my pack."

"Wait, I told you about that?"

"About what?"

"About self-portraiture. Being on my list. I don't remember telling you."

"That's because you didn't," Sam said, clearly bemused. "I just thought you might want to draw because you seem, how shall I say, a tad anxious. And, as the saying goes, 'art therapy is . . .'" He paused, waiting.

". . . good for the soul," Julia finished.

"Indeed. Besides, it'll give you something constructive to do with those fingers other than holding on to the seat like you might fly out the windshield any second." Sam smiled.

"Oh, sorry." Julia splayed her fingers like starfish off the edge of the seat.

"No worries. Thought drawing might help is all. Back-pack's right behind me." He tilted his head toward the space behind his seat. "It's pretty heavy. Probably don't want to pick it up. You can just grab stuff from the pocket."

Julia took a deep inhale, twisted in her seat, and saw the bag. Her thoughts turned to the envelopes of one-hundred-dollar bills filling the main pocket. She lifted it an inch or two off the ground, felt its weight. It wasn't as heavy as she thought it would be; Sam clearly didn't want her picking it up. She couldn't navigate opening the front zipper while strapped into her seatbelt, so she unbuckled. *Speed is of the essence.* Whatever she was going to do, she'd better do it quickly.

The front pocket contained more than the sketchpad and the leather pencil case. It also held a small sheaf of printed pages and the slender paperback with the graphic cover, squares divided diagonally in half—black and white—*The Myth of Sisyphus and Other Essays.*

"You find it?" Sam asked.

"Uh-huh," Julia said, pulling the sketchpad out from behind the book.

"Oh, and I put the Camus in there. Thought you could read later while we drive."

Julia placed the pack back down, leaving Camus in place. She slipped into her seat, clutching the sketchpad and leather pencil bag.

Within a few minutes she'd learned that, despite the X5's smooth drive, self-portraiture in a car was challenging. The mirror in the sun visor was small, limiting the reflected part of Julia to one third of her face at a time. Compounding this, looking up and down—from the little mirror to the sketchpad—made her sick to her stomach. When she mentioned this, Sam said, "I had a teacher once who made us draw without looking at the paper. Why don't you try that? See what you get."

So she did, working first on her eyes and eyebrows, then her nose, mouth, and chin, ending up with a self-portrait that resembled a cubist nightmare. She added a dialogue bubble on the upper-right-hand side reading "Sorry, I'm not myself." She held it up to Sam, who laughed.

Though Julia laughed along with him, the image was vaguely unsettling.

"Wait," Sam said. "Hold it up again." Julia obliged. "I kind of like it. It's Picasso-esque."

"Are you kidding?" Julia turned it back to give it another assessment. "It's awful."

"Well, something tells me these are not ideal conditions for accurate drawing of self. Good thing I brought the Camus. Why don't you grab it?" Sam's enthusiasm was obvious. "You're going to love it."

Julia unbuckled again and twisted in her seat to switch out the paperback in the pack with the sketchpad. She held the book lightly in her hands, her thumbs tracing over the lines delineating the black and white triangles that made up each square. *Albert Camus. Winner of the Nobel Prize in Literature.*

"Find it? I'm ready for some Audible-esque reading aloud."

Julia slid into her seat. "You want me to read aloud?"

"Well yes, yes, I do. I love being read to *and* I love the sound of your voice, so I can't imagine anything I'd rather do than drive across this beautiful country listening to you read seriously life-altering literature."

Julia exhaled audibly.

"Buckle up, babe," Sam said.

Julia did as Sam requested and opened *The Myth.*

"'An absurd reasoning: Absurdity and Suicide,'" she began, hesitantly. "'There is but one truly serious philosophical problem, and that is suicide.'" Julia stopped. "Are you sure this is a good idea?"

"It's philosophy, like a puzzle. Give it a chance."

Julia sighed. She'd had enough talk of suicide in her life.

"Want to start with something from your list instead?" Sam asked. "'Invictus' is in there, toward the top. Those first two lines have been running through my head: 'Out of the night that covers me/Black as a pit from pole to pole/I thank whatever gods may be for my unconquerable soul.' Intense shit. And those two last lines?"

Please help me. Julia shook her head. *Sam has no idea.*

"Maybe later." She was not ready to deal with "Invictus" in any way, not even to tell Sam it wasn't the poem on her list. Not that *The Myth* was proving to be any easier. The first two paragraphs referenced Nietzsche, Galileo, La Palisse, and Don Quixote, three of whom she'd heard of but had never studied and one that was a complete unknown.

She paused at the end of the second paragraph. "La Palisse?"

Sam kept his eyes on the road. "Ah, yes," he said, "that would be a reference to Jacques de La Palice, a French military officer who would have likely remained unknown but for his tombstone, which famously was mistaken to read 'Here lies La Palice. If he weren't dead, he would still be alive.'" Sam chuckled to himself. "Get it? If he weren't dead, he'd still be alive?"

"Oh," Julia said, getting it. "Right."

"Ironically, though, the actual inscription did not say this. It said 'If he weren't dead, he would still be envied.' If it'd been read correctly, his name would have slipped into the abyss of unknown French military officers."

Though this explanation did not help Julia understand the reference in Camus, she didn't ask Sam what he was talking about. She also did not keep reading. She sat there, thinking he knew things she didn't even know enough about to know she didn't know about them.

"But then," Sam went on, "the French would not have the term *lapalissade*, which basically means an utterly obvious truth, a truism. You know, like 'either it'll rain tomorrow, or it won't rain.' Or in the case of this book, 'one kills oneself because life is not worth living,' which, while true, is so obvious it's hardly worth saying."

Julia looked over at him and back at the book, now utterly convinced of two things: she was so fucking in over her head and Camus was not a good idea at all. She needed an excuse to stop.

"Honestly, Sam. I don't get most of this."

"I'm not surprised. I've read this stuff multiple times and I still don't get all of it." Sam's voice was sympathetic. "But each time, something becomes a little clearer." He smiled. "You may have to add it to your second-chance list. Trust me, it's worth it. Even this first time through, every once in a while, you'll read something and think, 'Yes, that's exactly right.' Please, keep trying."

So Julia read on.

Unfamiliar words took shape in her mouth, forming bewildering sentences that twisted in, on, and around themselves, with references to people and concepts she'd never heard of.

Nevertheless, Julia recognized Camus was brilliant. And Sam was right—just as she'd experienced the day before, reading outside the private bank—certain phrases resonated and caught at her heart, often ones highlighted in neon orange. Sentences about feeling lost, without illusions or light, longing for it all to end.

She recalled her own despair, the feeling of disconnectedness. Thinking about her father. Though she couldn't remember the pain itself, she felt a strange longing to cry, a tightness in her chest, a weariness seeping into her. Out of the corner of her eye, she saw Sam glancing at her.

"It gets better," he said softly. He reached for her hand and dropped a kiss on the inside of her wrist. "I promise."

She wasn't sure to what he was referring—life or the book.

She had only started to believe the former, and she had serious doubts about the latter.

The next paragraph stated the purpose of the book was to establish not whether suicide was an answer to the absurd, but "the degree" to which it was. Julia wanted to say something to Sam about this, about whether there were indeed times when suicide was a reasonable, even moral, choice. About how animals are spared from facing pain, but humans are not. But mostly, she wanted to stop reading Camus.

Julia turned to Sam. "This is your idea of getting better?"

"I know, it may not seem like it, but this is just the beginning. We're on what, page six?"

Julia nodded.

"So, page six, and page 123 is the last page, where you will find the best quote of all. The best, and I've given that a lot of thought. Here's a thing: A few years ago, I read this list of conversation-starters. You know, thought-provoking questions to get people talking."

"Mm-hmm," Julia half-murmured.

"Yeah, so the first one was 'What is your greatest fear?' which I thought was a pretty aggressive start, but the second was, 'If you could ask any one person three questions and be guaranteed truthful responses, who would you ask and what would the questions be?' which I loved, and the third one was even better: 'If you had to tattoo your arm with a message to yourself, what would you write?' My answer to that question is the second to last line on page 123. Go ahead." Sam looked down at the book.

As Julia turned to page 123, he repeated, "Second to the last line."

"'The struggle itself towards the heights is enough to fill a man's heart,'" Julia read.

Sam repeated the phrase and looked over to gauge her response before going on. "Right?" he said, as if he were sure she would agree. "I mean, obviously, Camus's referring to Sisyphus and his rock, but it applies to so many things. I knew this guy in college, a climber—you know, rocks, mountains. Anyway, his goal was to climb Everest and K2 someday, and people gave him shit all the time about the dangers involved, how selfish it was and such, and when I told him about this quote, he said it could be every climber's mantra. Truth is, it could be the mantra for writers and poets—anybody trying to create something from nothing—but also people with soul-sucking jobs they've got to do to pay the bills—stocking shelves all night, standing on an assembly line. It applies to all kinds of experiences."

"Even reading this book," Julia said.

"Yeah, even reading this book. Speaking of which," he said, giving her a looping "go-on" gesture, "I believe we were on page six."

Julia turned back to page six and found her place.

She read another four pages. She comprehended only a line here or there—or maybe not. Something told her that if a line seemed comprehensible, she was probably getting it wrong.

Julia closed the book with her right index finger holding her place. She turned in her seat to look directly at Sam.

"Before we go any further," she said, "full confession. I don't even understand what he means by the absurd, and I'm guessing that's critical."

"Yeah, it is," Sam said. "Do you want the 'back of the book' definition or mine?"

"Yours."

Sam nodded. "Okay." The car slowed. "Basically, it refers to the conflict between what we want from the universe and what we get. See, we want our existence to have meaning, but it doesn't. We want the universe to answer us, but all it gives us is chaos and silence."

Julia was herself silent, only for a moment.

"Well, *that's* fucking depressing," she said.

Sam gave a short laugh. "That's one way to look at it, but I heard this lecture on YouTube, and this guy, one of the students, described it as 'depressingly inspiring.' That's how I see it."

"Depressingly inspiring? Is that even a thing?"

"Yeah, see, Camus isn't making the argument that existentialists are right or wrong—it's not about the validity of Nietzsche's premise that 'God is dead' or Kierkegaardian leaps of faith. He's just saying we can only address what we *know*, and acknowledging the absurd is within the realm of known knowns."

Known knowns? A Kierkegaardian leap of faith?

Julia shook her head. "That still doesn't make sense."

"Okay, what about this? It's about accepting the *existence* of the conflict while still *rebelling against it* by choosing to live consciously aware of it rather than trying to escape it or transcend it."

"It?"

"The conflict. Between our desire for meaning and the universe's silence."

"Oh." Julia shook her head again.

"Still no, huh?" Sam paused. "All right, let me try another way. Remember how Tanya says we have the power to choose our thoughts and actions?"

Julia nodded.

"Yes. So then, in the face of certain death, choosing life is, in itself, a small, very personal victory. And if, despite the meaninglessness, we can still commit to passionately experiencing every moment—adventure and beauty and pain and darkness, a life full of moments—" Sam spoke with fervor, then his voice slowed. "If we can do this, then we can accept life has no meaning and still live lives of value."

Julia tried to take this in, but *choosing life in the face of certain death* had looped to a place she couldn't go. *Please help me.*

Sam turned and smiled. "But first, we've got to get past page, what, ten?"

Julia shivered. Checked the page number. It was, indeed, ten.

Sam gave the "go-on" gesture again.

Page ten continued with a paragraph comparing works of art with deep feelings and how our souls don't always understand the things we do or think, *or something like that*, ending with another highlighted phrase about how feelings can create their own universe, "splendid or abject."

Sam interrupted her. "You see? It's like Camus's describing exactly what I feel—the extremes that can be all-encompassing. I don't know how he'd view modern therapy, but the next few paragraphs could be part of one of Tanya's little talks. All about"—Sam's voice softened into his surprisingly accurate imitation of Tanya's marshmallow quality "—'behavior and thoughts and feelings.' It's like poetic CBT. Go on, you'll see."

But only a few lines later, Sam stopped her again. "Hold on." He repeated the last part of the line, something about knowing a person "by the totality of their deeds." "Right? It's what we do over a lifetime that matters."

Julia hoped this was true, that a person would not be judged solely by their last act.

Sam went on. "There's an overabundance of quotable quotes in this book. Check out the one on the bottom of the page, 'the last pages of a book . . .'"

Julia looked to the bottom of the page and located the line, highlighted and underlined: "'the last pages of a book are already contained in the first pages'?"

Sam knew the book well.

"Yes," Sam said, without providing the explanation Julia was hoping for. "Your Mr. Wardel would love this book."

"My art teacher?" Julia said.

"Yeah, your art teacher."

"I can't believe you remember his name."

"I remember everything you tell me." Sam placed his hand on Julia's thigh. "Don't you remember what I tell you?"

Julia felt cold wash over her as her thoughts turned to things she'd done that Sam didn't know—things she regretted and things she didn't, like how that morning, she'd done something Sam had told her specifically not to do.

Meeting Sheila in the elevator—

Sam gestured again to the book.

Julia heard herself continuing to read Camus's words aloud, but the words didn't register because memories and self-recrimination began to whirl. Her dad's face on the pillow. Sheila's trusting face as she listened to Julia spinning a tale about dropping her phone in the toilet.

She read as she tamped down guilt, recalling the rapid-fire typing and the duplicity of turning off the phone before handing it back to Sheila, murmuring "Oh, I'm sorry, habit," garnering herself time to escape.

Julia was a fraud, then . . . and now, reciting words of deep meaning about one's consciousness without paying attention.

She tried to concentrate on the words, knowing they meant so much to Sam. But after another few paragraphs, hearing herself say "If one is assured of these facts," she realized she wasn't assured of anything she'd read in the last few minutes, not a single line.

She stopped reading, thinking how she'd betrayed her mom, her dad, Sam, Tanya.

She was betraying everyone. Even Camus deserved better; philosophers probably hated non-attentive, superficial readings of their work.

She should go back.

Start from the beginning.

"Sam?" she said.

Sam's head did a quick shake, as if breaking a deep trance. Sam had been engaged; he was worthy of Camus. "What's up?" he said.

"I—" Her voice faltered. "I can't—it's just a lot. Can we take a break?"

"Sure, okay."

Julia could tell he was disappointed.

She turned her face toward the side window.

Outside, fields and farms and trees went by. Leaves blazing red and yellow and orange. Electrical poles forming geometrical patterns like mirrors self-reflecting into infinity. Fences. Billboards. Mileage markers. Exit signs. *When the time comes.* She thought about all the things she could not see or hear or understand. Death and life and the fine line between them. Wanting to live and wanting to die. *Please help me.* The people who lived in the few houses visible from the highway or in the towns beyond. She saw herself, gazing out on a world apart. She envisioned her mother sitting at the kitchen table, her favorite mug in front of her, one Julia had made, cobalt blue with a bronze glaze that made it shine, filled with coffee grown cold, coffee her mother had poured but hadn't wanted after all. She saw her mother look down at the phone in her hand, reading the message she'd sent from Sheila's phone. She imagined Tanya in her office, pushing a loose lock of hair behind her ear as she bent to place Julia's file in the back of a cabinet where patients who'd abandoned therapy were stored away. And Dr. Tarvas, removing Julia's pastel drawing from the top shelf, pulling back the protective wax paper cover and shaking her head softly as she contemplated what to do with it.

Julia sighed, filled with remorse. "Do you think they're worried about us?"

Sam was silent.

Julia wondered if perhaps she hadn't spoken the words. If she'd only thought she had. But then she noticed that the car had slowed.

"Sam?"

"Yeah, I heard you," he said. "Trying to decide how to answer. Who? Our moms?"

"Our moms, Tanya, Dr. Renner, Dr. Tarvas, Rita."

"Quite a list." Sam's voice was tinged with sarcasm. "No Brett or Claudia or Hannah, or, what was the name of that girl with the greasy hair?"

"Rachel?" Sam's tone bothered her, but then again, she hadn't been particularly empathetic toward Rachel either.

"Yeah, Rachel." Sam's sarcasm was even thicker. "I bet she can't get us out of her mind."

"I don't mean Rachel or Hannah. Seriously, Sam, I feel awful. Like I let people down. Leaving that way was kind of a shitty thing to do."

Julia watched Sam's jaw clench, his hands tighten on the steering wheel.

"Being there was your choice, Julia. So was leaving. It's your life. Yours and mine."

"I know," Julia said, "but our choices affect other people."

"Yeah, but it's still your life, and the truth is, they might be worried, your mom, mine, maybe even Tanya, though she's probably resigned to people leaving. But if we contact them, in any way, I'll tell you what'll happen—"

Julia could feel the car accelerating as Sam spoke faster and louder.

"They'll say we're crazy or this is crazy, though they won't use that word. They'll say something like 'ill-advised' or 'impetuous,' one of my mom's favorite words, 'impetuous,' like I don't understand what she means. The point is, they'll try to dissuade us, convince us they know what's best. They'll say we shouldn't be together. They'll want us to go back or say they're coming to get us and take us home. Is that what you want? To abandon this opportunity? Each other? 'Cause I've been down this road before, Julia, and I know we have a chance, right now, to live courageously—to accept who we are and choose our own path. Control our own lives."

Sam's voice began to vibrate like a string pulled tight. He turned to her, eyes glistening. "Are you willing to abandon that to do what *they* want us to do and be what *they think* we should be? Is that what you want?"

Julia shook her head, touched his forearm. "No, that's not what I want."

Yet as she picked up Camus, Julia allowed herself to acknowledge that, other than staying with Sam, she didn't actually know what she wanted. And she didn't feel in control of anything. What would Sam do if he knew all the things she'd done?

He's been down this road before. Was it with the girl in the photo? Who was she?

And what happened to her?

LAURA

AT 35,000 FEET, ONLY CLOUDS and blue sky were visible through the oval window of seat 2A. Nevertheless, Laura knew her emotionally fragile, physically shaky daughter was somewhere down there, putting her trust in a young man who was, at best, creative, impetuous, and mentally unstable, and, at worst, unhinged and deliberately dishonest, capable of stealing from the people who loved him most.

Laura focused on breathing in and out to stanch rising dread, somewhat perversely longing to be the version of her parents' daughter she'd been before—stoic, contained. At some point, however, a dam had been breached, and she was finding it difficult to stop the flow of emotions. So she sat quietly, consciously identifying each feeling as it came—as if by categorizing them, she could exert some control.

Toward the cool, collected woman seated one row up, on the other side of the aisle, Laura felt muted anger, pity, and begrudging gratitude. Arabella had made the last-minute airline reservations and insisted on paying for them.

"The important thing is getting there before they do, not how we do it or who pays for it," she'd said. "Besides, it's the least I can do. If it weren't for Sam, Julia would still be an hour away, not somewhere west of Bloomsburg, Pennsylvania, en route to Chicago."

West of Bloomsburg, Pennsylvania, en route to Chicago. Confirmation of Julia and Sam's whereabouts had been provided by a woman with a soft Southern accent named Sheila who, despite having only spoken with Julia for a few minutes, had given them enough to go on.

"Your daughter's lovely. So sweet. Just a wisp of a thing, isn't she?" she'd begun when she finally contacted Laura. "I sure hope she ended up eating something. She didn't even have a bite at breakfast, she was so intent on finding her young man. He was in the business center by the computers—least that's where I met him. Anyway, I'd had enough of the election, but Bob wanted to keep watching, so I headed up to the room alone, and that's when I saw your daughter again, in the elevator, and she asked to use my phone. She felt so bad not being able to reach you. Said she'd dropped her phone in the toilet and it wouldn't even turn on."

"Oh?" Laura managed to slip in. Julia's phone was sitting on her bedside table, right where Laura had placed it herself the morning after Julia was admitted to Brookfield. She pondered briefly if Julia had somehow gotten another phone, a new phone she promptly dropped in the toilet. This seemed unlikely.

"It was no trouble for her to use mine. Didn't occur to me 'til later I didn't see either of them with a phone and these young folks are so tied to them, aren't they? Sitting at dinner together, right across the table, not talking at all, just clicking away at their phones. It's a shame, really."

Laura didn't care about this woman's opinion on millennial cell-phone usage, but she also didn't want to be rude. "Are you still there, at the hotel?" she asked quickly, while Sheila was taking a breath.

"Oh, goodness no, we're long gone. Bob's a birder, and fall's migration viewing, so he was anxious to get on the road. Yesterday Delaware Water Gap, today Bald Eagle, and then on to our daughter's place, in Ohio, to see the kids." Laura could hear a man's voice murmur in the background and Sheila saying "I know she didn't ask," presumably directed at Bob, before coming back to Laura. "Sorry, I didn't see them after the elevator, your daughter or her young man. But seeing as they were in a hurry, I'm guessing they're long gone too."

"In a hurry?" Laura interjected.

"Definitely. He said they wanted to make it to Navy Pier in Chicago to ride the Ferris wheel. Some of these places have limited hours this time of year, and what with the long drive to Chicago, I told them there's a closer one, at Cedar Point, and maybe they could go there since they'd for sure make that one in time. But he said no, it had to be that specific one." Laura heard the man's voice again and Sheila responding "Oh really?" Then, "Bob says Cedar Point's closed now anyway, for the winter."

"Did she seem okay, Julia?" Laura asked, the words out of her mouth before she realized Sheila had no basis of comparison. Sheila was a perfect stranger with no idea of what an okay Julia looked or sounded like.

Laura wasn't sure she knew herself.

"Honest? She was a little shaky." Sheila paused. Laura could hear Bob murmuring again, then Sheila's voice half-muted, her hand over the microphone. "She asked, Bob. I'm not stirring things up. No, I'm not." And then she was back. "I'm not trying to make it sound serious, it's just, well, that's why I hoped she'd had something to eat. I was worried, wondered if she was okay, but she said she was fine, and she seemed better in the elevator, after she'd met up with her young man—"

"Sam," Laura interrupted. "His name is Sam."

"Really, Sam? Funny, we spoke for a while in that computer room and never did introduce ourselves. Sam, hmm," Sheila said, as if considering the appropriateness of his name.

"So you were saying you saw them in the elevator?"

"Oh, no, not the both of them. She was by herself, getting off on the second floor, and since our room was on the third, I waited while she finished texting you. I guess, now that I think about it, she wasn't shaking anymore, but she still seemed anxious." Another murmur. "Well, she did," directed at Bob again. "I just chalked it up to her being worried how you might react. She's young, what, eighteen, nineteen at the most?"

"She just turned eighteen."

"Mm-hmm, that's what I told Bob. I said, 'That girl couldn't be more than eighteen or so.'" Laura then heard Sheila telling Bob, "She just turned eighteen."

"Did she happen to say anything else about where they were going?" Laura glanced back and forth between Lilly and Arabella. Lilly motioned for her to put the call on speaker.

"She didn't say much, but he did, in the computer room," Sheila now told all three of them. "He was really excited, said they were heading to New Mexico and then to Yellowstone." More muted Bob. Laura held her breath, stifling her impatience with Sheila and her husband. "Right, no, not Yellowstone . . . Yosemite."

"Anywhere else?"

"Hmm, no, I don't recollect anywhere else. Bob, did I mention anywhere else? What do you mean, anywhere else where? Where Julia and her young man said they were going. I swear, sometimes, I do not understand you." Sheila made a huffing noise. "Men, you can't live with 'em, you can't shoot 'em. No, I'm pretty sure it was just Chicago and New Mexico. And Yell—Yosemite. I said I've always wanted to go out West. Get a camper and just go."

This time Bob was less muted. "Sheila, darling, no one wants to hear—"

"Fine, fine," Sheila said. "Listen, I wouldn't worry. She said she was going to get a new phone in Chicago. I'm sure she'll be in touch as soon as she can."

After they'd hung up, this was Lilly's argument: Julia was likely to reach out again. Laura and Arabella's well-intentioned scrambling to get to Chicago quickly was foolhardy.

"Honestly?" Lilly had said to Laura in the kitchen, out of Arabella's earshot. "The chance of the two of you being at the base of this Ferris wheel at exactly the same time as Julia and Sam strikes me as pie-in-the-sky thinking."

Laura bristled as she busied herself with washing the coffee mugs. *Pie-in-the-sky* was a Frances turn of phrase.

Though Lilly uttered the words with a gentle half smile, Laura heard her mother's voice. Felt her mother's instant judgment.

"That may be true," Laura had responded. "But I'm not going to do nothing. Not again."

A knock on the swinging door had interrupted them, followed by a push from the other side. Arabella appeared, a tablet in her hands.

"There are a few nonstops from Newark. If you can pack quickly and go with me to my home so I can do the same, my driver can get us there. It's a two-and a-half-hour flight and only about an hour to Navy Pier, so we could make it before Sam and Julia get there."

As it turned out, Arabella wasn't simply a pretty face. She was efficient and energetically take-charge. While Lilly and Laura had been arguing in the kitchen, Arabella had booked two first-class tickets from Newark to O'Hare, arranged for a rental car, looked up the operating hours for the Ferris wheel, and mapped the drive from Bloomsburg to Navy Pier. With the time change and driving time of nearly ten hours, she'd calculated Sam and Julia would probably arrive sometime between seven and nine o'clock.

Caught up in her own thoughts and the cascade of logistical explanations, Laura hadn't questioned why Arabella was so determined to find their children. The woman had a plan, and it sounded doable. Unfortunately, their flight had been delayed nearly an hour before being cancelled, and the next flight had also been delayed. So now, soaring somewhere over Ohio at 500-plus miles an hour, Laura realized their best-laid plans might not get them there in time, and she allowed herself to ponder the thought that had occurred to her back in her kitchen, a thought she didn't feel comfortable saying out loud: *If Sam was cleared to leave on his own, why is Arabella so desperate to find him?*

26

JULIA

IN THE STARBUCKS AT A TRAVEL plaza on the Ohio Turnpike, with the hubbub of ordering, coffee grinding, and milk steaming all around him, Sam stood in line, explaining the concept of philosophical authenticity. "It's a basic precept of existential thought, the idea of creating the self and then remaining true to that self despite external influences," he said, approaching the register. "Double espresso, no milk, and a Grande hot tea, Zen." He turned back to Julia. "Right?" She nodded as he went on. "It's about self-definition and continual self-reflection on whether you are, indeed, being authentic to your beliefs. Heidegger uses the word *Dasein*, which means 'being there.' He says we're continuously 'taking a stand'"—Sam added air quotes—"about who we are. Does that make sense?"

Julia nodded, thinking *I need this caffeine.*

Suppressed worries about what she'd done and was doing, combined with hours of Camus and extemporaneous conversations that seemed to run in circles, were exhausting her.

It seemed to have the reverse effect on Sam—he was energized. Other than brief stops like this one to refill the car, take a bathroom break, and buy drinks, they'd driven straight through. Sam wasn't hungry, he claimed, or tired.

Julia now understood the phrase "waxing philosophical." Throughout the day, as she'd read aloud, Sam had turned

alternately pensive, professorial, and attentive, asking her to
reread certain passages as he stared intently at the horizon or
stopping her so he could elaborate on specific philosophers—
Jaspers, Heidegger, Nietzsche—or try to make a concept
comprehensible. Asking Julia questions. Encouraging her to do
the same. And for every question she asked, he had a response:
an answer, an anecdote, another question, or a reference to a
book he'd read.

Back in the car, sipping green tea as a pink, orange, and
violet watercolor sunset arrived on the horizon, she'd followed
directions from Sam, turning to the back cover of the book
where he'd taken notes on each of the philosophers mentioned,
complete with dates of birth and death, theoretical concepts
introduced or expounded upon, publication titles, personal
details. The notes were written in fine-point black ink in
half-block print/half-script so tiny she often couldn't read it.
Every bit of white space on the last several pages was filled
with quotes, exclamation points, arrows and lines connecting
entries, and circles around certain phrases that reminded her
of her thought and dialogue bubbles. Julia couldn't help but
imagine Sam hunched over the book, pen in hand, frantically
annotating as he read.

*"Nietzsche, Friedrich Wilhelm (1844–1900) German
philosopher—suffered complete loss of mental function
at 44, BIPOLAR??; drew inspiration from Goethe,
Wagner and Schopenhauer [Arthur(1788–1860)
universe and everything in it driven by primordial
"will to live," ascetism (lifestyle characterized by
abstinence from worldly pleasures) did not live
according to his philosophy (p7)]—radical critique of
truth in favor of perspectivism; master-slave morality;
aesthetic affirmation of existence in response to "death
of God"; profound crisis of nihilism (MW: a viewpoint
that traditional values and beliefs are unfounded and
that existence is senseless and useless; will to power;
syphilis? Manic-depressive with periodic psychosis?*

*Human, all too Human; Beyond Good and Evil;
interpreted and misinterpreted; Adler . . . "Frenzy acts as
intoxication crucial for making of art?" Kirillov? "The
Possessed" Dostoevsky; C(S)hestov, Lev (1866–1938)
Russian philosopher; aphoristic style of Nietzsche and
Dostoevsky; "Everything is possible"!! not nihilism.
"We turn to God only to obtain the possible. As for the
possible, men suffice." (p34) Husserl, Edmund (1859–
1938) Phenomenology ("merely description of actual
experience" p43) "thinking is learning all over again
how to see . . ." studied math, physics and astronomy
Jaspers, Karl (1883–1969) existentialist; phenomenology;
philosophy and science; as subjective interpretation
of Being — being oneself — the potentiality to realize
one's freedom of being in the world! Wife was Jewish;
stayed behind in Germany; had suicide pact if arrested;
2 weeks before his scheduled deportation, Americans
occupied Heidelberg; cipher after WWII; world peace,
world confederation. Heidegger, Martin (1889–1976);
"Sein und Zeit" (Being and Time) — phen/exist, one of
the most important philosophical works, unfinished.*

"Nietzsche was bipolar?" Julia asked after skimming the
first section, deciding not to mention the 'complete loss of
mental function,' 'master-slave,' or 'suicide pact' notes.

"It's one theory out there. You'd be amazed at the controversy over what went on in some dead guy's mind. I gotta say,
though, he isn't the only creative person to be posthumously
diagnosed. Van Gogh, Beethoven, Tolstoy." Sam paused.
"O'Keeffe."

"Georgia O'Keeffe?"

"Yeah, and you know, I think that one might be right.
A while back I bought this book, *My Faraway One*, which
is this collection of letters she and Stieglitz wrote each other.
It's a fucking tome, like 700 pages and, catch this, it's only the
first volume. Turns out the two of them exchanged over 5,000
letters. Five thousand." Sam shook his head in wonder. "And

I'm talking real letters—paper, pen, stamps. Their relationship was kind of fucked up, but after he died, she put together this retrospective of his work. He was, like, the guy that pioneered the idea of photography as art. He held Ansel Adams's first show. Anyway, the book's fascinating, like a window into their minds. And her letters, well, someday, when we get back, you should read the book 'cause your letter—the one you wrote me at Brookfield—was another reason you remind me of O'Keeffe."

"My letter? Wait, you think I'm bipolar?" Julia said, immediately regretting both her tone, which somehow implied this would be a bad thing, and her choice of wording, remembering what Tanya had told her: "People are not their disease. One wouldn't say, 'I'm cancer.'" She hastily added, "I mean, not that that's bad."

Sam half-laughed.

"Don't worry. I get it. And no, I *don't* think you're bipolar, which, by the way, is bad and also not so bad, but that's a whole 'nother conversation. Want to know what I *do* think?"

"About me?"

"Yeah."

Julia nodded, acutely aware she both wanted to know and dreaded knowing.

Sam's voice took on a softer, gentler tone. "I think you got hit hard when your dad died and got dragged down somewhere you *do not* belong. And I think you're going to get out, in fact, I think you're *getting* out, and based on previous experience with the matters at hand, I'd say you've got a decent chance of staying out, which, full disclosure, is both fucking awesome and a little shitty for someone like me, who may never get out and stay out." *What would he think if he knew what I'd done*, Julia wondered as Sam went on, motioning with his head to the book. "I see you've turned over some corners."

Julia looked down at the paperback. *How did he notice that while driving?*

"Sorry, is that okay?"

"Totally. I do it all the time. What you got marked?"

"Mostly times when I think 'Yes, that's exactly right.'"

Sam smiled. "Want to read me one?"

Julia flipped, considering the options. "'The present and the succession of presents before a constantly conscious soul,'" she began, "'is the ideal of the absurd man.'"

"Yeah," he said, "I know that one."

"You highlighted it."

"Well, you know what they say, great minds think alike." Sam gave another half laugh.

"Mm-hmm," Julia said. "It reminds me of what they're always saying in yoga, about staying in the moment. And what you said that first day in the barn, about 'just being,' you know, right here, right now. Being fully aware, in the living present."

"I love that—'fully aware in the living present.' Though it is fucking hard, especially with a mind that tends to wander. And places like Brookfield don't make it easier. Other than Ashni and her vartamana"—Sam imitated the yoga teacher—"everyone's all about the past or future." Sam switched to his Tanya voice. "'How events have shaped you. Discharge plans. Medication checks.'" He dropped Tanya before continuing. "Even here, now, as amazing as these moments are with you, I find myself wondering about all the things I don't know about you, all the moments you've already had, without me."

Yes, Julia thought. *That's exactly right.* A host of questions she'd been storing up filled her head: *Did he love the girl in the photograph? Why did he try to kill himself? How many times? How far is he willing to go to avoid feeling too much or nothing at all? Was there a time when choosing nothing was the right choice?*

Julia wanted to know, and she didn't want to know.

Sam was still talking. "And then, there's tonight and tomorrow and the day after that, and that's only the start. Hard not to think about all that. Gotta say though, it's a beautiful goal—'the present and the succession of presents before a constantly conscious soul.' I'll have to share it with Ashni next time . . . See, there I go again."

"Yeah." Julia wondered how much she'd missed of Sam's monologue. "It's just—"

"Just what?"

"I don't know. This is probably going to sound stupid because I marked it and said it sounded good, but maybe it's not right. I mean, if we want to know ourselves, don't we have to look at who we've been and what we've done? Doesn't all of that have something to do with who we are now—who we want to be? I know you don't like discharge plans and medication checks, but all of that made me feel better about leaving, going back home, on my own."

Sam was silent.

Julia felt she'd disappointed him again. She turned back to another quote she'd flagged. "Here's another one . . . 'the mind that studies itself gets lost in a giddy whirling.'" Julia closed the book. "It's getting dark, and I don't think I can think about thinking anymore."

She waited.

Thankfully, Sam smiled. "Indeed, indeed. Point taken. Time to talk about something else. I've been wondering about your list all day."

How is this even remotely possible? He'd been, as Cheyenne would have said, "balls deep" in philosophy all day. With a mixture of relief and disbelief, she said, "You've been wondering about my list all day?"

"Yes, I have," Sam responded evenly. "Something tells me you're currently in no mood to discuss Holden Caulfield or college applications, so pick something else."

"Like what?"

"I don't know. Don't know the whole list. What else you got on there?"

Unlike Sam, Julia hadn't been wondering about her list while reading and discussing Camus. Nonetheless, it came back to her. She couldn't recall the exact order, except for the last two items—her mom and hope—which, to her surprise, she stopped short of sharing with Sam.

He did not seem to notice her hesitancy.

"What's a psalm of life?" he asked.

"It's a poem, by Longfellow."

"Ah, so two poems on the list."

"Actually, only one. 'Invictus' isn't on the list."

"Wait, what? Really? You sure? I could've sworn." He seemed incredulous that he'd gotten it wrong. "Wow, well, I guess that makes sense. I was trying to figure out why you wouldn't appreciate it the first time around. I mean, 'Under the bludgeoning of chance my head is bloody, but unbowed?' Talk about understanding how it feels. It's like the guy's been inside my head, bloody or not." He turned toward her. "All right then, hit me with the Longfellow."

"Hit you with the Longfellow?"

"I'm ready."

"You mean recite it?"

"Yeah."

"Oh, Sam, I don't have it memorized." Julia had a habit of knowing only the first and last lines of a poem. Sam, on the other hand, seemed to memorize everything. *Did he memorize "Invictus"?* "I only remember a few of the lines."

"Okay, gimme those."

Julia didn't respond. She didn't want to get into Longfellow. The poem wasn't exactly light.

"No? Want to just tell me what's it about? Why's it on the list or"—Sam smiled—"do you not want to go there either?"

"It's not that." It was that. Exactly that. She did not want to go there. However, Sam was waiting, filling the SUV with expectation. "My dad asked me to read it to him when he was really sick. And then my mom and her sister, my aunt Lilly, they insisted on having it as part of his memorial, which, well, kind of ruined it. My dad said it was a poem about living, but now, for me, it'll always be a poem about dying." Julia recalled how Aunt Lilly had slowed down reading the few lines now engraved in memory: *Lives of great men all remind us we can make our lives sublime, And, departing, leave behind us footprints on the sands of time.* She recalled how angry she'd felt that day: angry at her father for dying, angry with her mother for living, angry at some random stranger walking up to her and saying, "You are your father's footsteps," as if they knew anything about him, or her.

"Do you want to recite a different one?" Sam asked.

Regret overwhelmed her. She should have memorized "A Psalm of Life." And "Invictus." And "We Alone." Her father had. And he'd encouraged her to do the same. "I only know one poem by heart, 'Stopping by Woods on a Snowy Evening,' Robert Frost. You know, the one that ends with—"

"—miles to go before I sleep," she and Sam said together.

"Yeah, I guess I should have made more of an effort." Julia's voice was shaking.

"Hey, it's okay. I forget that memorizing isn't something that comes easily to everyone. Honestly, I wish I could forget stuff." Sam paused. "Let's try something else. Speaking of snow, why don't you tell me what happened with snowboarding. Or the snails."

Julia stared out the front window at the gray-brown road ahead of them as she recalled spending an entire day falling on her ass. How she'd been afraid of avalanches because she'd read this article about them online. How her wrists and abs ached, her brand-new, Christmas-present snowboarding pants were soaked, and she was cold and miserable and couldn't do a toe-side or a heel-side turn. The instructor's comments began to piss her off, and everyone around her seemed to be swishing by in an incredibly natural way, including her dad, and her mom, who kept insisting she needed to stop thinking so hard. It occurred to her now this advice was looking more and more appropriate all the time.

"Well, there isn't much to say about snowboarding other than that I sucked at it. The tragedy was I'd been really excited, and nothing I tried made any difference." Julia's voice faltered. "And snails are disgusting and slimy, and I can't even—"

"Oookayy—there's got to be something on this list you can talk about. How 'bout the pickle relish? Hot dog or burger?"

Julia shook her head. "Neither. It was tuna fish." She involuntarily shuddered.

"Tuna fish?"

"Yeah, at my grandma's house in Arizona, my dad's mom. I was little, maybe seven or eight, and we were visiting for Easter.

My mom doesn't like relish in tuna, so we never had it that way at home, but obviously, my dad grew up with it, so he dug right in. We were sitting outside, and it was hot and dry and windy. And the tuna salad was wet and mushy, and the color was awful—pale pink with these green bits in it. It was disgusting." Julia shuddered again. "It was one of the only times I recall my dad getting mad at me about anything. It was awful. I cried."

"So, no relish in tuna."

"No."

"Chalk one up for your mom, huh?"

"Yeah." Julia looked out the window. She hadn't really thought of it that way.

"Snails, mushy tuna, flan . . . sounds like you've got a texture thing going on, no? What's the verdict on pudding and Jell-O?"

Julia turned back. Sam was grinning.

"Seriously?" she asked.

"I am absolutely serious." Sam's grin grew broader.

Julia returned it. "As a matter of fact, I love chocolate pudding and strawberry Jell-O. My mom used to bring these Jell-O squares to my soccer practices, old school, and they were, like, my favorite snack. Ergo, your texture theory does not hold."

"Point taken. Again, go Mom. However, *mea culpa*, those were poor examples to establish proof, given that chocolate pudding is soft and delicious—and chocolate—and strawberry Jell-O in squares is definitely not flan."

"Definitely not."

"And you are adorable and this, this, is definitely living in the moment. I want to kiss you very badly—right now," Sam said. "We may have to pull over."

"Do we need to fill up?" Julia asked, leaning over to look at the gauge. It was just under the halfway mark.

"Indeed we do," Sam said.

As dusk turned to dark, Julia added another item to a new list, this one in her head—a growing list of firsts—sex in the backseat of a car.

She'd never felt so fiercely wanted, so connected to another person. Sam's hands on her body were more than a caress. It was as though he were creating her anew.

"Being with you might make me reconsider the meaning of transcendence," Sam said, burrowing his face into her neck. "You could make me reconsider a good many things."

Julia wished she could capture this moment in a bottle she could open whenever she felt empty or disconnected, and then she remembered the conflict she'd felt that morning opening a bottle with Sam's name on it.

What might you reconsider? Would you take this for me? Please, Julia. Stop. Stay here.

Julia ran her palms down over the muscles of Sam's back.

He shivered, pulled away, his expression inscrutable.

"Sam?"

Before she could react, he'd fully extricated himself from her embrace. He rubbed his arms with his hands, then moved them up to cover his face. Underneath his fingertips, she could see him scrunching his eyes as if pain accompanied an inexplicable chill.

Julia maneuvered to sit next to him.

"Are you okay?" she asked, instinctively putting her arm around his shoulder.

"Yeah," he said, ducking her touch and reaching for his shirt. "I'm fine."

He dressed even faster than he'd undressed only minutes earlier, leaving Julia feeling empty and disconnected with a rapidity she hadn't anticipated.

She turned her head away so he wouldn't see the tears forming in her eyes. Little chance of that—Sam had exited the car, leaving the door open. She could hear his footsteps crunching on loose gravel over cement, moving away, his voice low, mumbling into the darkness.

Julia dressed awkwardly in her Saks clothing, wishing for her own grungy sweatshirt and worn leggings. She wondered what she'd done. Had she said aloud the words in her head? Had she verbalized "Would you take this for me?"

As she slid to the edge of the backseat, Sam turned and walked slowly, solemnly toward her. She imagined him saying as he took her into his arms, *"No matter what I do or say, I need you. Finding you was the best thing I've ever done."*

Instead, he opened the driver's door and said, "It's getting late. We better get going if we want to catch that wheel."

ARABELLA

LAURA HADN'T SPOKEN MUCH since her sister's goodbye hug on the porch of her house, when Arabella had overheard Lilly saying, "Remember, be nice." At the time, the hug made Arabella feel a tinge of envy, and the advice merely confirmed what she'd already surmised—held in check by her younger sister, Laura was holding back her true feelings. The car rides to Brooklyn and the Newark airport, and the wait in the gate area, had been downright painful. Other than a few monosyllabic responses to questions Arabella posed in an increasingly artless effort to converse, Laura said nothing at all.

At least not to Arabella. The only one talking to Arabella was her British male Siri, summoned as soon as the rental car contract was safely stowed in the glove box.

However, Laura wasn't wholly silent. She called Lilly twice, once after they received news of the first flight delay, and then again when they landed in Chicago. She'd also received a call as their rental car exited the parking lot, her phone ringing as the tires crossed over the line of sharp red spokes that signaled no going back. Ironically, it quickly became clear the caller disapproved of the journey upon which she and Arabella had embarked.

A long pause after hello and then Laura's voice diminished, her tone indicating said disapproval was expected.

"We're leaving the airport. Yes, in Chicago. No, that's not how I see it. No. Well, it's not your decision, is it? Nor hers. Actually, that's not what she said, no — "

Laura drew an audible, intentional breath. She turned toward the window.

"No, what she said was that we might not find them." Her voice grew more strained with each phrase. "We might not find them, and I should be prepared for that. No, that is not — what?" Arabella looked over and saw that Laura's eyes were closed as she listened, her lips pursed, holding words in. "Honestly, Mother," she finally said.

Ah, Arabella thought, *of course.*

"Why are you calling?" Laura went on. "No. No. Fine."

Though she was concentrating on Siri's poorly pronounced instructions, bright green and white directional signs, and the crush of cars moving across multiple lanes, Arabella saw Laura drop the phone in her lap before wiping her nose and cheek with the back of her hand.

"Sorry about that," Laura said. "I shouldn't have taken the call."

"You needn't apologize," Arabella replied. "You all right?"

Laura sniffed, wiped at her nose again. "I'm fine."

Arabella returned her attention to the road as the car filled again with silence. She registered the digital time display on the dashboard.

8:24.

They might already be too late.

"Utterly absurd. A fool's errand." Laura's voice punctuated the quiet. "That's what my mother called this. She doesn't think we'll find them, of course, but that's not all. No, she also wanted to remind me of her strongly held opinion that Julia is just a rebellious young woman with a 'penchant for overwrought drama,' and I am a feckless pawn, failing to keep my emotions in check."

It wasn't clear to Arabella that a response was being sought, yet saying nothing felt wrong. "I'm sorry."

Laura was quiet. 8:25 became 8:26.

It was a long minute.

When Laura finally spoke, all she said was "Heavy traffic," leaving Arabella to assume the conversation was over.

Traffic *was* heavy, considering the hour. Perhaps there had been an accident. Red brake lights flashed all around, cars haltingly moving toward home, or work, or heaven knows where, but probably not the Ferris wheel at Navy Pier. Except Sam and Julia, if they were coming to Chicago at all. Arabella allowed her thoughts to drift. *Maybe Laura's mother is right. Maybe this is an absurd journey, a fool's errand.*

"She doesn't believe depression is an illness at all," Laura said suddenly, now in full-blown *can you fucking believe it* mode. "Won't even consider it." In her peripheral vision, Arabella saw Laura shaking her head. "Don't know why I'm surprised. She's always been this way, she and my stepfather. She wanted me to know how disappointed he would be. As if I'd ever *not* disappointed him."

To this, Arabella could relate. Nonetheless, she self-edited; spilling did not come naturally. It had taken years to open up to her therapist, and spilling to a woman who clearly bore her animosity was, as Sam would say, "a whole 'nother thing." Besides, Laura's shift from stone-cold silence to pissed-off true-confession was unsettling.

"Is *your* family supportive?" Laura asked. "Of you and Sam?"

Arabella was caught completely off guard. She hadn't thought Laura was interested in anything about Sam, or her. A car on her right flicked on the left blinker and began to drift into their lane. She slowed to allow it in, asking herself *How much should I share?*

"Supportive isn't the word I would choose," she answered. "I'm an only child, so it's just me and my parents, both of whom are British and in possession of the stiffest of stiff upper lips. Suffice to say mental illness is not part of their world. It doesn't enter their thoughts, and certainly doesn't enter conversations. My mother reaches out every so often, but we never discuss Sam. So, no, not supportive . . . not really."

"It seems we have something in common after all," Laura said, partially under her breath. She paused, then added, "I'm sorry. What about Sam's father?"

Another car, now on the left, aggressively edged in front of their car. Arabella shook her head. So much pointless evasive movement; everyone was moving at the same speed, a snail's pace. Flashing lights were visible up ahead on the right side of the road.

"Sam's father." This was even trickier than her parents. Arabella reviewed her options for sharing: full disclosure of familial history of genius, wealth, and suicidality; partial disclosure couching same behaviors as creativity, devotion to career, and poor personal decision-making; or no disclosure at all. "Also not terribly supportive," she began, "though for entirely different reasons. You see, my ex-husband, Max, generally seeks to escape anything unpleasant or emotionally difficult: obligations, growing old, family history." Arabella's voice slowed. "Weakness in those around him."

"And he views Sam's issues as a weakness."

"Yes, he does."

8:32.

As the car edged up to the flashing lights, Arabella could see a white pickup with a dented truck bed, a dark SUV with a pancaked front hood, broken windshield, and deflated airbags, a police car, and a tow truck off to her right. *A dark SUV.* She slowed, looking for a space in the far-right lane, but the cars were bumper to bumper at a standstill. She hit the brakes hard.

The driver behind her honked.

"Are you okay?" Laura asked.

Arabella strained to see if the car was a BMW X5. "Can you see?" she said, breathlessly. "Is it a BMW?"

"A BMW?" Laura said. "Oh my god. Is it them?"

Arabella craned her neck. The driver behind them laid on the horn.

"I don't know what to look for," Laura said.

Arabella did. She scanned the frame of the car, looking for the telltale markings of a BMW, finding none. Then she saw the stylized A. It was an Acura.

"It's okay." Arabella exhaled. "It's not them." She breathed, then repeated, more softly, "It's not them."

Traffic began moving in the lane to her left.

Arabella steered the rental into an opening, accelerated and went on, hoping to mask the predictable adrenaline hit she knew was coming and did not want to display to Laura.

Both women were silent for a few minutes.

"Are you sure you're okay?" Laura asked.

Arabella nodded. "I'm fine. Sorry, where were we?"

"You were telling me about your husband."

"I was? Oh yes. Right." She inhaled deeply.

"It's okay if you don't want to talk," Laura said.

"No, it's fine," Arabella replied. "It's complicated, because Max's dad, also a Sam Lorenzo, was very much like my Sam: creative, brilliant, with this incredible energy. If you'd met him, you'd understand—he was a force. Smart and funny. Captivating. When he spoke to you, you were the only one in the room. Of course, Max's experience was quite different. Growing up with someone like that was, well—complicated doesn't begin to describe it."

"And yet, you named Sam for him."

"No, well, sort of. You see, my ex-husband was named for his father, in reverse. Samuel Maximilian became Maximilian Samuel and then Max wanted his own son to carry his name forward, without any reversal, so Sam, my Sam? His official name is Maximilian Samuel, Junior. It wasn't until he was a teenager that he decided to use his middle name." Arabella shot a glance at Laura. "Did that make sense?"

Laura nodded.

Arabella went on. "Sam said the change was to honor his grandfather, but we all knew it was designed to hurt Max . . . for hurting him. Not physically, of course. It was more, how can I say this . . . Sam wasn't an easy child. A fussy baby. Hardly napped. Couldn't sit still. Always moving, bouncing, spinning. It drove Max to distraction, so his solution was to stay away—work late, travel. For a couple of years, in middle school, Sam took medication and settled down. He began to do well in school and sports, but it was too late to change the patterns with Max. By the time Sam had his first episode in college, followed by . . . Well, you don't want to hear all of this. The point is . . . by then, it wasn't difficult for Max to simply stay away altogether. We've been divorced for a couple of years now."

As she said these last words, Arabella wondered how she'd gotten so far in; maybe the adrenaline rush had swept her up. She gave Laura a tight smile, a "that's all there is to that" expression that brooked no further questions.

After driving in a cement, brick, and steel almost-city for miles, they were quite suddenly in the city itself.

"So, you've been on your own with all this." Laura's voice was soft.

Arabella could feel her staring.

"Yes," Arabella said, tightening her smile until it was no longer a smile. "Yes, I have."

Arabella's British Siri suggested a lane change, an exit up ahead.

"Well, not anymore, because like it or not"—Laura clearly didn't like it—"we're in this together. As much as I'd like to focus solely on Julia, I'm increasingly aware that, right now, your son has more influence over her than anything or anyone else. Which all goes to say, I do want to hear all of it. I want to know whatever you'll tell me."

28

JULIA

ABOUT 100 MILES OUT from Chicago, the inside of the SUV grew strangely quiet, leaving Julia alone with her thoughts—not a place she necessarily wanted to be. Post-ecstasy, the emotion, compounded by Camus-induced giddy whirling, left her thought/behavior/emotion triad in danger of imploding, and it seemed Sam's was in no better shape. His left leg was bouncing with barely contained energy.

As they drove into the city along the lake, Julia experienced brief relief when she caught a glimpse of the familiar dome of a planetarium. She'd been to many with her father; they'd been to the Hayden in New York City a bunch of times, but they'd also traveled to North Carolina, upstate New York, Washington D.C., and Chicago, specifically to make a visit to a dome. Of course, a planetarium wasn't necessary; sky watching could take place anywhere. "Just look up," her dad used to say.

There was magic in the darkness of a field, a sandy bluff, a campground, or even, on occasion, merely pulled over to the side of the road, far from ambient city lights. Crisp air that made outlines sharper, the smell of sand, salt, dirt, and leaves more pronounced. As a little girl, she'd stand next to a telescope with her hands behind her back as her father taught her, her eye up against the eyepiece, listening as her father or an astronomer described the planet, star cluster, or nebula in view. As she got older, she learned how to operate the telescopes herself, studying aperture, magnification, and power. Armed with her father's celestial calendar, she'd spread out star maps and make a plan for what she might see. She and her dad would discuss the plan, and when she saw his eyes light up, she'd know she'd read the maps correctly.

Julia remembered the waxing gibbous moon from the night before and recalled what had been lurking at the edges of her memory. She could picture her father, pointing to the calendar. "A mega moon," he'd said, "the closest one in nearly seventy years. There won't be another one 'til 2034." Julia leaned back and looked up. There was a moonroof in the SUV with a ceiling-fabric cover. The control was in a panel at the top of the center console. As she reached upward, she turned to ask Sam if he minded her opening it.

"Sure, but we're here," Sam said. He loosely pointed up ahead, off to the right.

There it was. Navy Pier.

Even at a distance, Julia could tell something was different from the last time she'd been there, and as they approached, she could see—it was the Ferris wheel itself. The one in front of her, ultra-sleek, modern, brightly lit in blue and white, was not the one she'd ridden with her father. That one had looked like a circus ride, red and white and boxy.

The underground garage wasn't full. Sam pulled the SUV into a spot next to two massive cement dividers that nearly obscured it from sight.

"Don't want to be too easy to spot," Sam said. "In case the view inspires us," he added, raising his eyebrows. Before she could respond, he leaned over and softly kissed the underside of her jaw. His fingertips brushed over the spot his lips had just vacated and trailed down her neck. "This may be my favorite part of you, though it's a tough call."

And then he was grabbing the backpack, opening his door, slamming it closed, and moving around to the back of the SUV. Julia turned in her seat as the rear door swooshed upward and Sam appeared in its frame. He was holding the black 35mm camera case. "Ready?"

Get your shit together.

She followed Sam's back through a doorway marked ENTRY 4 and then they were outside, a large body of water in front of them, a metal wave-shaped wall to their right.

"This way." Sam walked along the wave, then paused and announced dramatically, "And there it is."

Julia looked up to see the Ferris wheel, looming above. It was definitely not the same one. This was a massive white metal structure with dark, fully enclosed gondolas with floor-to-ceiling windows. It shimmered; white lights shot out from its core like continuous fireworks.

"Would you look at that," Sam said, squinting. He started up a curving staircase with wide wooden steps. "Now that's a Ferris wheel. I used to hear light displays like this when I was a kid."

"Sam, it's not—" Julia hesitated a few steps below him. *He'd hear light displays?* "It's not the one I rode with my dad."

"What do you mean?" Sam spun around. "Are you sure? 'Cause it's the only one here."

Julia couldn't tell if he was doubting her statement or making a joke.

"I'm sure. This must be new. It's way bigger."

It was huge, towering. A shiver began inside, spilling out into her arms and legs and head. Without awareness, her hand rose toward the hair at the back of her neck.

"Yeah, okay, but this one is amazing, no? The views are going to be fucking awesome." Sam grabbed the hair-pulling hand and continued climbing the staircase. "Let's do this. And then we'll find us some dogs," he added exuberantly in an accent she imagined he thought sounded Midwestern, though to her it sounded more like bad Texan. "With pickle relish and fries." He drew out the *i* sound in fries. *More Texan.*

Julia instinctively resisted Sam's forward motion. Reminded of the moment in Saks when he'd been pulling her across the cosmetics section, she said, "Wait, hold on, please."

She hoped he did not notice her clear lack of enthusiasm. She felt a pit opening in her belly. She needed a bathroom. Why had she allowed him to convince her to come here? This was dumb. She could not ride this new Ferris wheel, oohing and aahing over the silhouette of the skyline or view over the water, and somehow erase the time she fell limp to the floor.

She couldn't recreate and thereby correct the mistakes of the past.

She could not bring her father back.

"This is," Julia began, then she noticed Sam's face. It was as if the post-sex chill had never occurred. He was excited. He wanted her to eat relish and ride loops on the Ferris wheel. He wanted her to dedicate herself to the intensity of this moment. She reframed her answer. "Thank you for caring enough to bring me here. It *is* amazing—"

Sam retreated to stand next to her, bent to kiss her, hard. "I know. I told you. It's amazing. You're going to be glad you did this." He lifted the black case. "I'll memorialize everything and then we'll develop the film when we get back and put albums together—together. I've got a box of those photo books and rolls of those little triangles to mount them. You've seen those, right? Your parents probably made books like that for you. They did, didn't they?"

Julia watched the gondola cars rising skyward into the dark. *My mother did,* she thought.

Sam went on. "I've got this set of leather-bound ones that'll be perfect. And you can add some drawings. Speaking of which, we should stop and get some pastels. I'm sorry I only brought charcoal. I don't need any more color—"

Julia put her fingers up to his mouth. "Sam, stop."

"What?" He paused. "Why?"

"I can't do this."

Sam's head jerked backward, eyes scrunched, eyebrows knitted. "What?" he repeated.

"I can't do this. I can't go on the Ferris wheel."

"What do you mean, you can't go on the wheel? We came here specifically *to go* on *this Ferris wheel.*"

"I know. I'm sorry. It's just I'm already feeling dizzy and sick to my stomach, and I know it won't go well, and—"

Sam's look of incredulity softened but did not disappear.

"You don't know that," he said. "You don't know that it's not going to go well. I'm not letting you give up this easily. Courage, remember?"

The gondola cars rose behind him as Julia's hands dropped to press on the empty place inside her gut. She remembered her parents discussing how she'd been hungry the last time, that maybe she fainted from low blood sugar and the heat. "Maybe I just need some food. I haven't eaten much today."

Sam made a half turn away from her, shaking his head in the direction of the wheel.

"We came all this way," he said. "And it's right here. And it looks amazing, it really does."

"You can go," Julia said. "You should go."

Shadows caught on Sam's features. His expression transformed to something harsh.

"Yeah, except it's not *my* list," he said. "I'm doing this for you."

Julia's hands covered her face, her fingertips rubbing her forehead, up under her hairline, hard, almost to the point of hurting. She didn't want to see Sam's disappointment *or whatever it was he was feeling.* She felt her resolve wavering, her sense of surety about her decision dissipating. Maybe he was right. Maybe she needed courage. She tried to imagine what Tanya would say in this situation. Would it be "Go on the wheel. Your behavior can impact negative beliefs. If you behave as though you aren't afraid, you can conquer fear." Or would she say "Trust your emotions. You know yourself better than anyone else. If you have to remove yourself from a situation, do it." Or something else altogether?

Julia hadn't completed enough therapy to know which directional arrows on the thought/behavior/emotion triad to follow.

She shouldn't have left when she did. This was all her fault.

The words "I'm sorry," muffled against the inside of her wrists.

Sam's voice brought her back, his hands peeling hers away from her face. The harshness was gone. His voice was soft, kind. "Hey, hey . . . it's okay. Don't worry. Here's what we're going to do. There's got to be a hot dog place here. Let's find the food court, conquer your hunger, cross relish off the list, and give you some confidence. Confidence *and* sustenance for what, like twenty bucks? A bargain. And then we'll come back and tackle this big boy. All right?"

Julia nodded.

Sam took two steps back toward the path along the water and offered his hand. "Good, now come with me. Something tells me some truly fine dining awaits."

LAURA

THE PIER WAS RELATIVELY empty and there was no line at the Ferris wheel ticket booth, which was convenient since Arabella clearly had a strategy for engaging the woman inside. With an enchanting smile upon her face, she began telling a story about visiting from New York and how, having heard this was a must-do activity, she'd planned to meet her son and his girlfriend there, and she wasn't sure if maybe they'd already purchased tickets. "I know it's hard with so many people coming through," Arabella said, slipping a hundred-dollar bill through the slot under the window. "For your trouble. Perhaps you recognize him?" She held up her cell phone, displaying a photograph of Sam. "Or his girlfriend?" she added, holding up Laura's phone.

"Her hair is much shorter now," Laura said. The photo of Julia was over a year old, pre-dreadlocks and haircut, pre-piercings. "And she's a little older."

The woman rested her fingertips on the edge of the one-hundred-dollar bill, glancing around in a woefully conspicuous attempt at being surreptitious. She peered at the phones, shook her head. "Sorry, I don't think I've seen them. I took a break around seven o'clock, though. Maybe they were here then?"

Arabella's smile remained fixed, her tone gracious. "Of course. Or perhaps they haven't arrived yet. Thank you." She returned Laura's phone and slid another bill under the window. "I'll take four tickets, please."

Laura turned away to watch for Sam and Julia, taking in a carousel under a brightly striped circus tent and one of those huge swing rides under another, garden spaces wrapped by stone benches, and a wide sweeping staircase. The space was relatively empty, but Laura imagined it crowded in the summer, with happy tourists slurping snow cones and drinking beer. The Ferris wheel itself soared overhead, cobalt blue with white lights radiating outward, reminding her of the sparklers Paul used to buy for birthdays and the Fourth of July. She recalled watching him, Julia, and Julia's friend Jess dancing with abandon, twirling the sparklers, Julia calling out, "Look, Mom, we're making our own stars."

"We should find a place to sit where we can watch people getting on." Arabella gestured toward the graduated loading areas separated by a series of short staircases. "I think it might be best if we stayed out of sight. I'm not certain how Sam will react if he sees us."

This was becoming a familiar refrain. Laura wanted to ask *What, exactly, might he do?* As she and Arabella scoped out potential places to wait, Laura's thoughts turned to how fragile and vulnerable Julia had seemed the last time she saw her, the night of visiting hours two days earlier. *Two days ago. She was only just regaining her sense of self.* Laura remembered how easily swayed Julia had been by Cheyenne: the thrift-store clothing, the dreadlocks and piercings, and God knew what else. *What influence was Sam having on her, right now?*

When the two women had settled on a low cement wall tucked behind a churro concession near the base of the wheel, Laura turned to Arabella. "Perhaps this would be a good time to tell me about Sam."

"What would you like to know?"

"The doctors say Julia is clinically depressed. What do they say about Sam?"

Arabella looked up at the wheel and then higher, to the

night sky. "Currently?" she said. "Rapid cycling Bipolar 1, but it's been a long twisting road to arrive where we are."

"We may be waiting a while," Laura said. She tried not to focus on the word *currently*, but couldn't stop the thought: *How many diagnoses has he had?*

"The trouble is," Arabella was saying, "Sam's always been intense, so intense it's hard to know where the line is between his normal and his 'oh my god, something's wrong.' Even when he was young, he was never just happy, he was over the moon, and when he was sad, he was inconsolable—truly inconsolable, as if the world had come to an end. And there were signs, all along, that he experienced things differently. There was this one evening when he was eleven, he and I were in the garden, and there was a nearly full moon rising, not unlike the one tonight."

Arabella nodded toward the moon. It was nearly full, and it was enormous. Laura wondered if it was one of the supermoons Paul used to wait for, praying for cloudless nights.

"We could see the moon already in the sky. Sam held his arm aloft and then, in this quiet voice, he told me that some-times"—Arabella's own voice quieted and slowed—"sounds and tastes appeared like colors, and he could see feelings 'shimmering like auras.' That's how he talked. At eleven. Shimmering auras.'" She shook her head.

"It wasn't the vocabulary that surprised me, though, it was the underlying concept—the idea of his senses shifting somehow—that took time to wrap my head around. I remember he said the sound of a subway screeching could set off colorful fireworks in his head, that guitar music sometimes felt like brushstrokes on his skin, and happiness was a soap bubble.

"And all of a sudden, sitting there in my backyard garden, I found myself reevaluating events from his childhood that had baffled me when they occurred. Like once, when he was little, maybe five or six, we were at the park on this hot, hot summer day and I bought him an ice cream. He was standing there with his eyes half-closed, licking the cone, when he said, 'This is like touching the stars.' I asked him what he meant, and he opened his eyes all the way and said, 'You know, when you touch a star and it's cold, but it burns your finger.' So of course, I asked if he touched the stars often and, I remember vividly, he answered, 'Only when I hear the sky opening for me.'

"Or when he was a toddler, maybe two, if that. We were at a playground and this little boy showed up and started blowing bubbles with this little plastic bubble wand, nothing fancy, simply a little hoop on the end of a stick. Sam had been doing one of his favorite things, running around and spinning with his arms out wide until he fell down." Arabella smiled faintly. "But when he saw the bubbles, he stopped dead in his tracks and stood there, still as a stone, staring as they rose into the sky. I can see him now, standing there, transfixed, his hand outstretched."

Though she didn't raise her arm, Arabella's fingertips spread wide.

"Then a bubble floated by, and Sam touched it, and it popped and disappeared. And he began to wail. I know what you're thinking . . ." Arabella looking directly at Laura's face, making her wonder if her expression was too telling. "'He's certainly not the first child to cry when a bubble pops,' but it was more than that. He kept saying, 'I killed it, I killed it,' and I remember thinking I didn't know he knew the word 'kill,' or what it meant to kill something.

"Anyway, the night when he was eleven and he told me about his senses shifting, he explained that the world could be amazing, incandescent, and glorious, but it could also be overwhelming and frightening, because he knew in his soul, he was alone—no one understood him—other people didn't hear or see or feel things the way he did.

"And he was so terribly sad. So I said, 'Oh, Max'—he was still Max back then—'I'll always be here, and there must be other people that the world the way you do. You'll find them and then you won't be alone anymore.' And then he gave me this heartbreaking smile—obviously designed to make *me* feel better—and he said in an entirely unconvinced voice, 'Yeah, I'm sure you're right.'"

Laura was surprised to realize the look on Arabella's face made her want to weep.

"All along, he had such trouble in school. We knew he was smart, but he couldn't do the work—he never knew what was expected of him because he was either incredibly distracted or obsessively focused to the point he didn't hear or see anyone or anything outside his own head. Of course, Max had no tolerance for any of it. He was inpatient, angry . . . with Sam, with me. I remember him saying, 'You better do something before it's too late.'

"So, I took Sam to a learning specialist and a child psychologist and a doctor, and I filled out questionnaires, and they gave him all sorts of tests—IQ, response time, attention—most of which he hated, and then they prescribed a stimulant, which he ended up hating even more. At first, though, it was incredibly helpful, especially at school. Actually, it was more than helpful; it was the difference between night and day."

Arabella shook her head again. "But then, one day on the way home from school, he began crying. I asked what was wrong, and he said, 'I can't explain it.' I asked if the other kids were making fun or if he was in trouble. It was none of that, he said. He told me he just had to cry. And then it started happening every day, and on some level, I knew it was the medication, but I kept telling him it was going to get better. Looking back now, I feel awful, encouraging my son to take something that made him miserable, in part because it made my life easier."

Arabella's eyes shone with tears.

"Then one morning, he began crying when he took the little blue pill, and I broke. We tried another medication, and another, but each one had side effects and eventually, Sam refused to take them anymore.

"Things did get better in high school. There were fewer conflicts with teachers. He even made friends playing lacrosse, which was in its own way a lifesaver. At long last, running and spinning and intensity were good qualities; thank God, because by then, Sam was operating on a faster speed nearly all the time. I remember once he was reading while I made dinner, and to me it looked as though he was simply flipping pages, so I called him on it. I said something like, 'you can't possibly be getting anything out of that,' and he explained, in exquisite detail, exactly what he'd read. You see, all the signs were there. Yet even then, even after I'd seen his grandfather spiral out, I did not see the similarity in Sam's behavior. It's amazing what you can allow yourself to believe.

"And then, the proverbial shit hit the fan. A couple of months into his first semester at university, we learned he'd dropped into a dark place—weeks earlier. We'd arranged for him to have a single room, because of his erratic sleep patterns, which seemed like a good idea—until the depression hit. Apparently, for days, he hadn't showered or brushed his teeth, let alone gone to class. He barely left his room. Rarely ate. Wasn't sleeping. One day, his RA, a student himself, knocked on Sam's door when someone mentioned not seeing him for a while. He was sitting on the floor in the dark, staring at the wall."

Arabella looked up at the wheel. "That was his first hospitalization."

A trance broken, Laura realized she hadn't looked away from Arabella's face for several minutes. The narrative was compelling, and Arabella's face was captivating. Oddly, Laura heard Paul's voice saying, in relation to Keira Knightley, "the camera loves her, it's impossible to look away." She remembered not being jealous when her husband made this statement, because he'd been right—Keira Knightley held you in her spell.

Arabella had the same power.

Suddenly it occurred to her, what had she missed while staring at Arabella? Traffic was sparse in the space around the Ferris wheel and there was no line waiting to ride, yet a flush of fear spread across her chest, her shoulders, her neck. What if she'd missed seeing Julia?

Before Laura could ask her to hit pause, Arabella went on.

"They prescribed an antidepressant, which didn't do much, so they upped the dose. And he seemed better. But then, not long afterward, he spun out of control on the other end, and we didn't see it coming—because we didn't know what to look for. One afternoon, I was listening to him talk, and it was instantaneous, the realization that my son had gone over an edge I *could not see.* Later, he said it was as if his thoughts were caught on a loop, spinning and spinning until shards broke off and pierced the boundary of reality.

"What I remember is sitting there, trying to keep up with him, as he paced back and forth, faster and faster, not making sense. And suddenly my own thoughts started spinning—'What's happening?' and 'What do I do?'

"Of course, since then, at support groups, I've heard, over and over, it's difficult to know when behavior is within range and when your loved one has entered some unknown territory. People say, 'it was a stage' or 'it had seemed the medicine was working.'"

Laura understood this last statement. She felt rather than saw the closed bathroom door, heard herself calling Julia's name.

"At the beginning, hearing long-term survivors gave me hope but, in some ways, they were also the hardest to listen to. After a while, I stopped going. It was too painful. I remember this one young woman at a group in Brooklyn. She'd been with her boyfriend for twelve years—twelve years—cycling up and down, on medication, off medication, in therapy, out of therapy. She said it was like being in a sidecar attached to a motorcycle *he* was riding. She had no control—she had to go where *he* went, at the speed *he* chose, barreling down straightaways, careening around curves, knowing, at any time, he could break the connection between the bike and the sidecar, and she'd be left behind. She was so brave, well-informed, involved in advocacy . . . I knew it should have given me comfort to hear her . . ."

Arabella's voice grew small. She leaned back, shaking her head slowly. "But it didn't. I've never told anyone this—but for the longest time, I was certain Sam wasn't like the others. He was a genius. Creative. Empathic. I know now that sounds naïve." Arabella faltered and sighed. "Or deliberately obtuse. Like I'm wearing blinders. Even after the last time, when he—"

The sound of laughter punctuated the air. Recognizable laughter.

Both women shifted their gaze to the open space. Laura stood up, took three steps toward the wheel, looking in all directions. It was impossible to discern the source of the laughter before it ceased.

Laura turned to look back at Arabella.

"What happened to her?" Laura asked.

"Who?"

"The young woman from Brooklyn."

Arabella's translucent face was openly alarmed, her eyes wide. "Carolyn?"

"The one in the sidecar?"

Arabella exhaled. "Oh, yes, her, of course." She paused. "He died, her boyfriend. Last summer. I went back a few weeks ago, just once, and someone said she'd come only once afterward, for closure." Arabella paused again, this time a bit longer. "Apparently, she used the word 'relief' to describe how she felt. Relief and guilt. And despair, of course, because in the end, she couldn't save him."

Laura saw Julia in the hospital bed, lines on the monitor flashing to flat. Felt the ice pick hit her sternum.

"It's nearly ten." Arabella waved her hand to encompass the rides, the restaurants, the empty spaces. "Everything will be closing down soon."

She stood up, holding out a ticket in her hand.

"If they're still here, maybe we'll be able to see them from above."

JULIA

THE "CHICAGO DOG" CAME in a white cardboard box, with a dill pickle, mustard, tomato, celery salt, and, of course, the all-important, critical-to-the-whole-endeavor green relish. Sam upgraded to the "San Francisco Dog," which had so many toppings, it hardly looked like a hot dog: chili, ketchup, mustard, shredded cheese, lettuce, tomato—

"And relish," he said, licking a bit of chili from his lip. "Here, have a bite. It is, by far, the most glorious hot dog I've ever consumed."

"No thank you," Julia said. "I'm good."

Sam took another bite and said with his mouth full, "So, success? Cross this one off the list, yes?"

"Success." Julia smiled, placing the remainder of her hot dog back in the box. "I've been thinking of highlighting, though, instead of crossing things off. It feels more appropriate somehow, with my dad and all."

"Yeah," Sam said. "I like it. Speaking of which, how ya doing? Ready to ride?" He placed the last bite of the loaded San Francisco dog in his mouth.

Near-instantaneous terror struck, Julia's Chicago dog roiling inside. Her left hand migrated up to tug the short hair at the nape of her neck as her right hand covered her throat.

"I'm guessing no," Sam mumbled, his mouth still full.

"I'm so sorry. God, I thought I was doing better. Maybe we could look around first?"

Sam wiped his mouth with a paper napkin. "Sure. I don't know what time it is, but we've probably got a few minutes. Let's get some air. Better to let our stomachs settle anyway."

Jutting out into the lake, the pier was surrounded on three sides by water: a river, an inlet, and Lake Michigan. Tour boats of all shapes, sizes, and colors were tied up alongside. The air was cooler than when they'd arrived. Sam wrapped his arm around Julia's shoulder; she wrapped hers around his waist. His body radiated heat into hers.

They passed a large vertical sign reading "Shakespeare," across from an enormous black and white striped cruising vessel named "Odyssey," and then, there in front of them, was a banner reading "the Amazing Chicago Fun Maze."

"Hey, look at that," Sam said, gesturing with his head to the banner. "Too bad we're pressed for time."

"Oh, I don't like mazes," Julia said, thinking of the woods outside Brookfield. Turning, she could see the lights of the pier's attractions reflecting off the river, resembling oil paint floating on water. "Should we head back?"

"Wait, what?" Sam paused. "You don't like mazes?"

"No. I don't get them. How is it fun to purposefully get lost and twisted around?"

"Because it's a challenge," Sam said, though he turned to head back with her toward the Ferris wheel. "And there's satisfaction when you find your way out." Julia remembered then that Sam didn't just like mazes, he wanted to build one at Brookfield.

"So that's why you wanted to build one."

Sam slowed, staring at her.

"In the courtyard at Brookfield," she clarified.

"I don't want to build a maze in the courtyard at Brookfield. I want to build a labyrinth."

"Same thing, no?"

"No," Sam said, shaking his head. "No. Not at all." He stopped walking. "A maze is *designed* to get you lost. A labyrinth helps you *find yourself*. They both have twists and turns, but a labyrinth is one path; all the turns lead in one direction, to the center. It's a vast difference."

"I'm sorry," Julia said, leaning into him. "My bad."

"Okay, but now you get it, right? It's a vast difference," Sam repeated.

"Yes, I get it. It's a vast difference."

"Vast."

Vast. Julia thought of the vastness of Central Park, viewed from the Pierre. The vastness of the sky. She swerved unconsciously toward the flat wood-topped railing along the perimeter, directly across from the curving staircase that led to the Ferris wheel. She stopped. Gazed up. Inhaled deeply.

Sam moved alongside her. "What's up?" He chuckled under his breath at his own joke.

"There's going to be a full moon in a couple of days, a mega Beaver Moon."

She could feel Sam staring at her. "A what?"

"A mega Beaver Moon."

"A beaver moon?" Sam raised an eyebrow.

"Not that kind of beaver," Julia said, pushing his shoulder with her own. "It's what the Native Americans called the full moon in November because, you know, that's when they had to set their beaver traps, before the waters froze."

"No, I did *not* know that. Question is, why do you?"

"My dad." Julia sighed, staring at the night sky. "He studied astronomy in college. He used to take me out in the backyard at night, even when I was a baby. He'd lay me on his chest and recite poetry. Point out the constellations. He knew all the Indian names for the full moons: Wolf Moon, January; Strawberry Moon, June . . . Beaver Moon—"

"November," Sam said with her, pulling her closer, nuzzling the top of her head. "And I'm guessing a mega moon is, what, some kind of supermoon?"

"No, bigger. Supermoons are actually pretty common, just full moons when the moon's orbit brings it close to the Earth. A *mega* moon is really rare because the sun is in line with the earth in the exact right position to pull the moon even closer, so ..." Julia turned, saw Sam was still smiling. She shrugged. Looked back at the sky. "Anyway, it'll be closer, and bigger and brighter, than in like seventy years. My dad used to keep this calendar . . . and there was a point when he knew he wouldn't be here for it, so he made me promise I'd remember, which I almost didn't."

Julia was glad her father would never know she'd almost forgotten the mega Beaver Moon. That she'd been in an in-patient psychiatric facility because she'd given up on life. That she'd given up on so many things, long before she should.

She heard Sam say "Seventy years?" as she pivoted and took two steps toward the wheel circling above them.

"We should go on the ride," she said, trying to sound confident even as the pit in her stomach reopened and the possibility of losing her shit hit again. She needed a bathroom.

Sam remained by the railing. "Wait, hold on. *When* is this mega moon? Two days from now?"

"Two or three. It'll look full for a couple of days." Julia took a few more steps, approaching the bottom of the staircase. "I don't remember which night it's a hundred percent full. Why?"

Sam caught up to her, then silently lifted his hands, fingers wide, creating a right-angled frame around the moon. "And it'll be bigger and brighter than it's been for seventy years?"

"Mm-hmm. The next time it'll be this close will be 2034. I'll be thirty-six." Julia recalled her father hugging her after she'd done the calculation, murmuring in a voice that sounded far, far away, "Thirty-six, with children of your own." How could she have forgotten?

"Seriously?" Sam turned to her, his hands dropping. "2034? So this could be a once-in-a-lifetime thing? Like if you were born at the wrong time, you might never see one?"

"Yeah," Julia said, taking a few steps up, thinking *or if you died at the wrong time*. Despite her father's love for it, the universe didn't align for him to see a mega moon.

She couldn't dwell on these thoughts for long. She forced herself to keep walking, focusing on the wooden slats making up the staircase. Three to a stair. With each step up, her gut twisted, accelerating toward full churn. Abruptly, only a few steps from the top, her ascent was halted. Sam was gripping her by the shoulders, the blue and white lights of the Ferris wheel illuminating his face.

"So what you're saying is, the biggest, brightest moon in seventy years is occurring at exactly the time we could be taking pictures of the moon at one of the most iconic places to take pictures of the moon."

"I guess so."

"Goddamn." Sam shook his head slowly. "Don't you see? This is a sign."

"A sign?"

"Yeah, a sign. Definitely. A. Sign. Hear me out. I've got this book where Ansel Adams goes into his best-known photos—where they were taken, how they were taken—and one of them is a picture of the moon over Half Dome. Not the one I've got, that's in the book too, but another one, literally called 'Moon and Half Dome'—I'm sure you've seen it—anyway, he says each time you see Half Dome, it's different, 'it is never the *same* Half Dome, never the same light or the same mood.' His exact words, 'never the same mood.'"

Sam's voice took on the same intensity he'd had in the courtyard at Brookfield. "And now I get it. I can see it, in my mind's eye, the picture I'm supposed to take: 'Monolith' with a mega moon. And *you're the key to all of it*. Without you, I wouldn't be here, I wouldn't be doing this, now, this way."

The key to all of it. Julia's thoughts turned back to Camus, how she'd thought the book might be the key to Sam and how mostly it was confusing her.

He was lifting his face again to the sky, reframing the moon with his fingers. Julia felt herself swaying without the steadying presence of his hands on her shoulders.

"Two days?" he asked again, still framing.

"I think so." Julia hoped she was right.

"We can make it."

He tilted the frame again, this time toward the Ferris wheel, and then he froze. The harsh expression she'd seen when he was frustrated returned. "How—did you—"

"I'm sorry. We're too late to get on, aren't we?" she said.

Sam's whole body seemed to shudder. "It doesn't matter," he said. "We have to go." He turned away from her and the wheel and, reversing their progress, descended back toward the water. "We have to go now, or it'll all be for naught."

Julia tried to catch up with Sam, and his thoughts. "What will be for naught?"

Sam didn't answer.

"Sam, what will be for naught?"

Sam paused. "All of it," he said, looking back at her. "I'm not going to let anyone stop me, Julia. Not them. Not you. We can do this. We have to." His hand reached for hers. "We may have to change our plans, reorder things."

Julia nodded. She couldn't ride the Ferris wheel or bring her father back, but she could be there for Sam. She remembered her thoughts back at the Pierre Hotel: she could save Sam. She slipped her hand into his, but Sam wasn't looking at her anymore. His attention was focused somewhere ahead she couldn't identify, clearly not on the Ferris wheel. Risking the chance of tripping, Julia glanced back to see the wheel was no longer moving.

Relief washed through her, shadowed with regret. Unshed tears refracted and haloed the blue and white lights, creating an impressionistic blur as she turned away. Impressionism rapidly evolved into the surreal when, as she and Sam reached the bottom of the stairs, Julia could have sworn she heard the wheel itself calling her name: "Julia. Julia."

ARABELLA

THE SOUND OF AN AIRPLANE engine overhead woke Arabella from restless sleep. The alarm clock between her double bed and the other, empty one in the room read 3:30.

She wondered if Laura was sleeping. She wondered if Sam was sleeping.

Was anyone sleeping?

One thing was certain: Laura had been even more tightly wound than Arabella.

Tightly wound with pent-up fury.

Fury that they'd been too distracted. Fury that they'd gone on the Ferris wheel instead of remaining on the ground. She'd dismissed Arabella's suggestion that they might not have seen Sam and Julia at all if they hadn't spied them from the circling gondola. Clearly, Laura blamed her for their inability to physically encounter their wayward children, to stop them in their tracks. Arabella argued that even if they had done the former, the latter was not guaranteed.

"It's not like we can put them in restraints. They would have had to voluntarily decide to go with us."

Arabella knew all too well the drawbacks inherent in legislation designed to protect the rights of the mentally unwell; once a child turned eighteen, a parent's ability to make decisions in their child's best interests became incredibly difficult. As one mother had said during a support group, "Talk about letting the insane run the asylum," which had prompted a near meltdown of the session, accusations flying over politically correct terminology rapidly overwhelming the sentiment the poor woman had been trying to express: Is it reasonable and fair to expect an individual who is mentally unstable or unwell to make good decisions about their mental health?

Of course, Arabella hadn't gotten into any of that with Laura. It hadn't been the right time or place. Instead, holding herself in check, she'd listened to Laura, thinking sometimes it was helpful to be in possession of her hereditary stiff upper lip, even briefly considering how her parents must have felt when she'd brought up Sam's struggles.

With the intention of returning the rental car, Arabella had dropped Laura off at a hotel in possession of an airport shuttle for the morning transport back to O'Hare.

"I'll see you in the morning," Arabella had said, looking over her shoulder to where Laura stood outside the back passenger door, retrieving her overnight bag. "I am sorry things didn't go as you'd hoped."

Laura stood still for a few seconds, poised to close the door, the molded steel edge in her hand. "Honestly," she said, "I'm not sure what to hope for anymore."

She released the door with a slight push and turned away.

Arabella watched Laura take two steps and stop, her shoulders releasing with a sigh Arabella could not hear. Putting the car into drive, Arabella matched the sigh with one of her own. Then, before she could pull away from the curb, Laura reappeared in the front passenger window. Arabella lowered it.

"I wanted to tell you that I'm sorry too. And I appreciate your honesty, about Sam." Laura looked distinctly uncomfortable. "I just wanted to tell you that."

Arabella had nodded, her insides filling with another bubble of guilt. She'd told Laura quite a bit, but she'd left out what she worried about most.

That's what she thought about now, lying in the dark, listening to another airplane. The bubble returned—psychological indigestion. She sat up, thumped her sternum with the butt of her hand, and stared at the blank television screen as if the answers were hidden there.

Should I tell her what happened the last two times Sam attempted to make this trip?

The first time, Iliana, eighteen, a freshman at NYU. She and Sam made it to Ohio before he'd grown irritated—feeling, as he put it, "as though he were going to jump out of his skin if she said another word." Iliana's voice, her mannerisms, her very presence made him feel trapped, so he'd pulled off at an exit and left her at a gas station. Alone. Without a phone or any money. She'd promised payment to the clerk upon rescue, borrowed a phone, and called her father. He'd called Max because they worked together, which is how Iliana and Sam met in the first place, at the firm's partners' Labor Day celebration in East Hampton.

An idyllic setting for a young romance.

Max's partner had been furious that Sam convinced his daughter to skip out of her freshman year of college and embark on some wild-ass journey, only to leave her within days of their departure. "Jesus, Max, what kind of person leaves a girl on the side of the road? What's wrong with your son?"

"He's got some issues," Max had reported saying, followed by "He's working on them. What can we do to make it up to you, to Iliana?"

The partner had been relatively calm, Max said, "all things considered." His demands were simple: a spa day for Iliana and her mother, who was furious, and keep Sam away.

"Like I'd want to spend any more time with her," Sam said to Arabella. This comment had irked her, but it was the next one that caused her alarm. "I left her there for her own good."

He wouldn't explain what he meant.

"Does she want me to destroy the pictures?" he asked.

Apparently, photographs had been taken. In the style of Stieglitz. Iliana's hands. Her profile. Her breasts. It was art, Sam claimed, but it wasn't very good art. "There has to be a connection," he'd told Arabella. "And when all was said and done, I didn't feel one. She wasn't at all who I thought she was. She was a pampered pain in the ass. Demanding as hell. Her wanting a spa day doesn't surprise me in the least. I'm surprised she didn't ask for a week."

Arabella hadn't told Max about the photographs.

Or the pampered demanding character aspersions.

She'd called Iliana's mother and apologized profusely. Offered to meet for coffee. The invitation was politely declined, which didn't surprise Arabella; most of the friendships she'd thought she had through Max's work had ended with the divorce. Arabella had been relieved. She'd grown tired of the pitying glances and conversations that ended abruptly each time she entered the room, the whispers they thought she couldn't hear.

And Sam was probably right. It was highly likely Iliana was a pampered, demanding pain in the ass—but she was a pampered, demanding pain in the ass who could look out for herself. She'd missed a few classes. No harm had been done.

Second trip, Carolyn, a girl more like Julia: young, beautiful in an unusual way, emotionally fragile. Sam met Carolyn, age nineteen to his twenty-one, at a yoga class when she was two weeks into a ninety-day transition program from a dual-diagnosis rehabilitation program. Arabella met her only once and was never quite clear on Carolyn's underlying psych diagnosis nor the drug to which she'd been addicted, and Sam hadn't been much help in terms of information sharing.

What Arabella did know was that Sam thought Carolyn was a kindred soul: misunderstood, committed to finding her best self, and fully embracing alternative methods of healing—hence the yoga, along with mindfulness, philosophical study, and vegan-based cleanses. Sam informed Arabella shortly after they met that he and Carolyn had decided to journey cross-country with only what they could carry—which, as far as Arabella could determine, comprised backpacks and misplaced idealism. They intended to eschew technology, wealth, and "bougie trappings," Sam said, relying on the universe to provide, learning about the world from fellow wayfarers and travelers—or some such drivel. Arabella had tried to appeal to reason, had pleaded with Sam to at least take a phone, for emergencies.

"Don't worry," he'd said. "We're going to be fine. We've got this."

Then he'd fallen off the grid.

There'd been radio silence for four and a half weeks, until Arabella received a call from an acute-care hospital. Sam had been found in a parking lot—hungry, dehydrated, disoriented, agitated. And alone. Carolyn was not with him. When questioned after being given an IV and meds, Sam told Arabella he'd stopped sleeping completely for days. He and Carolyn had both fallen prey to phantoms and turned against each other. The last memory he had of her was in a weed-infused van with a surfboard on top and a mattress in back.

He never heard from Carolyn again. Though Arabella considered making an anonymous call to the police to see if a young woman named Carolyn had been reported missing, in the end she did nothing. Arabella told herself it wasn't her concern, but the truth was that a part of her did not want to know what had happened, and between the gallery and getting Sam back to Brookfield, she had enough on her plate.

After treatment, Sam had been better. He'd followed the medication regimen prescribed by Dr. Renner, given up veganism and cleanses, moderated the yoga and philosophizing. He'd taken photography classes, worked incessantly in his darkroom, managed to get a gallery in Chelsea to take a few of his pieces without Arabella making a call. He'd even talked about returning to school, but then, without warning it seemed, he went off the rails again.

And again.

Each time he left the hospital or Brookfield, Arabella got her hopes up. And now . . . How could she explain to Laura what she didn't understand herself? *What is going on inside my son's heart and mind? What really happened with Carolyn? What is he going to do next?*

JULIA

IT HAD BEEN ELEVEN HOURS SINCE they'd driven out of Chicago, and though they'd refueled, Sam didn't want to stop for food until Julia begged to pull off for a Denny's. She had been awake since dawn and needed a break from the monotony of the scenery: flat land dotted with hay bales and irrigation systems that resembled strings of airplane axles; an occasional forlorn tree or cluster of buildings around a horse or barn; wood fences, wire fences, wood and wire fences. She'd tried to pass time by freeze-framing images through the passenger window, imagining what she might sketch or draw to capture it, the palette that might be needed, a palette that varied little from image to image.

Unfortunately, other than the golden sign with red lettering, Denny's didn't add much in the way of color. Daylight shining through dirty windows made the interior of the restaurant appear dim and dingy, and the faded earth-tone decor did nothing to help: dull green walls, beige booths with pecan-colored pleather backs, a gray and brown carpet that reminded her of dried mud.

Same palette, she thought.

As soon as they were seated, Sam ordered coffee, pushed the menu away, and informed her he wasn't hungry, adding "We're wasting time."

Thinking his mood was likely to improve if he ate, Julia tried to tempt him, extolling the virtue of dining options and the menu itself, the only colorful thing of note. "Come on, Sam. I mean, look at these pictures. Even you have to admit the photography's impressive. How about a Grand Slam? You can customize it however you want—French toast, ham, Belgian waffles. And drinking coffee on an empty stomach can't be good for you."

She didn't mention how his hands seemed to be shaking whenever he wasn't using them purposefully.

She handed him his menu again, and he began flipping the pages back and forth, rapidly. "Hate to break your bubble, but the real food's not going to look anything like these pictures, and this isn't helping us achieve anything."

Julia smiled, kept her voice light. "Except that we need to eat."

The page flipping continued—back and forth, back and forth. "Yeah, okay, there is that."

"Yeah, there is that," Julia repeated. Still smiling, she reached out to touch his arm.

Sam flinched slightly, then looked up, took in her smile, and smiled back.

Thank God.

"Point taken," he said, continuing to flip pages. "But Denny's is of no use with your list. No blue cheese. No escargot. No flan. And no Brussels sprouts. Looks like every entrée comes with broccoli. Lots of broccoli." More page flipping. "They must get some kind of deal on it."

"Probably freezes well and clearly films well. I mean, look at the intensity of that green." A waitress three tables away was heading in their direction. Julia lowered her voice to a conspiratorial whisper. "Kind of a shame. We're in the middle of farmland, but I'm relatively certain Denny's serves frozen vegetables."

"Indubitably, given the intensity of the green." Sam's irritation seemed to dissipate further. He closed the menu and pushed it to the edge of the table. "You know, I'm thinking, after Yosemite, we should go to San Francisco before we head back to New Mexico. Have you been?"

Julia shook her head, half-listening, half-absorbed with deciding between French toast and pancakes.

"We'll be able to accomplish more there. The pedicure, for sure. We can get a copy of *The Catcher*. The snails, blue cheese, flan."

"We don't have any of those." The waitress had arrived. Youngish, maybe thirty. Circles under her eyes, sallow skin, a solid inch of brown roots, she looked tired and pissed off, like she'd been working all night and was ready to go home. She was wearing a wedding ring. A tattoo snuck out from under her shirt collar along her neck, a tail of some sort. Julia's mind wandered for a few seconds: Where did she live? What did her husband do for a living? Did they have children? Julia pictured a small house, a baby girl in a onesie asleep in a crib, her butt up in the air, a little boy in fire engine pajamas. She imagined the woman pulling into the driveway, looking forward to lying down, calculating the tips she'd earned—

"Julia, babe," Sam was saying, "what do you want?"

The waitress was staring at her, doing something odd with her mouth, clearly bored or annoyed, or both.

"Oh, sorry," Julia said. "I'll have the French toast slam. With bacon?"

"Eggs?"

"Scrambled, please."

"And?" The waitress turned to Sam, doing the odd thing with her mouth again, as if she were trying to extract something from a molar with her tongue. Maybe she had a cavity and couldn't afford to pay a dentist. Or it could be a habit, like Julia's hair pulling and thigh pressing, a need to spark sensation. Julia wondered about her own curiosity about this woman from Nebraska whose name tag read "Melanie," a woman Julia would probably never see again.

Sam ordered an omelet, no meat. Repeated his request for coffee. Asked for crayons.

Julia watched Melanie walk away. She had another tattoo, on the back of her right arm. Retreating, it looked like an elaborate brain on one side, a flower on the other, which startled

Julia. She realized she'd made judgments about Melanie from Nebraska—she would have thought a tattoo on the woman's arm would be a butterfly or a rose. Having dropped the menus in their appointed slot alongside the front register, tired, annoyed, elaborately inked Melanie grabbed a handful of used crayons and deposited them on their table with a sideways glance—disapproval mixed with something Julia couldn't decipher.

Sam had already flipped their paper place mats over. He picked up the crayons and distributed them across the table.

"Since we're here and this time will otherwise go entirely to waste—"

"Other than the food," Julia interrupted, redeploying her smile.

"Other than the food," Sam conceded. "My mom used to do this with me at restaurants when I was little. Quick draw," he said, holding his forearms parallel to the table—a gunslinger about to engage in a duel, his fingers twitching.

"Quick draw?"

"Yeah, we alternate calling out an object, say 'Draw,' and then whoever finishes first with a recognizable facsimile of said object wins. Keep it small so there's room for multiple rounds." Sam motioned to the crayons. "We'll start easy, ready? Bouquet of flowers and . . . draw."

Julia scooped up four crayons, thinking maybe Sam had seen Melanie's brain/flower. She began drawing looped petals with the intention of adding contrasting centers when Sam shouted "Done," ceremoniously dropping the crayons in his hands on the table before spinning his place mat to display a riot of curled color he'd created by holding three crayons at the same time, complete with a fury of green stems and a few leaves. It was quite beautiful.

"Wow," Julia said, looking up. "I don't know if I can—"

"No, no. I had a head start since I chose the object. Your turn."

Julia thought for a moment. "A horse, running and . . . draw."

"Shit, seriously?"

Julia nodded, her hand already moving across the bottom corner of her place mat. Sam drew a few lines then stopped. She could feel his eyes on her.

"Man, you're good," he said as she finished the hind quarters, the angled legs, the flowing mane and tail, all in motion. Julia lifted the crayon, whispered "Done."

Sam spun her place mat, shook his head. "With a fucking Denny's crayon." Holding his hands as if in prayer, he lifted them to his forehead and bowed. "To the greater talent," he said. "I concede defeat."

Julia felt her face flushing. "I've been drawing horses forever. It's like a thing, girls and horses." She reached for his hands, grasped them in her own in the same shape. She could feel a tremor radiating from his forearms. "Hands, arms, faces, torsos. Those are hard."

Sam nodded slowly, looking directly at her hands folded over his. "'Praying Hands,' Albrecht Dürer."

"Pen and ink."

"Yes." Sam pulled his hands out from within hers. "Another one of my favorites . . ." He picked up two crayons and then laid his hands flat on his place mat, the right hand on top, the left beneath, the crayons poised. "Escher's 'Drawing Hands.'"

Julia smiled, recalling the image to which he was referring, in which each three-dimensional hand is drawing a two-dimensional shirt cuff and wrist of the other hand, drawing one another into existence. She thought of other Escher images: a hand holding a reflective globe with the artist's hand, face, and the room behind him—literally holding the world in which he exists, a series of black and white shapes becoming birds flying from a city of light to a city in the dark that reminded her of *The Myth* cover art.

"I read an article about him, Escher," Sam said, his right hand now moving over the place mat, creating crayon curlicues. "About how he longed to express the impossible." He stopped mid-curlicue. "Apparently, he was a big fan of Camus."

Julia sat back. "Seriously?"

Sam smiled. "Yeah, you know his most famous piece, 'Ascending and Descending'? The one with the people walking on the staircase that seems to be going both up and down at the same time?" The curlicues became right angles.

Julia nodded.

"Yeah, well, he wrote this letter to a friend, right after Camus died in a car crash." Sam began shading the angles, creating steps. "He said 'Ascending and Descending' was about the absurdity of life, how we're all walking up and down, getting tired, and going nowhere."

Julia sighed, tilting her head.

"What's wrong?" Sam asked.

"Can this wait 'til after breakfast?"

"Indeed," he said. "Alas, I have digressed and risked ruining this splendid repast." This time it was his turn to use a smile to deflect. "Okay, I've got another one for you. Continue channeling 'famous pictures of hands.'" He turned his torso sideways in the booth and reclined, leaning on his left forearm. Then he lifted his right knee and rested his right arm upon it, fingers outstretched. Raising an eyebrow, he whispered, "Now, imagine me naked."

If I was blushing before, I must be bright red now, Julia thought as she glanced around. No one was looking at them. Melanie was nowhere to be seen.

"And there's another hand reaching for mine."

An image began to form in Julia's head.

Sam went on. "Artist known for meticulous drawings of the human form, and the divine."

It was suddenly clear.

"Michelangelo," Julia said. "Adam, the Sistine Chapel."

Sam gave her a shit-eating grin. "Yes!" He shot up to a sitting position, grabbed for her hands again. "You can see how this is going to be amazing, right?"

Melanie approached and placed plates in front of them, a little pitcher of syrup.

"This trip is only the beginning. It's bigger. It's both the end of one part of our lives and the beginning of the next, the culmination and the commencement."

And Sam was off, talking about how he'd mastered the car's navigation system while she was sleeping, how he'd forced it to calculate all the available routes, how he'd begun to envision the next journey from California to New Mexico, the museum, how they could make a new list, their list together. How many wondrous places there were to explore, and with his visualization come to fruition and her incredible natural talent, they would be unstoppable. She could study at NYU or Columbia while he opened a studio of his own. His energy was infectious. Julia found herself caught up in his excitement.

Or maybe it's the commencement of a super sugar high. Julia swallowed another mouthful of syrup-soaked French toast. *Denny's version of ecstasy.*

"The nav says we have another twenty-one hours to Yosemite, which probably means the edge of the park, and we have to drive in, probably another hour or so, to the head of the trail."

"Where *is* the head of the trail?"

Sam scooched forward in his seat and pulled folded paper from his back pocket. "I printed this while chatting with Sheila." He paused, tilted his head as if considering asking Julia a question, his expression solemn, grave even. Julia swallowed hard, held her breath, waiting, a forkful of eggs held aloft. After what seemed an eternity, but was probably five seconds, Sam said, "Like I said, she's a real talker. I imagine she might ruin things that require keeping silent." He paused again, looked right at Julia.

Was he referring to her talking to Sheila, using Sheila's phone?

"Like birding." He waited a beat before going on. "Humpty Dumpty. Those eggs are going to fall."

Julia put the fork in her mouth.

Sam unfolded the paper, moved his plate a few inches to the right, separated and smoothed the printed sheets. The top sheet displayed two black and white photographs, a copy of "Monolith" and a self-portrait of Ansel Adams. The artist stood in front of a rocky hillside, holding a remote shutter release attached to a bellowed camera that vaguely resembled the one Sam had used to photograph Julia in his apartment.

"He took the shot from the Diving Board, here." Sam turned the top sheet in Julia's direction, pointing to a spot on the first photograph, a snow-covered rock jutting up and out from the lower-right-hand corner of the image.

"Picture this," he began dramatically. "It's a cold, windy day in April 1927, and a skinny twenty-five-year-old photographer convinces his fiancé, Virginia, who he *married* later the next year"—Sam looked up, raising his eyebrow at Julia—"to go climbing with him so he can take pictures for a portfolio he's putting together for this guy Bender."

"Bender?"

"Yeah. See, about a year earlier, our young artist, Ansel Adams, was invited by a musician friend to play the piano at a party in San Francisco—"

"Ansel Adams played the piano?"

"Yeah, most people don't know it, but he was a super-talented pianist. In fact, for a while, he didn't know which to pursue—music or photography. Anyway, this musician friend tells him to bring along some photos because this wealthy business-guy-slash-art-collector, Albert Bender, is going to be there. So Ansel goes to the party, plays the piano, meets Albert Bender, and shows him a few of his photos. Bender's impressed, asks to meet again the very next day, and suggests he put together a portfolio Bender can sell to wealthy friends. Fifty bucks a pop, which is *huge* money, way more than Adams can make teaching piano, enough that he's convinced to go with photography over music. But on that fateful day in April—the day of the hike— he's only identified about half the images he needs and none of them are of Half Dome, so he decides to climb up to the Diving Board to get one. Now remember, there's no Patagonia back then—no fleece jackets or Vibram-soled boots—so even though there's still snow on the ground, he's wearing Keds basketball shoes, he's got window sash cord for rope, and he's carrying forty pounds of equipment—camera, tripod, lenses, glass plates. I told you about the plates, didn't I?"

Julia shook her head, put another bite in her mouth, thinking *that explains the Keds.*

"I didn't?" Sam said. "Really?"

Julia shook her head again, her brain catching up. *Will we need rope?*

"Well, this is a great story. See, he brought along these twelve glass plates, Wratten Panchromatic glass plates to be precise, which, unfortunately, are no longer available. Anyway, that day in April, Adams starts taking pictures on the way up, but because of the wind, the camera moves, ruining a couple of the negatives, and by the time they get to the Diving Board, he's already used seven of the plates."

Sam looked at her expectantly, waiting for a reaction.

"Seven plates," Julia said, hoping this response was sufficient.

"Exactly, seven plates, out of twelve. Then, when they get to the Diving Board, he takes a photograph of Virginia standing out on the edge—this lone figure in a vast expanse."

Julia thought of herself two nights ago, alone and anxious, high above the vastness of Central Park. *How high was this Diving Board? Was Virginia anxious?*

"Which means eight used. Then he ruins two by overexposing one and improperly seating the holder for the other, and now he's down to two and he hasn't taken a single shot of Half Dome, which, when they arrive, is still in the shadows. So they've got to wait for the light. They sit for a while, have lunch, and then Ansel sets up the camera, but he's in this precarious position, with an abyss on the one side and a bunch of rocks on the other."

Julia paused with the fork near her mouth. *An abyss?*

"Finally, the light is right. The face of the dome is half in shadow, half in light, and he takes the first photograph with a Wratten No. 8 yellow filter and exposure factor of 2, and he knows, pretty much right away, it's not right; it isn't going to have the 'emotional texture' he wants." Sam added air quotes. "But he's down to his last plate." Sam then slowed the pace of the story. "That twelfth plate, and he knows, he can see 'in his mind's eye,' what the image is supposed to look like, and he knows how to create it. A red filter instead of yellow, five-second exposure at f/22 and—" Sam pulled the copy of the

"Monolith" photograph back out from under the map with a mini-flourish. "We get to see what he saw, in perpetuity. And it's fucking beautiful."

"'Art is not what you see, but what you make others see.'"

"Yes. Exactly. Degas." Sam's eyes were shining. "The twelfth and final plate. The last one. The photograph that made him famous almost didn't happen."

Sam shook his head slowly. Julia looked down at her plate, the pooled syrup, a smaller pool of melted butter, the remains of the lone half strawberry that had been there purely for adornment. She compared it to Sam's plate, still holding more than half of his omelet.

"How many plates did you bring?"

"Me? None. I use sheet film, Ilford. It's good. Manufacturers stopped making dry plates a long time ago. It's next to impossible to get them. There're still a few commercial ones out there, places like Russia, Eastern Europe, some antique ones online, but no one'll guarantee you can capture an image on 'em. Can't be sure how they were stored. I considered making my own—websites out there that teach you how to do it—and there's been this revival for wet-plate collodion, but that requires instant developing, so it's incredibly hard to do in the field 'cause you need a portable darkroom—not impossible, but incredibly hard. Plus, the chemicals include some dangerous shit."

Julia recalled the brown bottles in Sam's darkroom, the box of medicine with the danger label. Visions of pills swam through her head: euphoria-inducing pink bunny pills; pills that were supposed to save her but made her want to die; medicine-cabinet leftovers with the power to kill; Sam's meds that made her feel better; the ones he should be taking—and wasn't.

His current medicine couldn't have been in the box. He wouldn't have had time to put it there. Does he still have it? Can I convince him to take it?

Julia looked directly at Sam. "Sam—"

"I know. Again, I digress. You wanted to know about the trail." Sam placed the paper with the photographs under the others, turning the top one toward Julia again. "It's a little complicated. There are a few ways to get to the Diving Board, but I think the best approach is here, Nevada Falls, off the Mist Trail, and then . . ." Sam traced his finger over a map with dozens of concentric squiggly lines. Julia tried to pay attention. She heard words like "gully" and "ridge," which she thought she knew, and other words she'd thought she knew that seemed to have different meanings altogether—words like "cairns" and "scrambling," which did not seem to refer to a dog breed or a method of egg preparation.

As with Kierkegaard and Camus, f-stops and filters, sheet film and Ilford, Sam was speaking a language Julia did not know.

He waved toward the waitress, indicating he wanted her to bring their check.

"I *am* sorry about the museum, Julia," he said, refolding the papers. "But as it is, we're barely going to make it. We'll have to start hiking as early as possible tomorrow to make it for the moonrise."

"Tomorrow? We're doing the hike tomorrow?"

"Yeah." Sam looked puzzled as to why she was puzzled. "You said the mega moon would be tomorrow night."

"And the next one too. Sam, we can't make it by tomorrow *and* hike up. We have to stop to sleep."

"Stop?" Sam said it as if this was the craziest idea he'd ever heard. "We've got miles to go before we sleep, babe. Miles to go before we sleep."

Sam smiled as he delivered this line. Julia bristled without quite knowing why.

Melanie approached and dropped a slip of paper on the table. She picked up Julia's plate, looked over at Sam's half-full one. "You done?"

"Yeah," Sam responded. Picking up the bill, he looked at Julia. "Listen, don't worry. We'll alternate driving. Sleep in the car. We'll be fine. Seriously, don't worry."

Two "don't worries" in the span of five seconds.

Sam slid to the edge of the booth seat, stood up. "We should probably use the bathrooms here, so we don't have to make another stop 'til we need gas again."

Julia stayed put. "I'll be right behind you," she said. "I'm going to ask for a to-go cup of water so I can take my meds."

If I'm going to get Sam to take his, Julia thought, *now is as good a time as any to bring it up.*

"And, Sam, maybe you could take yours too?"

Sam froze for an instant, the light from the window illuminating his profile. Then, without a word, he walked away.

JULIA

POST-DENNY'S, JULIA ATTEMPTED to take her Prozac in the SUV in a manner Sam wouldn't notice, holding the bottle off to her right side, next to her knee, as she opened the childproof top; palming the pill in her left hand as she tried to close the bottle and put it back into the pocket of the car door next to *The Myth* without a sound; turning her head toward the side window as she moved her left hand up to her mouth while sipping from the cup of water held in her right.

Silence filled the space between them. She heard Sam exhale sharply through his nose, kind of a short snort, and she turned to see him shaking his head in a gesture she interpreted as veiled disgust. He'd said he was glad she was getting out of the shit, so why did he want her to feel guilty for taking something that helped her?

And they were—the little white tablets with the FL | 20 on them were helping her.

Julia could feel her heart beating in her chest. "Sam, I get that you don't want to take anything, I do. I get that it's complicated, more than you know." *Please help me.* The image of an orange bottle tucked under a pillow floated on the edge of consciousness, then sitting at the edge of a full bathtub, opening bottle after bottle. "I want to understand."

Sam didn't respond.

"Sam?"

"We haven't finished Camus."

"What?"

"We haven't finished. I'll talk about it after we do."

"Why? Do you not take medicine because of Camus?"

"No, I don't—Holy shit!" Sam hit the brakes, veering the SUV off to the right shoulder. "Do you see that?"

Julia had no idea what he was referring to. There was nothing out of the ordinary, simply more pavement, painted lines, flat land, fences, road signs.

The tires spewed gravel as Sam brought the car to a halt. He shifted into park, unlatched his seatbelt and, without looking behind him for oncoming cars, threw the door open.

"Sam!" Julia's head spun to act as sentinel for him. A pickup truck swerved from the right lane to the left as Sam shut the front door and moved to the rear one.

"This'll only take a minute," Sam said, grabbing his backpack by the strap.

Before she could react, Sam disappeared behind the car. Julia slowly copied his actions, unlatching her own seatbelt and opening the door. Stepping down, she saw Sam jogging away behind the SUV. After about twenty paces, he turned, unzipped the pack, and removed the 35mm camera. He dropped the bag to the ground at his feet and stood motionless, his eyes in a semi-squint, his lips pursed.

Julia turned to gaze at the object in question, seeing nothing but a no-U-turn sign in the middle of the road.

In a smooth, practiced movement, Sam shook the flop of hair from his eyes and brought the camera up. Julia heard the click of the shutter followed by Sam muttering to himself. He dropped the camera slightly, tilted his head, and took a step backward, repeating the shutter click and murmuring. Click. Click.

And then, before she could say a word, he was passing her, walking rapidly.

"Got it. Let's go—" Sam's next words were enveloped by the sound of an eighteen-wheeler, also passing her, a whoosh of warm air in its wake.

Sam was already in the car when she climbed up, his eyes bright. He reached for her, cupped her jaw in both hands, and kissed her, hard.

"It's working, Julia," he whispered. "It's definitely working."

And in an instant, his hands were gone, the SUV in drive, the wheels crunching gravel again, this time as they peeled away.

After a moment, Julia asked, "What's working?"

"This," Sam replied, waving his arm in a tight circle between them. "You. Me. I'm seeing the images as they can be, their potential. And I can't wait to show you. Especially the third one. That was the one."

"What were you taking a picture of? The no-U-turn sign?"

"Yes. Of course. No turning back, don't you see?"

Julia could feel the SUV accelerating. She looked over at the speedometer, rapidly climbing then hovering near 95.

"Let's finish it," Sam said, gesturing with his head to the pocket in the side door where *The Myth* cover was peeking out. "Then we can discuss it all—everything that matters: courage and revolt and passion and mortality."

So Julia retrieved the slim paperback, flipped the pages open to locate where she'd left off, and began reading. It was clear Sam had known exactly where they were in the book when, several lines in, she came upon a passage about courage and revolt and passion ending with "Assured of his temporally limited freedom, of his revolt devoid of future, and of his mortal consciousness, he lives out his adventure within the span of his lifetime—"

"Yes, that's it," Sam interrupted. "Read that again."

She did.

"Good, yes. Do you get it? That's it, right there. Courage to live authentically, knowing your time is short, living adventurously here, now. Okay, go on."

Julia had read only one or two more lines when Sam interrupted her again, this time laying his hand on her arm, pulling down on the book.

"Hold on," he said. "I've got an idea. The highlights, read just the highlights, okay?"

Julia flipped the pages, assessing the highlighted sections, far fewer in this part of the book relative to the earlier chapters. "Okay," she said. "Just the highlights."

Three or four highlights in, Julia realized the book was oddly more cohesive. Far less bewildered, she was getting a window into Sam's view of the text, how he saw the world of Camus. Then, without warning, her body jerked against the seatbelt. The SUV was veering right again, followed by gravel-crunching, gear-shifting, the door thrown open without a backward glance, the backpack removed. But this time, Sam stood along the passenger side of the car to snap three or four pictures of a stylized white teepee behind a wood post fence, complete with lodge poles.

Upon returning to the car, Sam behaved as if the teepee episode hadn't happened. When Julia didn't immediately begin reading again, he turned and, seeing her confused expression, said, "Sacred space. Sacred space. Keep going, quickly. We're getting to the best part."

Six highlights later came a quote from Nietzsche: "We have art in order not to die of the truth." Two later: "Creating is living doubly." And then, three later: "The work of art . . . marks both the death of an experience and its multiplication."

Julia stopped, thinking *Yes, that is exactly right, but why?* Before she could ask this question aloud, Sam said, "Yes, yes. And the next?"

As Julia read, Sam quoted along: "The artist commits himself and becomes himself in his work."

Before she could think at all, Sam instructed her again. "Okay, now 115. Bottom of the page."

"Wait, do you have all of the highlights memorized?"

"Most of 'em," Sam said. "Though every reading, I add a few, so it's a constant work in progress. Did you find it?"

Flipping to page 115, Julia wondered, *If he has it all memorized, why is he having me read it aloud?*

"Yes." Julia read the highlight to herself.

"And?"

She read it out loud. "'Perhaps the great work of art has less importance in itself than in the ordeal it demands of a man and the opportunity it provides him of overcoming his phantoms—'"

"That," Sam interrupted, "that explains our quest. The only thing more important begins on page 119."

Julia turned two pages and there it was: "The Myth of Sisyphus."

"First, the whole thing, and then, just the highlights."

Julia had just began reading when the SUV veered and slowed once again. Julia stopped, anticipating Sam jumping out of the car. This time, however, he didn't. He shifted into park, closed his eyes. "Go on," he said. "I just want to hear every word."

Reading with care, it took less than ten minutes, including rereading the highlights. It was a story Julia thought she knew, a tale about futility and wretchedness, a man pushing a rock up a hill, every day, forever. But Camus's take on it surprised her; it was filled with a strange, melancholic hope. While reading, she began to tear up, not because she felt sorry for Sisyphus or Sam, but rather because there was something noble in Camus's interpretation. She reached the final paragraph:

> *I leave Sisyphus at the foot of the mountain! One always finds one's burden again. But Sisyphus teaches the higher fidelity that negates the gods and raises rocks. He too concludes that all is well. This universe henceforth without a master seems to him neither sterile nor futile. Each atom of that stone, each mineral flake of that night filled mountain, in itself forms a world. The struggle itself towards the heights is enough to fill a man's heart. One must imagine Sisyphus happy.*

Recognizing the words Sam had said he wanted to ink on his arm, she looked over at him. His eyes were still closed, his head against the headrest.

Remaining in that position, he said, "Now, ask me anything."

"Anything?"

"Anything."

Julia thought of all the questions she wanted to ask. And then, before she could edit herself, words spilled. "When we were at Brookfield, you said it was for recalibration, to figure out the right medicine. Which one are you *supposed* to be taking?"

"You mean which *ones*?"

"There's more than one?"

"Yeah, all the usual ones."

"Which are?"

"It doesn't matter, because I'm not taking them."

"I know you aren't taking them. What I don't know is why. Don't they help?"

Sam turned to look at her. Then he put the car in gear, checked his side mirror, and pulled out into the right lane, accelerating rapidly. For a moment, Julia thought he was evading her question, but then he said, "Depends on what you mean. If you consider it helpful to numb the self, to destroy one's creative spirit to conform to societal demands of appropriate behavior, then yeah, I suppose they're helpful. But I prefer to be authentic. To use your father's poem, I prefer to be 'the master of my fate.'"

"But—" was all Julia got out before he went on.

"No, I get it. It's tempting to look for easier answers, to take medication that alters the reality of now, to fill the emptiness or dull the overwhelming, to believe in God and angels, or heaven and hell, when you want your life to have meaning."

She'd heard "dull the overwhelming" before, in *The Myth*.

"So I was right. You don't take medicine because of Camus."

Sam laughed, though he didn't seem amused. "He didn't put the idea in my head. But, yeah, his views confirm my convictions. I don't *want* to dull the overwhelming, because some of my best days are overwhelming. Days when I can feel what I see. Days when I can smell the stars. Days like today when I can see what the images I'm creating are going to look like, when I know these moments are the ones I'm supposed to be having. Not because of God's will or because I'm in some perfect medicated state, but because I'm in the right place at the right time with the right person. Because I'm in this moment, just as I am, with you, just as you are."

"But I'm taking something, and I might not be here without it."

"Then you should keep taking it. If it works for you, take it. We aren't in the same situation. Meds don't make me better. They just mute me. No, that's not right . . . they deaden everything. They deaden me."

No, Julia thought, *no*.

"So, no," Sam went on, "I don't believe in it. I don't believe in any of it."

Julia suddenly felt nauseous—and lost. "You don't believe in any of it."

"No, I don't. I don't believe there is some magical answer. I don't believe medication is some cure-all, and I don't believe there is a god, at least not one that controls events in my life. I don't believe in physical places in the hereafter, some utopian world without pain or suffering—or the opposite. Obviously, it'd be easier to live this life, here and now, tied up in some hope of a better future one or convinced of a worse one—but to me, that's a complete cop-out, just a way to avoid the really difficult questions about who we are and why we're here, whether self-determination has any meaning at all."

Sam glanced over at Julia.

"So, if you don't believe in any of that, what *do* you believe in?" she asked.

"What *do* I believe in?" Sam repeated. "I believe this. Most days, I push my fucking rock up the mountain, knowing what will happen when I get to the top. The rock will not stay there, and Michelangelo's God will not be reaching down to take my hand and say, 'Job well done. Henceforth, you will be free from trial and tribulation.'" Julia couldn't help but notice Sam's God voice sounded like his father's basso profundo. "Because that isn't the way things work. That would be easy, and life isn't easy. No, every day, I push the rock up knowing it will slip back down. I know I'll have to turn around and start all over again. Up and down and up and down. That's what real life is about—perseverance, and truth, and trying like hell to be in the moment, even when I know the light isn't going to last.

"And when Camus says 'the mineral flake of the night-filled mountain,' it's like he's talking to me. Like he's describing what I feel. And Half Dome. I can see it, Julia, the flinty silver of the rock, its jagged edges and dense power. I can smell the earth under my feet and see your mega Beaver Moon rising, illuminating everything. I can imagine myself capturing the light, finding myself then and there, and I can't wait to show you not just what I see, but what I feel."

Sam's voice rose as he spoke. He turned to look at her again, his eyes now blazing. Julia knew that, had he physically been in a position to do so, he'd be pacing in a circle, coiled energy propelling him.

Sam went on. "So yeah, there are times when I struggle to control my brain. But I refuse to give control to some medication because, even though it might allow me to avoid the black pit of night, it also means giving up the splendid—which means giving up the best parts of who I am—and that I won't do. I know who I am, and I'm not going to let the world tell me who to be. It's all right there on page 123: 'There is no sun without shadow.' I'd rather live thirty years of a wildly creative, passionate life with the risk of darkness than fifty years as some diluted, deadened version of myself. I know the risk. I've got the scars. But the last couple of days with you have only convinced me that I'm right about this—this, right now, is worth it."

Sam reached for Julia's hand, gripping it tightly. His energy radiated outward, into her.

"But what about the people who love you?" Julia's voice was shaking. "Don't we have a say in it? If we lose you, we have to live with it for the rest of our lives—wondering if only we'd done that one thing, said that one thing, that maybe we could have saved you."

Even as she said these words, recognition dawned. Though her father might have been ready to die, her mother wanted every moment she could have with him. And though she'd felt she couldn't go on and that her mother would be better off without her, Julia knew she had caused her mother's already-broken heart to break again. In the silence between her statement and Sam's next words, Julia wanted her mother. She wanted her mother's arms around her. She wanted to tell her mother she was sorry—for everything.

"Wait," Sam said, drawing her attention back to him. He looked as vulnerable as she felt. "You love me?"

Julia swallowed, nodded. "I do."

Sam's face grew solemn. "Really?"

Julia nodded again. Waited for him to say "I love you, too."

"Well, then, in answer to your question, you can live the rest of your life knowing you saw, and loved, the very best of me." Sam glanced her way before Julia could wipe her face clean of dashed hopes. "I wish I could say what you want to hear, that I'll do whatever I have to do to make you happy, but I can't. I can't say it because if there's one thing I should be allowed to be selfish about, it's determining the destiny of my soul. Loving others shouldn't require you to give up yourself."

"I—" Julia tried to break in, to explain that wasn't what she meant.

"I deserve to choose to live the life I've been given with the neurotransmitters I've got and the moods those neurotransmitters dictate. I deserve to choose my life, Julia. I deserve to choose the highs even if I know the lows will follow."

The car slowed noticeably. Sam went on, in a different tone of voice, soft yet intense. "That's the answer to your question: I don't take medicine because I don't want to live a deadened life. I'm willing to risk the chance of dying, so I can truly live."

These words struck a chord deep within Julia's psyche, a place she'd been before that she no longer recognized fully. She remembered the moment when she was sitting in Dr. Stein's dusty office, thinking she had to want to die to get a chance to live, how getting into Brookfield had felt like the most important second chance she'd ever have, because without it, she wouldn't have a second chance at anything else.

"You know, not long ago," Sam continued, "my mom and I were arguing about this very thing, and I looked up the definition of courage—do you know what the dictionary says? 'The mental or moral strength to venture, persevere, and withstand danger, fear, or difficulty.' You want to know what I believe in? That's what I believe in. That's what I'm striving for—to live courageously."

Pulled back into Sam's orbit, Julia barely registered that his voice had intensified yet again, slowing in direct contrast to the accelerating speed of the SUV.

"To truly live every moment in the face of all the odds stacked against me. Because I understand that not only does creativity require courage, life requires courage. And sometimes, Julia, sometimes love requires courage."

There was a beat of silence and then "Holy shit!"

And with that, the car veered right again, accompanied by the blare of a truck horn and the screeching sounds of an eighteen-wheeler's brakes, gears, and tires trying desperately to avoid a collision.

34

LAURA

A PALE BLUE SKY WITH A STREAK of clouds. Purple-gray mountains.

Laura could imagine being out on one of the many trails she knew surrounded the city of Santa Fe—Paul up ahead, his trusty navy pack on his back, the pink-hued sand trails, the red rocks and green brush, sage and pine, Julia behind him, looking down, following in his steps. But Paul was dead, Julia was God-knows-where, and she was in another rental car, shading her eyes against light reflecting off stucco walls that seemed to be everywhere. She'd left her sunglasses somewhere and couldn't remember when she'd last had them—in yesterday's rental car, the hotel room, the airport shuttle. This misplacement was not something that would normally upset her, and yet she'd found herself silently crying when they landed in New Mexico and the glasses were nowhere to be found.

Her ability to *Stop* also seemed to be missing.

"You're tired," Arabella had said with sympathy, holding out a pair of designer glasses Laura instantly knew she herself could never have afforded to buy. "Here, take mine."

Laura had declined the offer. However, Arabella was right; weariness had settled in, filling her head, her limbs.

It was three o'clock. The Georgia O'Keeffe museum would close in two hours, and it was unlikely Sam and Julia would make it before then. Even with the time change, assuming they drove straight through in record time, it remained a nineteen-hour drive and they'd been at Navy Pier at ten o'clock the night before, on a staircase under the Ferris wheel.

Like a video on infinite repeat, Laura had been replaying the scene over and over in her head, wondering how she could have done it differently.

THE GONDOLA SLOWLY LOOPING DOWN. Laura blurting out, "There they are—oh my god, there they are!" Instinctively splaying her open hands on the floor-to-ceiling windowed door. Calling her daughter's name: "Julia. Julia."

Laura's eyes locking on them.

Sam lifting his hands into a half frame and looking directly at the gondola in which she and Arabella were standing. Sam turning, descending the stairs, faster and faster, pulling Julia along.

Laura asking, "Do you think they saw us?"

Arabella responding, quietly, appearing paler, older, her face sorrowful, her accent strong. "I think perhaps he did."

The gondola so close to stopping at the bottom. The tiered exit area right there.

Right . . . there.

The doors sliding open and Laura dashing out, continuing to call "Julia, Julia." She and Arabella running in the direction their children had gone, down a flight of stairs, into the same garage in which their rental car was parked. Laura's voice echoing off the cement, each repetition of her daughter's name quieter than the last, until . . .

Silence.

They were gone.

The words "if only we hadn't gone on the ride" echoing inside Laura's head long after she stopped saying them aloud. Joined by "if we'd run faster" and "if we'd split up and monitored the garage exit."

Arabella's calm reasoning, "at least we know we're on the right track," not helping.

SHE AND ARABELLA HAD REACHED A quiet détente, the support-group confessional "Hello, I'm Laura/Arabella, and my child has a mental illness" conversations placed on hold. For the time being, Laura needed to erect an emotional wall between them. She was close to a breaking point. Her own pain and helplessness had stretched her already-thin capacity for empathy. She was certain to say something hurtful she couldn't take back.

When Laura had politely requested that they drive directly to the museum, despite the timing calculations that made it nearly impossible for Sam and Julia to be there, Arabella had simply said, "Of course." She'd even offered to drop Laura off before parking. "If you want to go in, I'll wait outside, perhaps across the street, in case they turn up while you're inside."

As British Siri announced they'd arrived at their destination and Arabella pulled the car up to the curb, she said, "It's not what I expected."

Laura followed her gaze. The building was a simple adobe structure, stucco the color of sand, a large front window covered with simple iron bars, double French door entry, an unobtrusive sign to the left of the doors with opening times. If you didn't know it was there, you could easily walk or drive right by it.

"It's smaller than I thought it would be," Arabella went on. "Rather nondescript, isn't it."

Laura remembered from visiting with Paul that the façade was deceptive. She recalled the inside of the museum being filled with large light-filled rooms, expansive spaces displaying only a few pieces. In Paul, she'd had her own personal docent. He'd talked about O'Keeffe's unique style, modernism, her relationship with Alfred Stieglitz and other artists of the time, O'Keeffe's love for the landscape, and the questions that arose about the symbolism of some of her work.

"The light here is amazing," Arabella said. "It suffuses everything: the buildings, the clouds, the air itself. I can see why O'Keeffe, how did you say it yesterday, what your husband said . . . that this place was 'part of her soul'?"

"Yes," Laura said softly. "A part of her soul, and she a part of it."

"How poetic."

"He used to recite poetry all the time." Laura turned to stare at the entrance to the museum. "Drying the dishes. Sweeping the driveway. He loved the sounds of words, the rhythms, the senses they evoked. The emotions." Paul had never been uncomfortable with emotions. "He used to say poetry and literature and art all represented man's desire to describe the indescribable, to make sense of the world, make ourselves understood, understand others . . ." Her voice dropped off, her hand resting motionless on the door handle. He'd done that with her, and she'd failed him.

"Yes," Arabella said. After a long moment without a response or any movement from Laura, she added, "Are you all right?"

Laura didn't hear her. A memory she'd carefully locked away emerged: waking to a shimmer of early morning light in the guest room, Paul's voice saying "Please help me," and what she thought was the sound of someone in the hall. *The night nurse maybe?* Laura had rushed to Paul's side only to have him ask her to describe the beauty of the morning breaking. Though a simple task, it had been beyond her. Just as she had begun to cry, Julia had entered the room, and Laura had stepped back to give her space to say goodbye before leaving for school. This would be a point of contention later, that everyone had encouraged Julia to go to school that day. None of them had known Paul would have a series of seizures within an hour and slip into a coma.

Right after Julia had left, Laura had knelt next to his bed, weeping and apologizing for her inability to give him the dawn as pent-up emotions spilled along with words she instantly wished she could take back, guilt overflowing at her weakness, for looking to him for comfort when she should be comforting him. "It should be me," she'd said. "You should be the one here, not me. You know what Julia needs."

His voice had been quiet, strained. The words came slowly with long pauses between. "You know too. What she needs. What we all need. Love, understanding." The words came even slower. "Be there. Listen." Slower still, he said, "I was wrong to ask—"

"Ask what?"

Paul opened his mouth, then closed it, then said even more quietly, "Tell her." There was a long pause. "I didn't give up. Tell her . . . trying is enough." He tried to lift his arm, but he'd been too weak to even lift his hand. "Come. Lie. With me."

Fresh tears had fallen, for these four simple words were both a request and the first words of the poem that had become theirs: "Come lie with me and be my love." Found in a book titled *A Coney Island of the Mind*, by a Beat poet. Early in their courtship, Paul had taken to reciting it, in its entirety, until she knew it by heart as well. The first line was enough to invoke memories of Paul calling to her from the lumpy secondhand futon in their first apartment, his face appearing half-lit by the glow of the table lamp next to the couch where Laura would read in the middle of the night when she couldn't sleep, or behind her as she brushed her teeth, grinning at her reflection as he wrapped his arms around her waist. It was an invitation she rarely declined.

But kneeling next to the hospital bed she'd never gotten used to, fearing she might hurt him, Laura had hesitated.

"And be—" he'd gone on, "my love—"

Laura had called for the nurse on duty to ask for help. As they'd adjusted Paul onto his side, an orange plastic container of prescription medication had clattered onto the floor and rolled underfoot. The nurse had picked it up, given it a cursory glance, and frowned.

"Is everything okay?" Laura asked, and the nurse nodded, pocketing the container before helping Laura to climb in next to Paul. Laura had curved her body to Paul's as she'd done for decades, lifting his arms around her, holding him so he could hold her, and then she'd recited the entire poem, and slowly, so slowly, he had whispered, "Enough. Julia—"

The first seizure had come as he said their daughter's name . . .

"What?" Arabella's voice was tentative, the touch on Laura's arm even more so. "Are you all right?"

"I'm sorry," Laura said, her hand over her heart.

"What's enough?"

Laura took a deep breath, squared her shoulders, and exhaled. She looked over to Arabella. "Trying. Hopefully, trying is enough."

Laura opened the car door and began to step out when Arabella's voice stopped her.

"I have come to believe it must be enough," she said. "I'll be here when you come out."

The museum was relatively empty. Wandering through the white-walled galleries she'd remembered, this time alone, looking for her daughter, Laura nonetheless couldn't help but take in the art. Abstractions. Lines, spirals, colors, and shapes. Pale pink and deep purple, orange and yellow and blue. Irises and hollyhocks and lilies and poppies. Shells and leaves. Massive black crosses and stark white skulls. Skyscrapers and mountains. Walls and doors and frames. Empty spaces filled with energy and light and meaning.

O'Keeffe leaving "a part of her soul" on every canvas, an artist inviting you into her world, into herself.

Some pieces were inexplicable. Others felt like an invitation to see things in a new way. And Laura felt something new, something she couldn't describe. In the last few days, emotions she'd routinely suppressed had emerged, relocating close to the surface, set on a hair trigger. It was more than a little overwhelming. When she'd mentioned it to her sister on the phone the night before, Lilly had said, "Once you know Julia is okay, you'll feel like yourself again."

Laura realized now that she didn't want to feel like herself again; she hadn't felt good about herself for quite a while. She remembered a card they'd handed out at the one grief support group meeting she'd attended, a card she'd tucked away in her wallet that bore the quote "You may be whole again, but you won't be the same again. You shouldn't be nor should you want to be." At the time, though she'd kept it to be polite, Laura had disliked the quote, dismissing it as too maudlin, the sort of thing she pictured greeting-card authors sitting around drinking chamomile tea had thought up. Now, she realized it was spot on. She hadn't truly made herself whole after Paul died, and the broken parts and empty spaces had nearly sucked her under. It occurred to her now that maybe the emotions she'd suppressed—the ones that threatened to explode at a moment's notice—maybe once she found Julia, these would drift down and settle in place, filling the empty spaces.

She would be whole again, but she wouldn't be the same.

As she approached the last gallery and did not see Julia, Laura wished Paul were there with her, telling her everything would be okay, and yet she recognized a change in her grief, a shift in her thinking.

Paul was gone.

Julia was not.

Standing there in the open, empty gallery, Laura wanted to see Julia, not just to know she was okay, but also to hear her perspective on the art hanging on the walls, to watch her taking it all in, doe eyes wide, hands gesturing. Laura wanted to have another chance to try and truly know her daughter—what Julia saw, how she felt, who she was, and who she wanted to become.

And trying would have to be enough.

35

JULIA

"OH, FUCK," SAM SAID. "Now look what you've done."

"I didn't do anything," Julia said. But she had. She'd demanded he pull over. Threatened to open the window, wave her arms, and call for help. She'd been there, in the gravel at the edge of the highway, for three or four minutes, waiting for her breathing to return to normal after the second near collision with a truck. She'd involuntarily screamed when the dark red cab of the truck appeared mere inches from her window, the cursive white lettering that identified the transport company blurring. This time she hadn't had time to look up to see the driver but nonetheless sensed that he saw her clearly. She wondered how she'd appeared to him—what expression accompanies the moment when your life flashes before your eyes, rewind and fast forward operating together to create a dizzying display: her father reading to her in bed, Max, Jess, hitting her leg, pills in Cheyenne's palm, sinking into nothing, Sharpie on an index card, Tanya's neon sweater, dreadlocks falling to the ground, her mother reaching for her hand.

After Sam pulled over, instinct ruled her movement. She'd exited the car as quickly as she could. Then standing a few feet away, she'd made her case through the open door, her breath still short, the words staccato. "You haven't slept. It's not safe. I'm not. Getting back. In the car. Unless. I'm. Driving."

"Seriously?" Sam was irritated. "I'm not tired, Julia, and you're perfectly safe. You're being ridiculous. That could have happened to anyone."

"I mean it."

Silence had fallen between them. Julia had remained standing on the shoulder—lips pressed into a firm line that hurt, preventing her from saying anything more inflammatory; arms crossed tight, holding herself together. She'd felt her heart beating wildly, adrenaline coursing through her.

Sam's initial annoyance had morphed into something resembling anger. His right hand remained on the gearshift, his right foot poised over the pedals.

Wondering if he planned to drive off without her, Julia locked her eyes onto him. He assiduously avoided her gaze, staring out through the windshield.

And then, out of the corner of her eye, Julia had seen the flashing lights. She'd instinctively turned her head and just as quickly turned back, in time to see Sam look up into the rearview mirror.

"Fantastic," he said. "Now you've drawn their attention. They could already be looking for us, and you've put it all at risk."

"That's not fair, Sam," Julia said, the memory of her life flashing. "You're just as responsible. I told you I didn't feel safe. If you'd just let me drive—"

"And I told you I'm fine. If you hadn't—"

The trooper was stepping out of his car.

"Get out of the car," Julia said. "Make it look like we're switching drivers. Let me talk. Trust me, Sam. This one time, please." Following her own instructions, she walked toward the front of the SUV. She didn't have time to explain she'd been prepped for situations like this one, how her father's repeated warnings about dealing with officers of the law or, as he put it, "driving while Black, half-Black, or even a quarter-Black" had led to practice sessions on how to interact politely, how to deescalate a situation.

Sam glowered at her but did as she asked. By the time the trooper, a stocky guy in his thirties, was within striking distance, she was standing inside the open driver's door and Sam was in the passenger seat.

"Everything okay, here?" the trooper asked, hand resting on his holster.

Julia smiled. "Yes, thank you. All fine. Just switching drivers. I'm so sorry, I know we should've waited 'til an exit. It won't happen again."

The trooper peered around her to look at Sam. Sam acknowledged him with a half nod.

Looking Julia in the eye, the trooper repeated, "You're sure everything's okay?"

"Yes, thank you so much for stopping to check. We're all good," Julia said, slowly easing into the driver's seat. Later she would wonder at how calm she'd been. How calm—and how wrong.

"All right then," the trooper said. He patted the top of the car twice. "Be safe pulling out."

THOUGH SAM HAD BEEN PISSED OFF at first, and then restless, sleep had overtaken him faster than Julia had imagined it would. As for Julia, the interaction with the trooper and changing seat position had given her a new perspective. She liked being in control. She'd turned off the navigation display and, reluctant to turn on the radio for fear of waking him, had begun an imaginary therapy session with Tanya, posing questions to herself and scripting Tanya's replies. As Tanya, she reminded herself that her behaviors influenced her thoughts, and both influenced her emotions. Taking over driving and standing up for herself could lead to strengthening her views and feeling more confident and optimistic.

This "session" had segued into a revised version of the conversation with Sam from earlier in the day, with Julia saying in her head what she wished she'd said aloud, providing logical yet passionate arguments in favor of Sam following his treatment plan. In her head, she explained that she understood medicine was complicated, that sometimes it made things worse or could even lead to the worst possible outcome, but most of the time it worked. It could help clear the fog and darkness, and even things out. That most of the time, the benefits outweighed the losses.

In her head, she told Sam her love for him wasn't reliant on a profusion of genius and creativity—that she would love an even-keeled, modulated version of him. That she had the strong suspicion a modulated version of Sam would still be, using his word, "splendid." And that maybe, just maybe, Camus's view of the world wasn't the only valid one. That maybe there was more to life than pushing a fucking rock up a mountain.

She wanted the chance to use this more convincing script. She wondered how soon she could bring it up without making him angry.

She didn't think she'd like to see Sam truly angry.

What do you believe in? she'd asked him, and she realized it was a question she hadn't really answered herself. What did *she* believe in? Art? Poetry? Grace? Strength? Was Longfellow right, did we leave behind footsteps for others to follow? And if a person diverted their path at the end, did it negate their whole life? Did choosing how to live include choosing when to die? Was helping someone make that choice playing God or was it honoring their ability to determine their own fate?

Being true to oneself was easy to say, but was it more important than being there for others? Sam seemed to advocate this position. Perhaps she had even thought this herself, but now—on the receiving end—she saw it differently. Living a passionate life of moments sounded amazing, sure, but lots of moments would be awful and painful and others would be just ordinary. She'd thought she loved the Picasso quote about art washing away the dust of everyday life, but maybe the real challenge was finding beauty and meaning in everyday life— the raking of leaves and the washing of dishes, even the pain. Wasn't all of it meaningful?

Maybe this is what Camus meant about living each successive present—good or bad—knowing it won't last.

Past Denver, the landscape changed to rolling hills and craggy peaks, pine trees, streams of water, occasional walls of pale rock, and sand-colored shale interspersed with scrub. The light was softening at the edges.

A new palette, she thought. Julia glanced at the clock on the dash and then saw there wasn't much gas left in the tank. Sam had been sleeping for hours.

Thank God he's resting. Maybe this can actually work, driving straight through.

Even as this thought flitted in, Julia realized she was growing tired, her brain numb from focusing on an endless ribbon of road. She wondered how Sam had driven so long without a break. Julia wanted to stop, stretch her legs, get a drink.

Sam sighed in his sleep, and Julia looked over. At rest, his face looked younger, and Julia realized there was usually a tension there—in his jaw or across his cheekbones or around his eyes—a tension so much a part of Sam that she hadn't noticed it until it wasn't there. Sam stirred and his brow wrinkled, the tension returning. His demons . . . *roaring their terrible roars and gnashing their terrible teeth and rolling their terrible eyes and—*

Then, as if jolted with a bolt of electricity, Sam was awake.

"Where are we? Why is the nav off?" Adjusting his seat into an upright position, Sam leaned forward to turn the map function back on.

"I saw a sign a bit ago for Glenwood Springs."

"And where is that?"

"I don't know."

"You don't know." Sam had woken up in a foul mood.

"No," Julia said. "I didn't think it mattered. We're on I-70, heading west, and we've got like fourteen more hours to go. What difference does it make that I wasn't watching on a map?"

Sam was silent. Out of the corner of her eye, Julia could see him shaking his head. He retrieved a Red Bull from behind the driver's seat that Julia hadn't known was there, popped it open, and took a long pull. *When did he buy Red Bulls?* "I'm ready to drive again," he said, "make up some time." His leg began its infernal bouncing.

Julia tried to continue channeling her imaginary session with Tanya. She was not willing to give up control yet.

"If we can stop and get something to eat, I'm fine to drive a bit more if you need more rest."

"I don't need *more* rest, Julia. I didn't need *any* rest, and now we're behind schedule."

"It's just—"

"I told you, don't worry." His voice was harsh. "I'm fine. Take the next exit."

Silence filled the car.

Staring through the bug-splattered windshield, Julia marveled that for hours she'd been in a silent car, and it had been just that—fine—but now the silent interior was eerie and uncomfortable, like one of those proverbial moments of calm before a storm unleashes its fury.

ARABELLA

AS THE MUSEUM'S CLOSING TIME approached, Laura's disappointment was palpable.

At breakfast, she'd been bubbling with optimism, certain Sam and Julia would arrive sometime during the day. "Especially since they drove to Chicago so directly, don't you think?"

Though she herself hadn't been as confident, given her son's previous as yet undisclosed misadventures, Arabella hadn't wanted to say anything that might crush Laura's spirits. Besides, she rationalized it was possible that Julia actually was the positive influence Sam needed. Perhaps, this time, he would make it.

The night before, after consuming a "truly delicious margarita" in a salt-rimmed glass at the hotel restaurant, Laura had shared stories about her daughter, and from everything Arabella had learned thus far, Julia was exactly the kind of girl she'd envisioned as capable of saving her son: smart, kind, beautiful, artistic, with a dash of quirkiness that would appeal to Sam's nonconformist tendencies. Arabella had been particularly taken with Laura's description of Julia's efforts to find solutions for her own issues. However they might seem to others, the dreadlocks, bandanas, Internet research, and pottery throwing, her willingness to take medicine and commit herself to a residential treatment program—all these struck Arabella as quite brave.

"Brave," Laura had said when Arabella explained this viewpoint. "Yes, she is."

And then she'd ordered another margarita.

Despite the two-hour time difference from the East Coast and lack of a decent night's sleep in Chicago, as the restaurant had emptied of other patrons, the two women remained sitting under the ornate wrought-iron chandelier and fairy-lit trees, listening to the murmur of the indoor fountain and each other. Though Laura's stories focused on Julia, Arabella had heard enough about Paul to understand how deeply he'd been loved and had loved in return. Aware that her own marriage had fallen short, Arabella avoided speaking of her husband other than to mention how she understood how Julia might feel, being swept off her feet at such a young age.

"I'm quite envious of you," she'd said to Laura as they walked to their rooms, her arms wrapped around herself against the desert-night chill.

"What? You're envious of *me*?"

"Yes. You've had a great love in your life. Some of us never find that. And you have a sister, and a daughter who, by all accounts, is lovely."

Though her pace had slowed, Laura hadn't responded at first, but when they arrived at her door, she'd turned and awkwardly, wordlessly wrapped her arms around Arabella.

Now, standing across from the Georgia O'Keeffe museum at ten minutes to five, Arabella returned the embrace.

"Can we take a walk?" Laura said, pulling away gently. "I need to move. Maybe we could go to that church, the cathedral we saw last night."

The Cathedral Basilica of St. Francis of Assisi stood at the edge of the plaza adjacent to their hotel. The night before, in their margarita-induced haze, the church's stone exterior had appeared like gold with white light shining through the wheel window above the arched entryway. Arabella wasn't sure if Laura wanted to visit for spiritual reasons, artistic ones, or simply because, as she'd noted, "it looks like it's been here forever."

When they arrived, a service was about to begin. "Anticipatory Mass" according to the schedule, and it swiftly became obvious Laura wasn't seeking religious grounding. "Mass? That's unfortunate," she said. "Let's just look around outside. I'll come back tomorrow for the inside. I've been thinking we should do as you suggested. You know, split the day in half. That way, you can go see some of the galleries you mentioned, and I can take a hike. It would probably do me good. Oh, look." She pointed to an area to the left side of the church entrance, where paved stones were set in an elaborate circular design. "I wonder what that is."

Even in the fading light, Arabella could identify it in an instant. "It's a labyrinth."

In the next instant, Arabella could hear Sam's voice, righteous and insistent. "All I'm asking is to give purpose to an unused courtyard. It's a classic example of how this place operates. They'd rather dole out medicine than create opportunities for healing from within."

"Sam, that's not fair. They were very supportive of the art therapy."

"With your money. Which is another reason I don't get why they're fighting me on this. They let you build the barn, and they're all over yoga and breathwork. How is this any different?"

"A labyrinth," Laura was saying now as she moved toward it.

"Yes," Arabella said. "A walking meditation, designed to unwind your mind. Lots of churches have them. There's a theory that the pattern—the curves and folds—replicate the brain, so—"

Laura was looking at her skeptically. "Really? And how exactly does one execute a walking meditation?"

"That depends on who you ask. Some people set an intention beforehand, you know, finding an answer, letting go of something, looking for inspiration. Others meditate when they reach the center, sitting, even lying down." She shrugged gently. Sam had liked to do this. "And then, there are those who say it's about clearing expectations, simply being open to whatever comes as you journey to the center, that each of us will find what we're supposed to find, depending on where we are in life."

"What do you think?"

Arabella shrugged again. "I don't think there's a specific right way to do it."

Laura still looked skeptical, but game. As she listened to Arabella she'd moved to the entrance of the maze. She pulled a hair band out of her pocket, gathered her curls, and slipped the band around. "So I can just walk?"

"Yes, you can just walk."

"Are you going to join me?"

Arabella nodded. "I'll be right behind you."

"Here goes nothing." Laura walked around to the exterior of the circle to find the entrance. Her shoulders rose and fell, and then she began walking, her footfalls slow and deliberate, measured.

Arabella followed her to the start. Staring at the red brick path, defined by gray stone, she tried to quiet her mind. As she waited to give Laura space, she realized she was waiting for something else. *"Come on, Mum,"* she heard Sam calling to her, followed by the instruction, *"Relax. Just be."*

She exhaled and began to walk, placing one foot in front of the other, following the hairpin turns and curves. About twenty steps in, she passed Laura, going in the opposite direction. Neither of them looked up. As Arabella proceeded farther into the center, she turned inward, feeling a lightness of being she hadn't experienced in a long time. A memory floated of herself pregnant, lying in a huge bathtub, belly rising above the water line, supported in the bath the way "little Max" was supported inside her, heavy with child yet weightless.

Arabella approached the center, looked up, and saw Laura standing quietly in the middle, the bricks under her feet forming petals around her. Laura's eyes were closed, her arms at her sides, hands open, facing outward.

Arabella hesitated.

Without opening her eyes, Laura stepped to one side, motioning for Arabella to join her.

It only took a few small steps. The two women stood side by side, facing in opposite directions. Arabella closed her eyes. She could sense Laura next to her, could hear her breathing. The weightless feeling intensified. And then, as if to confirm her presence, Laura's hand found Arabella's.

Fingers entwined, they stood quietly as dusk settled around them.

37

JULIA

THROUGH A SMATTERING OF frost crystals on the window, Julia could see low mountains in the distance, fields of scrub, and the faded white line demarking the edge of the highway, the latter rushing by, creating a hypnotizing blur. Despite a posted speed limit of 80 miles per hour, Sam was intent on maintaining at least 95, and somewhere along this bleak section of Interstate 15 in western Utah his mood had shifted, bringing a change in his body language and vocabulary, now sprinkled with profanity.

"I did as you asked about the hotel," he said, clearly pissed off with another request to slow down. "Stopping four times in Richfield fucking Utah to find a room so you could shower and lie down took time, time we will not get back. We have at least nine hours to Yosemite and then the hike, and, trust me, it will be easier to make up time in a BMW than it will be climbing to the Diving Board, so if you're uncomfortable with the speed at which we are traveling may I suggest *again* that you close your eyes. You said you were tired."

"But—"

"But what," Sam said in a flat tone of voice. It did not seem like a question, so Julia didn't answer. "That's what I thought," Sam went on, leaving Julia wondering if it had been a question after all. She was still tired. So tired. Because despite Sam behaving as though he'd done her some huge favor stopping at a hotel in Richfield, Utah, he'd woken her less than an hour later, telling her they needed to pack up and go, right then. Right away. That if it hadn't taken them so fucking long to find a shitty hotel room, she could have slept longer. But, as it was, they were behind schedule.

He was right about it taking a long time to find a room. After the third "Sorry, we're full," he'd said, "Maybe it's not meant to be," prompting her to reply, without editing, "Or maybe it means everyone else found a place to sleep at a reasonable hour."

"We're not like everyone else," Sam had murmured, gunning the engine up the on-ramp.

"Speak for yourself," Julia had murmured in reply. Watching him aggressively changing lanes for no apparent reason, she'd recalled the feel of the steering wheel in her own hands and the strength she'd mustered in her imagined conversations. Channeling this, she'd pressed him, "I want to take a shower, Sam, and I need to lie down, and no," she added as he opened his mouth to interrupt her, "not in the back seat."

Though clearly annoyed, Sam had stopped at the fourth hotel option and there'd been a room. Carrying the duffle and the poster tube, Sam didn't hold her hand or place his on the small of her back as they walked to the elevator. The ride to the third floor and the walk down the dimly lit hallway to their room had been uncomfortably silent.

Sam dropped the duffle on the padded bench across from the double bed. "I need to take care of some things," he said. "I'll be back up in a little while. Don't wait for me."

But she had.

She'd taken a hot shower and then, standing in front of the steamy mirror while her hazy reflection cleared, she'd waited for Sam to come bounding through the door, to unwrap the thin white bath towel that smelled of bleach, and envelop her.

But he hadn't.

So she'd climbed into the bed closest to the door, tried to clear jangling thoughts, and succumbed to weariness beyond weariness.

It felt as if she'd only just closed her eyes when Sam had woken her in the dark, shaking her shoulder. "Wake up! Wake up!"

"What?" Julia squinted toward the bedside table, looking for a clock. "What time is it?"

"It's time to go. Now. We didn't have time for this stop." Sam backed away from her. In the darkness, two sheets of paper flew from his hands, floating and separating before landing on the end of the bed at her feet. "I was printing this . . . this 'Psalm of Life' for you when it occurred to me maybe you don't believe in me. In us. Maybe the 'I have to lie down' shit is just to stop me from getting there in time."

"What?" As Julia reached over to turn on the light, she realized Sam hadn't done so. He was still fully dressed. There was a thin sheen of sweat on his face as if he'd been running. His eyes were wide and red-rimmed. "Sam, that's not true. What are you talking about?"

"You heard me. Don't pretend."

"Yes. I heard you. I don't understand."

"That's not possible. You must understand. This isn't some game, some folly—it's the culmination and the commencement of everything I am supposed to be and do, and it's all aligning now—finding you, the mega Beaver Moon, the visualizations— everything peaking at the right moment. I can see it already. But it'll all be for nothing if we don't get there in time or let them stop us. So, unless that's what you want, unless you're trying to help *them*, I don't understand how you don't understand."

They'd argued while he paced back and forth. His words fast, furious. Hers shaky, conciliatory. Caught off guard, she struggled to pull out the reasoned arguments she'd developed while driving. It didn't matter. Past the point of appeasement, Sam had grabbed the duffle, flung it over his shoulder, and thrown open the door to the hallway. "We need to go. Now."

"Please—"

He'd turned back, eyes afire, a battle raging in the rest of his features.

"I need five minutes, Sam. You get the car. I'll be down in five minutes."

"Fine. Five minutes," he'd said gruffly, dropping the duffle inches inside the doorframe, already moving away.

She had the feeling the next five minutes were critical. Clumsily sifting through the duffle to find clean leggings and a hoodie, she tried to hear herself think over the psychic alarm bell going off in her head in its spiky dialogue bubble: "CLANG! CLANG!"

For the briefest of moments, seconds really, she saw herself from above, standing there at the foot of the unmade bed, weaving slightly. She wished she could hold herself there, out of body, long enough to gain better perspective. Maybe Sam had been right when he'd said they weren't like everyone else. Something told her most people didn't have out-of-body experiences on a regular basis or want to stay there when they happened.

Staring down at her weaving figure, Julia recalled how she'd mentioned these out-of-body experiences to Dr. Stein and then to Tanya, and how Tanya had explained it was a coping mechanism, a form of removing herself temporarily from stressful situations. She heard Tanya's soft, smooth voice making everything sound reasonable and less frightening. "All of us develop coping mechanisms—some healthy, others not so much. As you become more comfortable in your own skin, they may occur with less frequency, and you'll find you can control them. Do you remember when I told you, the first time we met, that self-awareness was one of your strengths?"

Julia nodded along with her recollected self. She heard Tanya repeat the well-worn phrases, "Recognizing the problem is the first step to solving it" and "Trite but true—you must be aware of your behaviors before you can change them. Each time you notice using a coping mechanism you no longer want to employ, remember you have a choice—you can decide to *do* something or to *not* do something. Remember that you control your thoughts and behaviors."

And then she recalled Tanya telling her the only person you can control is yourself, that while you can ask for certain behaviors from others, you cannot make them do anything. Julia thought of how she'd tried every possible rational argument with Sam against his drive-straight-through plan, how she'd begged him to lie down, even if only for an hour or so, how she'd told him full moons often appear for two nights, that they'd had more time than he thought.

Nothing worked.

She could not control Sam.

She could, however, control herself.

Not press on her cutting scars or pull on her hair.

Not go on the Ferris wheel.

Not listen to Sam and his "They won't understand what we have. They'll try to stop us."

The phone lay between the made and unmade beds.

Incidentals. Given his level of agitation, Julia wondered if Sam would've even thought to check out and collect the ubiquitous incidental deposit. She was willing to take that chance.

Five minutes later, the printed copy of "A Psalm of Life" hastily tucked into the pocket of her sweater, the duffle over her shoulder, Julia darted past the desk clerk, who'd called out, "Let him know it's all taken care of, it'll go out tomorrow." She'd walked out of the main entrance to find the SUV wasn't immediately visible and felt relieved—*maybe he's gone on without me.*

But he hadn't. The SUV was there, just past the entrance, engine running.

She'd barely gotten the door closed before he'd peeled out and yet, as the wheels cleared the exit curb, Sam reached over to rest his hand on her thigh, right over the scars. "I'm sorry, Julia. Really. It's just, this is everything—and I don't want to fuck it up."

She looked over at Sam now—hands tight around the wheel, his face stonelike in its focus in contrast to the constantly jittering leg. He did not notice her staring at him. It was as though he were in his own world, the bubble of Samness surrounding only him.

"Sam, are you okay?" she whispered, knowing he wouldn't answer.

She wasn't in Sam's bubble anymore, and she wasn't sure how or why or when she would be again.

Julia unbuckled, climbed into the backseat, reached over to unzip the duffle, and found a thick fleece belonging to Sam. Rolling it into a bulky pillow, she laid her head upon it and curled onto her side. Although enclosed in a steel shell, she was acutely aware of how fast her body was hurtling down the highway. She could see shadows in the night passing in the window at her feet, feel bumps in the road beneath her, sense the tension in Sam's body in the driver's seat only a foot or two away, and hear the echo of the psychic alarm in her brain. Awkwardly, she lifted her upper body to maneuver the middle seatbelt around her waist. Then she lay back down under the closed moonroof, imagining the vast sky above her as thoughts and voices from the past swirled and whispered before falling into the darkness: *miles to go before I sleep; I am the captain of my soul; you are his footsteps; trust your instincts; you can choose to not do something; love requires courage, love requires courage; let the wild rumpus start—*

LAURA

"WAIT, *WHERE* ARE THEY?" Arabella asked, blinking against the light in the hallway.

"Somewhere west of Richfield, Utah, on their way to Yosemite."

"So they *aren't* coming to Santa Fe." Arabella sighed. Her head and shoulders dropped. "Do they know we're here? That we've been following them?"

"No, I thought about telling her, but it didn't seem like a good idea. We only talked for a minute or two. Mostly her talking. I was just trying to listen."

Arabella nodded absently. "No, that makes sense. So they're still together,"

Laura paused. *Does Arabella think they'll no longer be together?*

"And they *are* going to Yosemite."

"Yes," Laura said. "She said they're going directly to Yosemite. No more stopping, because this month's moon is some kind of once-in-a-lifetime thing, and Sam says they have to be there—where the picture was taken—in time for moonrise tomorrow." Laura looked over to the clock on the bedside table. "No, *today*. And Arabella?" Laura couched her words. "Julia's worried—about Sam. He's not sleeping much, hardly at all." *Neither am I,* Laura thought, feeling herself swaying.

Arabella stepped back, reaching for Laura's arm, guiding her into the room as Laura continued speaking. "The hike he's talking about, the one they've got to take to get this picture? It's not a hike; it's a climb. She said Sam mentioned ropes and scrambling—and an abyss. That's the word she used, an abyss."

Laura shuddered. "And Julia's not a climber—she's barely a reluctant hiker. And I'm certain she's afraid of heights. She won't sit by the window on an airplane. Hates bridges. It's probably why she passed out on that damn Ferris wheel. She won't—" Laura cut herself off. "I asked if she was okay, and she said yes. She said *she* has medicine, which makes no sense. I mean, where would she get it? I could hear in her voice she was only trying to reassure me. I told her she doesn't have to do anything that seems unsafe, that she could leave, but she said she can't, that she has to stay with him, that getting this photograph is everything—and he needs *her* to do it. I told her I would come, that I wanted to be there for her, and she said I didn't need to, but she sounded relieved, I think, that I would come." Doubt entered Laura's mind. *Did Julia sound relieved or was it my own relief in hearing my daughter's voice?*

Arabella tugged the white comforter up, sat down on the edge of the bed, and picked up her tablet. "Does she know we're together?"

"No, I—" Laura struggled to recall what she'd said to Julia. The conversation had been disjointed. At one point, Julia had claimed the whole situation was her fault, saying "just like with Dad," which also made no sense, but before she could say so, Julia had gone on.

"No worries. It's probably better." Arabella's fingers danced across the screen. "Do you know how far it is—to Yosemite? Can we drive?"

"I don't know. It's not that close. We should probably fly." Laura thought again. "Except, I don't know, there's probably no flights 'til morning, so maybe we should drive." Laura felt oddly breathless. The room was seriously depleted of fresh air.

"Come, sit," Arabella said gently, gesturing with her head. "We'll figure it out."

Laura sat down but, feeling like a butterfly pinned to a board with its body and wings still fluttering, she stood back up. "I'm sorry. I can't. I need to do something. Pack or—"

Before Laura could take three steps away, Arabella had placed the tablet down, stood up herself, and grabbed Laura's upper arm, stopping her forward progress. "I understand," she said quietly. "I do. I've been at this for a while, and my first instinct has always been to *do something*, to *make it better.* The problem is, impulsively doing something to make it better often doesn't work. I'm only beginning to understand what I *need* to do is try to remain calm, try to behave rationally in the face of a host of irrationality, including my own. No, *particularly* my own."

"But—" Laura couldn't speak. Negative energy swirled around inside her, creating a destabilizing layer just under her skin, making her feel sick to her stomach. *Buck the*—the air thinned further. The soft glow in the room dimmed at the edges.

"Are you all right?" Arabella turned her so they were facing one another. "Laura, are you breathing?"

Laura recalled Dr. Renner's advice about the oxygen masks. Her thoughts turned to her sister. Should she call Lilly? *No.* She couldn't call her sister. What was she thinking? *It's two in the morning in New York. And what could Lilly do?*

"Laura?" Arabella's voice was calm but fuzzy. "Are you all right?"

Laura tried to shake her head.

"Let's sit down," Arabella said in the same calm, now even fuzzier voice. Laura allowed herself to be led. "All right, now lean forward, put your head between your knees. Excellent. And now I want you to breathe slowly—in and out. Yes, that's right. In . . . and out."

Upside down, eyes closed, arms draping, Laura tried to do as she was told.

"Yes, good, that's it. Just breathe," Arabella said slowly. Laura could feel Arabella's hand gently resting in the middle of her back. "It's going to be okay. I know it may be hard to see it, but we're in a better position than an hour ago: trying to sleep, waiting for them, uncertain as to where they were or where they were going. After all, uncertainty is the worst thing of all." Arabella paused. When she began speaking again, her voice had a confidence that was reassuring. "And now we know. We *know* where they're headed and we *know* the image he's trying to capture, so we *can* identify this hike or climb, or whatever it should be called, and we *will* get there. We *will* get there," she repeated.

After a few more cycles of in-and-out breaths, Arabella said, "Okay?" Laura opened her eyes to see the bedframe between her knees. Calmer, she placed her hands on her knees and began to roll up. "Slowly," Arabella said. "Better? Good. And now, a plan."

The first Internet search revealed driving would take at least fifteen hours. Clearly the best option was an early morning flight from Albuquerque—about an hour's drive from Santa Fe—to Fresno, with another drive of roughly two and a half hours into the park. If everything went smoothly, Laura and Arabella would be there early afternoon.

"And when will *they* be there?" Laura asked.

Arabella's fingers flew. Another map search.

"Around nine."

"So, they have at least three hours on us, maybe more."

Arabella had already moved on. "Mmm."

Laura watched as the screen turned from a search engine result to a page for the Ansel Adams gallery displaying a black and white image on the left the heading "New Release—Monolith, the Face of Half Dome as a Modern Replica." As Arabella had predicted when she first mentioned the photograph to Laura and Lilly, Laura recognized it straightaway—a stark yet lovely image of a dark, striated rock face that appeared to have been hewn by a giant axe, set against a lighter sky and pale snow.

"'On an April morning in 1927,'" Arabella read, "'Adams undertook a difficult four-thousand-foot climb through heavy snow to the granite outcropping known as the Diving Board . . .'" She stopped, clicked back a page, typed another search entry for Diving Board at Half Dome. Arabella was obviously

a faster reader than Laura or knew exactly what she was looking for, because she moved on again, typing "Hiking to spot
where Ansel Adams took Monolith."

Arabella's rapid navigation from page to page reactivated
Laura's anxiety. The sledgehammer was swinging, sending her
thoughts scattering. Laura caught only a few words here and
there on the screen: brooding; half in shadow, half in light;
difficult; route requires navigation; ever-steepening cliffs;
treacherous; bushwhacking. Many websites featured photographs of the Monolith or perhaps other sheer granite faces.
One image seemed to jump off the screen—an abyss, shown
from the top, rock pitched downward toward the floor of a
tree-filled valley, thousands of feet below. Dizzying. With one
hand hugging her own torso, the other tented over her eyes
and nose, Laura murmured, "Oh my god."

"It's—" Arabella hesitated for the first time. "You're certain
Julia is going to climb with him?"

"I think so. I don't know. I didn't ask her that specifically,
but yes, I think so. All she said was 'Sam needs me to be with
him.' But I should have asked her that, I should have told her—"

Arabella had continued to read. "Wait, hold on. This one
says it's *not* a dangerous trail. *Difficult*, but not dangerous. You
might get hurt, but—" Arabella stopped.

"But what?" Laura leaned over to read the page to herself.
"'Aside from the Diving Board itself, there are zero places on
this hike where you could plummet to your death.' Aside from
the Diving Board itself—but that's where they're headed."

"Yes, but the trail itself is not treacherous. Challenging
but not treacherous."

"I'm sorry, but that isn't reassuring at all. Not even a
little. There must be something we can do. Call the police or
the park rangers—"

"I wish it were that simple. But what would we tell them,
our adult children are planning to hike in Yosemite? I know
you want to stop them, Laura, but they haven't done anything
wrong, certainly nothing worthy of arrest. Experience tells me
getting help from authorities will be difficult."

Laura recalled her conversation with Dr. Renner. It was wrong—so wrong—but it was likely Arabella was right.

"At least we know where they're going," Arabella said. "And what they plan to do."

Do we? Laura thought but did not say. *I don't think we do.*

39

JULIA

TREES TOWERED OVERHEAD under a dome of blue sky, the scent of pine and wet earth permeating the crisp, cool air. In the trailhead parking lot, Julia watched Sam put on his black high-top Keds one at a time, resting first his right foot, then his left, on the tailgate of the SUV, rapidly tying the laces as if competing in a race. Noticing the substantial footwear of the other hikers preparing to embark from the lot and remembering the heavily treaded running shoes she'd always worn when she went out with her dad, she lifted one foot to glance at the relatively smooth rubber sole of her brand-new, strikingly white Keds.

"Sam?"

Sam had turned his attention to the duffle from which he'd removed and set aside a pair of much sturdier boots, a small clear water bottle with a Camelback top, a larger hard plastic bottle with a black screw-top lid, a thin blue tube printed with the words "LifeStraw," and a red zippered bag bearing a white cross and the label "FIRST AID KIT."

"Sam?" Julia said louder.

"What?" Sam looked at her like she'd popped up out of nowhere.

"You're sure these shoes are going to be okay?"

"What?" Sam repeated, clearly exasperated. Without waiting for an answer, he turned back to the task at hand, rummaging in the back of the SUV, for what, she didn't know.

"These sneakers, they're not really designed for hiking."

"Sneakers?" Sam continued to rummage and sort, packing items into the backpack and then removing them.

"Yes, the sneakers. On our feet," Julia said.

Sam did not turn around.

Julia pressed on. "I know Ansel Adams did the hike in sneakers, but—"

"Sneakers?" Sam spun around to face her. "He wasn't wearing sneakers. He was wearing Keds, Julia. Keds basketball shoes like these, only circa 1927. And he made it. He didn't have fancy boots or telescoping poles or any of this shit." Sam turned back to the SUV and its offensive pile of camping plenty. "He had his camera and tripod, plates, and Keds. That's it. None of this other shit." Sam began pulling items from the backpack as he named them. "No filtered straws. No maps. No shells."

He turned to look at Julia. She was wearing a jacket Sam had given her, a spare "shell" as he called it—too large, slate gray, wind resistant. She'd stuffed the pockets with the food she'd grabbed at the last gas station convenience store: a Snickers bar, a bag of trail mix, and three energy bars. *Is he going to ask for the shell?* she wondered. *Make me leave it behind?*

As it was, even with the shell, Julia knew her own outfit was inappropriate—the leggings and black-hooded cashmere sweater were more "walk in Central Park" than "strenuous hike to abyss overlooking Half Dome." Quietly, she moved the bars and Snickers to the pocket of the sweater with the folded-up poem, regretting the trail mix bag would not fit.

But Sam did not ask for the shell. He was on to something else. And though he still hadn't answered her question about the adequacy of the Keds' treads, Julia gave up asking. Clearly, he was on some mission to preserve the purity of his Adams-inspired ideals.

She wished the Keds were her biggest concern.

But they weren't. Far from it.

Vying for positions near the top of her latest list, "Alarming things that could lead to disaster," were lack of adequate food and the fact that the route Sam intended to take to the Diving Board seemed to be loosely defined. When she'd looked over the directions printed back in Bloomsburg that she found on the front seat that morning, she saw the words *scrambling* and *bushwhacking* (which she imagined were exactly as they sounded) along with mileage markers and numbers for latitude and longitude (useless as she did not know the first thing about the system to which these numbers referred).

What if something happens to Sam and I'm out there on my own?

And something happening to Sam was at the absolute top of this new list, because something was already happening with Sam. Julia worried he was slipping over an invisible edge. She'd sparked a deluge of fury when she insisted on driving after the final stop for gas before entering the park and dared suggest he rest. And then another deluge when they'd arrived at the valley floor and she asked if they could stop in the visitor center to make sure the route was legit. Sam had grown more and more agitated with each request, claiming she was trying to sabotage his dream. She'd denied this, telling him she wanted him to get the image more than anything she'd ever wanted for herself. While this wasn't an untruth, she also hadn't been completely honest; a part of her did want someone to stop Sam. He hadn't slept, and he was scaring her. He'd started repeating phrases, speaking more and more quickly, resulting in rapid-fire, bizarre speech that had a different quality from the monologues she'd heard up until now. Actively listening to the CLANGING psychic alarm bells, she tried to recollect the worst of bipolar disorder she'd researched online pre-Brookfield and, more than wishing he would get the picture, she wished that she'd brought the whole box of darkroom medicine—that she could convince Sam to take something, anything.

Now, as he took items *out* of the backpack, he'd moved on from berating himself about having modern gear to a rehash of their conversation earlier, in the SUV, on the way to the parking lot.

"We've got plenty of food because, as I've said, I'm not hungry. And it *is* a trail; the Mist Trail is one of the most traveled in the park. We take that up to Nevada Falls to the use trail. Point-six miles past the new restrooms to the metal sign, then another 100 yards to the first cairn. And a use trail is a trail that people have followed before, and they've left cairns to guide the next traveler like the bloody footsteps in the sand in your bloody poem. Bloody heads, bloody footsteps. 'Tell me not in mournful numbers/Life is but an empty dream . . .'"

Julia stared at him. Had Sam memorized "A Psalm of Life"?

"Empty dreams. That's it, isn't it? You want to delay. Make it an empty dream. Well, I'm not going to let that happen, so no, we won't be going to talk to a ranger because we can do it. All we have to do is follow the trail and the cairns, verify coordinates and mileages and references committed to memory, because commitment is required: west, northwest, small creek, meet the gully between Broderick and Liberty Cap—"

Julia had heard Sam mumbling when she woke, and now she knew what he'd been going over: the route—the coordinates and mileages and references. She remembered his notations at the back of *The Myth*, details critical to Sam but nearly incomprehensible to anyone else.

"Shortcuts require experience. Variation A: follow the gully instead of circling Liberty Cap, and so on—so no, we don't need to ask about the route, challenging, as it should be, as it must be." Sam paused, went on in a more formal tone, a recitation. "'The great work of art is less important in itself than in the ordeal it demands of a man.'"

Julia thought she recognized this last line.

"Overcoming phantoms, capturing the seen, the unseen. Adams and Stieglitz and Weston. This," Sam said, closing the back of the SUV and flinging the now-bulky full backpack onto his back for emphasis, "this is why we are here. The whole point. The whole fucking point."

Julia peered into the back of the SUV. The black camera case and poster tube were gone, the leather case empty. But she could see the items he'd removed from the backpack included the water bottles and first-aid kit.

Sam went on. "To see, yes, but also to show others what we see. To be courageous. Overcome fucking phantoms. My rock. Your moon. The struggle toward the heights isn't just enough—it's everything. Everything."

Julia interrupted. "Water, Sam—what about water?"

"Option one: Merced River after Nevada Falls. Option two: creek at route junction before Lost Lake. Option three: Lost Lake, swampy, but large enough. Option four: spring on Manzanita slopes below Diving Board."

Julia vaguely recalled seeing a bullet list of water sources on one of the printouts. He wasn't exaggerating: *He'd memorized all of it.* Nonetheless, she was referring to the water bottles it seemed he intended to leave behind.

Sam stepped away from the SUV, bumped into her, and turned. Quite unexpectedly, he gripped her shoulders, leaned in, eyes shining, and said, "You. With me. Here. In this moment. Vartamana. Together, this is going to work." He broke away, on to another tangent. "Six to eight hours if we leave right now and make good time, which we can. Sunset at 4:57. Civil twilight 5:24. Nautical 5:55. And we'll be there, where they stood, on the Diving Board that day in April 1927. We'll be there at the moonrise. We'll be there."

Sam began walking away, still talking, now to himself. "It's going to be fucking amazing. Amazing. But we have to go. Now."

Julia didn't move. "Sam, wait. We need the water bottles." She didn't know what a LifeStraw was, but it sounded like something they should have with them. "And the LifeStraw. I'm not going without them. Sam! Stop."

Sam stopped, paused for only a second or two before wheeling around, his face transformed with a wild fury. "No!"

They roared their terrible roars—

"No more delays. Nothing's going to stop me from making it."

Julia stood her ground. "Sam, I want you to make it. I want you to get this picture more than anything." *What will convince him?* Julia took two steps toward him, holding out her hands, staring at his eyes, hoping to hold his attention. "Please, Sam, listen. I know it's going to be amazing. But I want you to be safe. I want us both to be safe. I *know* Ansel Adams and his wife didn't have all this. I know they used window cord and glass plates—"

"Wratten Panchromatic plates," Sam interjected, shaking his head.

"Yes, Wratten Panchromatic plates. But they had water, Sam. Ansel Adams had water. It will only take me a minute to get the bottles and fill them. Please."

Without saying a word, Sam pulled the keys from his pocket and threw them. As they arced in the air toward her, she reacted. Too late. The keys fell to the ground at her feet. "I'm not putting liquid in this pack, not with the cameras and the film. Take what you want."

"Sam, please."

"We have to go."

"One minute."

"You'll catch up."

Watching Sam walk away, Julia wasn't at all sure she would. She was aware of each second as she retrieved the water bottles, the LifeStraw, and the first-aid kit, all the while considering how to carry it all. The LifeStraw had a string attached, but the other items would need to be toted, and the duffle bags were too large, too heavy. There was a thin plastic bag from the last gas station convenience store in the backseat. *Totally impractical,* she thought. *Likely to rip and I'd have to hold it in my hand the entire time.* Then she saw a compact coil of blue and gray rope under the duffle with a bunch of rings or hitches attached. *Ansel Adams had rope.* Julia envisioned looping it around her body under the shell, with the water bottles and the kit attached to the rings. *It will have to work.*

It may be up to me to keep us safe.

Please let it work.

She reached up, hit the lock button, and hearing the tail-gate close with a hush behind her, hurried after Sam.

ARABELLA

TWO PARK RANGERS IN CLASSIC gray and green uniforms stood behind the information counter. There was a line three-deep to speak with them. The time estimates she and Laura had formulated in Santa Fe were proving to be entirely inaccurate. Everything was taking longer: renting the car; the drive from the airport to Yosemite's valley floor; finding a parking place; and now, waiting to speak with a ranger. Though Arabella had always considered herself patient, she was learning that Laura was not, at least not today. Having insisted on renting the car and driving, Laura had been frustrated with the rental car company employee who she swore was moving slowly to taunt her; she'd been infuriated by the RV driver who insisted on obeying the speed limit inside the park; and now, she was clearly vexed by the time and attention the rangers were giving to the people in front of them.

"Seriously?" she said as the young couple ahead of them unfolded an elaborate map on the counter. "We should just go."

"We *could* just go, but this will only take a few minutes, and it might save us far more than that," Arabella said quietly, not wanting to add fuel to Laura's fire. They'd decided it would be unwise to try to find Sam and Julia by following the confusing preponderance of online advice, so as they'd trailed behind the slow RV, Arabella attempted to contact the

Park Ranger office by phone. Her efforts had been for naught. First, she'd been unable to reach a human, continuously being circled back to the main menu and then, when she finally got through, she lost the call going around a curve under an impressive canopy of trees.

"Shit," Arabella had said, looking down at the No Service message.

"Oh my god," Laura had replied. "Is that it?"

The valley had opened before them, the steep hooked face of Half Dome at the far end, framed by a series of peaks and towering rocks. "It is," Arabella answered. "Spectacular, isn't it?"

Laura's head bob was somewhere between a nod and a shake.

Any marginally positive vibes generated were ephemeral and Laura's impatience had returned. Traffic had gotten heavier, parking was a "bitch," and while standing in line, Laura noticed a video about bear activity in the park on a screen next to the information desk. Each of these developments had inspired a "Seriously?" a one-word utterance of dismay now replaced by a "*Finally*," as the young couple lifted and refolded the elaborate map.

The ranger, a middle-aged man with a weather-worn face and a badge with "Mike" on it, gave the couple a nod and smile, saying "Stay safe out there," before turning to Laura and Arabella. "Good afternoon. How can I help?"

"We think our kids are in trouble," Laura said quickly. "They're out there." She flung her right arm out wide. "And we can't reach them."

"Ooookay," he said. "Let's start with the basics. How old are these kids?"

Arabella interrupted, placing her hand softly on Laura's arm. "They're not children. They're young adults, 18 and 23. They're just *our* children."

"Gotcha," Ranger Mike said with a subdued smile. "Got a couple of those myself."

Arabella returned a subdued smile. Laura looked perturbed. "And you think they're in trouble because . . . ?"

"They set out on a hike this morning, off trail," Laura said. "And we can't reach them."

"What time did they leave?"

"Around nine," Arabella replied.

"And you've tried to call them?"

"They don't have phones," Laura said. "But you must have a protocol for this, right? For tracking hikers off trail?"

Ranger Mike had dropped the smile, replacing it with an "I'm listening" expression, nodding slowly as Laura spoke. "Well, yes, ma'am, we've got protocols for all sorts of things, but we don't really track hikers off trail. Simply wouldn't be practical. Folks are allowed to hike anywhere within the park not marked restricted, and thousands of people do just that every year." Before Laura could say anything, he went on. "You know where your hikers are headed?"

"The Diving Board," Laura said.

"I'm sorry?" Ranger Mike asked.

"The Diving Board. Where Ansel Adams took his famous photograph."

The ranger's smile returned. "He took quite a few pictures here at Yosemite."

Laura's perturbed look resurfaced.

Arabella pulled out her iPad and opened it. "Yes, he did," she said, engaging her "be nice" voice. "The one we're referring to is called 'Monolith.' It's of Half Dome, taken from this spot, here, the Diving Board." Arabella pointed to her screen. "Apparently, there's a number of possible routes."

Within a few minutes, Laura had additional reasons to be displeased with Ranger Mike: he wasn't familiar with the location of the Diving Board; the routes Arabella described had "exposure" and required climbing skills; and he wouldn't recommend them as one-day climbs this time of year, when days were short, and temperatures dropped rapidly as soon as the sun went down.

"We're wasting time," Laura said to Arabella under her breath, turning away. "We should just go up after them."

"I wouldn't recommend that, ma'am," the ranger said, glancing at his watch. "You're unlikely to make it before dark and you'll need a wilderness permit to camp."

Laura turned to Arabella. "Camp? Oh my god, I hadn't even thought of that." She turned back to the ranger before Arabella could answer. "So what *can* we do?"

Ranger Mike paused. "At this point, ma'am, your hikers aren't even late. Even if they weren't back this evening, given they could be camping, we wouldn't send anyone out until tomorrow, earliest." He raised his hands slightly as if to calm her as he went on. "I know you're worried, but you've got to understand, we simply don't have the manpower to send out backcountry teams for every off-trail hiker. We do have volunteers on major trails—yellow shirts—who'll reach out to hikers heading up, ask about preparedness, describe hazards, that sort of thing. It's possible your kids received some guidance. Are they experienced hikers?"

The two women exchanged a glance, followed by competing replies: a "yes" from Arabella, a "sort of" from Laura.

"Properly equipped?" He gestured to a poster, rattling off the list it contained. "Map, compass, water, food, first aid kit, storm gear, flashlight, matches, knife, cell phone?"

Sam had a knife.

"They don't have a cell phone," Laura said. "That's why we can't reach them." She turned toward Arabella. "Sam had supplies, though, right?"

Arabella chose her words carefully. "He has some of those items."

"Right, so no cell phone, and a maybe on the rest," the ranger said. "What about the two of you—are you properly equipped?" He began rattling off the list again, stopping after food. "Search and rescue often ends with more people to help when Good Samaritans get in trouble. Won't help anyone if you end up needing help yourself."

"Put on your own oxygen mask," Laura said.

"Precisely," the ranger said.

Laura exhaled audibly, shaking her head.

"For what it's worth," Ranger Mike went on, his voice calm, conciliatory. "Most people enjoy hiking without incident. Your kids are probably fine."

"What if they're not fine," Laura began. "What if . . ." She looked over to Arabella before going on. "What if they're unwell, mentally unwell. Would that change anything?"

Arabella sucked in her breath.

The other ranger turned from the conversation he was having with an elderly man who looked like a walking advertisement for an outdoor adventure store. The elderly man turned too. Both men bore expressions of curiosity and concern.

Ranger Mike matched his tone to Laura's. "Well, ma'am, I'm not sure exactly what you mean, but physical and mental illness are certainly factors that could change our approach. If you believe your young people are in imminent danger, we can contact law enforcement here at the park or call 911, and they'll connect you with Yosemite dispatch, who'll take it from there."

"And they'll send out a team?"

Arabella's gentle touch on Laura's arm had become a firm grasp.

"They'll work with you, assess the situation, and then—"

Laura interrupted the ranger. "Then they'll send out a team."

The other ranger and the old man were watching, listening.

"That's one of several options."

"Such as?"

"There's the ranger BOLO, a 'be on the lookout.' And then, if necessary, they could call in YOSAR."

Laura shot a questioning glance.

"Yosemite Search and Rescue," Mike said.

Sighing, her hand at her throat, Laura looked at Arabella, then back at the ranger. "I—"

"Ma'am," Ranger Mike added slowly, carefully. "I don't know your hikers, but if you believe they are in imminent danger—"

"Thank you. You've been so helpful," Arabella said, placing her hand on Laura's shoulder. "Can you give us a moment?"

"But—" Laura said.

"One moment," Arabella said. She turned Laura and guided her past a giant relief map of the park and out the front door.

A few steps outside, Laura stopped and stood still, closing her eyes.

Standing next to her, Arabella's eyes were, in contrast, wide open. She was staring at the building that housed the Ansel Adams Gallery, the place from which she'd purchased Sam's pristine, now missing, "Monolith" photograph for nearly $30,000, the gift that may have landed them all here. Arabella tried to corral the thoughts racing through her head, spinning and ricocheting against each other—Sam and his rock; the promise and curse of experiencing the world with brilliant intensity, saying "there must be some good to come of all this"; believing that, someday, his creativity would peak at the right moment, and he could start living the life he longed for. *This could be the moment.* She wanted to see what he saw. And he'd seemed so well on his birthday. He could be fine and calling in rangers would only ruin things. Worse still, he'd be gutted if she took away this chance; he'd think she no longer believed in him and pull away, and that could destroy them both. Then again, if he wasn't sleeping, his synapses could be going haywire, leading to bad decisions. And yet, as she'd heard other loved ones say, "You can't wrap them in bubble wrap" and "They deserve to live their lives—"

Laura's voice broke her reverie. "I know he's your son and you want to do what's best for him, but it's *my* daughter he's bringing up there and I think we need to call 911."

Arabella's thoughts spun to Julia, to Iliana and Carolyn. *Falling prey to phantoms. The missing knife.* Turning to look at Laura, she acknowledged an uncomfortable yet undeniable truth: *Doing nothing could put someone else's child at risk. This might be Sam's moment, but he could also be a danger to himself—and Julia—in more ways than one.*

JULIA

THE HIKE WAS TURNING OUT to be nothing like Julia had imagined. No holding hands. No posing for pictures or pausing to take a breath. After employing a pace somewhere between a jog and walk-as-fast-as-you-can to catch up to Sam, Julia could barely keep up with him. And other than asking, "You wanted to fill up those bottles?" at a water station just past a footbridge with an amazing waterfall view about a mile in, Sam hadn't really said anything *to her* at all.

At first, the trail consisted of a steep paved walkway with a man-made wall on one side and a nature-made slope on the other. Steep, but safe. Keeping one eye on Sam's back, the tripod jutting out of his backpack, Julia had commanded herself to live in the moment. *Put one foot in front of the other and be here, now.*

Because even under duress, Julia recognized her surroundings were spectacular. It was the sort of place that cried out to be captured on film or canvas or paper, even as awareness would inevitably strike the capturer of the impossibility of truly doing it justice. It was the sort of place her father would have loved—and her mother would love still: massive tree trunks and curling roots that resembled thick, sinewy spiderwebs; the smells of wet earth and bark; the vibrant greens, amber, ochre, and crimson, peerless blue and shimmering silver; alternating patches of sun and shadow as they passed under a thin cover of trees. She could see her father pre-cancer strong, striding along as he expounded on how all of it had been here long before humans came along and would be here long after they were gone, undoubtedly coming up with a poem or a quote to illuminate his point. And she could see her mother, gently shaking her head, saying, "It's just a hike, Paul."

Julia wished she could reengage Sam in the philosophical debate they'd had in the car, sharing her parents' imagined exchange, and explaining how she was beginning to understand that maybe Sam and her dad, and Camus, and Frost and Longfellow, and Tanya were all a little right. That there was a time and place for existential angst and the search for meaning, times and places for poetry and philosophy and metaphor and analysis—but maybe her mom was right too, maybe sometimes it *was* just a hike. Left to her own thoughts, Julia considered whether that was what "just being" was all about, that maybe she was right about Picasso. Maybe he hadn't meant to disparage everyday life but to inspire us to find art and beauty in each moment, even the dusty, ordinary ones. Maybe, Julia thought, Sam's swinging from the splendid to the abject at the whim of his neurotransmitters wasn't noble. She wanted to say, "Yes, we're all going to die, and life can be shitty and absurd. But looking at it as a series of unending days futilely pushing rocks up mountains isn't depressingly inspiring, it's just depressing, and I don't want to be depressed anymore. I want to live. I want to try to be happy."

She hadn't had the chance to say any of this, however, since Sam remained several feet in front of her no matter how fast she walked.

And then, shortly after the footbridge and the filling of the water bottles, the trail had changed to a series of staircases. Making an argument against the whole rock-pushing-uphill bit was abandoned, partly because now she needed to concentrate on putting one foot in front of the other lest she slip and fall, and partly because what she and Sam were engaged in was, in fact, a daunting uphill climb—surrounded by rocks. Julia had never seen so many rocks. Underfoot, a superfine mist from the waterfall dampened the steep steps hewn from stone. Soaring above them were glistening sheer-cut gray and white rock faces, lined with cracks and ledges. Decomposed granite and small stones covered the ground. Boulders lay alongside the trail—car- and minivan-sized individual ones, others in various sizes forming haphazard piles.

Rather incredibly, Sam's pace seemed to constantly accelerate, as if there were an inverse formula at work involving adversity of conditions versus level of exertion—the harder the terrain and steeper the climb, the faster he moved. His self-talk, though nearly incessant, had become irregular, sometimes an indecipherable whisper, other times clear and loud. And whatever Sam was feeling, it wasn't shaking his commitment to the task at hand. At one point, Julia heard him repeating the text of his future tattoo like a mantra: "the struggle itself towards the heights is enough, the struggle itself towards the heights is enough."

As they approached the top of the waterfall they'd seen from the bridge, he moved so far ahead she could scarcely hear him at all, yet she could see his mouth moving, and she could tell from his body language he was irritated and jittery, unhappy having to wait for her.

And then, while navigating around a group of French-speaking tourists who'd stopped along a particularly narrow set of granite stairs to pose in front of the falls across the gully, her thoughts on Sam and his mantra instead of her own internal survival instructions, Julia made a disastrous error—she looked down over the edge.

Instant vertigo struck as the floor dropped away beneath her. Dizziness seeped into her head; even when she closed her eyes, the world continued to spin. Nausea brought a cold sweat, clutching at her gut like an innards-devouring gremlin. Julia opened her eyes to a whir of purple and green and gray and blue, the vista a smear of trees and rocks, rushing water and sky. Unzipping the shell partway, she leaned up against a large sloping rock wall on her right, wanting to feel something stable, to ground herself, even while her psyche told her that grounding was impossible. Aware she was doing everything wrong, she nonetheless sucked at the air, gulping for oxygen.

She blinked, then looked up the trail. Sam continued to climb, completely unaware, unconcerned.

"Sam! Wait—"

He turned. Paused. Looked up the trail himself, then back at her. He shook his head and began to descend back to where she stood. His face resembled the stone all around them, his movements tense and deliberate. He stopped one foot away and, surprising her, reached for her right hand. Then he raised two fingers of his other hand and moved them back and forth frenetically between his eyes and hers. "Look at me," he said. "No stopping. Only climbing." His fingers continued to move. "Look at me. Eyes here. Here." This command was not at all like the last time he had asked her to look into his eyes, for the toast at Per Se. *Was that only days ago?* "No fear. No phantoms. Courage. We must keep climbing." He grabbed her shoulders, hard. "Up. Up, not down. We must keep climbing. No turning back. No looking down. I need you. Look at my shoes. Look at my shoes and climb. Up. Up. The struggle is enough."

With that, he turned again and began walking up and up, repeating this new, shorter mantra, assuming she would follow. The unease Julia had felt on and off for the last two days settled, festering in her lungs before circulating in her blood, feeding her organs, muscles, and nerves with anxiety-laced oxygen. She stood there, in shock, for a few seconds, but then, unable to think clearly for herself, she did follow him, keeping her eyes on the back of his Keds. Within a few minutes of dizzyingly steep steps carved into a massive ledge, they arrived atop a huge sloping slab of rock that led to the river and the top of the falls, populated with clusters of hikers taking photos and making videos, reclining on the ground, picnicking.

Enjoying the moment.

Impossible. Julia stopped to breathe. *Just stay away from the edge.*

Sam did not stop. Julia darted after him, noticing people staring as they passed, undoubtedly wondering about a guy moving so fast, muttering to himself—and the girl scampering after him, staring at his heels.

As they passed a large pool of water tinged green, Sam narrated aloud. "Emerald Pool and Silver Apron, illegal, dangerous to swim, extremely hazardous current," repeating it twice before saying "Cross the Merced River on the trail footbridge," now clearly reciting route guidance he'd memorized.

Route guidance they were following for they did exactly as he said, crossing another smaller, narrower, higher wooden footbridge—*Don't look down*—and then wrapping around a boulder onto a relatively flat sandy trail.

Sam's recitation continued. "Shortcut option A: Leave the trail behind and follow the drainage between Liberty Cap and Mount Broderick."

Shortcut?

As they left the trail behind, they entered a wooded area. *Whose woods these are,* Julia thought, trying to recall what Sam had said about the shortcuts earlier. A thick layer of branches, leaves, and trunks obscured the geographical landmarks he must have been referring to. *Liberty Cap and what was the other one? Mount something?* "Class 3, difficult, only experienced scramblers, bushwhacking required," Sam said, stopping Julia in her tracks. She spun around, thinking *Where is the trail?* Sam kept walking, continuing deeper into the trees, the distance between them growing, Sam's audible guidance fainter to her ears. *Where is the trail?* Everywhere she turned the tree trunks, fallen logs, bushes, pinecones, sticks, and rocks all looked remarkably similar and treacherous.

Bushwhacking and scrambling through this—this shortcut—with hours still ahead of them was downright insane.

"Sam," she called to his back. "This doesn't look right. This isn't a trail."

He turned. Yelled, "Don't worry, come on!"

Listen to your instincts. This place is nothing like the woods at Brookfield.

"Sam," she yelled in return. "No. Stop. I'm not doing this. I am not an experienced scrambler. And we don't need a shortcut because we're not short on time. You said so yourself. Sam! Come back."

He plunged ahead.

"Sam!"

He turned. Stared at her.

"We're not short on time. Come back," she repeated. *Please let him listen to me.* "You said you need me. I'll be waiting for you back on the trail." She said these words with more confidence than she felt.

Julia made her way out of the woods, hoping the light ahead indicated the path they'd left. *Look for the light, that's where I'll be.* She heard Sam behind her, his footfalls on pine needles, bark and stone, rambling words she chose not to hear.

Before she reached the edge of the tree line, Sam passed her, moving fast. And then keeping up became even more difficult. The sound of rushing water intensified as the trail steepened again, the staircases now a series of square-ended switchbacks, ever upward, reminding Julia of the stairs in "Ascending and Descending," Escher's existential image of people going nowhere. Struggling to breathe, her legs leaden, Julia marveled at Sam's energy. His pace did not waver, the murmuring did not cease.

Just when she thought she couldn't go any farther, they reached another plateau.

With more park signs: Nevada Falls and the John Muir Trail to the right. Half Dome and Merced Lake to the right. A restroom hut.

"Thank God," she said aloud "I need to stop."

Sam walked on, without her, in the direction of a sign reading Half Dome—4.

"Sam, wait!" Julia called. *Jesus, is he kidding?* Seeing him pause, head shaking and face shadowed, she turned back to the hut, removed the shell, and dropped it onto a log bench near the restroom door.

Maybe sixty seconds later, contemplating an unfortunate train of thought from permanent port-a-potties cleaning methodology to her pink shovel and standing at the edge of a pile of shit, Julia came out of the restroom shaking her head.

"Four more miles," she said to no one in particular. "You can do this."

"You know the cables are down, right?" A young guy with a full beard wearing a yellow shirt was perched on the log bench. He gestured with his head to the rope crisscrossed over her torso. "You're not planning to climb it, are you?"

"I don't think so," Julia said. *Are we?* "We're headed to the Diving Board."

"Really?" the guy said, doubtful or impressed, Julia couldn't tell. "Who's we?"

Julia looked back toward where she'd last seen Sam. There was no sign of him.

"Oh, shit, I have to go," she said, taking off at a jog.

"Hey!"

Glancing over her shoulder, Julia saw the young man rising to his feet.

"Be careful out there," he called after her.

It took a couple of minutes to catch up, and Sam was strangely silent. Looking for something along the dusty trail, he didn't seem to notice her presence, even after she'd said his name twice.

"Sam," she tried again, breathless.

"There's no sign," he said, expression and voice both disappointed and indignant. "There's supposed to be a sign."

"You mean . . . an actual sign . . . one of those metal ones?" Julia's words came out in spurts as she tried to find her breath.

"How'd you know it was supposed to be metal?"

"All . . . of the signs . . . are metal, Sam."

"All of the signs are metal?" he repeated. "No, not all signs are metal. They're not. Definitely not. Not all signs are metal." The indignant tone now bordered on angry.

Why would this make him angry? "You're right," Julia said, trying to defuse the situation. "They're not. There are other kinds of signs."

Sam didn't notice. He was clearly back to reciting. "100 yards after the sign, 100 yards, leave the trail for unofficial one marked by a cairn—"

Leave the trail?

"Can we slow down, just a little?" Julia asked. Every few steps, she had to jog to stay even with Sam.

"No! No, we can't slow down." Sam's words were coming faster. *Angrier.* "We can't slow down," he repeated, before going off on another tangent of directions, speaking so rapidly it was nearly incoherent.

"The cables are down," she said loudly, over him. "This guy back at the restrooms, he said the cables are down. Whatever that means."

Sam stopped on a dime. He grabbed Julia's arm and spun her toward him, placing both hands on her shoulders. "What guy? Who were you talking to? Who is he?" His fingers dug into her, pressing into her bones. "Where'd you get this?" With one hand, Sam yanked on the rope. Julia realized she'd forgotten the shell, and the snacks, on the log bench. "Where'd you get this?"

"Sam, stop." Julia tried to pull away. "You're hurting me. The rope is yours. It was under the duffle. In the car."

"Who is he?"

Julia could feel a tremor in his hands. She could see his body shaking, his eyes wild, flitting back and forth from the trail ahead to the trail behind.

"No one. Just some guy by the restroom."

"Some guy? You wanna go with him, don't you, that's what this is about. All the same, you, Carolyn, leaving me."

Carolyn. The other girl in the picture. She'd left him.

Julia reached up to cover his hands with her own, trying to engage his eyes. "Sam, no, I'm not leaving you. I don't even know the guy. I said something about it being four miles to Half Dome, and he must have heard me, so he said, 'the cables are down.' That was it, Sam. That was all it was." Slowly loosening his grip, she added, "It didn't mean *anything*."

"You want to be with him. You're going to leave me."

"No." Julia pulled his hands down slowly. "I want to be with you. I'm here with you, Sam. I believe in *you*."

Even as she said these words, Julia wondered if they were true. She wanted them to be; she wanted to believe in Sam. *Isn't that why I'm up here, doing this?*

"You don't," Sam said. She couldn't tell if he was enraged, dubious, or sad. Tears were forming in his eyes. "You don't."

"Yes, I do." He was sobbing now. *Oh my god, what do I do?* Hoping to calm him with her touch and her words, Julia held his hands tightly as she heard herself saying, "I believe in you and us and this." *What else can I say?* Her father's words floated up: "I believe the stars will shine tonight and the sun will rise tomorrow." Words so at odds with *when the time comes.* Had she done the right thing? *What was the right thing?*

Still shaking, Sam yanked his hands from hers to place them on either side of his open mouth, pulling the skin back as he exhaled sharply. The gesture looked painful.

Julia kept talking, words spilling, her hands still suspended toward him. "I believe there will always be things we cannot know and that that's okay."

"You don't understand."

"No, but I'm trying, and that's what matters. I'm trying to understand, Sam."

Sam took a step back toward the restroom, turned, took two steps forward, turned again.

"Maybe we should go back? I left the food back by the restroom, in the jacket. Do you want to go back?" Julia asked, hoping he'd say yes. *We should go back.*

Sam ducked his head down, his hands now raking through his hair. Julia felt her own hands migrating upward. *No*, she told herself as they reached the edge of her hairline. She consciously lowered them, brushing against the water bottle. She'd only gotten him to take a few gulps of water so far. Maybe he was dehydrated.

"Do you want some water?" Julia said, unhooking the bottle.

Sam lifted his face, his fingers still entwined. He was still crying.

"Sam," Julia said softly, reaching for him.

Sam jerked backward as if her touch would burn him.

"No. No." Sam's voice changed yet again, louder now, angry. "No, we must go forward, not back, no U-turns. We're going to find the sign and the cairns and the trail and the creek." He was off, both physically and verbally, walking fast in the direction of Half Dome, talking to himself under his breath.

Maybe I should go back, get help, Julia thought, even as her feet began moving in the direction Sam had gone. Up ahead there was a metal sign marking a fork in the path. As they approached, Julia could see it bore some of the words Sam had been muttering: Merced Lake, Little Yosemite Valley. Sam was counting aloud in time with rapid, deliberately lengthened paces. "Eighty-one, eighty-two, eighty-three . . ."

What is he doing? she wondered, until she remembered him saying "100 yards past the metal sign." *He's counting the yards.*

"Ninety-eight, ninety-nine, one hundred." Sam stopped, looking around, his face streaked with dusty, smudged trails from his tears. "Where are they? Where are the cairns?"

"The cairns?" Julia asked.

"The rocks. Where are the rocks marking the way?"

Where were the rocks? They were fucking *everywhere.*

"There!" Sam said, pointing to a rock the size of a misshapen grapefruit lying sideways atop a boulder off to the left, several feet up. "This is it. This is it."

Julia watched as Sam rushed up the hillside with kamikaze recklessness, repeating "This is it" over and over. She acknowledged it was a trail, of sorts, up to the top of a small ridge where it disappeared into low brush.

"Yes, this is it," Sam said, swiping at the brush with a stiff arm. "This is it. Look," he went on, pointing to another small pile of stones in a small forest below. "Cairns. It's the trail. I told you. Follow the cairns. That's all we need to do, follow the cairns."

Julia could see a huge, curved dome of rock ahead of them; the sheared-off face in the iconic image must be on the other side, the side with the gaping emptiness Sam had extolled. They were looking at the back of Half Dome, and it was really fucking far away. She looked back down. There was no trail. The sandy ground was covered with crisp pine needles. Lime-green patches of moss. And more rocks. Everywhere. From where she was standing, she could see three piles of granite stones, varying in size from ones that might fit in the palm of her hand to the size of a flat-bottomed bowling ball. The three piles were not in a line nor did they seem to form any kind of pattern. *Were these cairns?*

"Which ones are we supposed to follow?" she called to Sam.

But he was off, moving quickly down the hillside, already passing one of the piles of stones. She watched him pause, spin around, take several steps in one direction only to pause again. Then she heard him say, quite clearly, "West, northwest."

"Sam?"

He looked up at her for the briefest moment before taking off in a new direction. Julia began to traverse the "path" he'd taken.

"Sam, wait."

When she reached where he'd just been, she couldn't see any cairns, and yet Sam was plunging ahead, gaining ground. She heard him say, "Step over small creek to your right. 37.734380, skirt the shore of Lost Lake."

She could not see a creek or lake.

"There's no creek, Sam, there's no lake," she called out. "I don't think this way is right."

Up ahead, Sam was repeating, for the fourth or fifth time, "West, northwest." Perhaps hearing her, he stopped again. "Don't be afraid. West, northwest. It was all there: The trail becomes difficult. Backtracking necessary. Go back to last cairn. Difficult trail-finding, scrambling, all right there, right there. The ordeal. Must be committed, like Stieglitz and Adams. Virginia. Heidegger. Sein und Zeit. Go back to last cairn." Sam looked away.

Backtracking also proved difficult, however, and a search for where they'd just been led them to a place Julia didn't recognize at all. Spindly pine trees. Dead tree trunks standing. More on the ground. Rocks, but no cairns. Not a single cairn. No trail.

This is crazy, she thought. *Worse than a maze.*

"I don't see any cairns," she said quietly. "Sam, there're no cairns."

Sam turned. "What?"

"Is this where we were?"

"Where we were?" Sam's head and body turned in opposition: body left, head right; body right, head left; back and forth. The backpack jostled. "Where we were? No. We can never be where we were, never again. No one can. Sein und Zeit. Time waits for no one. No one. Not where we were because we have to go up." He stepped deliberately toward a thick, low bush with shiny red bark. "Bushwhacking. Limit exposure. Always risks. We're not where we were because we must go up. Commit. Pacts and promises. Decades of letters. Decades, my faraway one. Virginia on the edge of the abyss for him." Sam's face was damp, the dust streaks more pronounced. Eyes bright, he looked the way he had in the hotel room in the middle of the night. Confused. Enraged.

Had he just said "on the edge of the abyss for him"? Did he mean *she* needed to go out on the edge of an abyss? She could not do that.

She needed to stop this madness, stop him.

"Stop, please. Sam, stop, listen to me." She needed to exude confidence, yet she could hear the desperation in her voice. "This isn't a good idea. We should go back, Sam." Julia moved directly in front of him, raising her hands to calm him. "I know this is really important, but we should go back down and wait—"

"Wait?!" Sam was yelling now. "For what? It's going to be years. Thirty-four years! That's what you said."

Shit. Julia wished she'd never told him about the mega moon. *Shit.*

"No, I meant wait until you can do the hike with someone experienced, someone who knows the trail."

"I don't need someone else only you I know the trail I know it." Sam sputtered, along with more memorized bits of the route, the words melting together. "But you don't believe me you don't think I can do it say it." He spun away from her, eyes wide, arms flailing, contacting her shoulder. Accidental, but hard.

Julia stumbled backward, but Sam didn't notice. She held up her hands again, took one step toward him.

"Please, Sam, listen to me. I *do* think you can do it, just not today." Julia spoke over Sam's continued stream of words. "You're not okay, Sam. I know you want to do this, but we can come back another time, when things are clearer—"

"What?" Sam shouted, his right hand flying up, this time with an intentional sideways swipe to bat hers down, making impact with the bone on the outside of her wrist. Sharp pain radiated into her hand. "I'm not okay? Clearer fuck clearer I knew it I saw it ohhh ohhh." Sam's hands went back up to pull at his face. "That's what it was all the questions why aren't you taking it why won't you take it ohhh now I see it was all a big fucking act you don't love me it's a big fucking act." His voice a venomous snapping snarl, he took a step toward her, leaning in. "You don't love me don't believe in me don't believe in anything."

"No, Sam. You're wrong. I do believe in you." Julia lifted her hands again, attempting to place them on Sam's upper arms. "But you're not okay. You're not thinking clearly."

"Clearly not thinking clearly." Sam's voice raised, his hands swatting hers away again. "Never more clearly in my life wasting my time all this time explaining it to you—"

"I'm trying to understand—"

Before Julia saw it coming, Sam strong-armed her and she stumbled backward again, this time falling to the ground. Breaking the impact with her right arm, she landed awkwardly on the side of her hip and thigh. Sam looked at his hands as if they didn't belong to him, then at Julia. "You understand nothing. Nothing. You called them you called them you called them the first day you told them where to go on the Ferris wheel

watching from above no pact with you you don't know about
struggling struggling." Sam's voice trailed off as he raised his
eyes, swiveling, looking for something above them.

Julia looked up too, trying to follow what he was saying.
They hadn't gone on the Ferris wheel. *What does he mean,*
she thought, *watching from above?* She searched for the dome
through the trees. She could find her way if she located it, or
the ridge they'd crossed, if she could recognize it. Would she
recognize it? Before she could do anything, Sam took three
firm strides away in what seemed to be a totally new direction,
not where they'd been. Julia's thoughts turned to the woods
outside of Brookfield, Sam drawing a path on her palm.

Julia got to her feet, ignoring the radiating pain in her hip,
her wrist. "Sam! Stop!"

Sam did not turn. She heard him murmuring a string of
words set to a cadence that, even if she were closer, she doubted
she'd be able to keep up with. His movements were quicker
still, frenetic—nearly running, jumping over fallen logs, arms
up like wings.

"Sam, please stop!" she called, taking two steps toward
his retreating figure. "Sam!" she called over and over, as he
disappeared into the trees.

LAURA

LAURA STOOD OUTSIDE THE VISITOR center, staring at Arabella, when her phone rang in her pocket, displaying yet another unknown number. It was Julia, distraught, speaking in spurts punctuated with "oh my gods." Any relief Laura felt at the sound of her daughter's voice quickly dissipated watching Arabella's face wash with dread as she listened to Laura's side of the conversation.

"Slow down, honey. Where are you?"

"At the top of the falls. But Sam's not here. I don't know where he is. He kept driving and wouldn't sleep and it's all my fault. If I hadn't left with him in the first place, none of this would have happened. I told him about the stupid moon, and everything went sideways, and I didn't know what to do, and then, then I left him." She went on rapidly. "And now, what if he gets lost or he doesn't get the picture and he—oh my god, this is all my fault. I can't do anything right."

"That's not true, Julia. You're doing the right thing right now, calling me," Laura had said. "Arabella and I are here, and we can help you. We can help Sam."

"Arabella?"

"Yes, she's here with me and we can help you."

"Wait, what—Arabella's *with* you?"

"Yes, we're together. We've been trying to find you, since that first text. We saw you in Chicago—"

"You were in Chicago?"

"Yes, we talked to Sheila. We found your list—"

"You were in Chicago. You were on the Ferris wheel. Oh my god." Julia's words tumbled out. "That's what he was talking about. He saw you. I thought he was losing his mind, but he wasn't. Oh my god, this is all my fault. First Dad, now Sam."

"Honey, this isn't your fault."

"He didn't want us to hurt anymore."

"Sam?"

"No. Dad, Dad. I heard you arguing. I heard him say he wanted to stop all the hurting. He wanted you to help him end it, but you said no. So I did it. I heard him say 'Please help me' that morning, and I did. I brought him those pain meds and he died. Because of me."

"Pain meds?" Laura's thoughts swooped and swirled to the memory she'd had just the day before: Julia saying goodbye, the orange bottle appearing out of nowhere, dropping onto the floor, the nurse picking it up. Paul had been asking her to help him see the sunrise that morning, *not to help him die.* But Julia must have misunderstood. She must have placed the medication there for Paul, but he'd been too weak to lift his hand, let alone open a childproof bottle. *Don't give up. Make sure to tell her I'll keep trying.* Laura hadn't told Julia any of this. She hadn't known what it meant and was having trouble processing it now. *Does Julia think she had a role in Paul's death?* "Oh my god. Julia, honey, is that what you've thought? Oh my god, no. No. He was asking me to help him see the sunrise, not—it doesn't matter. Oh, sweetheart, I'm so sorry. You've been carrying this. All this time. And, oh—" This explained so much: the pain, the guilt, *maybe even the suicide attempt.* "No, no. Julia, please listen to me. You aren't responsible at all. Dad never took that pain medication. He told me to tell you, but I didn't know what he meant."

Julia was weeping, gasping for breath.

"Julia, he didn't take the medication you left."

"How do you know? How do you know he didn't take it?"

"I was there the whole time. He didn't take it. The nurse took it away."

"What? She took it away?"

"Yes, he didn't take it, and he told me to tell you. He told me to tell you he didn't give up. It was the seizures. The cancer. Not you. None of this is your fault. Not Dad. Not Sam." Laura looked over at Arabella. Her face was pale. There was so much more to say, but it would have to wait. "And you're not alone, not anymore. I'm putting you on speaker. Arabella and I, we're here for you, and we can get help—for Sam—if he's in danger." Laura lowered the phone, pressed the speaker button. "Do you think Sam's in danger, Julia?"

Hearing Julia continue gasping for air, Arabella shook her head, lips pressed between her teeth. Laura repeated her promise. "We'll do everything we can to get someone up there to help, to keep him safe, okay?" Julia did not answer. "Julia?"

"I didn't know what to do. Something's happened to him. He's not making sense anymore. I wanted him to be okay. I *wanted* him to take his medicine. I wanted him to sleep. But he wouldn't. I didn't know what to do. We need to help him."

"Okay, okay," Laura said, though nothing was okay. "We're in the valley, by the visitor center." Instinctively, she reached out to touch Arabella's forearm. "We'll go inside and get help for Sam. Do you want to stay on the phone?"

"I can't. They're almost out of power. I have to give them their phone back."

"Okay, okay, but I don't want you to be alone. Can these people stay with you, the people you borrowed the phone from? Or maybe you can start hiking down with them? I'll hike up. Meet you halfway."

"I can't leave," Julia said. "I can't."

Laura recalled saying these same words herself, only days earlier. She could feel the desperate hope she'd clung to the night she'd heard Julia had gone missing, how she'd wanted to remain at home—to be there, where Julia might return.

Empathy fought with selfish longing; Laura ached to hold Julia again, to protect her. "I understand," she said, "but we need to be able to reach you. Can they stay with you until we know what we're going to do?"

Laura listened to her daughter asking for help from total strangers. And then she went inside with Arabella to speak with Ranger Mike. They were shown into a stark, utilitarian room, thinly lit by shaded sun through a single window and a florescent fixture overhead. The only decorations were two notices, *Safety in the Workplace* and *The Ten Essentials*, aka Ranger Mike's memorized list, along with three vintage Yosemite advertisement posters in wooden frames that had seen better days. The supervising park ranger on duty, Luis, sat across from them, papers on the desk labeled Search Urgency Chart and Missing Person Questionnaire. "Standard forms," he said. Filling out the former was quick, circles drawn around numbers 1 through 4. Though Sam was young, fit and dressed somewhat appropriately, he also had a known mental illness, was unreliable, unfamiliar with the area, and the route had known hazards.

Shockingly, to Laura, these conditions did not add up to an "urgent response."

And a "measured response" included completion of the MPQ and other relevant paperwork: name, address, date of birth, height, weight, hair and eye color, automobile being driven. As Luis asked about the make, model and color of the vehicle Sam was driving, Arabella's jaw clenched, and with each additional question, her accent became more pronounced.

In contrast, Luis continued in the calm, neutral tone he'd used ever since meeting Laura and Arabella. "Any distinguishing marks, tattoos?"

Aware how easily it could have been herself answering these questions, Laura felt the clutch in her gut as she watched Arabella try to contain her emotions: shoulders raised, lips tight, hands clenched into a twisted knot in her lap.

"Nothing you can see from a distance." Arabella's voice was strained. "I'm not sure how this is relevant."

"The more information we have," Luis said, "the more accurate our response will be."

On one level, Laura understood that the ranger's matter-of-fact, stick-to-the-script interview style was meant to modulate the situation, keep things even-keeled. But she felt the urge to pull Luis outside and say, *My daughter is up there, desperate, and this woman's son is losing his mind as he climbs toward a literal abyss, and you want to know about birthmarks and the model of his car?*

Arabella exhaled, her eyelids fluttering. "He has scars on his wrists, each about an inch and a half long, running vertically along the tendon."

"Nothing else, no tattoos?"

Arabella shook her head.

"Are the scars you mentioned the result of a recent event?"

"No, they are not. That particular event occurred over a year ago. His most recent attempt, about two months ago, involved an overdose . . . of prescription medications."

The ranger flipped pages, jotted something down. "These medications, were they prescribed *for him* and might he have them in his possession?"

"Excuse me," Arabella interrupted, lifting her hands as if to repel an attack. "I understand you're following protocol, but please, can't this wait? I explained to the first ranger—Mike?—that my son has *not* been taking anything, according to the young woman with him, Julia. He hasn't been sleeping, eating, or drinking enough water. He's no longer making sense. Displaying erratic behavior." Arabella leaned forward, placing her hands on the desk, her upper arms, shoulders, even the cords in her long neck, tense. Her fingertips blanched white as she tightened her grip, holding on to the edge of the desk. "I promise you, I will give you every detail you could possibly want as soon as someone's gone up after him. Please."

Ranger Luis sighed, shaking his head. He stood, unfolding to his full height. Well over six feet, Luis had hair like a military recruit and a barrel-chested physique that, under normal circumstances, would have inspired confidence. Yet now, Laura feared his appearance might indicate he was the sort of man who loathed the vagaries of mental illness, a man not unlike her father. "Let me check with Dispatch. I'll be right back."

Arabella leaned back, closed her eyes.

Other than the dull drone of an attic fan in the hallway, the room was silent.

In the silence, Laura's thoughts drifted. Paul had wanted to die to stop hurting them. Julia had believed she'd helped her father die, all these months. *All these months.* Laura looked down at her phone, wanting to call her, to talk to her. "It's going to be okay," she said aloud to herself. To Arabella. From her chair near the open door, she could hear Luis's muted voice in a nearby room, conversing on a radio or the telephone: words, silence, words, silence. The offending forms sat on the desk, waiting.

"I'm so sorry," Laura added softly.

And Luis was back, speaking as he came through the doorway, as he walked around the desk to face them again. "Okay, some good news. A yellow shirt up at Nevada Falls heading down trail says he spoke with your daughter near the restroom before she headed up toward Half Dome. When he heard the BOLO, he turned around and headed back up, which puts him much closer in terms of where your son went off trail.

"If we'd had to send someone from here in the valley, we'd be hours behind. But now, well, we'll see, but this yellow shirt's heading up. If it's all right with you," he said, turning to Laura, "we'd like to have him speak with your daughter on the phone. You mentioned she's still at the falls, is that right? And you've got that number?"

Laura nodded. She pulled up her recent calls and slid her phone across the desk. "It's the last call."

As Luis wrote the number at the top edge of the Search Urgency form, there was a knock on the doorframe. A young female ranger with a slight build stood in the open doorway. "Ms. Reeves, Ms. Lorenzo, this is Rebecca. She'll be your point person going forward. I'll remain involved logistically, but Rebecca'll help you finish up the paperwork, stay with you, keep you abreast of what's happening. She's got a lot of experience in situations like this."

The severe bun at the nape of Rebecca's neck amplified the serious expression on her unlined face. Laura thought she didn't look old enough to have experience in anything.

"Rebecca, Ms. Lorenzo is the young man's mother. Ms. Reeves is Julia's." Luis nodded in succession. Moving around the desk, passing behind Laura and Arabella, he said, "I'll leave you to it, then. Rebecca—"

Within minutes, Laura had to admit her prejudgment about the young female ranger had been incorrect. Rebecca revealed she was a licensed social worker, a wilderness EMT, and a mother of two little girls, and when Laura begged to be allowed to "do something," the young ranger had listened. Within a half hour, she'd not only okayed a plan for Laura and Arabella to proceed up the trail, with her and a radio, toward Julia and Sam, she'd also procured granola bars, water bottles, a couple of fleece jackets, and headlamps.

Laura had been wrong about Luis as well. Rebecca said he'd recommended a helicopter search of the area where Sam went off trail, now, before darkness fell. "If we can locate him from above, it'll be easier for the PSAR, Jason, and the YOSAR team now heading up." Luis had also spoken directly with Julia and convinced her to come down before dark, to stay safe herself. And Julia would not be alone. The couple she'd borrowed the phone from, the Burnhams, had agreed to stay and hike Julia down. They were locals, Rebecca explained, familiar with the trails and well provisioned, with extra food and flashlights.

"Like you," Rebecca said, addressing Laura, "Julia wants to help, so she's going to accompany Jason to the point at which she and Sam left the trail and give him whatever info she can on Sam's intended route. Also, you should know, just now Julia told Luis she had a bit of an episode on the way up. Some vertigo, nausea"—Rebecca held up her hands palms out—"which she handled, but Jason and Luis suggested she take a different trail down, the John Muir trail. It's wider, more gradual, with a wall much of the way. One snafu: The

Burnhams' phone is nearly out of power, so they're going to turn it off and check in periodically for messages. Julia's in good hands, though, and with the moon and these clear skies . . ." Rebecca gave them a tight smile. "For what it's worth, we have park-sponsored moonlit hikes. A full moon provides a surprising amount of light."

Time and space blurred: en route to the trailhead, they passed campsites filled with tents and RVs; Laura barely registered the forested scenery; they set a brisk pace up a paved trail, across a wooden bridge over a boulder and rapid-filled river with a view of a waterfall; and then, shortly thereafter, they peeled off the trail, heading away from the water. Laura, Arabella, and Rebecca hiked in silence, broken only by sporadic sighs and periodic radio exchanges between Rebecca and voices without faces. Taking up the last position in line, mechanically placing one foot in front of the other, Laura tried to decipher the coded radio exchanges, only a smattering of which were accompanied by translations from Rebecca: "Jason's reached Lost Lake"; "The helicopter's circling the area"; and "Julia's heading down with the Burnhams. We should meet up in about an hour."

An hour. Laura would see Julia in an hour. A rush of adrenaline pulsed through her, followed by a shiver that struck hard and lingered like lightning trapped in a web, stopping her dead in her tracks. An hour sounded like a lifetime. Laura began to count her steps, measuring the minutes in distance to Julia, each switchback a 180-degree turn bringing her closer to her daughter. At sixty times sixty, she began to look ahead. The vistas opened to commanding panoramic views of rocks and trees, water falling, and an ever-changing sky, now lighter at the horizon, deep bluish purple above. At sixty times seventy, tears began to form, and she paused, listening for voices.

And then, Julia was there—face drawn and wet, eyes red and puffy, body lost inside a large dark gray jacket—and then she was running awkwardly toward Laura. Passing Rebecca and Arabella, Laura ran toward her, and for one brief moment, nothing else mattered. All the steps and turns and doubts and fears, the bottled-up emotions and empty spaces and closed doors, even the towering pines, granite peaks, and setting sun— all of it disappeared. Tears poured down her face, unchecked. The only thing Laura knew or cared about was her daughter in her arms. However, all too quickly Julia pulled away, saying, "Have you heard anything? Did they find him? Did they see him from the helicopter?" Letting go of everything except Julia's left hand, which Laura gripped tightly in her right, there was a pause as reality returned: the older couple standing behind Julia, Rebecca and Arabella standing behind Laura, the stone wall between all of them, the drop to the landscape below.

Laura shook her head slowly.

Rebecca spoke up. "Hey, Julia, I'm Becky, with the park service. First, I want to tell you, you did the right thing, getting help. Truly. It was the brave thing. The right thing. I know you have a lot of questions, and I'll try to answer all of them. So, no, they couldn't see Sam from the chopper, but Jason is nearly at the Diving Board and a second YOSAR team is on the way up. Jason said you were really helpful, that you gave him a lot of locator cues. He said he couldn't have done it without you." She paused, giving Julia a chance to absorb what she'd said. "How're you doing?"

Julia shrugged, her shoulders overwhelmed by the jacket. Laura didn't recognize any of the clothing Julia was wearing. *Of course,* Laura thought, *she'd left everything behind.*

"I just want to know that he's okay," Julia said. She turned to Laura. "I didn't know what to do." And then to Arabella: "I'm so sorry," her voice broke. Dropping her hand, Laura put her arm around Julia's shoulders. Julia leaned into her as they both wiped away tears.

Standing only a foot or two away, Arabella nodded ever so slightly. She was clearly holding everything in, her expression grave, face quivering. "I know," she said, reaching out to briefly grasp Julia's free hand. "I know. So am I."

Looking past Arabella and Laura to the view beyond the gray stone wall, Julia said, "The moon. It must be after five.

That's when we were supposed to be up there. Is that it?" She turned to Rebecca, pointing to a jagged rock peak to the left of a waterfall. "Is that Half Dome?"

Rebecca shook her head. "No, that's Liberty Cap, then Mount Broderick." She raised her own hand to point in succession as Julia nodded along. "And then, the curved one, that's the back of the dome. We can't see the face from here, or the Diving Board. We wouldn't be able to see anything up there from this distance."

Julia wiped her cheeks again. "He wanted to be there now."

Mr. Burnham spoke. "It's getting dark. Maybe we should head down—"

Laura wasn't sure if he was referring to himself and his wife, or all of them. She also realized she hadn't spoken to them yet, this couple that had helped save her daughter. Still holding on to Julia, Laura turned and said quietly, "I'm sorry. I haven't thanked you for everything you've done for Julia."

The man said something in return, but his words were eclipsed by Julia asking, "Can't we stay here a little longer? I know we can't see him, but—"

As if an unspoken agreement had been reached, all five of them stood quietly watching the moon rising in the color-washed sky.

Then Rebecca's radio squawked, and Laura felt Julia stiffen beside her. Rebecca took several steps down the trail and, with her hand over the mouthpiece, answered in a low voice. After another exchange, she returned to where the other four stood waiting. "Jason's up on the ridge. He says there's someone fitting Sam's description on the Diving Board. Whoever it is, they're moving around a lot, but Jason said it appears they're setting up some kind of pole, maybe a tripod. Luis is going to step him through the contact protocol."

Laura felt the adrenaline rush and web of lightning strike again as Julia whispered, "He made it." All eyes locked on the round back of Half Dome as she repeated the phrase. "He made it."

JULIA

WITH HER NOW-DUSTY KEDS SOLIDLY on the ground, Julia wished she could orchestrate an overhead out-of-body experience. Not there, where she was—standing behind a low stone wall with a view of the back of Half Dome, watching the moon climb in the sky—but rather on the other side of the valley, above the Diving Board itself. Short of that, Julia had to imagine what she might see: Sam positioning the tripod, lifting his head from the camera's eyepiece as she'd seen him do with the U-turn sign and the white teepee, shaking his head to clear the flop of dark hair over his forehead, his eyes narrowing as he envisioned the exact image he wanted to capture, seeing what he wanted the world to see, smiling as he set the aperture, shutter speed and ISO, and then, pressing his finger on the shutter release, hearing the click—

"And he's sure? Yes. No. I understand. Yes, I see." The tone of Becky's voice shifted from conversational to clipped, almost stern, bringing it from calming background noise forward into focus. Julia turned to glance at the ranger, aware her mother and Arabella had done the same. As though a screen had closed over her features, Becky's face became a neutral mask.

"What is it?" Julia asked.

Stowing her radio, Becky took a slow tentative step toward the three women. She glanced down, blinked slowly, her hands slowly rubbing up and down the outside of her gray pants.

"Luis wants us to start heading down." Seeing Julia shake her head, Becky went on, "I know you want to stay, but I think he's right. For safety, we should head down. Everyone okay with that?"

Out of her peripheral vision, Julia saw Mr. Burnham nodding his head in agreement.

Arabella said nothing.

"They'll be bringing Sam down," Laura said softly to Julia. She felt her mother's arm wrapping around her waist. Laura directed the next comment to both Julia and Arabella. "We'll meet him in the village." Turning to Becky, she added, "Right?"

Julia watched as Becky leaned over, unzipping the backpack she'd placed at the base of the wall when they'd first stopped. She removed a number of black straps from a middle pocket and, straightening up, handed them to Laura, Arabella, and Julia. "Headlamps," she said. "If you press and release the red button, they flash, so you'll want to hold it in for a second or two, then it'll stay on. I also have a couple of flashlights if anyone wants more light."

Mimicking Becky's actions, the three women depressed and held the buttons until circles of bright-grayish-blue white light flooded the stone path, wall, and sloping granite behind them. Julia placed the strap over her head as Becky said, "Anybody need something to eat or drink before we start?"

Julia realized she hadn't even thought about eating since leaving Sam on the forest floor. Becky was loading the pack on her back. "No? Okay, well, at least remember to keep drinking water. All good?"

Julia turned back to stare again at the back of Half Dome. Arabella did the same.

Sam is up there, Julie told herself. *He saw the moonrise of his epic moon. And my dad only wanted to see the sunrise, an ordinary sunrise.*

Becky's voice broke through her thoughts. She was moving toward the downhill trail. "I'll lead, then how about you follow me, Arabella, then maybe Julia, and Laura. Mr. and Mrs. Burnham, would you mind taking up the rear?"

Nodding, Mr. Burnham said, "Please, Frank and Liesl."

Julia knew their names already. The couple had done their best to keep her distracted while they'd been waiting for Jason and then again on the trek down from the falls, also sharing the names of their four children and a bunch of grandchildren, and stories Julia knew they were carefully curating to keep her mind off where she was and what was going on somewhere high above them. On some level, Julia had appreciated their efforts. Moreover, she'd recognized the fact that she could appreciate these efforts was another sign her return to self was real. Nevertheless, she'd found keeping up her end of the conversation difficult. Finally, Liesl had silenced Frank with "I think Julia's a bit overwhelmed, hon. Am I right?" She'd glanced to Julia. "Would you like a little quiet?"

Now, descending in the intersecting glow of the head-lamps and softer diffuse moonlight filtering through the trees, Julia was grateful for the low murmur of Frank and Liesl talking behind her. She was torn between wanting silence and wanting it to be filled, between wanting to be alone with thoughts of Sam and what her mom had said about her dad, and wanting not to think at all. As she turned around a curve in the serpentine path, she was reminded of Sam and his lab-yrinth. Did he feel he'd made it to the center today? *Had he found himself there, even if only for a moment?* She hoped he'd understand the decision she'd made, that eventually he'd come around to seeing it the way she did: she wanted to keep him safe, not because she didn't believe in him, but because she did. Somehow, knowing he'd made it to the top without her allowed her to consider that maybe he didn't need her as much as he'd professed. At first this realization made her sad, yet, in a way, it was also freeing. Her dad hadn't needed her either. She wasn't sure how to think about all of it. *Maybe Tanya will agree to see me when I get home,* she thought.

And then, Julia understood—she wanted to go home, with her mom. She wasn't ready to be on her own, with Sam, not just yet. She sighed.

"You okay?" her mom asked, coming alongside her.

Julia shrugged. Shook her head.

Her mother reached for her hand and, for the next several steps, they walked together, hand in hand, in silence.

Turning another corner, listening to the sounds of their footfalls on stone, sticks and needles underfoot, the hum of the night around them, Julia saw Becky below her moving in the opposite direction and it occurred to her that the radio had gone completely quiet. No more updates. Becky hadn't received a message or spoken into it since they began to head down.

And with a suddenness that caused her whirling thoughts to still and the air to cease moving in her lungs, Julia knew something had gone wrong up on the Diving Board. She stopped walking.

"Julia?" her mother said, as her hand jerked loose. "What is it?"

Becky and Arabella stopped and turned. Julia stared at Becky. And in that second, caught without the mask of neutrality she'd been wearing earlier, Julia saw in Becky's face that her suspicions were correct. *Something happened to Sam.* Something had happened before they started down.

"The radio. There's been nothing. Tell us," Julia said, gulping. "Tell us what happened."

From her position on the path, she could see Frank and Liesl on the trail above, looking back and forth between her face and that of the ranger.

"What happened?' Laura said. "Something happened?"

Julia looked directly at Arabella as fear and recognition crossed her face. Wrapping her arms around her own torso, all Arabella said was "Sam," in a quiet voice, a single word that spoke volumes.

Becky took three or four steps back up the trail and reached out to touch Arabella's crossed arms. Julia felt her mother's arm come up and around her waist, lifting her and holding her.

"Luis wanted me to wait until we were down."

"Is Sam okay?" Julia asked.

"Please, let me explain." Becky swallowed. "Jason saw Sam up on the Diving Board, shortly after sunset."

A wave of heat swept through Julia's head. *That was at least an hour ago.*

"He was several feet away when Jason began to go through the protocol, with Luis on the radio. Sam was jittery, excited, talking fast. He kept repeating this phrase—"

"What, what was he saying?" Julia interrupted.

Becky fixed her gaze on Julia's face. "He was saying 'Tell her I got it.'" Seeing Julia's eyes open wider, Becky went on quickly. "So, Jason said he would, as soon as they both got down, but Sam was insistent that 'she'—Jason assumed he meant you—needed to know." Becky's eyes darted over to Arabella before returning to Julia. "Jason said he'd radio down. Sam was getting agitated, so Jason had his right hand out." Becky demonstrated. "So he was using his left hand to get his radio. He fumbled it and—" Becky looked back and forth from Arabella to Julia. "He said he only looked down for a second, but when he looked back up . . . When he looked back up, Sam was gone."

What does she mean? thought Julia. *That can't be right. No.*

"No," Arabella whispered.

"Jason thinks it was an accident, maybe he tripped or took a wrong step. His backpack was right there under his feet, by the tripod—"

Arabella inhaled sharply, audibly. "An accident?"

Sam was gone.

"I'm so sorry," Becky said softly and slowly. "We are all so very sorry."

With that, Arabella began to weep. Silent sobs that wracked her slight frame. Instinctively, Julia curled toward her, feeling her mom's arms around them both.

There were no words.

ARABELLA

IT WAS ALL IMPOSSIBLE: acknowledging she would never hug Sam again, never hear his voice, or see his smile; wondering how things might be different if she'd only called 911 earlier; thinking about Sam's last moments; dealing with the emotions that flooded over her on both an unexpected and a regular basis. Guilt, horror, disbelief, sorrow that defied description. Begging the universe for any comfort, she hoped Sam's thoughts had spun into shards well before he was aware of what was happening when he fell.

A part of her hadn't wanted to leave Yosemite, where her son had been alive, looking up at the same moon, but in the end, she had to return to face the reality of a life without him. On the plane home, a random part of her brain screamed she should have prepared herself better, that if she had, it might have been easier. All those trial runs. But nothing compared. The first time she walked into her foyer, the finality of the silence from downstairs was painful in ways she couldn't have ever imagined.

A stack of mail sat atop the side table, neatly sorted by Arabella's cleaning lady in her absence. Arabella's eyes drifted down to the floor where a gray poster tube sat on one rounded end, sloppily sealed with silver duct tape. The cardboard bore her name and address in Sam's instantly recognizable handwriting. She could barely make out the shipping label that indicated it had been sent from Richfield, Utah. Dropping her bags, Arabella held the tube in her hands for a while, she had no idea how long, allowing the flood to subside enough to contemplate walking into the kitchen, where she found scissors to slice open the tape. Inside was Sam's copy of "Monolith," rolled inside a few sheets of hotel letterhead. An outside layer was covered with Sam's increasingly loopy combination of script and print:

Mum—

Enclosing inspiration . . .

I can't wait for you to see the images I'm capturing. Everything is coming together in this amazing way, and I know you're going to love them, because you will see me. You, of all people, will see what I see.

So, if for some reason something happens to me, please get them developed. Don't worry, I'm not planning on anything happening, but you know how it is, better than anyone else.

Since we're on the topic, though, if something does happen, please take care of Julia. She reminds me of what you must have been like when you had me, but I'm not sure she has your strength—not yet— and she just might need it someday. I don't want her to get lost somewhere she doesn't belong. Besides, I think she'll be good for you.

Which brings me to the main reason for this note . . . In this incomprehensible world, when nothing else made sense, I've always known one thing for sure—what love could be—because of you. When I couldn't believe in myself, I knew you believed in me, and that's worth more than I'll ever be able to repay. I've put you through too much and no apologies will ever be enough . . . but I'm going to say it anyway—I'm sorry. I only hope I also bring you joy. Wait 'til you see these prints!

The life you've given me has been more than most people will ever experience and I've never wanted to be anyone other than exactly who I am.
Always,
Your son, Sam
ps Now I'm off to touch a crazy-ass moon and some stars
pps Sorry for the crappy stationery

JULIA

MID-AFTERNOON SUNLIGHT reflected off the pale stone edifice of Butler Library, its Ionic pillars creating arched frames around square-paned windows that stretched several stories high. Come evening, these windows would shine with a warm, golden glow, and they'd remain lit throughout the night, welcoming insomniacs and anxious students twenty-four-seven. Every time she walked past, Julia recalled knowing Columbia was the place she wanted to be when, one month after Sam's memorial service, she'd toured the campus with her mom as part of her easier-on-paper-than-in-execution Tanya-assisted life plan and seen the names of philosophers, thinkers, and writers inscribed over the entrance: Homer, Herodotus, Sophocles, Plato . . . It was a sign, she decided, a sign that had been confirmed when she found Longfellow's name inscribed under one of the windows, along with Emerson, Thoreau, and Whitman. A sign that provided motivation—and just enough justification for turning grief into material—to write an essay on "A Psalm of Life": self-determination, her dad, Sam, and her ever-evolving understanding of the world.

Now crossing the aptly named College Walk, Julia took it all in—hedges and grass trimmed to the perfect length, well-dressed students purposefully crossing campus or meandering in groups, conversing, and laughing—it was so picturesque, it didn't seem real. She imagined what Sam might say if he were by her side, instead of only in her head. He'd be talking about some obscure topic about which she knew little and then he'd stop and, with a dramatic sweep of his arm, say, "Behold, your world as a college catalogue cover. Just like a Denny's menu, unlikely to hold up to reality."

Questioning reality was a fairly common occurrence for Julia since Sam had died. Ironically, though, she rarely lost herself anymore. The last time she distinctly remembered floating above her own head had been four months ago, and then only for a minute, as she walked in the last room of a pop-up show of Sam's work at a Soho gallery. The event had evolved organically, as if led by an outside force. It had its genesis when Arabella decided to hire a photographer to develop the last few photographs Sam had taken. A week or so later, she'd asked to meet with Julia, her mom, and Aunt Lilly, to show them the images, offering to give Julia copies of any she liked.

Viewing the photos in Arabella's gallery had been ridiculously hard, particularly the last one. A study in contrasts—black and white and every shade in between, filled with depth and texture. It was a picture Julia would never grow tired of: the rock stark and unyielding, the emptiness of its missing half, the moon shining directly into her soul. *Forever*, she'd thought, *I'll be able to see the place Sam found himself and then lost himself, exactly the way he had seen it . . . if I can bear to look at it.* Half-remembered quotes from Camus pinged in her brain like text messages: a piece of art as both the death and multiplication of an experience, life being a succession of presents, imagining Sisyphus happy. She wanted to believe Sam was happy the moment he took the picture, knowing he'd done what he set out to do, that the struggle to the heights was enough. But she couldn't get past the thought that *capturing this photo was supposed to be the beginning, not the end.* Through tears, she'd told Arabella, Aunt Lilly, and her mom about Sam's plans and dreams: San Francisco and Santa Fe, memorializing journeys with photographs in leather albums, working through her list, creating art together.

Ten days or so later, Arabella reached out again to say that a fellow gallery owner had seen a copy of the third teepee print propped up in her office and asked to see more. Arabella wondered if Julia would be interested in helping. Julia was torn, but then she recalled Sam telling her how O'Keeffe created a retrospective of Stieglitz's work after his death. So, over a long weekend, the two of them had worked side by side, talking and laughing and crying as they sorted through negatives and prints to create a series that felt like Sam. Arabella even convinced Julia to include a few of the photographs Sam had taken of her, saying "these represent how he saw love."

Julia shared with Arabella the story of her exchange of quotes with Sam that first day in the barn, how much the space had meant to her, and how true "Art is healing, and healing is an art" had turned out to be. In turn, Arabella had shared the story of the quotes with the gallery owner, who shared it with his curator, who'd asked Julia to calligraph some of them, with appropriate attributions, onto museum mounting board, to be displayed amongst the photographs at the show.

In the final room, an open space with white walls and a cement floor, the curator had designed a labyrinth of light with overhead projectors, using the sketchpad drawing Julia had first seen Sam creating in the cafeteria. It was there Julia last saw herself from above, watching the top of her head, her shadows floating as she walked and turned. She wondered, *Is this how my dad and Sam see me now?* And then, *What would Sam think of all of this?* Which led to the rumors that had circulated around the opening of the show—about Sam's life, his creative genius, and his death—which reminded her of the controversy over Nietzsche and the debate about what had gone on in some dead guy's mind. *To the list of Nietzsche, Van Gogh, Beethoven, Tolstoy, O'Keeffe—add Lorenzo.*

We can never truly know what's going on inside someone else's head or soul.

As she made the final turn, Julia thought of the two quotes she hadn't inked onto museum board, the ones she'd shared only with Arabella, admitting they might not have been exact since her memory wasn't as good as Sam's. However, the sentiments were all Sam: "If there is one thing I wish, it would be to never break my mother's heart again," and "You can live the rest of your life knowing you saw, and loved, the very best of me."

Then, reaching the center of the labyrinth, feeling the light on her face, Julia's perspective had seamlessly shifted. Grounded in the moment, standing in stillness in the heart of Sam's six-petal flower, surrounded by the curving paths he'd drawn, she was exquisitely conscious of herself in time and space.

Out of the corner of her eye, she'd seen her mom and Arabella in the doorway, side by side, watching her. Arabella looked ineffably sad, but Julia recognized in her mother's expression the look she'd seen on her father's face while Julia stared at peaches, the look Sam had worn at Per Se. She recalled asking her mom only days earlier, "What do you and Arabella talk about?"

"You. And Sam," Laura had said, her voice slowing. "Your dad. Losing someone you love and finding a way to go on. Sorrow. Hope. Everything really and, sometimes"—she paused, her eyes wet with tears—"nothing. Sometimes, we just are."

Just being wasn't easy. And it didn't last. Julia had left the center of the labyrinth doubting she'd ever experience that exact feeling again.

The show had not been an overnight success, but little by little, word spread, and when it closed three weeks later, all of the prints had been sold: the curve of Julia's body under a sheet; the silhouette of her hands in front of a window; a no-U-turn sign in the middle of a barren road; a photograph of a photographic print, curled at the edges; a night-filled mountain under a glimmering moon.

Julia hung her copy of Sam's own "Monolith" image next to the drawing she'd recovered in her things at Brookfield—the Matisse-like sketch of her face with the oil-stained cheek.

Love, loss, going on.

None of it was easy.

Julia missed Sam. She missed her father. She missed them every day, with a depth that shattered her at times. She wondered if maybe she'd always be defined by this, the missing. She knew she thought about death more than the average person, but somehow this didn't bother her because she also thought more about life. About what it meant and how she wanted hers to go.

She committed herself to memorizing poems in their entirety and rereading Camus—in short installments. She tried to remain conscious of each day as a "succession of presents," whether they were dusty, ordinary experiences, memories, or moments of splendid amazingness. She started working on the graphic novel she'd dreamed about when she was younger and continued to work through her list. Though most attempts at a self-portrait had, thus far, ended in a crumpled heap, and the easy comfort she'd shared with her best friend, Jess, might never return . . . on these, Julia refused to give up. Not so with the edible list items because, while it turned out she loved Brussels sprouts, she intensely disliked flan, blue cheese, and snails, and had no desire to ever try them again.

Sam might have been right about the texture thing.

Sam had been right about many things.

And wrong about others.

For months, Julia dwelled on what she hadn't been able to do, wishing she could go back and convince Sam to turn around. To sleep. To stay with her curled up in soft sheets. To take the medicine prescribed for him. To consider dulling the overwhelming. Yet, over time, she'd begun to understand that even though life wouldn't necessarily give her the second chances she longed for most—she could make the most of the ones she got.

So she continued to do what helped her stay out of the dark: practicing yoga, taking Prozac for the time being, and following her plan, which included contacting the Counseling and Psychology department her first week on campus. After a phone session, Julia had been given an appointment, to which she was now headed, on the eighth floor of Lerner Hall.

How will this all go? Am I ready?

She'd asked Tanya these questions during their last meeting two weeks ago.

"It will go as it will go, and yes, you're ready."

"What about my roommate, Alyssa from South Carolina? What if I don't like her?"

"You might not like Alyssa from South Carolina, and that will be okay. But you probably will, Julia. You're very accepting and, believe it or not, super easy to be around."

"And all the work?"

"Definitely ready," Tanya had said with a smile. "You're really smart, Julia."

"And what if I get sad and lonely?" Julia heard her voice crack, felt fear seeping under her skin, reminding her of the fog.

"You *will* get sad and lonely sometimes, Julia. We *all* get sad and lonely sometimes. You're going to be happy, and sad, and confident, and scared, and bewildered, and grounded, and then, hopefully, you're going to remember that all these feelings are valid and totally part of being human, and you're going to remember that you get to choose how to think about things, that you can reframe your thoughts. And when you get overwhelmed, which, again, we all do, you'll know to ask for help because, as I've told you many times, you're incredibly self-aware, and that is a strength. If you need me, call. I'm not going anywhere. Now, go be you. You're enough."

The same words her mother had said repeatedly in the last few weeks, words which had seemed believable that day, in Tanya's office, listening to her marshmallow voice, watching her steepled fingers, smelling the lavender-diffused air. Feeling hope without freaking the fuck out. Now, sitting in a waiting room she didn't recognize, contemplating how to tell her story to Susan Konemann, Doctor of Philosophy, Julia realized how far she had come.

And she realized she had miles to go.

Leaves to rake. Dishes to wash. Hills to climb. Hands to draw.

A life to live.

"Julia?" Dr. Konemann was tall, youngish, wearing a pink blouse, a tailored skirt, and a sympathetic expression. "Come on in."

Taking a seat in the offered chair, Julia placed her black portfolio on the floor, gave a curl of her hair a gentle pull, turned, and with the hint of a smile, waited for the question she knew was coming.

"So, Julia, tell me, why are you here?"

AUTHOR'S NOTE

ASTUTE READERS MAY NOTICE THAT the first line of the first chapter and the last line of the last chapter are one and the same, "Why are you here?"

It's one of the simplest and most difficult questions ever—and one I hope readers will come away thoughtfully considering.

The idea for this book came to me after my nephew attempted to die by suicide. Devastated, his parents, siblings, and those of us in his extended family were struck by how fragile life is, how important it is to be there for each other, and how critical it is to talk openly about mental health—and yet, we were often at a loss as to how to discuss what had happened, with my nephew or with each other. We often made the mistake of saying nothing because we were afraid of saying the wrong thing, not realizing that our silence on the matter left those struggling to understand it feeling more alone than ever.

Talking with my sister about her experiences opened my eyes to the struggles facing those who love those struggling with mental illness. (Yes, I know that it's a confusing sentence, but a struggle to unpack it seems appropriate somehow.) I learned that suicide is not a casserole disease and there are no cards wishing you a speedy recovery from surviving a suicide. I learned that people don't really want to hear about the pain of being supervised during a visit with your loved one after they attempt (in case you are the reason), or about not recognizing that a sudden lift in mood in a depressed person might be a sign of an imminent attempt (the elevation in mood being due to knowing an end to the pain is coming soon). I learned that helping someone struggling with mental illness is filled with obstacles: there can be interminably long wait times for appointments; medications are poorly understood and may not work or, worse, make the situation more desperate; decision-making is often left with the individual whose thinking is clearly compromised by the mental illness; society continues to treat mental illness as a taboo topic; and even among those willing to discuss it, folks often do not know what to say.

Little did I know during these discussions with my sister that I would soon face the struggle of a young adult child longing to end her pain with suicide or that, two years later, I would believe my family would be better off without me and seek to end to my own life. Speaking from personal experience, living within the heads of severely depressed characters or characters obsessed with existential and absurdist philosophy may contribute to or exacerbate existing clinical depression.

On a positive note, my daughter reported that reading an early version of this book led to her taking an antidepressant and reaching out to a therapist. And more than a few of my early readers have thanked me for writing the book.

All of which is to say this book may bring up strong emotions. If you are suffering from depression, dramatic mood swings, or disordered/scattered thinking, or are thinking of hurting yourself or others—OR if you know someone who is—please seek help. Call a hotline. Call a friend or family member. Call your doctor. You matter.

Here are a few resources:

988 SUICIDE AND CRISIS LIFELINE
Call or text 988.
Chat at 988lifeline.org.
Connect with a trained crisis counselor. 988 is confidential, free, and available 24/7/365.
Visit the 988 Suicide and Crisis Lifeline for more information at 988lifeline.org.

CENTER FOR DISEASE CONTROL AND PREVENTION
https://www.cdc.gov/suicide/resources/index.html

NAMI HELPLINE
The NAMI HelpLine can be reached Monday through Friday, 10 a.m.–10 p.m., Eastern time. Call 1-800-950-NAMI (6264), text "HelpLine" to 62640, or email us at helpline@nami.org, or visit https://www.nami.org/help.

ACKNOWLEDGMENTS

I WOULD LIKE TO EXPRESS MY deepest gratitude to the following people, without whom this book would not exist:

My daughter, Olivia, who took time off work to drive with me from New York City to Yosemite in four short days as research for this book; read one of the earliest drafts; made practical and emotional contributions to the text; continues to listen and help me reflect on what it all means; and supports me every step of the way.

My son, Jack, who, as another early reader and twenty-three-year-old, gave me feedback on how an exceedingly philosophical young man might see the world and express himself, and then, as an older young man, advised me on edits, cover design, and the art of letting go. Another brilliant listener and always a loving voice of reason.

My sister, Amy, who shared with me her experiences as a mother with a young adult child that survived a suicide attempt; provided invaluable insight on countless versions of the book; was there for me during my struggles as a mother of a young adult struggling to find meaning in life, and regardless of the circumstances, continually helps me to see the light on the other side.

My sister, Tricia, who read chapters, synopses, and elevator pitches, dares me to dream big, and has a gift for talking me through moments of anxiety-fueled sheer terror.

My dear friend, inspiration, and life-saver, Deborah, who challenges me to think harder, write better, and live more authentically; takes me on writing retreats that renew my soul; and reminds me to find joy in the creative process.

Writing coach extraordinaire and dear friend, Marni Freedman, who believes in me when I do not believe in myself, pushes me to go beyond my comfort zone (and is there to pick me up if I fall), and refuses to let me give up.

The patient, wise, and understanding members of my writing and reading community, all of whom have helped me develop as a writer, author, poet, leader, and human being:

The women in my longstanding read and critique group (you know who you are);

The San Diego Writers Festival and Memoir Showcase team (in particular, Marni Freedman, Jeniffer Thompson, Caroline Gilman, Lindsey Salatka, and Tracy J. Jones);

Countless beta readers and other authors who've helped me polish my work;

Podcasters, publishers, and industry professionals; and

The women in my book clubs (too many to name), who've shown me the countless ways a book can be analyzed, loved, disliked—and sometimes ignored in favor of wine and conversations about life.

My Smith friends, Alicia, Andrea, and Gretchen, who've given me support from afar and weighed in on matters small and large with enthusiasm and love.

My publisher, Brooke Warner, and her team at She Writes Press, including my project manager, Shannon Green, cover designer, Julie Metz, interior designer, Tabitha Lahr, and copy editor, Jill Angel.

My publicist, Caitlin Hamilton Summie, another fellow Smithie, who has served as a guide into the world of public relations and marketing with a spectacular blend of idealism, realism, and grace.

The park rangers at Yosemite National Park, who gave generously of their time, thoughtfully answered questions, and pointed me in the right direction.

Albert Camus, for writing *The Myth of Sisyphus*, which has earned a permanent spot on the pile of books next to my bed. Each time I pick it up, I marvel at how words can be placed one after the other in such a remarkable way.

And last, but certainly not least, my husband, Tom, who gave up a Half Dome lottery win to explore the path Sam and Julia might have taken to the Diving Board; listens (mostly without complaint) to my wild tangents and readings from Camus, Stieglitz, and *Off the Wall: Death at Yosemite*; finds me when I am lost; and is there for me in every way I need, even when I don't know what I need.

ABOUT THE AUTHOR

ANASTASIA ZADEIK is a writer, editor, and storyteller. After graduating summa cum laude, Phi Beta Kappa, with a BA in psychology from Smith College, she had an international career in neuropsychological research while raising her children. She now serves as Director of Communications for the San Diego Writers Festival, as a coproducer of the San Diego Memoir Showcase, and as a mentor for the literary nonprofit So Say We All. She also sits on the board of the International Memoir Writers Association.

Her debut novel, *Blurred Fates* (She Writes Press, August 2022), won the 2023 Sarton Award for Contemporary Fiction and the 2023 National Indie Excellence Award in Contemporary Fiction.

Learn more at www.anastasiazadeik.com or follow her @ anastasiazadeik on Instagram, Facebook, and Threads.

Author photo © Michelle Goane

SELECTED TITLES FROM SHE WRITES PRESS

She Writes Press is an independent publishing
company founded to serve women writers everywhere.
Visit us at www.shewritespress.com.

Blurred Fates: A Novel by Anastasia Zadeik. $16.95, 978-1-64742-379-7. When suburban mom Kate Whittier's husband admits one night to a drunken sexual indiscretion, the beautiful life they've built together begins to crumble, unearthing long-buried memories and revealing deceits that threaten to shatter Kate's world, inside and out.

Finding Grace: A Novel by Maren Cooper. $16.95, 978-1-64742-385-8. When Caroline, a gifted ornithologist who wants a life of travel and adventure, gets pregnant against her wishes, her husband, Chuck, assumes she will change her mind. She doesn't—and as their daughter, Grace, grows up, she falls through the devastating schism that grows between them.

The Way You Sleep by Christine Meade. $16.95, 978-1-63152-691-6. When David's determined search for meaning and independence drives him to decide to live in an isolated New Hampshire cabin inherited from his recently deceased grandfather, his girlfriend's dark past and his family's long-buried secrets prove to be the greatest tests of his resilience.

The Nine by Jeanne McWilliams Blasberg. $16.95, 978-1-63152-652-7. When well-meaning helicopter mom Hannah Webber enrolls her brilliant son and the center of her world, Sam, into the boarding school of her dreams, neither of them is prepared for what awaits: an illicit underworld where decades of privileged conspiracy threaten not only Sam but also his fragile family.

Adult Conversation by Brandy Ferner. $16.95, 978-1-63152-842-2. A frazzled suburban mom, pushed too far by the ruthlessness of modern motherhood, goes on a do-or-die road trip to Las Vegas with her therapist—but neither one is prepared for how tested, and tempted, they will be along the way, or for the life-altering choices their journey will force them to make.

So Happy Together by Deborah K. Shepherd. $16.95, 978-1-64742-026-0. In Tucson in the 1960s, drama students Caro and Peter are inseparable, but Caro ends up marrying someone else. Twenty years and three children later, with her marriage failing, Caro drops the kids off at summer camp and sets out on a road trip to find Peter, her creative spirit, and her true self.